Ladies Prefer Rogues

Janet Chapman
Sandra Hill
Veronica Wolff
Trish Jensen

BERKLEY SENSATION, NEW YORK

THE BERKLEY PUBLISHING GROUP
Published by the Penguin Group
Penguin Group (USA) Inc.
375 Hudson Street, New York, New York 10014, USA
Penguin Group (Canada), 90 Eglinton Avenue East, Suite 700, Toronto, Ontario M4P 2Y3, Canada
(a division of Pearson Penguin Canada Inc.)
Penguin Books Ltd., 80 Strand, London WC2R 0RL, England
Penguin Group Ireland, 25 St. Stephen's Green, Dublin 2, Ireland (a division of Penguin Books Ltd.)
Penguin Group (Australia), 250 Camberwell Road, Camberwell, Victoria 3124, Australia
(a division of Pearson Australia Group Pty. Ltd.)
Penguin Books India Pvt. Ltd., 11 Community Centre, Panchsheel Park, New Delhi—110 017, India
Penguin Group (NZ), 67 Apollo Drive, Rosedale, North Shore 0632, New Zealand
(a division of Pearson New Zealand Ltd.)
Penguin Books (South Africa) (Pty.) Ltd., 24 Sturdee Avenue, Rosebank, Johannesburg 2196,
South Africa

Penguin Books Ltd., Registered Offices: 80 Strand, London WC2R 0RL, England

This is a work of fiction. Names, characters, places, and incidents either are the product of the author's imagination or are used fictitiously, and any resemblance to actual persons, living or dead, business establishments, events, or locales is entirely coincidental. The publisher does not have any control over and does not assume any responsibility for author or third-party websites or their content.

LADIES PREFER ROGUES

A Berkley Sensation Book / published by arrangement with the authors

PRINTING HISTORY
Berkley Sensation mass-market edition / February 2010

Copyright © 2010 by Penguin Group (USA) Inc.
"Man from the Moon" by Janet Chapman copyright © 2010 by Janet Chapman.
"Tomorrow Is Another Day" by Sandra Hill copyright © 2010 by Sandra Hill.
"The Drowning Sea" by Veronica Wolff copyright © 2010 by Veronica Wolff.
"Sixteen Decades" by Trish Jensen copyright © 2010 by Trish Jensen.
Excerpt from *Even Vikings Get the Blues* by Sandra Hill copyright © by Sandra Hill.
Excerpt from *Devil's Highlander* by Veronica Wolff copyright © by Veronica Wolff.
Cover art and design by George Cornell.
Interior text design by Laura K. Corless.

ISBN: 978-0-425-23381-8

BERKLEY® SENSATION
Berkley Sensation Books are published by The Berkley Publishing Group,
a division of Penguin Group (USA) Inc.,
375 Hudson Street, New York, New York 10014.
BERKLEY® SENSATION and the "B" design are trademarks of Penguin Group (USA) Inc.

PRINTED IN THE UNITED STATES OF AMERICA

10 9 8 7 6 5 4 3 2 1

Praise for *New York Times* bestselling author
Janet Chapman

"Janet Chapman is a keeper."
—*New York Times* bestselling author Linda Howard

"Chapman is unmatched and unforgettable." —*Romantic Times*

Praise for *New York Times* bestselling author
Sandra Hill

"Hill writes stories that tickle the funny bone and touch the heart." —*New York Times* bestselling author Susan Wiggs

"Sandra Hill always delivers."
—*New York Times* bestselling author Christine Feehan

Praise for national bestselling author
Veronica Wolff

"A fresh, exciting voice in Scottish time-travel romance."
—bestselling author Penelope Williamson

"Extraordinary! . . . A must-read page-turner . . . Powerful, riveting, and vibrant."
—*USA Today* bestselling author Sue-Ellen Welfonder

Praise for *USA Today* bestselling author
Trish Jensen

"One of the best writers of contemporary comedy around."
—*All About Romance*

"[Jensen's] got a great comic touch." —*The Romance Reader*

CONTENTS

Man from the Moon

Janet Chapman

For all of you who have ever looked up
at that big, bright full moon and wondered,
what if?

One

Isobel plunked her purchases down on the counter, causing the store clerk to look up from her magazine with a smile. "Hi, Doc," the gum-snapping teenager chirped. She suddenly recoiled, pointing at Isobel's chest. "Eww, that's not guts, is it?"

Isobel looked down and brushed at her work coat. "Nah, it's just cow snot."

The young clerk leaned on the counter, her smile back in place. "I heard you finally gave Whiny Wayne his walking papers," she said in a conspirator's whisper, darting a glance at the man in the snack aisle before arching her pencil-thin eyebrows at Isobel. "That's a record for you, isn't it? You dated him what . . . a whole month?"

"Whiny Wayne?"

The girl straightened with a shrug. "Everyone knows that ever since Wayne Thompson's mama kicked him out, he's been looking for a new place to plug in his umbilical cord." She pointed the scanner at the pint of ice cream, then aimed it at the six pack of soda. "You gotta stop being such a push-

over, Doc. I mean, really, a guy just has to look at you with
sad old puppy-dog eyes, and you practically trip over yourself running to his rescue."

"I do not."

"No? What about Fred Baker? It's no secret you checked
him into the rehab center in Ellsworth, but that he started dating Lacey Briggs the day he came out." She hit some buttons
on the register, then leaned over the counter and lowered her
voice again. "And everyone knows you had to get a restraining
order against Clive Jenkins, when he camped out on your lawn
because you wouldn't go on another date with him."

Isobel swiped her debit card through the machine somewhat forcefully and punched in her password. "You make me
sound pathetic."

"No, you're not pathetic! The guys you date are," the girl
said, instantly contrite. She snapped open a paper bag with a
dramatic sigh. "You're too softhearted for your own good,
Doc. I swear it's like you go around wearing a sign that says 'I
Date Losers.'" She packed Isobel's purchases but didn't hand
them over. "There's a bean supper at the church tonight.
Maybe you'd have better luck finding a boyfriend there."

Isobel gaped at the audacious twit, then grabbed the bag
out of her hands and strode to the door. "I have a date with
some maple fudge ice cream tonight."

"You know what they say, Doc," the girl called after her.
"The best way to get over one man is to get under another
one!"

Utterly mortified, Isobel began searching through her
purse when the man who'd been in the snack aisle reached
past her and opened the door, allowing her to precede him
out. "Thank you," she muttered, juggling her ice cream and
soda as she continued searching for her keys. She couldn't
bring herself to look up to see if she knew the man, especially since she'd heard him chuckling.

Dammit, she didn't date losers!

At least not once she found out they were losers.

Isobel got in her truck and continued searching for her
keys. She finally found them in her coat pocket and was try-

ing to cram the key in the ignition when her passenger door
opened and a man slid in beside her. She didn't immediately
panic, since there was a good chance it was someone she
knew who needed a ride.

But she did yelp in surprise. "Hey, you startled me!"

"Don't scream," he said, his hand snaking around her
head to cover her mouth.

Okay, *now* she panicked. She didn't know this creep!

His other hand moved in a blur, catching her fist when she
tried to drive her key into his thigh as she groped at her door
handle. His fingers dug into her jaw when she tried to buck
him off, and he jerked her back toward him.

"Don't fight me; I don't want to hurt you," he said, guiding her hand to slide the key in the ignition. He started the
truck. "Drive east. Slowly," he ordered, his fingers wrapping
around her neck like a manacle.

Isobel tried to look toward the store, but he held her facing forward, his thumb pressing into her pulse. "Drive, Doctor. Do as I tell you, and you won't be hurt."

Yeah, like she believed that!

"Now!" he snapped.

Her heart pounding violently and her hands shaking un-
controllably, Isobel put the truck in gear as she tried to come
up with a plan. Hadn't she heard that letting an assailant take
her to another location was the worst thing she could do?

Maybe she should crash into the light pole.

"Don't try anything," he said, as if he'd read her mind.
His hand on her neck tightened. "Just do as I tell you, and
we'll be gone by morning."

We? Oh God, he had buddies!

Isobel's foot jerked on the accelerator and the truck lurched
forward. She immediately stomped on the brake when he
squeezed her throat so tightly that she started gagging.

"You need to stay calm." He adjusted his grip, settling his
thumb on her carotid artery. "You'll be released unharmed if
you do as you're told. Now, *slowly*, pull onto the road and
head east."

Isobel took a shuddering breath, which caused her to inhale his scent. He smelled . . . pleasant, actually. Like the ocean. And spruce trees.

For some unexplainable reason, that calmed her more than his assurance that he wouldn't harm her. She took another steadying breath, slowly eased out of the parking lot, and turned east onto Route One.

They'd traveled less than half a mile when he said, "Pull over here, but don't shut off the engine."

No sooner had she lifted the shifting lever into park when the passenger door opened and a man leaned in. Isobel inched her hand toward her door handle, prepared to make a run for it the moment he relaxed his grip.

"Bring Daniel," he said to the new man. "She's a doctor."

Isobel stilled. He'd kidnapped her because he thought she was a doctor?

"No, wait," she said, twisting to see when the rear passenger door opened and two more men appeared. "I'm not a—"

His thumb pressed into her pulse, cutting her off. "How far to your office?" he asked, releasing the pressure slightly.

"T-three miles. But I'm not—"

She snapped her mouth shut when his fingers tightened again. There was a commotion in the backseat, and somebody groaned as the truck rocked slightly. The back door shut and one of the men climbed in the front seat beside her assailant.

"She's a doctor?" the new man asked.

"No," Isobel rasped, clawing at the fingers around her neck. "I'm a veterinarian!"

The hand on her throat slackened. "A what?"

"I'm an animal doctor. If you'd looked at the door of my truck, you would have seen the DVM at the end of my name. As in Doctor of *Veterinary* Medicine."

"Damn," he muttered under his breath.

A much more colorful curse came from the backseat, accompanied by a pained moan. She glanced over her shoulder and saw a man sprawled across the seat, resting up against another man.

"It's bad enough we have to rely on their crude medicine," the guy beside her assailant hissed. "We can't let an animal doctor work on Daniel."

"It's her or nothing, if you don't want him to bleed out."

"I have an idea," Isobel offered. "I can drive you to the hospital in Ellsworth."

"How far?"

"Sixty miles. But it's Saturday night, so traffic's light. It shouldn't take us more than an hour to get there." She glanced over her shoulder again. "But if he's bleeding, I need to put a pressure bandage on him first."

"We already have," the man in the backseat said.

"We'll go to your office," her assailant said, forcing her to face forward. "Drive."

"But—"

"Now!"

Isobel pulled back out onto the road. The only reason she could think of as to why they wouldn't let her take their buddy to the hospital was because he'd been shot. Gunshot wounds had to be reported, and apparently letting their friend bleed to death was preferable to alerting the authorities.

Oh, God. What if *she* killed him?

Isobel tried to think back to the last gunshot wound she'd treated. "Do you know if the bullet's still in him?" she asked, remembering the difficult time she'd had with Jane Hay's horse four years ago, when a hunter had mistaken the poor animal for a moose.

The hand on her throat twitched. "Bullet?"

Isobel squirmed, moving his thumb off her throbbing artery. "I'm trying to figure out what I have to do when we get to my surgery. Where was he hit? Is there an exit wound?"

"Daniel wasn't shot," the man in the backseat said. "He fell. We aren't sure if he has any broken bones; it's the tree branch in his side that seems to be putting him in immediate danger."

"Is the branch still in him?"

"Yes. We packed a pressure bandage around it."

"Then let me drive you to the hospital. He needs a real doctor!"

Instead of tightening again, the thumb on her pulse moved soothingly. "We mean you no harm. You help Daniel, and the four of us will be gone by morning."

And if Daniel died on her operating table—would they still feel the same way about not harming her?

Two

Isobel got straight down to business the moment she pulled up to the front of her surgery and shut off the engine. "Carry him in and lay him on the table in the back room," she instructed, opening her truck door.

Her assailant's grip tightened, and Isobel fell back with a yelp.

"That's enough!" she cried, clawing his hand as she drove her elbow into his ribs. "If you don't quit manhandling me, I swear I'll let your buddy bleed out."

"Let her go, Micah," came a pained growl from the back-seat.

Micah's grip only slackened. "What if someone's in the house?"

"Chase will check it out. If he finds anyone, he has my permission to kill them."

Though he might be bleeding to death, apparently Daniel was coherent enough to realize that threatening a loved one would gain her cooperation far better than manhandling her would. "There's no one inside," she whispered. "But I have a pet rabbit!" she rushed to say when the man sitting beside Micah got out. She was worried he might hurt Snuggles if her pet took him by surprise.

The fingers around her neck suddenly opened, but instead of bolting for the woods like she wanted to, Isobel cautiously got out. Rubbing her sore throat, she opened the back door and leaned inside to see the extent of Daniel's injury. Only, when she tried to move his jacket aside, his hand shot out and captured hers, and Isobel found herself looking into piercing, arctic blue eyes.

"Go prep your surgery, Doctor," he said quietly, though he continued to hold on to her. "And don't bother trying to call for help. Chase will have cut your phone line."

She started to back out, but he still didn't let her go. Isobel arched a brow. "Postponing going inside isn't going to make it hurt less."

One corner of his mouth lifted in a tight smile. "What's your name?"

"Isobel."

"You won't be harmed, Isobel."

"Even if you die?" she whispered.

His eyelids dropped momentarily before his gaze locked on hers again. "I have no intention of dying. You take the branch out and sew me up, and tomorrow it will be as if we were never here," he said, finally releasing her.

This time Isobel did bolt, but for her surgery instead of the woods. She didn't know who in hell these guys were, but they obviously meant business. They didn't appear to be common criminals but had more of a . . . military air about them.

Special ops, maybe? Navy SEALs?

If so, then what in hell were they doing here in coastal Maine?

❖   ❖   ❖

Isobel slammed through the door of her surgery and snapped on the lights, only to scream when she saw Chase standing in the hallway to her house.

In an almost mirror image of Daniel, one corner of his mouth turned upward. She shed her coat as she rushed to the back room, giving a cursory glance at the phone on her way by. Had he already cut the line?

"It no longer works," he said from right behind her.

She continued on to her desk, took out a set of keys, then unlocked her medicine cabinet and began reading labels.

"No drugs," Chase said over her shoulder.

She looked up in surprise. "You expect me to pull a branch out of your friend while he's *awake*?"

When he merely nodded, she grabbed a bottle of anesthesia. "Yeah, well, Daniel might be a tough guy, but I'm not. I refuse to work on a conscious patient."

He reached past her and pulled out a different bottle, swapped it for the one she was holding, and put the anesthesia back in the cabinet.

"You know medicine?" She shoved the bottle at him. "Then you pull out the branch, and I'll assist."

"I know chemicals," he said, walking away. "Daniel stays awake."

Micah and the man from the backseat came through the door, Daniel shouldered between them.

Isobel rushed to her operating table, gathered up the books piled on it, and tossed them onto a nearby counter.

Chase startled her by lunging after the books, catching several of the journals as they slid off the counter. "Have a care, woman!" he snapped, shooting her a glare that should have turned her to toast.

Isobel gaped at him, only to realize the other men had also stilled, looking equally horrified. "They're just old monthly journals," she said as Chase carefully set them on the counter, his hands hovering to make sure they didn't slide off again. She took down two surgical gowns. "You planning to hold him up while I pull out that branch or are you going to lay him down? Chase, you're scrubbing up with me." She tossed the men a surgical blanket. "Take off all his clothes, then you two are leaving so you don't contaminate my OR." She waved toward the reception room.

"There's a hallway that leads into my house; just watch out for Snuggles."

"Snuggles?" Micah said, looking up from unlacing Daniel's boot.

"My pet bunny. But instead of running from strangers like a proper rabbit, she likes to dart out at people so she can watch them trip over themselves," she explained, slipping into her gown. "You can make a pot of coffee if you want, and help yourselves to whatever's in the fridge. Oh, my ice cream! Would one of you go out to the truck and get it before it melts and put it in the freezer?"

The men stopped undressing Daniel to look at her.

She smiled, rather proud that she had finally stopped shaking despite the fact that there were four threatening giants in her surgery. "I know the kidnappee doesn't usually give orders to her kidnappers, but these are unusual circumstances, wouldn't you say, gentlemen?"

A weak chuckle came from the table. "Her surgery, her rules, *gentlemen*," Daniel said. "Get Isobel's ice cream."

Micah leaned down next to his ear. "What's ice cream?" he whispered.

Isobel stopped halfway to the sink. He hadn't really just asked that, had he?

"You'll know when you find something that's melting," she heard Daniel whisper.

Isobel clutched the rim of the sink and closed her eyes. She might be acting like she was in control, but honest to God, she felt as if she'd stepped out of that store and into the twilight zone. Who in hell were these brutes?

She jumped when Chase set his hand on her shoulder. "You're doing fine, Isobel. This will be over in a few hours."

"My patients are dogs and cats and horses and cows, not humans."

He gave her shoulder a squeeze. "The biology is similar. Think of Daniel as a horse, if you like. Surely you've treated equine puncture wounds."

"But if I can't stem the bleeding when we pull out that

branch, he could go into shock and die. I have no way of replacing the blood he's going to lose."

"We can give him a transfusion."

"But I can't test for his type," she cried softly. "And even if I knew what it was, I don't have any blood to give him."

"The three of us can supply what you need."

Isobel leaned away in surprise. "You *know* you're all the same type?"

He turned on the water, then nudged her around to face the sink. "We're a match," he said, filling his hands with soap. "Wash up, Doctor. The sooner we begin, the sooner we'll be gone."

Isobel scrubbed up, slipped into her gloves, then grabbed two surgical masks and handed one to Chase. She walked over to her operating table as she tied her own mask in place, folded down the blanket covering Daniel, and immediately started shaking again. A piece of wood as thick as her thumb was sticking out of what looked like a shirt wrapped tightly around his midsection, leaving two inches of the branch exposed. She was relieved to see there wasn't much blood seeping out.

Chase walked up on the opposite side of the table and started to unwrap the bandage, but Isobel stilled his hand. "I want to give him an exam first." She moved to Daniel's head and found him looking intently at her. "Where else do you hurt?"

"No place else. It wasn't a long fall, and the tree . . . slowed me down."

She touched an angry bruise on the inside of his shoulder. He tightened defensively. But when she fingered the thick metal collar he was wearing, Chase pulled her hand away.

"Don't touch that, please," he said.

"What is it; some sort of communication device or something?" She couldn't tell if Chase was also wearing one, as he had on a black turtleneck—just like the other two men were wearing. She looked him right in the eyes. "Are you guys Navy SEALs? Not that it matters, because that collar needs to come off."

"It stays."

She noticed he hadn't answered her question about whether they were SEALs. "But his clavicle might be broken, and the swelling could choke him."

"It stays," Daniel echoed. "Just get the damn branch out of me."

"My surgery, my rules," she reminded him.

All that got her was another tight smile. "Except in this instance."

She looked at Chase again. "Okay, let's knock him out."

Daniel also looked at Chase. "No."

"Not completely," Chase assured him. "Just enough to keep you manageable."

"No drugs. I need for my head to be clear."

Isobel carefully pressed on his shoulder, and he snapped his gaze to her with a growl. "It won't knock you out, it'll just make you not care. So what do you weigh, big guy?" she asked.

"He's around a hundred kilos," Chase answered.

Isobel arched a brow. "What's that in good old American pounds?"

"Approximately two hundred and twenty."

She did a quick calculation in her head, filled a syringe with the tranquilizer Chase had chosen, and gently slid the needle directly into Daniel's vein.

She handed Chase a pair of surgical scissors. "You can cut off the bandage while waiting for the medicine to kick in. I'm going to x-ray that shoulder and his torso." She rolled her portable X-ray machine over to the table. "Um . . . could you look under the blanket at his lower extremities?" she asked, fighting the blush creeping into her cheeks. "I need to make sure he doesn't have any injuries we're overlooking."

Chase lifted the blanket and Isobel immediately got busy positioning the X-ray machine over Daniel's shoulder, leaning down to make sure it was aimed correctly.

"You have unusual eyes," Daniel said.

She turned her head in surprise.

"They're a mixture of green and gold," he continued, his

own blue gaze locked on hers. "And very beautiful and . . . expressive."

She shot him a smile, then remembered she was wearing a mask. "You're the first patient I've ever had tell me that." She started positioning the X-ray machine again. "Unless you count slobbering kisses and wagging tails."

She draped a lead apron over the lower half of his body, then stepped away, pulling Chase with her. She depressed the button in her hand, repositioned the machine along Daniel's torso and stepped back, and depressed the button again. "So, did you find anything interesting below his waist?" she asked, only to wince at the way that sounded.

Dammit, she wasn't used to working on *humans*, much less handsome giants!

Chase's eyes crinkled with amusement as he finished removing the bandage. "I can't say that I found anything particularly interesting," he drawled.

Isobel studied the digital X-ray screen, wishing she'd given *herself* the tranquilizer. Honest to God, if her cheeks got any hotter she was going to burst into flames. She jumped when Daniel suddenly wrapped his fingers around her wrist.

He smiled up at her, his eyes glazed and unfocused. "You should look for yourself, Isobel," he said, guiding her hand toward the blanket with surprising strength. "Maybe *you* will find something interesting down there."

"Christ, how much tranquilizer did you give him?" Chase growled, prying Daniel's hand off her wrist.

"Not enough, apparently," she said with a slightly hysterical laugh, stepping away. She quickly sobered, however, when she finally got a good look at the fully exposed wound just below his ribs—that was now bleeding profusely. She studied the digital X-ray, positioned the screen so Chase could see it, and half filled another syringe with tranquilizer.

"It's deep, Chase," she said softly, sticking the needle in Daniel's arm before either of them could stop her. "And not only are there fragments of wood floating around in there, it looks as if that branch may have nicked his kidney." She took a steadying breath. "This is beyond my expertise. He needs a real doctor. Let me stabilize him and call for an ambulance to take him to Ellsworth."

Chase looked from the screen to Daniel, then to her. "No. You will take out the branch."

"Dammit. Don't you understand that I could kill him! Is whatever you guys are hiding from so important that you'd risk your friend's life?"

"Yes."

The hairs on the back of her neck rose at his softly spoken answer. Whoever these men were, and whatever they were doing here, apparently was worth dying for.

And killing for?

Isobel looked down at the branch sticking out of Daniel's side, took another steadying breath, and finally picked up her scalpel. Not that it mattered if they did kill her, because the moment she'd stuck that needle in Daniel's arm, her life as she knew it was over. If the authorities ever found out she'd performed surgery on a human being, not only could she lose her veterinary license, she could also go to jail.

Which certainly put her dating losers into perspective, didn't it?

Three

Isobel scooped another spoonful of ice cream out of the pint container, only absently aware of dribbling some on Snuggles sitting on her lap. Honest to God, she felt as if she'd spent the last five hours wrestling Daniel away from the devil.

And the frightening thing was, she still didn't know if she'd won.

Her patient was sleeping peacefully—thanks to the third injection of tranquilizer she'd given him half an hour ago—and she was trying to come to terms with the fact that she had actually poked around inside a live human being.

Which was something she never, ever, wanted to do again.

Slurping down more of her ice cream, Isobel studied her surprisingly competent surgical assistant. Chase looked nearly as battered as she felt, his feet propped on the bed as he quietly slept in a chair on the opposite side of her guest room. He'd thrown his blood-stained surgical gown and turtleneck in the trash, and was left wearing a black T-shirt. There was a small bandage on his heavily muscled arm from where she'd set up a direct blood transfusion, and his hair had specks of dried blood in it.

But it was the thick metal collar around his neck, exactly like the one Daniel was wearing, that truly puzzled her. If these guys were military, she hoped to God they were on *her* side.

They certainly had the physiques of soldiers. But even stranger than dressing alike, they could almost be clones. All four of them had piercing blue eyes and short dark hair, they were all the same height—which she estimated at six-three—and they all appeared to weigh within ten pounds of one another.

Oh yeah, she'd definitely stepped into the twilight zone.

Isobel folded Snuggles' ear around so the rabbit could clean off the mess she'd made, and wondered how grown men could not know what ice cream was. As soon as she'd finished supervising settling Daniel into bed, she'd gone straight to the kitchen to get her ice cream, fully intending to pour a liberal dose of Baileys Irish Cream over the top of it. Only she hadn't found the pint of maple fudge in the freezer, but in the fridge!

Nor had they made any coffee, despite her asking for some at least twice during the five-hour surgery. She'd had to settle for caffeine-laced soda instead—which had been lukewarm because apparently they didn't know what soda was, either.

As soon as they'd helped carry Daniel to bed and assured themselves she hadn't killed him, Noah and Micah had disappeared back into her den, where they seemed to methodically be working their way through her library of textbooks and journals. One or both of them had come into the bedroom several times in the last hour and asked her to explain the physiology of some animal they were reading about.

And if that wasn't strange enough, when she'd finally asked them why they were interested in the autoimmune systems of cats, dogs, mice, and squirrels, they'd both suddenly clammed up and left and hadn't returned since.

Isobel drank the last of the ice cream right out of the cardboard container, then set it on the floor beside her chair. She wiped her mouth on her sleeve with a sigh, set Snuggles down, and stood up. After feeling Daniel's forehead and checking his pulse, she headed toward the hall.

"Where are you going?" Chase asked.

She stopped in the doorway and looked back to find he hadn't moved a muscle except to open his eyes. "I have a horse in the barn that lost a fight with a barbed wire fence, and I need to go check on him."

Chase dropped his feet to the floor and stood up. "I'll come with you."

Isobel held up her hand. "No, you have to stay here and let me know if Daniel so much as moans. He's still in critical condition and needs constant supervision."

"Then Micah will go to the barn with you."

"Look," she said tiredly. "You don't have to worry I'm going to escape and alert the authorities about what's going on here. Whether you realize it or not, my saving your friend has put my career in jeopardy. You disappear just as soon as it's safe for Daniel to travel, and I will simply pretend this has all been a bad dream."

"What do you mean, in jeopardy?"

She waved toward the bed. "If anyone finds out what I've done, at the very least I might lose my veterinary license, and at the worst I could get arrested for performing surgery on a human." She shot him a tight smile. "So I promise, I won't tell if you don't."

"Tell what?" Micah asked from right behind her.

Isobel jumped in surprise and turned to find Micah holding yet another one of her textbooks, open to a page on . . . now he was reading about raccoons?

"You will accompany Isobel while she checks on a horse in the barn," Chase said, also feeling Daniel's pulse before walking over to them. "Then take her upstairs and have her pack whatever she'll need for the next five days." He moved his gaze to Isobel when she gasped. "Make sure you include warm clothes, as the cabin has only a woodstove for heat."

"Excuse me?" she whispered. "W-what cabin?"

"You intend to take her to the island?" Micah asked, apparently as surprised as she was. "But why? It's bad enough we were forced to break our rule of not engaging the locals; you can't mean to continue doing so."

Chase nodded toward Daniel. "He's in danger of dying if we don't. Tell Noah to pack some food for them." He looked at Isobel again. "When you're done upstairs, gather whatever medical supplies you'll need."

"That wasn't our deal. You said if I patched him up, you'd all be gone by morning. You have enough medical knowledge to take care of Daniel yourself."

"The three of us can't stay with him, so that leaves only you."

"Then why can't I take care of him *here*?" she cried. "I promise, I won't tell anyone!"

Chase stepped past her into the hall. "I will allow you to make one phone call before we leave, to someone who can come tend your animals for the next five days."

"Dammit, no! That wasn't our deal."

His entire countenance suddenly changed, his features hardening and his eyes turning dangerously cold. Isobel took a step back at the realization that Daniel hadn't been bluffing when he'd said Chase would have killed anyone in the house.

"Our deal, Doctor, was for you to save Daniel's life. And since that has not yet been accomplished, I have no choice but to take you to the island so that the three of us can continue our mission." He reached down and scooped up Snuggles when she came hopping into the hall, and gently wrapped his fingers around the rabbit's neck. "Continue cooperating, Doctor, and both your career and your pet," he said ever so softly, "will remain intact."

"You wouldn't," she gasped. "She's just an innocent animal!"

"Do not test me, Isobel. All of us have sworn to do whatever we must to achieve our goal, at whatever cost to us— or anyone or any *thing* we encounter."

Four

Isobel hugged Snuggles inside her coat, blinking back tears as she shivered in the stark silence broken only by the snap of cedar catching fire in the woodstove. She wasn't in the twilight zone anymore, she decided; she was in hell. And hell was cold and dark and smelled of decay, and was so damned isolated that she doubted even God would hear her scream.

"You don't have to worry about my bringing home any more losers," she told Snuggles, rubbing her quivering chin against the rabbit's fur. "Because as of today, I am swearing off all men. If Prince Charming himself walked in here right now and asked me for a date, I'd turn him down flat. I would," she muttered, tilting Snuggles so her pet could see how serious she was. "Men are pigs. No, I take that back; pigs are more civilized. You never see a pig reassuring you everything's going to be okay one minute, then threatening to kill someone you love the next."

She hugged her pet to her chest again. "Don't worry, I wouldn't have let those mean men hurt you. I made them let me bring you with me, didn't I? Threatening not to give

Daniel any pain medication certainly made Chase change his tune."

"Then how about keeping your word."

Isobel yelped in surprise, spinning to look at the bed in the corner.

"Christ, woman, what in hell did you do to me?" Daniel growled. He tried to move, then stilled on a sharp groan. "It feels as if you cut me clean in half. And why is my left arm bound to my chest?"

"Because your collarbone is broken."

"My side is on fire. I swear the branch didn't cause this much pain."

"I can shove it back in you, if you want," she offered sweetly.

There was a heartbeat of silence, and then she heard him sigh. "Isobel, I'm sorry you were brought here against your will."

"I'm sure you are." She stood up and walked to the bed, just so she could glare down at him. "Now that you realize your pal Chase has left you at my mercy for the next five days. Which means that I'm in charge. You got that, big man?"

The kerosene lamp on the bedside table gave off enough light for her to see one corner of his mouth lift in a grimace. "Yes, ma'am."

Isobel walked over to the supplies the men had carried up from the boat and unceremoniously piled in the corner. She set Snuggles on the floor and opened the box of food. Good Lord, it appeared as if Noah had thrown *everything* from her fridge into the box—including some four-day-old pizza, the bag of beef bones she kept for recuperating dogs, and the baking soda!

She turned at the sound of the bed creaking, then jumped to her feet and ran across the room. "What do you think you're doing?" She took hold of Daniel's good shoulder and pushed him back down. "You can't move; you're going to pull out your stitches and start bleeding inside again."

"I need to get up," he growled in a winded whisper. "I have to use the latrine."

Isobel straightened and closed her eyes. Damn. She hadn't thought about that particular aspect of caring for him. She rarely put catheters in her patients; they just wet on their bedding, which she would simply crumple up and toss away.

But she doubted Daniel was into piddling on newspaper.

"You can't get out of bed yet," she said, walking to the counter on the side wall of the cabin. She found a dusty old gallon jar and carried it back to him. "So you're going to have to settle for peeing in a jug."

His cheeks darkened as he eyed the jar.

"Look, being shy about this isn't an option. I just spent five hours getting personal with your internal organs, and you're going to burst that kidney wide open if you don't . . . go." She set the jar on the bed beside him, then headed back to the supplies.

"Remind me again what planet you guys are from?" she muttered. "Because I gotta tell you, your pal Noah doesn't seem to know that eggs don't go in the bottom of the box, or that the Geneva Convention outlawed feeding moldy pizza to prisoners."

She stared out the dusty window at the breaking dawn. "And Micah acted like he'd never seen a horse before. When I asked him to hold Clyde while I gave him an injection, you'd have thought I was asking him to hold a lion by the whiskers. And he nearly came unglued when one of the barn cats rubbed up against his leg."

"I'm done," Daniel said, a distinct growl still in his voice.

Isobel carried the carton of broken eggs to the counter, then wiped her fingers on her coat as she walked over to the bed. "So what's up with you guys, anyway? Aren't there any horses on Mars? Or ice cream? Or refrigeration? Or *books*?"

"Everyone knows Mars is uninhabitable. And refrigeration is a waste of energy."

"Only if you like fungi growing on your food. Where's the jug?"

"I slid it under the bed on the other side. So how about some of that pain medication you bargained for? Chase kept his word; are you going to keep yours?"

The only reason she didn't demand he hand over the jug was because she could see beads of sweat had broken out on his forehead. And considering he probably had the pain threshold of a rhinoceros, and that he'd rather die than ask her for anything, Isobel guessed he must truly be hurting.

And there was always the added bonus that a drugged patient would be much easier to deal with than a growling one. She headed back to the pile of boxes and started searching through her medical supplies. "So if Mars is uninhabitable, which planet did you fly in from?" she continued conversationally. She filled a syringe with pain medication and returned to the bed to find Daniel glowering at her.

Apparently extraterrestrials didn't have senses of humor, either.

He captured her hand when she tried to slide the needle in his arm. "What is that you're giving me? I don't want to be knocked out again."

"You don't have to worry that I'll take advantage of you in your sleep. You're not my type. Ohmigod, look at that giant spider!" she cried, pointing at the wall beside him.

The moment he turned to look, she jabbed the needle in his arm and pushed the plunger, then skittered away when he tried to grab her again.

"Dammit, woman! That was dishonorable!" he hissed, rubbing his arm.

"But effective." She shot him a smug smile. "It works every time—at least on dogs. Cats just look at my finger." She shrugged. "You're welcome to sue me for malpractice, if you'd like."

"I need to stay awake."

"Will you chill out? Since it appears we're stuck with each other for the next five days, how about you stop growling at me like a wounded dog, and I'll stop treating you like one." She stepped closer so he could see her smile was perfectly sincere. "And to pass the time, you can tell me all about life on whatever planet it is you flew in from, and I'll explain how things work here on Earth."

"I'm not from a planet; I'm from the moon," he said, only

to snap his mouth shut with a scowl. "Dammit, you can't give me any more drugs! I need to remain lucid."

Isobel patted his arm. "Don't worry, I have no intention of telling anyone you're the man on the moon." She frowned. "And I'll lower the dose next time. It's obvious your metabolism is abnormally fast. That injection already seems to be working, despite my not even hitting a vein.

"So," she said, walking back to the supplies. "What brought you four moon men to Earth? Are you on vacation, or is this a business trip?" she asked, carrying more of the food over to the counter. Hell, maybe she could boil the bones and make soup. She glanced toward the bed when he didn't answer. "Five days is a long time to stare up at the rafters in silence."

Not to mention how long it would seem for her. She really would have to lower his doses, because even a growling patient was better than stark silence. "Hey, wait. Isn't the moon's gravity a lot less than Earth's? Like half or something? So if you live up there, how come you can even walk down here?"

"Our gravity is one-sixth of Earth's," he growled. But then she heard him sigh. "And if we hadn't worn weight suits all our lives, our bones would have snapped the moment we landed."

Isobel stilled. Was he *serious*?

He sure as hell sounded serious. And rather knowledgeable.

"Um . . . how did the four of you get here?" she asked.

"We used one of our old cargo transports," he said, still staring up at the rafters, his voice slightly slurred. He touched the collar around his neck and looked over at her. "But once we got to Earth, we came back to this century via our time links. That's why we couldn't let you remove mine; it's my only means of returning."

"R-returning to when?" she whispered.

"To the year 2243."

Ohh-kay. This was getting really weird. "So you're not only from the moon, but from the future as well?"

He looked back up at the rafters with a heavy sigh and closed his eyes. "Yes, from the future," he murmured. "Only we'll not survive another decade if our mission isn't successful. The four of us are our colony's only hope."

Utterly intrigued despite herself, Isobel walked to the bed and gently shook him. "What colony?" she asked. "Are there people living on the moon in 2243?" His eyes opened slightly, but she could see he was quickly fading. "What about Earth? It's still full of people in 2243, isn't it?"

"No," he murmured. "Humanity got wiped out in the middle of the last century. And it's taken Earth almost a hundred years to be habitable again."

She gave him another gentle shake. "What happened to all the people?"

"Plague."

Isobel stepped back and rubbed her hand on her coat.

"Which is why we must find the . . . animal," he said, his eyes closing again.

"What animal?" She pulled her sleeve down over her hand and shook him again. "What animal?"

"We don't know, exactly. One of your small mammals, we believe."

"Daniel!" she cried, shaking him again. "What do you need this mammal for?"

He swatted at her arm, missing by a mile. "Go away, woman. I'm not supposed to engage any of the locals."

She gave a slightly hysterical laugh. "Don't I wish," she muttered, walking over to the door. She opened it to stare at the ocean surrounding the small coastal island they'd brought her to, and let out a shuddering sigh.

She'd been kidnapped by aliens?

No, by moon men from two hundred and thirty or so years into future.

Either that, or horse tranquillizers made people creatively delusional.

She rubbed her hand on her coat again. But what if it were true?

It *could* be true, she supposed. Man could be living on the moon two hundred and thirty years from now.

And have learned how to travel back in time.

But Daniel said humanity got wiped out in the middle of the twenty-second century.

Except for the people living on the moon, apparently, who had then been forced to wait almost a hundred years to return home.

But that would mean *generations* would have been born there.

She looked back at the bed. Including Daniel? And Chase and Noah and Micah?

They couldn't really be from the moon—could they?

Isobel snorted and stepped out into the slowly warming October morning, deciding to explore the tiny island that would be her prison for the next five days. This is what she got for dating Paul Stanford for almost a year, who had been a certifiable Star Trek groupie. And she really had to stop watching the Syfy channel, as she was damn close to *believing* Daniel's drug-induced delusion.

It certainly explained a lot of the men's strange behavior.

Five

Daniel fought his way through the shroud of fog imprisoning him, alarmed to realize that his muscles were even less responsive than his mind as he tried to remember where he was and why he felt drunk. He stilled at the sound of movement to his left, the spike of adrenaline sharpening his senses.

He cracked his eyelids, then relaxed when he saw Isobel crouched in front of the woodstove, feeding it fuel. Her pet rabbit, that he'd caught only a glimpse of peeking out of her coat earlier, was on the floor beside her, and the two of them seemed to be having a whispered conversation.

Which surprised him, as he hadn't realized people talked to animals.

Could the creature talk back?

While he listened to see if the rabbit responded, Daniel silently flexed his muscles. His shoulder seemed back to normal despite the binding immobilizing his left arm, but his side still felt as if it were on fire—though the flame had dulled appreciably since he'd last been awake.

He wracked his mind trying to remember *his* conversation

with Isobel, and feared he had revealed the reason the four of them were here. He winced, remembering that he'd told her what year they were from, too, as well as from where.

He'd have to be more guarded; for hadn't it been drilled into them over a lifetime of preparing to come here that people of this century would be unable to comprehend their ability to breach time? And that if they did expose their presence, not only could it put their mission in jeopardy, but the future of mankind as well.

Daniel smiled faintly. He would also have to keep guard against Isobel's trickery. Her smugness hadn't been lost on him after she'd turned his attention away from her crude method of administering medicine by pretending to see a spider.

Not that he could remember what a spider was, exactly. An insect, he thought.

Daniel concluded the conversation taking place across the room was one-sided, as the rabbit had yet to respond to Isobel's long-winded monologue disparaging men in general and several ex-boyfriends in particular.

His smile widened as he began freeing his left arm from its binding. Was that why she'd chosen a pet with such long ears? His history lessons had included what role animals had played in people's lives before the Cataclysm, though cats and dogs were thought to have been the most common household pets. Maybe the fact that Isobel was an animal doctor had led her to choose a more unique companion. Then again, maybe she simply needed a pet with long ears that would quietly listen without comment.

The woman did like to talk.

She was quite pleasant on the eyes, as well; much plumper than Moonlander women, and far healthier looking than the Earth women he'd seen pictures of from a hundred years ago. Daniel guessed that if Isobel had been alive at the time, she might have survived the plague. For they knew now that society's obsession with thinness had been its ultimate demise, everyone having grown so gaunt that they hadn't been able to fight the super-germ that had spread around the world like wildfire. Only by the time the scientists had realized their irrevocably weakened immune systems were to blame, the entire human race had disappeared in one generation.

Having witnessed the Cataclysm from afar, the colony that had at first been quarantined and then eventually stranded on the moon had spent the next four generations trying to fatten itself up in preparation of returning to their homeland—though limited resources had made it difficult. And if the four of them were unsuccessful this week, the last humans in the universe could be gone within the decade. Which was why it was imperative they find at least one species of animal that could provide a vaccine to make Earth safe again, so they could transport all the Moonlanders home before their aging infrastructure finally collapsed.

"I'm serious, Snugs. If a date ever darkens my doorstep again, you have my permission to trip him flat on his face," he heard Isobel say, her voice rising at the prospect. "And just to save you boyfriend troubles of your own, I'm not going to put off neutering you any longer. That way we can grow old and fat and happy together, and eat ice cream until it's coming out our ears." She gave a musical laugh, lifting the rabbit's ears playfully. "Which would take at least a pint for you, Snug-a-bug."

She suddenly looked toward the bed, and Daniel closed his eyes to slits, to pretend he was still sleeping. Apparently satisfied that he was, she scooped the rabbit into her arms and stood up.

"But you can't trip Daniel," she said, her voice lowered back to a whisper. "I'm going to have to get him walking by tomorrow at the latest, and I don't need him falling and bursting open his side. You stay well clear of that growling bear, you hear?" she said, holding her pet at eye level, facing her. "For all we know, they eat bunny rabbits for breakfast on the moon."

"We don't have bunny rabbits on the moon," Daniel said.

She turned toward the bed with a gasp. "How long have you been awake?"

Daniel sighed. Since she already knew more than she should, maybe she could help them discover exactly which small mammal they were looking for.

"In fact," he continued, "we don't have any animals on the moon."

"None?" she asked, her expression turning appalled. "That is really, really sad."

"Sad? How so?"

She approached the bed, cradling the rabbit to her chest. "Well, because it's a proven fact that animals play an integral role in human health. We *need* to love something that will love us back unconditionally." She snorted. "Because men sure as hell don't know how to love a woman just for herself."

"So are you saying Micah misinterpreted the conversation between you and the young girl in the store?" he asked, watching her expressive face turn a lovely pink. "You don't dump your boyfriends just as soon as they become enamored with you, then get over them by getting . . . under another one?"

She gasped so hard the rabbit flinched. "Micah *told* you what that little twit said? But when? I've been with you almost the whole time."

"In your truck after you ran for your surgery, when I asked him what he knew about you."

She set the squirming rabbit on the floor in order to cross her arms under her breasts, and stepped closer to the bed— presumably so he could better see her glare. "For your information, I do *not* sleep with every man I date. And not one of them was ever enamored with *me*; they were only interested in the DVM at the end of my name."

"How so?" he asked, intrigued by how serious she was.

"In these parts, marrying a doctor—even a veterinarian— is tantamount to winning the lottery. One jerk even suggested that if we got married, he should take *my* name instead of me taking his, so that our stationery could read 'Dr. and Mr. Briggs.'"

Daniel couldn't believe what he was hearing. Had she

ever looked in the mirror? Or did she simply not realize that when a man looked at her, prestige would be the last thing on his mind.

It sure as hell was the last thing on his at the moment.

She was absolutely beautiful, with her disheveled blonde hair falling down around her green gold eyes and suntanned face. She exuded health and vitality, not to mention a hint of potentially explosive passion. And that was above the neck. When he let his gaze drop lower, she was better than flawless; she was perfect.

He wouldn't mind helping her get over her last boyfriend by letting her get under *him*.

"Hey!" she suddenly cried, pouncing.

Daniel actually flinched, afraid she'd read his mind, but then sighed in relief when she grabbed the bandage that had been binding his left arm.

"You have to leave this on," she scolded, trying to wrap it around him again, which caused her to lean close enough that tendrils of her hair tickled his neck. "If you don't, you're going to finish breaking that clavicle."

Daniel captured her hand in his. "It's already mended."

"It can't be," she said, pulling his shirt aside. Her eyes widened in surprised and returned to his. "How is that possible?" she whispered. "I know it was only a hairline fracture, but the swelling is completely gone and even the bruising has faded."

She tried to straighten away, but he held her leaning over him. "As you noted earlier, I have an unusually fast metabolism." He reached up with his other hand, captured one of her escaping tendrils of hair, and rubbed it between his fingers. "It is as soft as it looks." He returned his eyes to hers and smiled. "Moonlander women all have dark hair and must keep it short out of necessity."

"M-moonlander women?"

He ran his thumb down the side of her cheek. "Your skin is also soft and carries the kiss of the sun." He pressed his palm against her cheek. "Do that again."

"D-do what again?" she whispered.

"Blush with that beautiful glow of passion. I wonder if your lips are as soft as they look? And as sweet," he murmured, gently cupping her head and urging her closer.

Her fingers kneaded into his shirt as she at first resisted, before she suddenly softened, allowing him to lower her mouth to his. Mindful not to overwhelm her, Daniel carefully captured her lips in a gentle kiss. His restraint was rewarded when she softly moaned, and her delicate hands cupped his cheeks. She tasted even sweeter than he'd expected and exuded the sensual energy of an expanding pulsar.

Which made him wonder how she thought she could ever swear off men.

But just as he was about to deepen the kiss, she suddenly jerked upright with a yelp, shaking one of her hands violently. "Eww!" she cried, swiping at the pillow beside his head. "That is a monstrous spider!"

More than a little confounded by her antics, Daniel arched a brow at her.

"No, really," she said, rubbing the back of her hand on her leg before pointing past his head. "There was an honest-to-God spider crawling on my hand. And then I saw it go scurrying up the bedpost." Her eyes dropped to his slackened mouth, and her cheeks turned bright pink again. "That was . . . we shouldn't have . . . you can't do . . ."

She suddenly turned and strode to the stove, but just as suddenly stormed back. "What in hell is a Moonlander?" she asked rather aggressively.

The poor woman appeared more confounded than he was. Apparently Isobel didn't have a clue how to handle the frustration of thwarted passion—something every male learned to deal with by the age of fourteen. "Me," he told her calmly. "I'm a Moonlander. And Chase and Micah and Noah. It's the name that was given to those living on the moon, especially those of us born there."

He saw her hands ball into fists at her sides. "Are you going to continue with that crazy story?" she growled. "Because I gotta tell you, it's starting to give me the creeps."

He arched a brow again. "How so?"

"People can't live on the moon, much less be born there. It's nothing but a dead rock. There's no air to breathe and no water to drink. And if the gravity really is only one-sixth of ours, then you should have the bone density of a thirty-seven-pound person—which means you couldn't be walking upright right now."

"I believe I explained that we wear weight suits to compensate for the difference. Every Moonlander does—only the four of us wore suits that would replicate the weight of a three hundred-pound man here on Earth to make us even stronger."

She crossed her arms under her breasts again and rested back on her hips. "Do you think I just crawled out from under a rock or something? A suit that heavy would have to be so bulky you wouldn't be able to move in it."

"Not if it's made out of Tricarblyster."

"What's Tri . . . tri-whatever?"

"It's a material that was developed early in the twenty-second century so the scientists living on the moon wouldn't lose bone mass on extended stays." He lifted the blanket at his waist. "It's no bulkier than this material."

She rolled her eyes with a snort and marched to the woodstove. "I made you some beef broth," she said, lifting the cover off a steaming pot on the stove. She turned just enough to look at him. "Or will it upset your stomach because you've never had animal-based protein before? What with there not being any animals on the moon," she drawled, looking rather smug again.

"I have no idea," he said. He tossed back the blanket, gritted his teeth against the pain he knew was coming, then slid his legs over the side of the bed and pushed himself into a sitting position.

"Hey!" she cried, dropping the lid and rushing to him. "You have to stay in bed!"

He resisted her attempt to ease him back down. "What was that term you used earlier?" he asked. "Chill out? If it means to relax, then you must chill out, Isobel. If I don't start moving around, I'll grow weak."

Her fingers flexed on his shoulders as she gave a small laugh. "Not in a month of Sundays, big guy. You have more muscle than a boa constrictor." She let him go when she realized she had no hope of laying him back down. "Okay, then. Let's see if we can get you on your feet," she said, lifting his arm over her shoulder as she tucked herself into his side. "I don't know why Chase had to kidnap me," she muttered. "At the rate you're healing, you'll be swimming to shore in a couple of hours."

She actually attempted to lift him, but Daniel didn't budge. "I can get myself up," he said, trying to pull his arm away—which she refused to let go of. "I don't know how steady my legs are, Isobel. If I fall, I could crush you."

She repositioned her grip on the back of his pants and gave another tug. "I'm stronger than I look. I handle large domestic animals for a living, remember? Don't worry, I won't let you fall."

Daniel didn't know whether to laugh or roar. He did know he'd like to meet a few of her old boyfriends and ask them if she was this stubborn and bossy in bed.

Bracing himself against the pain, he pushed off the bed to his feet. Only his knees buckled the moment he stood, and he ended up in a wrestling match with Isobel when she tried to support him and he tried to push her out of the way. They fell back on the bed together; Isobel giving a yelp that ended in a whoosh of expelled air, and Daniel giving a roar at the jarring pain.

"Ohmigod, your side!" she cried, holding him on top of her instead of pushing him away. "Dammit, I told you it was too soon to get up. But oh, no. Mr. Macho Moon Man had to prove how big and strong and—"

He covered her mouth with his hand to keep himself from wrapping it around her neck. "Hush, woman," he whispered through gritted teeth, closing his eyes against the fire raging in his side as he adjusted his weight slightly off her.

"Dnt-mve-r-ymyby."

"Silence!"

She went perfectly still beneath him, her eyes widening in alarm.

Daniel dropped his forehead to hers. "Just lay quietly Isobel, and let me get my bearings." He slackened his hand to see if she intended to comply, then took it away completely when she remained silent. A minute later, he lifted his head. "Did you get hurt when we fell?"

She gave a frantic—and utterly mute—quick shake of her head.

He took a steadying breath as the pain in his side finally eased to a dull throb, and brushed her hair away from her pale face with an apologetic smile. "I'm sorry, Isobel. I would never hurt you."

She said nothing. She did, however, hesitantly shift beneath him.

And every drop of testosterone in Daniel's body roared to life.

Which set off a far more pleasant fire deep in his gut. After giving a quick scan of the bedposts for anything that might resemble a spider, he dipped his head and kissed her, fanning the flames of his desire even as he fought to keep them in check. Only instead of the soft, pliant woman he'd kissed just minutes ago, Isobel held herself perfectly stiff. He felt her hands slowly creep up to his chest, and she hesitantly tried to push him away.

Daniel broke the kiss to run his lips over her forehead before rising up enough to look her in the eyes. "I swear, Isobel, I would cut off my arm before I'd ever hurt you."

She blinked up at him, then tried pushing him away again. He rolled off her with a groan, but when she tried to slide off the bed, he captured her arm and held her lying beside him. "Please, don't run off. It's important to me that you believe I won't hurt you." He laced his fingers through hers. "Let's stare at the rafters together and . . . talk. Go on, ask me something about life on the moon in 2243."

There were several heartbeats of silence, then Daniel heard her mutter something under her breath. He smiled, realizing he'd been right; Isobel's apparent need to fill the silence was much stronger than her fright.

"Do the women of your colony allow men to shout at

them?" she asked. "And if they were to shout back at you, what would happen?"

"Our women give as good as they get, if not better. However," he said, giving her hand a squeeze, "they are wise enough not to test the limits of a warrior's patience."

He looked over to find her eyes had gone huge again. "Are you a warrior?"

He nodded. "Chase, Micah, Noah, and I were bred especially for this mission."

"Bred? How do you mean?"

"We were designed to produce more testosterone than the average man, to give us the strength, endurance, and aggression it would take to succeed."

"Designed? As in a lab? Is that how babies are made in the future?"

"No, it still requires a man and a woman and a good deal of privacy, and is one of the few pleasures left to us. In fact, you might say Moonlanders have perfected the art of lovemaking."

When her jaw slackened, Daniel returned to looking at the rafters to hide his smile. He wouldn't gain her cooperation if she was afraid of him, and apparently the subject of male-female relationships was of great interest to her. "But when certain traits are sought," he continued, "then sometimes certain people are . . . encouraged to mate. The four of us are the results of several generations of selective breeding."

She rolled toward him, her curiosity finally winning out completely. "Does that mean the four of you are brothers?"

"Yes."

"And was your father a warrior?"

"No. Our parents are scientists, as are most Moonlanders."

She arched a brow. "Exactly how many Moonlanders are there?"

"One hundred and twenty three.

She blinked. "That's it?"

"Our infrastructure was designed to support only a hundred, but we've managed to make room for more in the last generation, in preparation of repopulating Earth."

Her eyes widened again. "Are those extra twenty-three people just like you?"

"No, there's only ten of us warriors altogether. We have another brother who traveled from the moon to Earth with us, along with our mother and father. But Neil and our parents stayed in the year 2243 to maintain the energy supply supporting our links. The other five warriors from a different family remained on the moon . . . in case the seven of us failed."

"That's it?" she repeated. "You only have an army of ten protecting the moon?"

He arched a brow. "Exactly who would we be protecting ourselves from? There is no one left to war against, Isobel. The last men on Earth died in 2156."

She rolled onto her back and stared up at the rafters again. "What about aliens?" she whispered. She looked over at him. "In over two hundred years, no other life form has ever been discovered in the universe?"

"We are it for our solar system." He shrugged. "And if there is life elsewhere, we haven't found it."

"Or it hasn't found us," she drawled. She suddenly let out a yawn, immediately covering her mouth. "Oh God, this lumpy old bed feels good," she murmured, her eyelashes dropping to her cheeks. "I didn't get a wink of sleep last night. So tell me more about the four of you," she continued drowsily. "If there isn't any need for an army on the moon, then who taught you guys how to be warriors?"

"Our mother."

She opened her eyes in surprise. "A woman taught you about fighting and stuff?"

Daniel chuckled. "Mom is a historian and the keeper of our colony's precious book collection. Using ancient texts, she taught the ten of us the art of war, educated us in the ways of twenty-first century Earth, and helped us grow strong by making sure we got extra portions of protein. In fact, it was her idea that we should wear heavier weight suits." He chuckled. "She also helped get us excused whenever we got into trouble growing up, by explaining to the Elders that creative intelligence and aggression were an integral part of a warrior's make up. And that the pranks we pulled were proof enough that we would eventually save the colony."

Isobel's eyes narrowed. "So you're really saying the ten of you were spoiled rotten." She snorted. "And your mama wouldn't let anyone even shake a finger at her boys. You turned into a bunch of bullies, didn't you, throwing your size and strength around like . . . like you did with me just now," she said, pushing his hand holding hers away and sitting up. "Well, Mr. Moon Man, *your* women might get all ga-ga over a macho attitude and bulging muscles, but women in *this* century don't particularly like intimidating brutes."

She started to leave the bed, but Daniel wrapped his arm across the front of her shoulders and pushed her back onto the pillow, all the time wondering how their conversation had gone so terribly wrong so quickly.

"Hey!" she cried, struggling to sit up again—even as she was careful not to bump against his side. "Let me up!"

"Go to sleep, Isobel. You can't nurse me to health if you're falling-down tired."

"You're a bully," she whispered, lying stiffly beneath his arm.

"No, I'm simply a man in pain who would like a few minutes of quiet."

"You started the conversation."

He gave her a squeeze. "Which we will continue *after* you've slept."

She remained silent for all of sixty seconds. "I have to get Snuggles."

"The rabbit sleeps with you?" He lifted his head. "Does she do so when your boyfriends are . . . visiting?"

Isobel returned to glaring up at the rafters. "She gets cold easily, and she's scared and confused to be here. And rabbits are social creatures, and they get lonely."

Just like you, he refrained from saying. "Then call your cold and frightened little friend and pick her up," he offered, freeing one of her arms. "And I will keep the both of you warm and safe while you sleep."

Six

Isobel wound back her arm and threw the rock as far as she could, then watched it land in the ocean with a plop. *Perfected the art of lovemaking*, she thought with a snort, picking up another rock.

Yeah, well, he better not try any of his fancy moves on her!

She threw the next rock at a piece of exposed ledge, then watched in horror as it ricocheted off the granite and nearly hit a seagull floating on the swells. The bird rose into the air with a squawk of surprise, its scolding caws carried away on the breeze.

"Sorry! I didn't see you swimming there!" Isobel called after it. She picked up another rock worn smooth by the surf and began searching for another target.

If Daniel tried to kiss her again, so help her God, she would . . . dammit, she was tempted to kiss him back! Just to prove that he didn't intimidate her one itsy-bitsy bit, she decided, this time aiming at some floating seaweed.

It was bad enough Snuggles hadn't left his arms all afternoon. Didn't the little traitor know that his fawning over her soft fur and long ears was nothing but a veneer, hiding a don't-test-me-or-I'll-wring-your-neck liar just like his brother Chase?

About the only part of Daniel's story Isobel believed was that he really did have an overabundance of testosterone. The guy had shown up with a branch sticking out of his side, for crying out loud; but not only was he already walking around on his own, he apparently felt well enough to kiss her. Twice! And when she'd awakened from her nap this afternoon, it had been to find him cupping her breast in his sleep!

Were horse tranquilizers aphrodisiacs for men, or what?

Isobel picked up another rock, this one the size of her fist. So what if she'd slept like a dead woman in his arms? She'd been up for almost two days. And getting kidnapped was stressful. So was being forced to perform surgery on a human, only to be kidnapped again, then stranded on this stupid island with a man who snapped at her one minute and turned into a horny-toad the next.

And if Daniel thought she believed he was from the future, he was dumber than he obviously thought she was. His story was riddled with holes big enough to drive a truck through. If he and his brothers were on such an important mission to save mankind from becoming extinct, why did he seem more interested in kissing her than helping his brothers search for their precious animal?

She suddenly gasped in midthrow and lowered her hand. "Ohmigod, he's playing me. If his story is even remotely true, then he's been buttering me up in hopes that I'll help them find the animal they need. The no-good, conniving sneak," she muttered, winding her arm back and spiking the rock at the ledge again.

This time it hit so hard it shattered into pieces and sent tiny missiles flying in every direction. One of the pieces sailed into the air and smacked a seagull soaring in to see if it was food she was throwing. The bird gave a strangled squawk and tumbled straight into the ocean, only to bob to the surface in bewilderment as several more gulls landed beside it, thinking their friend had found something to eat.

"Jeesh, I'm sorry!" Isobel shouted, shoving her hands in her pockets.

"Is it customary to apologize to an animal you're trying to kill?" Daniel asked.

Isobel turned with a gasp, tripped over her own feet, and fell into the surf just as a wave slammed into her back and washed over her head. "Dammit, you can't sneak up on a person like that!" she cried, getting to her feet and slogging back onto the beach.

But then she had to scramble up the bluff and grab his arm when she realized he'd started down to rescue her. "You're not well enough to be out here. I don't care how good you feel, you're going to burst your kidney wide open."

He wrapped his arm over her shoulder for support and allowed her to lead him to a boulder to sit down. "I'm sorry I startled you," he said, unzipping his jacket and peeking inside.

Isobel saw Snuggles peeking up at him.

"Can I set her down out here?" he asked, eyeing the gulls edging closer in hopes the new arrival had brought food. "Or will those large birds carry her off and have her for dinner?" He looked up at Isobel. "Aren't rabbits prey animals?"

"Yes. But seagulls are not raptors. They eat mostly crustaceans—or whatever food they can beg or steal from people. It's okay to set Snugs down. She won't go far."

Isobel shed her soaked jacket and tossed it on the pebbled beach. Then she pulled her hair free, bent over, and began fluffing the water out of it with her fingers.

"You're shivering," he said. "Here, let me give you my jacket."

She straightened to glare at him. "Keep it. The last thing I need is for you to catch pneumonia."

"You're still angry," he said, sincerely surprised. "I apologized for groping you during our nap." He shot her a boyish grin. "But you were so warm and plump and inviting, my hand instinctively wandered to you without my permission."

She stopped fluffing her hair again. "Did you just call me plump?"

His boyish grin turned outright lecherous, and he actually

nodded. "Trust me, Isobel, if you were not so beautifully plump, I wouldn't be spending every moment wanting to run my mouth over every centimeter of you," he said, his voice dropping several octaves. "Or imagining how sweet your skin must taste or what it would feel like to have you writhing beneath me as I slid deep inside your heat, and let your soft, plump body consume me."

Despite being soaked to the skin and standing in fifty-degree air, Isobel felt like an ice cube in a pot of boiling water. Was this guy for real? Because, honest to God, she could practically *feel* herself consuming him.

"You're the most beautiful woman I've ever laid eyes on," he continued gutturally, his piercing gaze holding her trapped in a realm of salacious possibilities. "And like an explorer, I want to map every line and curve and dip of your body, and turn the passion of your blushes into flames of desire," he whispered, the deep cadence of his voice sharpening the mental image of his words. "And hear your cries of ecstasy as you shudder around me with the force of an exploding nova."

He dropped his gaze to her blouse plastered against her breasts, then his darkened eyes returned to hers. "I want you, Isobel. Badly. So I suggest that you run while you still can."

"W-what?"

"Because if you don't leave immediately, I will have you right here on the beach."

He thought she could run? Hell, it was all she could do to *breathe.*

"Go!" he snapped, making her flinch and effectively getting her moving.

Isobel frantically scrambled up over the bluff in a daze of confusion and no small amount of horror—both of which were aimed at herself. Because, honest to God, she had wanted him to make love to her right there on the beach, so she could shudder around him like an exploding nova.

She was halfway to the cabin before she suddenly stopped, turned around, and marched back to the bluff. "For your information," she called down to him, "I am not plump. I have a body mass index of twenty-two, and that's considered perfect. And I wouldn't have let you have me, anyway, because I've sworn off men."

He stood up. "Do not test me, Isobel," he said roughly. "As I am determined to keep my promise not to hurt you."

She took a step back, preparing to make a run for it again, but something in his voice gave her pause. He was fighting more than an overabundance of testosterone; it sounded as if he was equally determined not to hurt . . . himself?

She turned and quietly walked to the cabin, no longer fleeing in horror but still confused. Was it possible Daniel was coming to actually like her?

Impossible. They'd known each other less than twenty-four hours.

But she had saved his life. Could he have one of those syndromes—like the Stockholm syndrome, where captives came to feel affection for their captors—that was making him feel affection for her? Maybe he was battling a misguided sense of gratitude, or even adoration, that had manifested as . . . lust.

But *she* was the captive; she should be the one enamored with *him*.

Isobel stepped into the warmth of the cabin and softly closed the door. "So what if I do think he's to-die-for good looking and totally hot?" she said into the silence as she took off her blouse. "Other than his tall tale that he's from the moon, he's certainly a far cry from the losers I've been dating." She unzipped her wet jeans and peeled them down with a snort. "Which isn't saying much. I've dated every eligible male in a fifty-mile radius, and not one of them ever made my heart race the way Daniel does just by looking at me."

She kicked her pants toward the woodstove, went to the supplies in the corner, and found the duffle bag she'd packed. "My God," she muttered, "I damn near had an orgasm just *picturing* him sliding into me."

And she probably would have had three by now, if he'd followed through instead of chased her off.

She took a shuddering breath and pulled a sweater down

over her head. "Okay, young lady, get a grip on yourself. You've sworn off men, remember?"

She paused in the act of stepping into a pair of dry jeans. If she was facing a prolonged bout of dates with pint containers of ice cream, and Daniel would be disappearing back into the ether in a few days, why not kick off her celibacy by having a torrid little affair with him?

He sure as hell seemed willing. And he certainly seemed physically capable, considering how fast he'd healed. And maybe Moonlanders really had perfected the art of lovemaking, and he could give her some really hot memories to keep her warm on the long, lonely nights ahead. And who knew, maybe there was even a thing or two she could teach him.

Yeah, she didn't have to swear off *all* men.

Isobel finished pulling up her pants with a smile of anticipation. "So I guess that means you better start sleeping with one eye open, Mr. Moonlander, because you're no longer the only person on this island with wandering hands."

*   *   *

Daniel sat back down on the boulder and hung his head in his hands with a heavy sigh. Christ, that had been close. He really had been seconds away from stripping Isobel naked and making rough, unrestrained love to her right here on the beach.

After which he would have carried her to the cabin and made love to her again.

And then he would have spent the next four days trying to persuade her that he wasn't a brute.

He snorted. "Say it enough times and maybe you'll eventually persuade yourself."

The tiny black rabbit hopped over and sat up on her haunches, nudging his leg with her front paws. Daniel picked her up and tucked her inside his jacket with a humorless laugh. "I can see why Isobel is fond of you, little one. You've even managed to get *me* talking to myself. It must be your long ears," he murmured, stroking her ears against the soft fur of her back. "They encourage speech. And now I also understand Isobel's claim that pets have health benefits, as I am growing calm just holding you."

He ducked his head to look the rabbit in the eye. "Isobel stirs my senses like no other woman ever has. And it's not just her beauty. Even when she's not especially pleased with me she's still tender and caring, her concern for my welfare always winning over her anger."

Daniel looked out at the ocean, once again awed by the vast expanse of water, and took a deep breath of fresh, fragrant air that was being filtered by nature instead of machines. He couldn't wait for his people to come here and witness such colorful beauty and abundance for themselves.

"So, my little friend," he said, stroking the rabbit's fur as he eyed the large birds edging closer, "do you have any suggestions as to how I can keep my hands off Isobel?" He rubbed his stubbled chin on the rabbit's head. "For it's not physically that I fear I might hurt her, but emotionally. I know only too well that when a woman gives her body to a man, there is a danger that her heart will follow. And it's obvious that Isobel is a passionately generous and caring woman, and I worry she may come to care for me more than she should."

He lifted the rabbit to look into her dark, fluid eyes. "And in four days, when I have no choice but to return to my natural time, she could be heartbroken." He hugged Snuggles to his neck and closed his eyes. "Just as I fear I may be."

Seven

Daniel eyed the plate Isobel had set in front of him, then leaned to the side and eyed the plate she'd set on the floor for Snuggles. And then he scowled at the bowl of delicious-smelling broth sitting in front of her. "Is there any particular reason the rabbit and I are eating the same food, but you are not?" he asked.

"Yup," she said, taking a noisy slurp of the broth. She closed her eyes and made a sound of pleasure, then dipped her spoon into the broth again.

Daniel reached across the table and stilled her hand on its way to her mouth. "And that reason would be?" he asked.

She lowered the spoon to her bowl. "Because recovering from major surgery is not exactly the best time to introduce a body to new food." She arched a delicate brow. "You said there aren't any animals on the moon, so that means your digestive system has only had plant-based protein."

She reached across the table and picked up his fork, drove it into the pile of green foliage and diced orange . . . things, and held it up to his mouth. "Like Snuggles, you are essentially a herbivore, and the only thing I had in my fridge when Noah raided it was lettuce and carrots. It's this or nothing." She set the fork on his plate when he refused to open his mouth and be fed like an infant. "Or, you can chance having your intestines blow up," she said, taking another loud slurp of broth.

Daniel finally picked up his fork but hesitated. "What is making it wet?"

"Olive oil." She nodded toward the floor where the rabbit was eagerly munching her dinner. "Eat up. It'll make your chest hair soft and shiny, just like Snugs' fur."

Daniel hid his consternation by filling his mouth with foliage. Something had changed between the time he'd sent Isobel running from the beach and when he'd returned to the cabin an hour later. She hadn't been leery of him as he'd expected; in fact, she'd been outright solicitous. And smiley. And unusually quiet.

Which only served to put him on guard.

"So your parents and brother are waiting for you back—I mean forward—in 2243?" she asked. "Where are they, exactly, location-wise?"

"Right here," he said after swallowing, deciding that he liked the earthy taste of olive oil—though not the bitter aftertaste it left. "Wherever we're standing when we activate our links is where we will be standing when we arrive in our new time. We left from this island."

"But then how did you get to the mainland when you arrived here? You couldn't know there would be a boat on the island, could you?"

"We swam the eight kilometers to the mainland." He grinned. "Apparently Micah found a boat to borrow to bring us here this morning."

"But how did you know this island wouldn't be inhabited when you suddenly . . . what, do you step out of the ether or something?"

Daniel swallowed his next bite. "We don't step out of anything, we simply materialize. And we took an educated guess the island would be deserted, based on what we knew of this time and this area." He grinned. "Though it's quite run down, the cabin being here was a pleasant surprise."

She leaned forward. "Okay, I can understand why you picked the sparsely populated Maine coast, but why this particular year?"

"Because it was far enough back in time from when the first strain of the plague showed up, which made it our best chance of finding the animal we need without contaminating ourselves."

"Why couldn't someone from the twenty-second century simply come back and stop the plague from happening to begin with?"

"Breaching time wasn't possible back then. Moonlander scientists developed the technology just thirty years ago."

"Then why didn't one of the Moonlanders come back and warn everyone about what was happening, so they could create a vaccine before it was too late?"

"Time travel is still a very new technology, and we haven't yet explored all the ramifications of using it. But our scientists believe it's imperative that we not alter the past in any substantial way, because we can't predict what rippling effect it could cause. We dare use time travel only to impact our own futures.

She set down her spoon. "When all the people die, do the animals die, too?"

"Not all species. But when the last humans disappeared, the nuclear energy reactors eventually deteriorated and spread radiation into the atmosphere, and the Earth went through what we've been calling a Cataclysm." He shrugged. "Which in turned altered the DNA of many of the animals that did survive. So we made sure we came back both before the super germ existed and the animals hadn't mutated. But we also had to make sure it was late enough that we would have access to science advanced enough to help us find which animal we need."

"Um . . . if you're worried the plague is still hanging around in 2243, aren't you afraid that you and your family could get infected?" She gasped. "And that you'd bring it to this century and infect us?" she asked, her eyes widening in alarm.

Daniel shook his head. "We know the four of us didn't carry it back to this time."

"How can you possibly know that?"

"Because we exist. Mankind wouldn't have survived more than a decade if we brought it here, so there never would have been a colony on the moon to begin with." He set his fork down to rest his elbows on the table. "That's what I meant about not altering the past, Isobel; if we have an impact during one of our visits, it would then be part of recorded history."

"Can you travel *forward* in time?"

He picked up his fork again. "We don't know for certain, but all our data points to it being possible, although it does appear to be a one-way journey."

"Why do you believe that?"

"Because anyone who has ever activated a time link set on a future date has never returned."

*   *   *

Isobel started devising her plan of seduction right after dinner, even though she was pretty sure starting an affair with Daniel wouldn't require any more effort than taking off her clothes. Still, there wasn't any reason her soft, plump, inviting body—that he wanted to feel writhing beneath him—couldn't be presented in its best light.

And what better light was there for lovemaking than the soft glow of a kerosene lamp? Especially if she set it on the table in the center of the cabin, well away from the bed, so it could cast interesting shadows over every line and curve and dip of her body that he wanted to map like an explorer.

Isobel splashed some of the spring water she was using to wash the dishes onto her face, then ran her wet hand down her neck. Good Lord, she was growing hot again just remembering the sensuous images he'd conjured up on the beach this afternoon. If he could make her melt with just *words*, there was a very real danger she'd go off like a

Fourth of July rocket if he did run his mouth over every square centimeter of her.

"I'm going outside to sit and watch the moon come up," he said from behind her.

Isobel yelped, spinning in surprise and splashing water all over herself, and him, and Snuggles pecking out of his jacket.

"I'm sorry," he said, though his grin said he was anything but. "I don't mean to keep startling you."

"You walk like a cat," she muttered, wiping her face on her sleeve. "Why don't you whistle or something to warn a person you're around."

"Whistle?"

She dropped her arm and blinked up at him. "You don't know how to whistle?"

"I assume it's some sort of noise I should make?"

Isobel puckered her lips and whistled a few notes of *Twinkle, Twinkle, Little Star*, but stopped the moment she realized he'd locked his gaze on her mouth and his eyes had darkened. "Er, that's whistling," she whispered, her own gaze going to *his* mouth as she imagined those lips kissing every square centimeter of her body.

"I may be gone awhile," he growled, turning away and striding to the door.

She gripped the counter and closed her eyes on a sigh. Maybe having an affair with him wasn't such a good idea. Since she couldn't remember ever being this flustered over a man before . . . well, what if he ruined her for *all* men? What if after making love to Daniel, every other man paled in comparison?

"Yeah, right," she said with a snort, squaring her shoulders. "He puts his pants on one leg at a time, just like every other man."

But he sure filled them out nicer than most. And she couldn't have helped but notice how ripped his body was when she'd been rooting around inside it. She honestly hadn't found one ounce of extraneous fat, though she had found plenty of muscle. And a blind woman couldn't miss how broad his shoulders are.

Or how soft his shadowy chest hair looks.

God, she loved chest hair on a man. It made her want to run her fingers all through it, and kiss it, and feel it tickling her naked breasts as . . .

Isobel pushed away from the counter with renewed resolve and ran to the bed and straightened the blankets Micah had suggested she bring. She fluffed the pillows *she* had insisted on bringing, then grabbed the lamp and carried it over to the table. Then she went over and dug through her duffle bag to find her toiletries, and after a peek out the window to see Daniel making his way toward the bluff, she stripped off her clothes.

Washing up in spring water certainly cooled her down, and brushing out her hair until it flowed like silk calmed her considerably. She stuffed everything back in her ditty bag, gathered her clothes off the floor, then carried them to the corner.

She stopped in midstep. "Damn. Snuggles," she muttered. She pulled everything out of her duffle bag, arranged a sweater in it like a nest, then carried it over to the bed and set it on the table where the lamp had been. But then she rotated it so the opening was facing the counter. "Sorry, Snug-a-bug, but last I knew, lovemaking wasn't a spectator sport."

She ran to the window to see Daniel sitting on a log, watching the sun drop into the ocean as Snuggles sniffed through the crisp leaves at his feet. She lit the kerosene lamp on the table, then looked around. It was a rickety old cabin someone had built half a century ago, and the Maine coastal storms had taken their toll. Still, it kept out the weather, and she couldn't think of a cozier place to cozy up to a Moonlander.

Well, except maybe her comfortable bed at home.

She added two of the punky old logs she'd found out back to the woodstove, closed the damper to keep them from burning up too quickly, then looked around again. "What else?" she asked out loud. "Think of the five senses," she instructed, holding up a finger for each. "Sight; the kerosene lamp will do nicely. Sound; let's hope my cries of ecstasy are music to his ears. Smell." She snorted. "I hope Daniel gets turned on by the odor of deodorant soap. As for touch and taste, those are a given." She suddenly gasped. "Ohmigod. Protection!"

She ran back to the pile of clothes and started searching though her toiletries again. "Come on, please let there be some condoms in the bottom," she pleaded, digging deeper as she tried to remember her last sleepover. Only sleepovers were usually at *her* house, since half the men she dated still lived with their mothers. "Yes!" she cried, pulling out a sleeve of three. But then she went rooting through the bottom of the bag again. "Three condoms for a four-day affair just isn't going to cut it."

Coming up empty but for the three in her hand, Isobel stood up with a sigh. "I don't suppose time-traveling warriors pack that kind of protection, so I guess that means I'm about to find out how creative Moonlanders really are when it comes to lovemaking."

Taking a deep breath, she walked back to the bed, tucked one of the condoms under her pillow, then stuffed the other two in the duffle bag under Snug's nest. "There, the stage is set and we're ready for the show to begin, folks."

She crawled into bed, fanned her hair across the pillow, arranged her boobs—that she had to admit were pleasingly plump— so that a good deal of cleavage showed just above the blanket, then settled in to wait for the leading man to arrive.

And she waited.

And waited.

Until she eventually fell asleep.

Eight

Isobel woke up with a scream when something brushed her arm, and she came up swinging at the dark shadow looming above her.

"Dammit, woman, would you stop!" Daniel snapped, catching her fist before it could make contact with his belly. "You're starting to give me a complex."

"You're supposed to *whistle*," she snapped back, tugging her hand free to pull the blanket higher around her.

"I've been trying to for the last hour, but I can't seem to make my lips work the way you do. Here, I fear Snuggles may have gotten chilled," he said, trying to tuck the rabbit under the blanket again.

"No, put her in the duffle bag," Isobel told him, gesturing toward the bedside table. "She likes cuddling up in my sweater."

Daniel frowned at her, hugging Snuggles back to his chest. He looked around the dimly lit cabin, and sighed. "She can sleep with me, then," he said, heading toward the pile of clothes in the corner.

"No, wait," Isobel called out. She took a fortifying breath

and scooted over and patted the bed beside her. "There's no reason we can't share the bed." When he stopped and turned to her, she let the blanket slip just enough to reveal one naked shoulder and lowered her voice to what she hoped was a sultry tone. "There's plenty of room for both of us. And it's going to be chilly in here by morning, so I thought we could share our . . . our body heat," she ended in a whisper, her courage deserting her when she saw his eyes darken—not with lust, but with . . . oh, God, he actually looked angry.

"Go back to sleep, Isobel."

She immediately recoiled, prickles of heat rushing to her cheeks as she realized he had just flat-out rejected her. Suddenly feeling her chin starting to quiver, she turned onto her stomach and pulled the blanket over her head to bury her face in her pillow. What in hell had she been thinking! No wonder only losers dated her; she obviously had the seductive wiles of a gnat. Isobel pressed deeper into the pillow to muffle a sob when she heard him mutter something nasty under his breath.

So now how was she supposed to get up and get dressed, if he was lying on her clothes? Because there was no way she was going to let him sleep on the floor after she'd spent five hours sweating bullets to save his sorry, miserable life.

The no-good, ungrateful jerk.

She felt the bed dip, and his hand settle across her back. "Isobel. Look at me."

"G go away," she sniffled into the pillow.

"I need to—Christ, are you crying?"

"No Go away!"

"Isobel."

She tightened her grip on the blanket when he attempted to pull it down. "I've decided I deserve the bed tonight for saving your miserable life," she said, trying to sound appropriately dismissive. "Go sleep in the corner with your new best friend."

He stopped tugging on the blanket and his hand returned to her back, only lower, settling on her backside. "Are you not concerned I might catch a chill on the floor and take a turn for the worse?"

She tried to slide out from under his touch, but he pressed heavier, then started caressing her. So she reared up to her hands and knees as she pulled the blanket around herself, then scooted backward off the end of the bed. "Fine! *You* take the bed and I'll sleep in the corner."

Her toes hadn't quite touched the floor when she suddenly found herself swept off her feet and plastered against his chest. "What the—Are you nuts? You're going to burst open your side!"

"Hush, Isobel," he whispered, just before his mouth came down on hers.

Oh, great. A *consolation* kiss!

Keeping her lips tightly pursed, and being careful not to smack his clavicle or lose her grip on her blanket, she tried to push him away. But he effortlessly held her cradled against him and kept right on kissing her until she started getting dizzy from lack of air.

Totally and utterly humiliated now, and fighting to keep from bursting out in loud sobs, Isobel gave a shudder of defeat and went limp. And when he finally lifted his head, she hid her face in his neck.

"You will not cry," he whispered. "I don't like it."

Oh, then by all means she should stop, shouldn't she? "Put me down," she said against his neck. "Because I swear if you bust open your side, I'm not sewing you back up again."

"I will put you down when you stop crying."

She gave a quick swipe of her eyes, then lifted her head to glare at him. But the moment she looked into his beautiful blue eyes, her chin started quivering again and she turned away. "Will you please put me down?"

He laid her on the bed, but then he lay down beside her, somehow managing to keep her locked in the crook of his arm. "I want you to look at me, Isobel."

"Yeah, well, I want to go home, but that's not happening," she muttered, yanking the blanket up around her shoulders.

He cupped her jaw to force her head up, and then threaded his fingers through her hair to keep her looking at him. "Six months before we left the moon to come here, the entire colony gathered together for a grand and solemn ceremony," he said calmly, "to hear myself and my brothers give our warriors' vows. And a part of those vows was our promise to become celibate, and remain so until we chose a wife."

Isobel dropped her gaze to the metal collar around his neck. "A-and that's why you don't want to ... why we ... ?" She looked into his eyes. "We can't make love because you've vowed to have sex with only your future wife?"

"If I make love to you tonight, Isobel, we won't leave this bed for the next four days, and when I return to my time, I will never touch another woman."

"Then why did you tell me down on the beach that you wanted me?"

"Because I do."

She dropped her gaze to his collar again and released a shuddering sigh. "Oh. Okay. I understand. You want to, but you can't," she said, trying to pull away.

His arm around her tightened, and he forced her to look at him again. "I have a duty to my people, Isobel, not only to help make Earth safe for them to come here, but to help repopulate it. Our warrior genes are mankind's best hope for survival, and my destiny lies in the year 2243."

"I *understand*," she repeated, this time trying to sound like she meant it.

She also tried to roll away again, but he continued to hold her facing him even as she continued to struggle. "If I could, I would take you with me."

She went perfectly still. "You ... that's quite ... you're assuming ... you want to take me with you?" she squeaked.

He nodded.

"But you can't!"

"I know," he said, closing his eyes on a sigh. "But I am tempted to anyway."

She untangled a hand from her blanket and poked him in the chest—well away from his injury—to make him look at her. "That's a pretty arrogant thing to say, considering you haven't even asked me if I *want* to go with you."

One side of his mouth lifted, and his eyes crinkled at the corners. "I don't have to ask; warriors have been granted the power to take."

"Take what?"

"You," he said, smiling openly when she gasped. "If I want."

She blinked at him, trying to decide if he was serious or just making up another tall tale to distract her from his flat-out rejection, afraid she might start crying again. Yeah, well, she was certainly past that; she wouldn't make love to him now if he was the last man on Earth!

"That might be a rule or law or something in *2243*, but it sure as hell doesn't apply to women in *this* time." She poked him again. "I mean, really, where are you getting all these harebrained notions, anyway? To begin with, soldiers haven't been called warriors for centuries." She arched a brow. "Are you telling me that instead of becoming enlightened, mankind regresses over the next two hundred years? Vows of celibacy are positively ancient even *now*."

He captured her hand so she couldn't poke him again. "I told you my mother was a historian, and that she's also the keeper of our book collection. By the middle of the twenty-second century, printed books had become relics, as all knowledge was stored digitally. But when Earth died, everything was lost. So when it came time for us to train, the only military information we had access to was in the few printed books some of the scientists had brought with them to the moon."

He grinned. "And my mother's grandmother had a thing for ancient warriors, apparently, so she brought her small personal collection of novels. They were penned in your century—which is one reason we decided to come to this time—but were set anywhere from the tenth century to the fifteenth."

"Novels?" Isobel whispered in disbelief. "Your mother taught the ten of you how to conduct yourselves from historical *fiction*?"

"They were set in a very noble time."

"It was a barbaric time."

He sighed. "Which isn't far from where Earth is now, in 2243. There's nothing left, Isobel. In the eighty years since the Cataclysm, nearly all signs of humanity have disappeared. The land and the oceans are as if man never existed." His arm around her tightened. "Which is why I am reluctant to take you with me."

"Are we back to that?"

"I believe *that* is exactly what this conversation has been about," he growled. But then he sighed again. "What I've been trying to explain, Isobel, is that just like your boyfriends are looking for the prestige marrying you would bring them, I must also guard against women who want only to be a warrior's wife." He snorted. "In the six months before we came here, I and my brothers would come home to find women in our beds, hoping we would choose them as our wives. Oh, and while we were at it, could we please impregnate them before we left?"

Isobel felt prickles of heat rising into her cheeks again, and she hid her face in his shirt. No wonder he'd gotten angry to find her waiting for him; she had acted just like all those conniving, blood-sucking, no-good, rotten Moonlander tramps.

Oh God, that made *her* the loser!

He canted her head back to look at him again. "You're the only woman to ever tempt me, Isobel. And if it wasn't for the uncertainty of having you travel forward in time, we wouldn't be having this conversation at all, because we would right now be setting this bed on fire."

Okay, she had to get at least some of her dignity back here, before she totally humiliated herself. She shot him a rather sad smile and patted his chest. "Yeah, well, sorry to burst your bubble, big guy, but I'm really not into alpha males carrying me off into the ether." She tried to roll away, but when he still refused to let her go, she added, "But it's very sweet of you to *want* to take me with you, and I am honored. Truly."

She felt him stiffen, and his eyes sharpened with suspicion.

Isobel kicked her smile up a notch. "It's just that . . . you

see . . . I have a pretty good life here. I enjoy being a veterinarian, and my four-legged clients need me. And I like running water and electricity and indoor plumbing. And though
I'm not a vegetarian, I don't think I could actually kill my
own food, and I can't grow a tomato to save my life. So you
see, I'd really make a lousy twenty-third century wife, anyway."

When his only response was for his complexion to
darken, she patted his chest again. "And really, when you
think about it, we've only known each other one day," she
said with a soft laugh—that she hoped sounded lighthearted
rather than hysterical.

Because, honest to God, the idea of starting out fresh in a
pristine new world with Daniel was actually starting to appeal to her. And really, that was just too crazy even for her.
Wasn't it?

"And for all you know," she continued, keeping her smile
shining brightly and her tone light, "within a month of bringing me home to meet your parents, you would be bugging
your scientist buddies to find a way to send me back when
you discovered that under all this wonderful plumpness, I'm
really not the woman you thought I was."

He still said nothing, and it took Isobel several heartbeats
to realize he'd opened his arm and freed her. She immediately rolled away and scooted down to the foot of the bed to
leave.

Only the blanket didn't appear to be leaving with her. She
looked over her shoulder to find Daniel holding on to it, his
expression . . . unreadable.

She gave a sharp tug on the blanket.

Daniel tugged back. And despite scrambling to catch it,
the blanket flew off her and onto the pillow beside him, leaving her utterly naked.

"What did you do that for!" she cried, hunching her
shoulders to hug herself protectively, glaring back at him.

"Because I wanted to. And because I could."

Like he could take her with him if he wanted to?

Isobel stood up and calmly walked across the cabin to the

corner. She gathered up several pieces of her clothes, then walked to the door, stepped outside into the cold night air, and closed it softly behind her.

Apparently when a twenty-third-century warrior found himself on the receiving end of a flat-out rejection, he didn't get disappointed, or humiliated, or want to burst into tears.

He simply got even.

Nine

Isobel woke up to sunlight hitting her face and immediately closed her eyes with a stifled groan. How in hell was she going to survive being trapped on this stupid island with Daniel for three more excruciating days? She had made such a fool of herself last night, she was probably going to develop a permanent sunburn from blushing every time she looked at him.

Opening one eye and finding the cabin empty, she groaned out loud. Never mind looking at Daniel; she was going to have to touch him, too. Because if she didn't change the bandage on his side, his sutures could get infected. She'd shot him full of dog antibiotics right after the surgery, and mixed some with the olive oil she'd put on his salad, but considering what the horse tranquilizer had done to him, there was a good chance his body didn't have a clue what to do with twenty-first-century antibiotics.

Then he'd get a fever she had no way of fighting.

And then he'd die.

And Chase and Noah and Micah would return and find

out she'd killed their brother, and Chase would wring *her* neck instead of Snuggles'.

Assuming she didn't die of embarrassment first.

Isobel pulled the blanket over her head with another groan. The moment she'd come back in the cabin last night and curled up in the corner, Daniel had picked her up and carried her to the bed, covered her with the blanket, then gone outside.

All without saying a word.

And apparently without coming back in, either.

She suddenly bolted upright. "Ohmigod! What if he thought he was well enough to join his brothers and swam to shore like he did before?" She threw off the blanket, jumped out of bed, and went hunting for her shoes. "He better not have drowned himself. How in hell am I going to explain to Chase that I *lost* his brother?" she cried, hopping to the door as she pulled on one sneaker and then the other. "Honest to God, I've treated snarling *wild* animals that didn't give me this much trouble," she muttered as she tore outside.

Only to slam head-on into a large, solid chest.

"Hey, there," the owner of the large, solid chest said with a grunt, grabbing her shoulders when she bounced off him and nearly fell back.

Isobel looked up and gasped. "Chase!"

"What are you saying about wild animals?"

She took a calming breath, stepped out of his clutches, then took another step back for insurance. "I . . . um . . . I lost your brother," she whispered, inching toward the side of the cabin as she kept an eye on his neck-wringing hands.

"Which brother?"

She finally worked up the nerve to look up. "Daniel."

"Oh, him," he said with a shrug. "That's okay. I've always wanted to be the oldest. So what were you saying about wild animals?"

Isobel took a step *toward* him this time. "That's a terrible thing to say! Brothers are precious."

"Do you have a brother?"

"No. But if I did, I certainly wouldn't want to find out someone had *lost* him."

"What about a sister? And parents? Do your parents live near you?"

Isobel scowled at him. "My parents are dead. But what are we talking about me for, when Daniel's out there somewhere?" she said, angrily waving toward the ocean. "Probably drowning, because he thinks he's such a warrior that he can swim to shore two days after having major surgery."

She stepped around him and strode toward the bluff. "Okay, if you won't go find him, then I will. Honest to God, if everyone's counting on you guys to keep the human race from becoming extinct, mankind is in really big trouble," she continued when he fell into step beside her. "Maybe along with the animal, you should take back some *nonfiction* books." She stopped when they reached the bluff and she saw the beach was empty. "Dammit, where's your boat?" she asked, turning around and heading to the beach on the other side of the island. "I need it to go find your no-good, rotten brother."

"I can see by your concern that you've obviously grown quite fond of Daniel," Chase said, falling in step beside her again.

Isobel stopped and shot him a brilliant smile. "Oh yes, how can anyone not grow fond of a man who leads a girl to believe he wants her, then totally humiliates her by flat-out rejecting her when she works up the nerve to accept what he'd been offering all day?"

"It certainly wasn't Daniel's intention to humiliate you, Isobel. He was trying to protect you."

"Protect me from what?"

"From yourself." He grabbed her shoulders when she gasped and took a step back. "Isobel, Daniel knows that when a woman gives herself to a man, her heart usually follows. He was protecting you from getting your heart broken."

Of all the arrogant, outrageous, condescending things he could have said, the idea that Daniel was protecting her from herself was . . . it was . . .

Oh God, there were those prickles of heat climbing into

her cheeks again, and damn if her chin wasn't starting to quiver. Without even thinking about what she was doing, much less *who* she was doing it to, she punched Chase in the belly hard enough to make him grunt and let go of her.

And then she ran as if the hounds of hell were after her.

But she didn't make it ten feet before she was stopped by another large, solid chest—only this time she knew instantly who it belonged to.

"Daniel! You didn't drown!"

Not answering because he was too busy glaring past her shoulder, he pulled her into his arms and held her against his chest. Isobel didn't even protest, because . . . well, because she just as soon not let him see her blushing to high heaven.

"Why was she running?" he asked over her head. "What did you do to her?"

"Hey, she punched me," Chase said, walking to them. "She was so distraught that you might be drowning and we weren't going to look for you that her emotions obviously got in the way of her judgment."

Wonderful. She could hear the amusement in Chase's voice, as well as feel the tension humming through Daniel. So how in hell was she supposed to get out of *this* mess without utterly humiliating herself again?

"Eww! What a monstrous snake!" she cried, pointing at the ground as she stamped her feet in alarm and struggled to get free.

Daniel's arms merely tightened. "Fool me once, shame on you; fool me twice, shame on me," he whispered into her hair.

She snorted. "Did you get that one out of one of your great great-grandmother's books?"

His arms relaxed but didn't let her go.

That was okay with her; she still wasn't quite up to facing him yet.

"Where's the snake?" Noah asked, running toward them. "I want to see it."

"There is no snake," Daniel said. "Isobel pretends to see things to distract unsuspecting dogs before she pokes them with a needle. Only apparently it doesn't work on cats." He gave her a warning squeeze. "Or on men."

"It sure as hell worked on you the first time," she muttered into his shirt.

"So, have you asked her yet?" Micah asked, having run up with Noah.

"No," Daniel said.

Isobel tilted her head back to look up at him. But when she found herself staring into his beautiful, ocean blue eyes, she immediately buried her face in his shirt again. "Ask me what?"

"We want you to help us catch a raccoon," Micah said.

Isobel leaned back in surprise, but having learned her lesson, she looked at Micah instead of Daniel. "You think the animal you need is a raccoon?" She suddenly pulled free and walked over to Micah. "What happened to you?" She looked at Noah. "And you!" She stepped closer and squinted up at his face. "Are those claw marks? From a raccoon?"

Noah nodded.

"Well, come on then," she said, taking his arm and leading him toward the cabin, figuring that as distractions went, this one worked. "You, too, Micah. I have to clean those scratches before they get infected. There's a whole world of nasty bacteria growing under animal claws."

Noah freed himself from her clutches but continued walking with her, Micah and Daniel and Chase following behind.

"If they have bacteria under their claws, how come they don't infect themselves?" Noah asked. "We saw them putting their little hands in their mouths."

"You did? Where?"

"Just fifty meters behind your house, down by the stream." He grinned over at her. "We found some bread in one of your cupboards and filled a large can you had in your shed with it, then set it beside a tree down by the stream."

She arched a brow. "So you know what bread is, but you didn't think to pack any for *us*?" She shook her head. "Never mind. Okay, you filled a trash can with bread and then lugged it into the woods. But why?"

"Because one of your books said raccoons like to sneak in when it's dark and lift off the covers to get to the food inside. So we lured them with the bread, then waited in the bushes for them."

She stopped walking and eyed the scratches on his face. "And what did you do when they showed up?" she asked, even though she had a pretty good idea already.

"We jumped out and grabbed them," Micah interjected, holding up his battered hands as proof. He shook his head. "They're not as friendly as your rabbit."

Isobel looked at Chase, noticing he didn't have a scratch on him. "And just what were you doing while Micah and Noah were wrestling raccoons?" she drawled.

"I was in your den, reading," he drawled back. "Because I do not believe a raccoon is the animal we need."

"Why not?"

"Because it's not from the family of Lepor-something. I don't know the rest of the word, but I did find that raccoons are of the Procyonidae genus, which isn't even close."

The hairs on the back of Isobel's neck rose in alarm. "You're looking for a member of a genus that begins with the letters l-e-p-o-r?" she whispered. "Um . . . what makes you think that?"

When Chase's eyes sharpened on her, Isobel realized she probably looked as if she'd just seen a ghost. She started for the cabin again.

"The only thing our medical scientists on the moon were able to come up with is four or five Latin genera for which animal it might be," Chase told her, falling in beside her again. "But they aren't sure of the spelling; the data uploads they got from Earth were garbled, because radiation was already leaking out of some of the nuclear reactors and causing interference. But even though I've been scouring your books, I still haven't been able to narrow it down, much less translate it to a common name. We can't afford to mess this up, Isobel," he said gravely, "because if we don't find an animal with the proper attributes that can fight this particular germ, then we have nothing."

"Did your scientists send you here with actual data, or is it all in your head?"

Pulling her to a stop, Chase reached in his pocket and took out what looked like an iPod, touched a button that caused the screen to light up, then handed it to her. "It's been difficult for them to solve a problem from over four hundred thousand kilometers away, especially with no animals to study. The scientists on Earth sent us what they had on developing a vaccine, but our worry is that just like the animals mutated, so did the germ."   •

Isobel frowned at the notations on the tiny screen, then turned to face all four of them. "How about I make a deal with you? You take me home right now and let me go over this information," she said, holding up the iPod-like device, "and let's see if I can't help you decide exactly which animal you need." She shot them what she hoped was a reassuring smile. "And once I do, then I will help you catch that animal."

"We only have nine hours," Chase said, "and then we must leave, with or without the animal."

"But I thought you had four more days?"

"Our time links have been signaling us that they're running low on power," Daniel interjected. "If we don't return to 2243 in nine hours, we won't be able to return at all."

"Then go plug them into a charger or something, and come back."

He shook his head. "It's not that simple, Isobel. The cargo transport we used to come here from the moon is supplying the energy for our links." He smiled sadly. "And I'm sure Neil and our parents are right now working to get every last drop of that energy out of its antiquated fuel source. If we don't activate our links ourselves, Neil will do it for us in exactly nine hours."

"Then come on," she said, heading back to the beach. "We're burning daylight!"

Daniel grabbed her arm to stop her. "We must find Snuggles first. She hopped away from me earlier and is exploring the woods," he said, pointing to her left.

"We don't have time," Isobel told him, pulling away and

heading for the beach again. "She's a rabbit; she'll be fine. I'll come back and get her . . . later."

But Snuggles chose that exact moment to come tearing out of the bushes at Micah—causing him to trip over himself to avoid stepping on her. Then the little imp ran right over to Daniel, sat up on her haunches, and begged him to pick her up.

Which he did, immediately tucking her inside his jacket with a laugh. "Okay, let's go," he said, clasping Isobel's hand and leading her to the beach.

And sure enough, her face started prickling again at the feel of his large, warm, and rather proprietary hand holding hers.

*   *   *

Eight hours and two pots of coffee later, Isobel had most of the books in her den strewn over every available surface, including the floor. Micah and Noah were quietly following her around, picking up the books she would snap shut and shove away, and silently piling them into neat stacks that she would then dismantle as she went digging for something she'd read in one of them.

Chase was also following her around, reading over her shoulder.

And Daniel? Well, he was roaming through her house and surgery and barn, to study what type of structures they should build in 2243, he'd told her just before he and Snuggles—who seemed way too content in his arms—had disappeared.

Meanwhile, she was getting more than a little frantic as she searched in vain for something—anything—that would help her find another species of animal that would satisfy the barely decipherable formulas on Chase's device.

But try as she might, for some stupid, insane, no good, rotten reason, the only genus of mammal that appeared even close to what they needed was Leporidae.

Or in layman terms, a *rabbit*.

Or in more personal terms, Snuggles.

And if Chase had known how to work backward from the

Latin genus, she didn't doubt that she'd be standing in an empty den right now, in absolute, stark silence, minus her pet.

"We have less than an hour, Isobel," he said, straightening with a sigh and closing the book they were reading. "Do you or do you not agree with me that of the five names they gave us, it's the Lepor-something family we are looking for? Because if it is, you need to tell us what animal that is exactly, so we can go catch one *now*."

She also sighed, rubbing her eyes with her fists, then finally looked directly at him. "Yes, I agree with you," she said softly, just as Daniel walked into the room. She looked at each of the four men in turn, who were all looking at her expectantly, then settled her gaze on Chase. "Um . . . they don't intend to kill this animal, do they, to develop the vaccine?"

"No. They need to keep it alive, to draw its blood."

Isobel took a shuddering breath. "Then the genus is Leporidae, and the animal you're looking for, is a rabbit."

The room suddenly went silent enough that they could have heard a mouse sneeze, and almost as one, all four men stopped breathing.

When she felt silent tears streaming down her cheeks, Isobel hugged herself and nodded toward Daniel. "I guess mankind's salvation has been r-right here under our noses all . . . all along."

"Are there no other rabbits we could take?" Daniel whispered, placing his hand over Snuggles' ears, as if protecting her from their conversation. "A wild one, or . . . some other one we could find?"

"There's a chance one of the pet shelters might have a rabbit," she said, even as she swiped at her cheek and shook her head. "But the closest shelter is in Ellsworth, and even if they did have one, it would take several hours to get there, fill out the paperwork they require, and then get back to your island."

"We don't have several hours," Chase interjected softly.

"I-I know."

Chase pulled a tiny metal collar out of his pocket as he

walked over to Daniel and held out his hands. "At any cost, brother; to us, or anyone, or any thing," he said quietly.

Daniel glanced at Isobel, his dark-as-the-ocean eyes locking on hers briefly before he looked back at Chase. "We can come back," he growled tightly. "Isobel will find us several rabbits, and we will come back and get them."

"We can't," Chase said, shaking his head. "The transport might not have the energy for another trip. As it is, we can't even get back to the moon. We'll have to develop the vaccine ourselves and have it waiting for the others when they arrive."

"Dammit, Daniel! Just give him Snuggles and go!" Isobel cried, turning away. "All of you, just get the hell out of my house. Now!"

She ran out of the den, down the hall, and into her surgery, slamming the door behind her so hard the windows rattled. She blindly groped her way along the reception counter and fell into one of the waiting-room chairs, then bent at the waist, buried her face in her hands on her knees, and broke into loud, gut-wrenching sobs.

Honest to God, she wanted to die.

No, she wanted to go with them!

She could help them. She knew stuff they couldn't possibly know about Earth, and animals, and vaccines, and medicine! And weather. And fishing. And what plants were edible. Dammit, she could help.

No, she just wanted to die!

She was so distraught that she didn't even scream when she was suddenly plucked out of the chair, slammed against a solid chest, and hugged so tightly that her last sob came out as a strangled squeak.

"Stop crying, Isobel," Daniel growled, sitting down in one of the chairs to cradle her against his chest. "I don't like it."

Realizing that he was shaking nearly as badly as she was, she bunched his shirt in her fists and cried harder.

"I'm sorry, Isobel," he whispered. "For everything. You have been nothing but kind and generous to us, and so brave through all we forced upon you; I'm sorry we hurt you. But mostly I'm sorry that I have hurt you," he continued gutturally, stroking her hair. "And by all that I hold dear, I will find a way to make this up to you, I swear."

"You can't! You're going to disappear into the ether!" she wailed, struggling against him because she was afraid she'd start begging him to take her with them.

"I'll come back!" he snapped. "I will find a way."

"I won't be here!" she snapped right back, lifting her head to glare at him. "So don't waste your precious energy. Save it for your colony."

His mouth came down on hers in a searing, heart-stealing kiss, and Isobel clasped his face in her hands and put everything she couldn't say into kissing him back.

And that's when she knew; without their ever making love, this sexy, arrogant, growling man had ruined her for all men. She would never again find anyone who made her heart race the way Daniel did, or make her hot all over just by describing what he wanted to do to her, or make her so angry and crazy and excited all at once that she wanted to smack him.

No, she couldn't imagine ever falling in love with anyone except Daniel.

Isobel suddenly felt herself tumbling, her arms windmilling wildly as she tried to catch herself. She banged into the chair then fell to the floor with a jarring thud, her cry of surprise lost in the deafening boom throbbing through the heavy, shimmering air.

"Nooo, take me with you!" she screamed in a keening wail, curling into a tight ball right there on the floor, in her utterly empty waiting room. "Oh, Daniel, I want to love you," she quietly sobbed into the stark silence.

Ten

Isobel sat cross-legged on the floor in front of the crackling fireplace in her den, listening to the blizzard-force winds bang a shutter on one of the upstairs windows as she slurped down a spoonful of soupy ice cream. She glanced around at the empty shelves with a shuddering sigh and tried to work up some enthusiasm at the thought of her books reverently lined up in her new den, in her new house, attached to her new surgery in Kansas.

It had taken her two months to find a veterinarian practice for sale that was as far from Maine as she could get while still being a thousand miles from the ocean. Then it had taken her another month to buy it, and two weeks to pack her belongings. At nine o'clock this morning, she'd signed the papers selling this practice to a starry-eyed young woman just out of veterinarian school, then watched the moving van disappear down her driveway an hour later with all her belongings.

And tomorrow morning at seven o'clock sharp, blizzard or no blizzard, she was leaving for Kansas herself.

She'd tried getting her life back to normal after her little . . . adventure into the twilight zone, but right in the middle of her second date with the last available man in the
county, she had suddenly realized it was time to stop pretending that she would ever feel normal again.

She had borrowed a boat and gone to the island at least
twice a week until the winter storms had put an end to her
sitting on a log and looking around, trying to picture Daniel
and his family on that exact same island two hundred and
thirty years in the future. She would imagine them cooking
their meals over a campfire, drinking out of the freshwater
spring that bubbled up next to the stunted pine tree, and
learning to catch fish and dig clams and avoid marauding
seagulls.

She hoped they took their time introducing themselves to
new proteins.

There was so much she could teach them about life on
Earth; like how to prepare for the change of seasons, and
how they could learn from the animals what worked and
what didn't when it came to choosing a site to build their
home.

It was at that last thought, after one of her last trips to the
island, that Isobel had realized they'd probably moved to the
mainland shortly after the men had returned. She'd sat in her
dooryard, staring out the windshield at her home, and wondered if maybe they might choose to build *their* home on the
exact same site. It was a good piece of land, with a stream
running behind the low knoll that was sheltered from the
fierce Gulf of Maine storms by towering pines and hemlock.

Which would actually be a whole new generation of trees
in 2243.

She dipped her spoon in the semimelted maple fudge
again, but then stopped with it poised halfway to her mouth
when she suddenly realized she was no longer alone in the
house. She slowly turned her head to see Daniel standing in
the doorway, silently watching her. She just as slowly looked
away to set the spoon back in the ice cream, took a shuddering breath, and looked at the doorway again.

He was still there, as big and strong and larger-than-life as she remembered; only his hair was longer and he had the beginnings of a beard, but his shoulders were just as broad, his body just as ripped, and his eyes just as stunningly, piercingly blue.

"H-how long have you been standing there?"

"No more than five minutes."

She set the ice cream on the floor and slowly stood up, not once taking her eyes off him; afraid that if she did, he would disappear. She stood right where she'd been sitting and faced him, shoving her hands in her pockets so he wouldn't see how badly they were trembling.

"How long are you s-staying?"

"No more than five more minutes."

She took a step back at the feeling of being punched in the gut and pulled her hands out and crossed her arms under her breasts to hug herself. "That's it? You came all the way back here for only ten minutes?" she whispered, fighting the tremors threatening to buckle her knees.

"Ten minutes is all I need."

"To do . . . did you bring Snuggles back?"

"No. I told you, Isobel, traveling into the future is a one-way journey. We can travel back and then return to our own time, but we cannot travel forward and then return to our natural time. I couldn't bring Snuggles with me."

"Th-then why did you come back here?" she whispered, fighting the lump in her throat that was threatening to strangle her.

"I came back for you."

She locked every last muscle in her body, afraid to move or even breathe when he stretched open his arms toward her, as it was then that she noticed the thick metal collar in his hand, exactly like the one he was wearing around his neck.

"But you must come to me, Isobel," he said softly, "because, like your pet, it will be a one-way journey for you as well." When several seconds passed and she hadn't moved, one side of his mouth lifted. "Take your time," he drawled. "You have four minutes to get from there to here."

"Four minutes isn't very much time for a girl to decide if she's willing to give up maple fudge ice cream for the rest of her life."

His smile disappeared, his complexion darkened, and his eyes hardened. "I gave you four months." But then he sighed, motioning to her with his still outstretched hands. "Come to me, Isobel."

"E-everything I own is on a truck headed to Kansas."

"It doesn't matter; you can't bring anything with you, anyway." One corner of his mouth lifted again. "In fact, there's a very good chance the twenty-first-century clothes you're wearing won't travel into the future with you."

She took a step back. "I'm going to arrive in 2243 *naked*?"

"My mother has let out a few of her outfits for you to wear." His grin turned into a full-blown smile. "And I made sure she added extra material in certain . . . areas." He motioned with his outstretched hands again. "Come to me, Isobel."

She took a hesitant step forward. "I-is it going to hurt?"

"No more than having a needle stuck in your arm. Three minutes, Isobel."

She took another step toward him. And then another one. "What if your mother decides she doesn't like me?" she whispered. She stopped. "Because if she's expecting me to put up with your bullying just because you're some spoiled-rotten warrior . . . well, I don't think I can pretend to be appropriately awed, Daniel."

"My mother is going to love you."

She started slowly walking toward him again, not because she didn't want to run but because her entire body had turned to quivering mush. Yet she somehow managed to end up between his outstretched arms, only he didn't close them around her.

"And your father? And Neil?" She eyed him worriedly. "And what about Chase? Does he know you came back here to get me?" She took a step back. "It's not like you can just . . . dump me or something, if this doesn't work out."

Daniel looked over her right shoulder and his eyes suddenly widened in horror. "Holy Christ, what is that!" he shouted, pointing behind her.

She spun around to look at where he was pointing, only to gasp when she felt the collar close around her neck with a loud snap. And Isobel suddenly felt herself tumbling again, and windmilled her arms in surprise as a deafening boom throbbed through the heavy, shimmering air. Only instead of landing with a jarring thud, she was *pulled* into the strong, secure, unbreakable embrace of a twenty-third-century Moonlander warrior as they *both* disappeared into the ether.

Tomorrow Is Another Day

Sandra Hill

One

Not so easy in the Big Easy . . .

"Life is just a box of pecan pralines, *cher*. Sometimes you get a rotten nut."

Larry Wilson stopped dead in his tracks and glared at his Cajun friend, Justin LeBlanc. Larry was real good at glaring. Probably why his nickname was "Scary Larry."

"Really, Larry, it's been five years since your wife died. My Mawmaw allus says ya gotta put the bad times behind ya and move on."

Larry gritted his teeth. He did not discuss Bethany and her drowning, ever, but he knew Cage meant well. So, instead of punching his lights out, he said, "Honest to God, Cage! What are you . . . some kind of frickin' Forrest Gump now?"

From his other side, a scoffing sound came from Sylvester "Sly" Simms, a big black dude from Harlem. As they strolled down Bourbon Street—forget strolling, I'm limping—Sly was gaining a fair amount of attention for the three of them, all Navy SEALs. Hell, no wonder! Sly was so good looking he used to model men's tighty-whities for Esquire. Sly laughed. "Just so long as his Cajun Mrs. Gump . . . uh, Mawmaw . . . doesn't say 'stupid is as stupid does.'"

"I *am* stupid . . . to have come to New Orleans with you two. I could have handled—"

"No, my friend." Sly put up a halting hand. "We're going to help correct the problem. We caused it."

That was for damn sure. The two dingbats had concocted this idea of signing him up for an Internet dating service . . . Extreme Dating, a New Orleans–based company that employed some unique methods. The people who paid overinflated prices to subscribe had to be engaged in the extremes of their professions. Olympic swimmer. Mountain climber. Celebrity divorce lawyer. Erotica author. Special forces. Stunt man and woman. Paratrooper. Flying doctor. NASCAR driver. Rockette. Firefighter. Blue Angel.

What better candidate than a Navy SEAL! Or so Cage and Sly had thought. Unfortunately, they hadn't signed up themselves, but used his name and photos instead. Also unfortunate was the response . . . a huge response. Women stalking him at home and on the base. His Internet server threatening to shut him down. He'd become the laughing-stock of all the SEAL teams. And him limping around with a severely bruised hamstring after tripping over a woman camped out on his doorstep. He was thinking about making a bonfire of the bags full of mail piled in the foyer of the house he shared in Coronado, California with these two morons.

He'd tried by telephone and mail to resolve the issue, and, although Extreme Dating had taken his info off the website, the problem continued. Now he had an appointment with the company owner to see what could be done.

Sly interrupted his musings with an elbow to the ribs. He was gawking at something across the street. "Lookee there. It's a bare-naked woman. Just standin' in the doorway."

But, whoa! She wasn't just standing there now. She was waving at the three of them, beckoning.

Cage grabbed Sly by the back of his belt, preventing him

from moving. "It's a cat house, you idiot. Holy crawfish! Ya must have hookers in New York City."

"Sure, but they don't stand bare naked on Forty-second Street flashin' their goodies to every passerby."

"This is N'awleans. We do things different. And, believe me, thass the least of what you'll see if you come in the nighttime. Talk about!" Cage rolled his eyes. "I'm thirsty. Let's stop for a Hurricane."

"I am not stopping again. Not for frou-frou drinks, or gumbo, or voodoo shops, or to stare at some moldering statue or naked women, even if they're standing on their fool heads," Larry asserted, continuing to limp along. "Unless Ms. Marguerite Baptiste herself is naked." Now there was a horrific thought. She was probably fifty and broad as a barn door. "No matter! It's almost seven. Do or die time."

         ❀   ❀   ❀

Signed, sealed and delivered, baby . . .

Marguerite Baptiste was swearing at her computer, which had frozen again, when she heard a noise in the outer office of Extreme Dating, her Internet matchmaking company. Through the open door, she could see three men enter, and her assistant, Sandy Cuzzins, speaking to them.

"Master Chief Lawrence Wilson to see you," Sandy said into Margo's intercom, although she could have just spoken a little louder, and Margo would have heard her. The office was that small.

"If the tech guy from Deak's Geeks finally shows up, let him start on your computer," she replied. The computer technician had promised to be here at nine A.M., then noon, then two P.M., then had made no promises at all as only voice mail picked up. People in the South, and New Orleans was definitely the South, tended to move at their own slower pace. She should know, having lived here her entire life. Like, "I'll be there shortly," or "by and by, chère," could mean today or next week.

She inhaled and exhaled for calm to prepare for her next appointment. No one liked to admit they were wrong, least of all her. And her company could not withstand any more financial crises, not in this economy. "Send Mr. Wilson in."

All the air she'd just exhaled came back in on a gasp as she got her first real look at her Navy SEAL from hell who limped in. Not a good sign. Was the limp comparable to a neck brace for accident victims? *No, no, no! I am not going to think negative thoughts. Be positive, Margo. Put a smile on. That is your motto.*

But, really, this guy's pictures did not do him justice. And she had seen some super hotties in this business. He was tall, over six feet, and buff as you would expect from a special forces member. That was evident even in the button-down denim shirt he wore with faded jeans. In his early or mid-thirties, his black hair was military short, almost shaved on the sides, but it was his eyes that caught and held her attention. They were an eerie pale blue, almost gray, and rather haunting. No, not haunting . . . haunted.

"Hello, Mr. Wilson," she said, rising to stand behind her desk and motioning for him to come forward. "What can I do for you?"

He gave her an insolent once-over survey. "You know damn well what I want. Fix the problem you caused, sweetheart, or I'm going to sue your ass off."

"There's no need for threats."

"No?" He arched his brows at her as he braced his arms on her desk and leaned forward. She could almost smell his anger.

She was no fool. She sank back into her chair.

"My lawyer and I have been doing everything possible. We removed your name and data from the website. We posted a newsflash that your name had been accidentally entered without your permission and that all attempts to contact you would be futile."

"What about all those files already downloaded? What am I supposed to do with the hordes of women who are jumping me like a piece of prime meat?"

Her lips twitched with a smile.

"Think it's funny, do you, cupcake?"

She bristled at the deliberately insulting "cupcake" but decided not to take offense. *Pick your battles, Margo.* "Some men would consider it a compliment."

"Some men are assholes."

Now I am definitely insulted. "Nice talk!"

He shrugged. "I'm way past the polite stage, honey."

"Do not call me honey, or cupcake. That is sexual harassment."

"And what kind of harassment is it when a nutcase Internet dating service puts my name and address and picture up for a couple thousand loser women to drool over? And some men, too." He straightened his body and eased himself with a wince into the chair in front of her desk. His leg was probably hurting. Hopefully, he hadn't walked up the three flights to her office. The elevator had been as wonky today as her computer. But that was the consequence of being located in an old building in the historic French Quarter.

"Number one, we never put up addresses of any of our clients."

"Hah! 'Navy SEAL.' 'Trains in Coronado, California.' 'Runs on the beach at dawn every morning,'" he quoted. "Do you have any idea how small a town Coronado is, sweet cheeks?"

She bared her teeth at the disgusting endearment. "Number two, none of the men and women who sign up for our service are losers. They are highly successful people engaged in extreme positions of power or celebrity."

"Blah, blah, blah."

"Have you thought about taking advantage of this opportunity? Meeting some exceptional women?"

"Get real!"

Okay, so he's not looking for a woman. Or maybe it's just extreme women on his non-radar.

"Are you anorexic, by the way?" he asked.

"Whaaat?"

"Your arms are like sticks."

She could feel her face heat. "They are not!"

"I like a little flesh on my women."

"Good thing I'm not one of your women. And, for the record, I'm slim because of metabolism, not starvation. And I work out every day." *Well, every couple days.*

He didn't smile, but an expression resembling satisfaction flicked across his face, and she realized that he was purposely goading her.

"Not that you're not hot." His eyes locked on her breasts, clearly visible in her silk tank top.

Her warm face got warmer, but that wasn't what he'd meant by hot. "Listen . . . if you've come here to insult me—"

"It was a compliment. Jeesh! Since when is being considered sexy an insult?"

"Let's start over. My name is Marguerite Baptiste. I am the president of Extreme Dating. My friends call me Margo." She leaned across the desk, extending a hand for him to shake.

At first, he just stared at her. Then he took her hand and shook it. His big calloused palm engulfed hers, causing her skin to tingle, even when he released her hand. "My name is Larry Wilson. My teammates call me Scary Larry."

This guy was scary, all right . . . scary gorgeous, scary irresistible, scary like crazy to a twenty-seven-year-old woman who hadn't been involved in a relationship for so long her birth control pills had long passed their expiration date. It was the eyes. And the lines between his eyes and bracketing his mouth . . . definitely not smile lines. Something bad had happened to this man, she just knew it, to put that perpetual glower there.

"Larry, I promise you. I am going to do everything in my power to make you happy."

❀　❀　❀

Was it heartache, or heartburn? . . .

Larry was stunned speechless at that promise because, frankly, his warped mind was already conjuring some things she could do to make him happy, and none had a thing to do with her dating service.

From the moment he'd laid eyes on Ms. I-am-the-president-la-de-da Baptiste, Larry had felt the oddest sensation in his chest. Like someone was squeezing his heart, making him breathless. And he was tingling in some interesting places. Even worse, he'd been practically floored by a spontaneous, knee-buckling, mind-numbing hard-on, which was why he'd just sat down. It was amazing because he hadn't been turned on—in fact, he'd been practically a eunuch—since Bethany.

She was a little above average in height, probably five-seven, and although he'd remarked on her being skinny, she was just fine. More than fine. Slender but well-formed in brown linen slacks, with a beige silk tank top outlining high, full breasts. She'd attempted to tame her long, curly blonde hair into a knot on top of her head with one of those claw thingees. To no avail. Tendrils had come loose and framed a heart-shaped face and a pouty rosebud mouth. Yeah, he was referring to her mouth as a rosebud like some frickin' girly guy. Next he would be quoting poetry.

He shook his head to clear it, feeling like a total dork. He was a thirty-three-year-old Navy SEAL who had been around the block more times than one of Sly's Forty-second Street hookers, and here he was tossing out silly insults like a clumsy teenager in heat, practically panting.

Cage had talked him into this fool trip to the Crescent City. "Listen, *cher*. My Mawmaw, she allus sez, 'ya cain't cook a gumbo if yer drivin' down the highway,' " Cage had told him.

To which he'd snapped, "What the hell does that mean?"

"Means ya gotta settle this matter face-ta-face. Not by telephone or email or snail mail. No one's gonna take ya seriously if they doan know who they're dealin' with. Glare at her jist like yer doin' now, and she'll prob'ly jump up and down tryin' ta handle yer bizness, lickedy split. Talk about!"

So, here he was, using insults as a method of persuasion. Did he really think pissing her off would make his embarrassing dilemma go away? He was about to try a different tact when she asked, "Why do they call you Scary Larry?"

Huh? "Look at me."

"You are drop-dead gorgeous. I'm not surprised that so many women want to connect with you."

His jaw dropped, and he turned to see if there was someone

behind him. *She likes me? Me?* "Are you blind? I was only passably good looking before . . . well, just before. Now, more than one person has told me that I'm scary-bad looking."

"Whoever told you that was lying. What happened?"

"I was married. My wife . . . my pregnant wife died in a freak ferry collision, and—" He shook his head like a wet dog at having spoken aloud what he'd been only thinking. "I never discuss Bethany. Never."

"I am so sorry, Larry. Have you tried grief counseling?"

"Hell, no! I handle my rage by killing tangos. Lots of them. And I'm damn good at it, too." *I must be more rattled by this crap than I realized to be spilling my guts like this.*

"Tangos?"

"Bad guys. Terrorists."

She nodded, as if she understood, which she couldn't possibly.

Enough of this nonsense! "I want this situation cleared up now. I'm drowning in mail . . . two thousand letters and growing. My computer mailbox has crashed from overload a dozen times. Women are breaking into the special forces training grounds looking for me, and half the sailors on the North Island Naval Air Station are laughing their BDUs off at the joke of the year . . . me. Not to mention this bruised hamstring"— he patted his pain-ridden thigh near the knee—"caused by a forced handspring over a woman who'd made my doorstep a home away from home, probably the loony bin. It's an injury that might very well land me on permanent desk duty."

"I had no idea it was that bad. I'm so sor—"

"And, by the way, what the hell were you doing on *Good Morning America*?"

She blushed prettily. "That was a mistake. I realize that now. Classic bait and switch. They lured me on to the show saying they were interested in the concept of extreme dating, then made it be all about you. I should have known better."

"Damn straight you should have. And I don't give a rat's ass who was at fault. Just fix it."

"Are you sure you wouldn't like to avail yourself of our services?"

"Hell, no!" *Unless you're offering yourself, baby.*

"I have an idea."

So do I, baby. So do I. But then he realized that it wasn't Margo who had spoken but Cage, who stood in the doorway. He looked like an idiot in a cowboy hat and boots, but women seemed to go for the image. Sly was sitting on the secretary's desk in the other office, doing his usual thing . . . charming her panties off, no doubt.

Larry waved him in and said, "Cage, this is Margo Baptiste, owner of this screwball company."

She bristled.

Good! "And, Margo, meet my friend and teammate, Justin LeBlanc. A dingbat Louisiana cowboy."

Cage wasn't at all insulted. In fact, he preened as if he'd just said he had golden nuts. "Jist call me Cage, sugah," he said in an exaggerated Cajun drawl.

Margo didn't seem as insulted by Cage's endearment as she had been by his.

Dammit!

"So what's your big idea?"

"You've been lettin' the tail wag the dog so far. The only way ta get rid of all this publicity is ta give them somethin' else ta feed on." Cage sank down into the other chair in front of the desk and flashed Margo a smile and a wink.

She smiled back.

Dammit!

"You two are gonna get engaged," Cage said.

"What?" he and Margo both shouted.

"Now, now, it's jist fer make believe, but ya gotta use yer website ta publicize every little thing, Margo, darlin'."

"Margo, darlin' " ? What the hell!

"I can see the banners proclaiming, 'Brave Navy SEAL Falls for Beautiful Matchmaker.' Every day ya kin feed them a bit more news. 'The Ring.' 'The Betrothal Party.' 'The Wedding Plans.'"

"You are an idiot." He glowered at Cage, even more than usual.

"I don't know. He might have a point," Margo said, tapping her lips with a forefinger thoughtfully.

"Huh?"

"If women who log on to my website see that you're taken, they'll eventually fade away. And the press will give it only a fifteen-minutes-of-fame type of attention after the initial announcement."

"I am not getting married again. No way!"

"Who asked you to?" she snapped back.

"This is the dumbest idea I've ever heard of."

After that, Cage and Margo ignored him as they made the most god-awful plans. "I have to be back at Coronado in three days," he interjected finally.

"Well then I guess we'll have to work fast," Margo said. "Can you be here tomorrow at eleven? I'll get a photographer and my webmaster in here. Hopefully my computer system will be fixed by then."

"I haven't agreed to all this crap," he said, but he did agree, grudgingly, to come in the next morning . . . to think about it overnight. Yeah, right. He was going to go get blitzed.

As he limped down Bourbon Street with Cage a short time later—Sly already had a date with the secretary—Cage looked at him and laughed.

"What now?"

"We're gonna turn you into Happy Larry yet. Guar-an-teed!"

❊   ❊   ❊

She was gone with the wind . . . uh, elevator . . .

Guilt tugged at Margo's conscience as she stuffed her briefcase, turned off the office lights, locked the door, and headed for the elevator.

But more than that, she was stunned by the effect the sad Navy SEAL had on her. Her heart literally ached for him. Even worse, she felt an overpowering sexual attraction, and she never ever got involved with her clients. Not that he was a client.

From the time she had been a dirt-poor kid living with a druggie mother in a fourth-ward project apartment, Margo had vowed to make enough money when she was grown up that she would never have to struggle again. And she had been successful . . .

Until recently. But the downturn in the economy had affected more than banks, real estate, restaurants, car dealers, and upscale purchases, like yachts and vacations. Yep, expensive dating agencies were a luxury in a time of depression. For the first time since she had left home at fourteen, Margo was nervous about her future.

So, yes, she had been careless, especially in agreeing to the *Good Morning America* interview. She was a smart cookie. She should have crossed her t's and dotted her i's before ever hopping on that plane to New York City.

The question was how far she could, or would, go to make him good again. How much bad publicity could she afford? Would their last-minute damage control work?

It had to. Look at how he's being harassed. His life has been turned upside down, at no fault of his own. That was the good side of her brain speaking. Her conscience.

He isn't really hurt by the publicity. Just a lot of women chasing him, which will die down once he shows he isn't available. Jeesh! It's not like anyone died or anything. This from the logical, more ambitious side of her personality.

Don't you care that he's a private man, still grieving over the death of his wife?

Absolutely. My heart goes out to him. I can see why he looks so haunted. But that's not my fault.

And the joke he's become? The subject of ridicule on the navy base?

Those guys making fun of him are just jealous. Plus, he needs to get over himself. Lighten up. Have a sense of humor.

Okay, so I go ahead with this fake engagement idea. I do

my best to make sure he's buffered from the publicity. It might even be fun.

But what if I fall for him? I haven't been attracted to a man like this in, like, forever.

I can handle it.

Margo could swear she heard laughter in her head.

The elevator started making weird, clacking noises. "Here we go again," she muttered. Honestly, she was going to have to make another call to the landlord. He either needed to replace the antiquated elevator or fix it better than he had the last six times.

There was charm in being located in the heart of the Crescent City in a building that had once been the fashionable Vieux Carre Hotel, but not when it resisted modern technology.

This elevator in itself was a relic . . . all dark mahogany with its deep patina offset by polished brass. At one time there would have been a uniformed elevator operator. She'd seen the pictures in the lobby showing the way the hotel had once looked just after the Civil War.

For a second, the elevator seemed to stall. Then, before she could press the call button, it shot downward, and crashed.

Screaming, she hit one wall, then another, before falling to the carpeted floor.

Then everything went black.

❈ ❈ ❈

Some dreams are really scary . . .

She awakened a short time later . . . or she assumed it was a short time . . . to find herself reclining on a plush velvet sofa in the lobby with a bunch of people looking down at her with concern. Strange people. Wearing strange clothing . . . clothing that would have been more appropriate in the 1800s. Women in long dresses, carrying frilly parasols, men in dark suits with fancy satin brocade vests. Several men in what looked like Yankee Civil War uniforms.

Her eyes darted about, and she began to panic. It was the lobby of her office building, but as it had been when it had been the Vieux Carre Hotel. A hundred and forty years ago! Period furniture. Flocked wallpaper. Heavy red draperies with gold braiding. Thick Brussels carpeting.

Voices began to penetrate her frozen mind.

"Miss, are you all right?"

"I think she hit her head. Someone should call a physician or take her over to Charity Hospital."

"Look at her clothing. It's scandalous."

"Maybe she's one of the girls from Simone's House of Pleasure."

"A prostitute? In a respectable hotel like this? Outrageous! Where's the hotel manager?"

Margo blinked with confusion and put a hand to the back of her head. There was a bump there. But what was going on? She must be dreaming. *A dream in color? Wow!* Yes, she must have a concussion.

Closing her eyes, she succumbed to the darkness again.

It was no better the next time she opened her eyes. If anything, there were more people, and none of them looked friendly, or familiar.

But wait, there, walking by on the edge of the crowd, heading toward the front door. It was a tall man with longish black hair and a mustache, wearing a rather worn dark suit . . . no brocade vests here. He glanced her way, then immediately forward again, finding her of no interest, apparently. Still, it was enough time for her to notice that he had strange grayish blue eyes. And he walked with a slight limp. It was Larry Wilson. Sort of.

Holy cow! Scary Larry in her dream.

How scary was that?

Two

Dream lovers they were not . . . yet . . .

Laurent Duvall was limping across the lobby of the Hotel Vieux Carre after a most unsatisfactory meeting with his banker, whom he had once considered a friend. No more.

At the Battle of Bentonville five years ago, the last full-scale Confederate offensive of the whole damn war, Laurent had suffered a leg wound which acted up on him on occasion, like when he was stressed. He was very stressed today and in no mood to stop and watch the ruckus being created by some crazy woman wearing trousers and little else. This was New Orleans; you never knew what you would see.

"Hey, you!" he heard her shout to someone.

He kept going, already worried about how he was going to buy all the supplies he would need before returning to Rosylyn, his small sugar cane plantation up the river, about thirty miles from New Orleans. If it weren't for his sister Lettie and the eight or so blacks remaining, mostly old or crippled, he would chuck it all and head for the California gold fields.

"Larry! Wait up!" The woman was still shouting behind him.

He was almost to the door leading out to Royal Street when he felt someone grab his upper arm. He turned, and just his luck, it was the crazy woman.

Her blonde hair was half falling out of a comb atop her head. Her slim figure and long legs were encased in brown linen breeches. On her upper half a sort of silk camisole, cream colored, barely covered her bosoms and left bare her arms and shoulders. A diamond hung from a thin chain around her neck, probably just glass, and she wore a new-fangled watch bracelet, which you did not see often on women. Possibly a gift from a satisfied customer. His upper lip curled with distaste. A wanton, or else a prostitute working for one of the sporting houses. Either way, he was not in the market for her particular wares. Shrugging off her hand, he started to walk away again.

She was not to be deterred. This time she jumped in front of him, blocking his way, walking backward. "Larry? Don't you know me?"

"Bloody hell, no, I don't know . . . Margaret? Is that you . . . Margaret Dubois? I thought you moved north to Pennsylvania with your family before the war." Margaret had been a skinny little thing with a heart-shaped mouth that had a tendency to pout in a most annoying fashion. Margo was still a mite skinny, but she had breasts now, and her pouty mouth was no longer unappealing.

About six years younger than he was, she had always been a bit *different* as a child, doing unsuitable things. Like setting up a stall at the French Market selling necklaces made of dried peas and acorns. Like pretending to be a boy in a horse race. Like smoking one of her father's cigars in public. Like interfering at a slave auction. Well, that last he did not disagree with, but her methods had been scandalous.

But, heavens above! A prostitute? Could she have sunk so low?

"My name is Margo . . . that's short for Marguerite, not Margaret, and my last name is Baptiste, and I've never lived anywhere but Louisiana."

They were drawing an audience . . . well, not a new audience; the same crowd that had surrounded her before had just followed in her wake. He did not have time for this, but her family had been neighbors for many years. He did not want to be impolite. "Is your family with you?"

"I have no family."

"Oh. My sympathies." They must have died. Like so many in the South, so many deaths! In fact, now that he thought on it, he seemed to recall that her father and brother had fallen at Gettysburg. "I heard that your old plantation was sold for taxes."

"Huh?"

"Where are you staying?"

"I don't know."

"Relatives?"

"I have none that I know of."

"Friends?"

"Just you, although we're not really friends. More like acquaintances, or you could say, business associates."

Uh-oh! "What are you doing here . . . at the hotel, I mean?"

"I was in the elevator, and it crashed. Next thing I knew, I was waking from a dead faint with a goose egg on the back of my head."

That explained her craziness, he supposed. Or her latest craziness.

"Why have you not finished dressing?"

"Huh? What's wrong with my clothing?"

"Margo! You're half-dressed."

"I am not!" She studied him closer. "You know, you look like Larry Wilson, but then you don't. Your hair is longer, and your clothing is way out of date, but your eyes are the same. You limp the same. And the frowny face, of course."

"Frowny . . ." *Oh, shit! She thinks I'm someone else. Hmmm.* Maybe that's a good thing. "Sorry, Miss Baptiste, but it appears we don't know each other after all. I am Laurent Duvall."

She tilted her head, uncertain.

"It has been nice meeting you, Miss Baptiste," he said, shaking her hand. "But I must be off now."

He had turned onto Dumaine Street, heading toward the river, when he noticed her running to catch up with him. He did not stop walking along the brick banquette but turned his head to glare at her.

"I'm going with you."

"You are not!"

"Hey, it's your fault that I'm here."

"I beg your pardon!"

"Listen, Larry—"

"Laurent."

"Don't they call you Larry for a nickname?"

"My *friends* call me Laurie."

"Sounds like a girl's name to me."

He growled.

"Okay, okay. I'll just call you Laurent then. Where are we going, Laurent?"

"*We* are not going anywhere."

"Oh, my God! This is amazing!"

"What?" He swiveled to see what she was looking at. Nothing out of the ordinary that he could see.

A horse-drawn milk wagon came to a halt in front of them as the Creole lady of one of the narrow houses stood at the iron-laced railing of the house's upper gallery, calling for the driver to stop. Down below, a servant ran out to have the daily order of milk filled from the spigot into a large can.

Turban clad black women with baskets atop their heads called out their wares:

"Strawberries, raspberries, cherries! Fresh-picked and sweet!"

"Come get yer pralines! Sweet and crisp!"

"Fresh baked beignets! Come buy my beignets!"

"Flowers, flowers! Roses, gardenias, lilies, and violets."

Still others peddled their products from push carts.

Here and there, tall, forest green shutters flew open on the houses, which were painted bright colors, like grand rouge, which he knew from experience came from a combination of brick dust and buttermilk. His father had once used it on the *garconniére* quarters, with great success. Housewives leaned

out the windows and invited the venders into their courtyards
to display their goods.

Another wagon passing by had a small boy in back yelling out, "Ice! Ice! Nice and cold!"

In the background the hourly bells from St. Louis Cathe-
dral on nearby Place d'Armes could be heard. Two o'clock!
Bloody hell, he was wasting time. "Go away!" he ordered
Margo, figuring rudeness might be the only method at this
point. "I don't know you, and you are wasting my time."

"Lighten up, Laurent. It's my dream, and it goes any way
I want."

He rolled his eyes, grabbed her by the upper arm, and
dragged her into a restaurant farther down Dumaine. She was
attracting too much attention with her outrageous attire. He
took her into an inner courtyard where a fountain bubbled
and tropical flowers in big pots scented the air. He shoved
her into a chair at one of the tables while he dropped into the
opposite chair. Other restaurant patrons stared at them, including a few white-robed Ursuline nuns from the convent
on Chartes Street, but then everyone resumed eating and
talking in low voices.

She picked up a parchment menu. "Isn't this nice. Hand-
made. Fine calligraphy. But not efficient, cost-wise. I could
recommend a good printer to the owners. Of course this is
not really a restaurant. Just in my dream. I know the family
who lives here. They spent a fortune restoring it last year."
Fanning her face, she smiled at him.

He was not going to be swayed by pity over her delusional state. He was not going to be swayed by a smile . . .
even though it was a very nice smile. Swearing under his
breath, he exhaled with disgust at the predicament he found
himself in.

"No wonder they call you Scary Larry! Do you ever stop
scowling?"

"Scary Larry? You are incredible. Is that how you attempt
to sway me . . . with insults?"

She shrugged and fanned herself some more. He would
like to fan her all right . . . fan her bottom. With the palm of

his hand. *Now there's an image that does not bear dwelling on. Watch yourself, Laurent,* he warned himself. The fountain and the shade alleviated some of the heat, but this was New Orleans in summertime. Humid heat was the norm. He hated being in the city. He was needed back at Rosylyn. He should not be wasting money on high-priced restaurant food.

Another clump of her hair fell out of its claw comb. Without hesitation, she raised her arms to let her hair loose into a million wavy curls. Fascinated, he watched as she finger combed her hair and redid the knot on top of her head. Belatedly, he clicked his gaping mouth shut.

But not before that wanton pose caused his blood to race and lodge between his legs, almost with a bang. He hadn't been this aroused in years. Probably because he hadn't been with a woman in a year, or was it two? This was too much! Was she deliberately tempting him? Was that her plan now . . . to entice him to help her by offering sex?

No, he did not think that was the case. Still, maybe he was being too polite. Maybe more direct methods were called for.

"I can see your nipples," he said, leaning back in his chair.

Her arms were still upraised and she froze in place. The position caused her breasts to arch out against the thin fabric of her camisole . . . *What kind of woman wears a camisole in public?*

Her breasts were high and surprisingly full for her slender frame. Very nice!

"That was certainly rude." She lowered her arms. Her cheeks bloomed with color. Apparently, despite her dementedness and wantonness, she could still blush.

"And your underarms are hairless."

"I shave there."

He arched his eyebrows. "Is that a new trend in the North?"

"I wouldn't know. I've lived in Louisiana all my life."

He placed orders for the two of them. Just gumbo, crusty bread, and thick Creole chicory coffee. Leaving it to her, she would probably order the most expensive thing, which he could not afford. Which of course she did. Adding a shrimp éfouffeé, lemonade, and later a café au lait for herself and bread pudding to share.

He braced his chin in one of his hands, elbow on the table. "Let us start over. Who are you, and what are you doing here?"

She gave him an exasperated glance, as if he already knew. Placing one of her hands over one of his resting on the table, she told him that she understood how confusing this was for him, that she was confused, too, but all he could think about . . . all he could feel . . . was the ripple of sensation that stemmed from their touching skin out to all parts of his body, making the blood drain from his head. It was torture. It was pleasure.

She was staring at him with parted lips and glazed eyes. He could tell she was equally affected by this strange sizzle between them.

But then he jerked his hand back.

She shook her head, as if in wonder.

"I repeat," he said. "Who are you, and what are you doing here?"

"Right." She inhaled and exhaled with a whooshy sound. "You are a Navy SEAL. You came into my office today. I am a matchmaker, who made a teeny tiny mistake regarding you, which I plan to correct ASAP."

He covered his eyes, then counted to ten before looking at her again. "Let me see if I understand. I am an animal. A seal. You are a matchmaker. And you're going to do something with sap, like sap in a tree?" Or was she referring to the sap rising in him like hot erotic syrup?

She waved a hand dismissively. "Of course not, but not to worry. This is only a dream."

If only that were true!

❖   ❖   ❖

She was going to be a damn Rachel Ray or die trying . . .

The waiter brought their bill, and Margo could see Laurent carefully counting out several coins. They looked like silver . . . antique silver. That, and the condition of his clothing, gave her a message loud and clear.

Reaching into her handbag, she pulled out a crisp new fifty and slapped it on the table. She'd been to the bank yesterday and had nothing smaller. "My treat," she said with a smile.

"What is that?" he asked, picking up the bill to examine it more closely.

She frowned. "Money."

"With Ulysses S. Grant on it? Pfff! Didn't take long for the general to get his face plastered everywhere, and only one year in office."

She continued to be disconcerted by his faint French accent. Creole, she supposed. Not as strong a patois as the Cajuns but distinct nonetheless. Then his words sunk in. "What? I don't understand."

He ignored her as he studied the bill closer. "What in bloody hell is this date here? Two thousand and ten. Is that meant to be a year?"

She nodded, hesitantly, and picked up his coins as well. Several 1870 G octagonal half dollars, 1870 liberty dimes, and 1870 Indianhead cents. Raising her eyes to Laurent's equally puzzled ones, which she again noted with a bit of hysterical irrelevance were blue gray with thick black lashes, against the framework of his olive skin, she asked softly, "What year is this?"

"What kind of game do you play now? It's 1870, of course."

She nodded, beginning to understand. "No, it's not, honey."

"I am not your honey."

She shrugged. Taking one of his hands, trying to ignore the weird electricity they generated, she told him, "This is 2010, one hundred and forty years into the future." She patted the hand now. "But it's only a dream. Imagine that, me dreaming myself into history?"

"I've got news for you, *honey*," he said. "This is not a dream. And it's not some future time. It's 1870, reconstruction, Yankee-military-governed, bloody damn New Orleans, and I am sick of this nonsense. I am going home." With that he tossed her bill back at her, left his coins on the table, and stomped out.

Margo was stunned at first. Time travel didn't exist. Of course it didn't. But she found herself more observant and less certain as she rushed after him.

First, there were no cars. Just horses, and horse-drawn carts, and horse-drawn omnibuses. And the smells. Manure and sewage waste running down the edge of the road. Now, New Orleans was not the best-smelling city at times, especially late night on Bourbon Street, or anywhere after Mardi Gras, but this was different.

Color dreams with sound and smell? *I don't think so!*

She ran in her attempt to catch up with Laurent.

"You know, it's interesting that New Orleans is looking so battered but in the process of rebuilding after the war. Just like after Katrina."

She could tell he wanted to ignore her but was intrigued. So, he stopped. "Katrina?"

"Hurricane Katrina. It hit the Gulf Coast in August, 2005. The worst natural disaster in American history. Eighty percent of the city was hit, and a lot of the coastal towns, as the levees broke. Sixteen hundred people died. Floods filled the city. People had to be rescued from their rooftops."

He stared at her with wide eyes. Then he shook his head and resumed walking. "You do tell tall tales!"

"It's the truth," she asserted, rushing to catch up with him again. When they neared the French Market, he approached a young woman—younger than him, closer to her own age—who stood next to an old-fashioned buckboard wagon with a harnessed horse. Her long black hair was braided and pinned on top of her head in a sort of coronet. She wore a short-sleeved, ankle-length dress of faded blue imprinted with once pink, tiny roses.

"Laurent!" she said, rushing up to give the man a hug. He hugged her back.

Margo felt an odd constriction in her chest, watching that embrace.

"What happened?" the woman asked anxiously. "Oh, no! You didn't get the loan?"

He shook his head, his expression grim. Then he took out

the remaining coins in his pocket, handing them to her. "You'll have to take back anything that isn't absolutely necessary," he said, pointing at the back of the wagon where supplies were heaped. In particular he told her to remove rolls of fabric, several pairs of shoes, and a half-dozen books.

They had no money, Margo realized, tears welling in her eyes. "Wait! Laurent!" she said, all of a sudden. She didn't know why, but she felt the need to help. If this was time travel, and she was sure it wasn't, she was for damn sure going to carry her own weight.

Laurent and the woman turned to looked at her. He groaned. The woman stared at her, first with shock at her attire, then with question, glancing back and forth between her and Laurent. Was it his wife? She gulped. She hadn't thought to ask. And why it should matter, she had no idea. Well, she had an idea, but still it shouldn't matter.

"Hi!" Margo said, reaching out to shake the lady's hand. "I'm Marguerite Baptiste. You can call me Margo."

"And I'm Letitia Duvall, Laurent's sister. You can call me Lettie."

"Sister?" She couldn't help the grin that twitched at her lips. But she had things to do. "Wait right here," she said to both of them. "Don't return anything yet."

Laurent looked outraged that she would order him so. Lettie was amused. But they both followed after her.

She soon found what she was looking for: a man with a jewelry booth. "I have a piece of jewelry I would like to sell."

The kindly looking man holding a magnifying glass, who identified himself as Mr. Goldstein, raised his head with a sigh. "Miss, everyone has jewelry to sell these days. What I want is a buyer." His eyes went wide, though, as they latched onto her wristwatch . . . a Cartier.

"Now that is interesting," he said. "A watch bracelet?"

"A wristwatch," she corrected. "But this is not for sale. It once belonged to my grandmother." Instead she undid the clasp on her neck chain and handed it to him. "This is a flawless, emerald cut, two-carat yellow diamond."

He picked it up and studied it with his magnifying glass. "Very nice." With a shrewd cast in his rheumy eyes, he asked, "How much do you want, not that I am really in the market for more jewels?"

He couldn't fool her. Margo knew she was in for a bout of what she did exceedingly well: haggling. A short time later, she was walking away with five hundred dollars in gold coins. She had declined his paper money. Of course, the diamond was worth more like ten thousand dollars, but beggars couldn't be choosers.

"That was amazing," Lettie said.

Not so impressed, Laurent demanded, "Where did you get that diamond?"

He probably thought she'd robbed a store.

"It was an engagement ring from my boyfriend five years ago, but he decided he liked men better, broke our engagement, and told me to keep the ring. I had it remounted into a necklace. No big loss."

"What does she mean that her boyfriend liked men?" Lettie whispered to her brother.

With color shading his cheeks, Laurent replied, "Never mind. I'll explain later."

Margo handed half of the coins to Laurent.

He glanced down at them heaped in the palm of his hand as if they were poison. "What? Why are you giving me these?"

"Listen, I don't understand where I am, or why. I just know that it's somehow connected to you."

"You're plumb crazy."

"Probably. But I'm going with you . . . wherever you're going. I don't care what you say. I'll buy a horse and follow you if I have to." Not that she knew how to ride or even how much a horse cost. "And I don't want to be a burden. If I'm going to stay here in the past, even temporarily, I insist on doing my part."

He tried to hand the coins back to her, but she folded her arms over her chest and turned to Lettie, who was practically jumping up and down with glee. "You're coming home with us? Oh, this is wonderful! We haven't had guests in ever so long. And we've never had a fancy lady."

Before Margo could protest being called a fancy lady, another term for a whore, or before Laurent could voice further protests to her accompanying them, Margo put her arm through Lettie's and said, "Let's go shopping. Your brother doesn't approve of my clothing. Is there anywhere I can buy a readymade dress?"

Lettie was already tugging her in the opposite direction, but before she followed, Margo had to talk with Laurent. "Is it all right if I go with you and Lettie?"

He hesitated. "Does it matter what I think?" Then, "Can you cook?"

"Like a chef," she lied. "For how many?"

"Ten. My cook died."

Ten? Oh boy! "Piece o' cake."

"Huh?"

"No problem. Is one of the ten your wife?"

"Pfff! I have no wife. That is all I would need on top of my other problems."

She couldn't help but be elated at that news. How pitiful was that? "Did your wife die by any chance?"

He bristled. "You have no right to ask that."

She shrugged. "I was just asking because I knew this guy whose wife drowned five years ago. Your twin, if you must know."

"Scary Larry?" he scoffed.

"Actually, yes."

"Elizabeth did not drown. She was taken by the summer fever."

Elizabeth? Beth? Bethany? Close enough! Is this a coincidence, or what? "I am so sorry. I shouldn't have asked." He looked so miserable that Margo just wanted to hug him, but she did not dare. *Good Lord! I am falling fast for a dream guy. Scary Larry, but worse.*

"I need to protect my sister. I better not find out you are listed in the Blue Book."

Her face heated. "I know what that was. A listing of all the prostitutes in the red-light district, with all their specialties detailed. For your information, that book was outlawed at the turn of the century. Original copies are real collectors' items." Margo, like any other New Orleans native, knew its history well, especially the bawdy stuff, and most compelling had been the section of town noted for the ruby glass lanterns hung on the buildings. Just in case some fool wasn't sure where the "parlor houses" were located.

"What century?"

"The twentieth. It's now the twenty-first century."

He crossed his eyes in the cutest way.

"But, no, Laurent, I am not a hooker. Oh, I keep forgetting that you don't understand modern language. A hooker is another word for a lady of the night."

"I know what a hooker is, for God's sake!"

"You do?"

"Yes, General Joe Hooker visited the New Orleans brothels so often during the war they named the girls after him."

"You're making that up."

"Why would I make up that kind of story?"

She wanted to ask him if he'd visited any of those houses but sensed that now was not the time.

"You're not going to try to tell me you're a virgin!"

"Give me a break. I'm twenty-seven years old. How about you, bozo? Are you a virgin?"

He smiled at her then. A wide, dimple flashing with an I-could-melt-your-bones-if-I-wanted-to smile.

Jeesh! Why not just mow me down? I am a dead duck if he beckons me closer with his finger.

He didn't. Instead, he said, "I apologize."

"So, can I come?"

He nodded with obvious reluctance.

"You won't be sorry, I promise."

She thought he muttered, "I'm already sorry."

Three

Gone with the Wind *was never like this* . . .

As he drove the wagon the twenty miles back to Rosylyn, occasionally having to prod the aged horse, Lightning, who hadn't had the energy his name denoted in more than ten years, Laurent had plenty of time to regret his impulsive decision. He and Lettie bracketed the demented woman on the buckboard bench seat as she talked. And talked. And talked.

Lettie was fascinated.

He was not buying her addled notions. Not one bit.

But she was probably harmless. So, he let her go on about how the plantation homes along River Road had changed, some no longer there, except for ones like Elmwood, which they passed. She talked about how women wore britches as often as they did skirts and some of the skirts rose inches above the knee. And all homes had electricity for light and heat and, important in the south, air-conditioning. "I couldn't live with this humidity without my thermostat set at fifty."

"It appears you'll have to." Not that he had a clue what a thermostat was.

She just smiled at him with a secret smile, which annoyed the hell out of him, more than when she had an answer for everything. Plus, he was way too conscious of her thigh pressed against his thigh. Innocent, but tempting.

She looked totally different but still attractive in a different sort of way. She wore a yellow and white gingham dress with short puffed sleeves, a scooped neckline that exposed skin almost to the top of her breasts, and a tight white cloth belt that accentuated her small waist and tied into a bow behind her back. Not that he had noticed much.

"No horses, except for pleasure riding?" he exclaimed then. "Only horseless wagons made of metal? Really! If you were halfway sane, you would know how ridiculous that sounds."

"If I were halfway sane, I wouldn't be dreaming in all these dimensions . . . sound, sight, color, smell. Nor would I have plopped myself down in steam heat Loo-zee-anna in 1870, carrying a fringed parasol, wearing an ankle-length dress with a bonnet. And a crinoline, for heaven's sake! Nor would I have chosen an always-scowling, no-sense-of-humor hero."

"Hah! You are sadly mistaken if you think I am going to be your hero. And I do not scowl all the time."

"You do scowl," Lettie interrupted.

He scowled at his sister.

"I mean if God was going to send me back to this time and place, he could have at least sent me a Rhett Butler."

"Rat who?" *First, she says I am a seal. Now she wants me to be a rat.*

"Not rat, silly. Rhett. Butler."

If she calls me silly again, I am going to push her off the wagon. "The only Butler I know is that Yankee monster Beast Butler who ruled N'awleans with an iron hand durin' the war."

She waved a hand dismissively. "Rhett Butler was a fictional hero, and Scarlett O'Hara was the heroine. He saved her butt on more than one occasion."

"Saved her butt?" He had to smile at some of her expressions.

"You are really hot when you smile," she remarked to him.

"Hot?" Lettie's brow furrowed with confusion.

"Drop-dead gorgeous," she explained.

"As if I care!" he said. *She thinks I am gorgeous. How . . . interesting!*

The idiot then went on to tell the most outrageous . . . and, yes, intriguing . . . story about a plantation called Tara during the Civil War, and how the people fared during Sherman's march on Savannah. Scarlett was famous for her expressions, like, "tomorrow is another day," and "fiddle-dec-dee!"

Lettie giggled. "Fiddle-dee-dee?"

"Yes. She said that whenever she was exasperated or annoyed."

Turning to him, Lettie teased, "That is going to be my new favorite word, Laurie. Whenever you go cursing over the state of my garden or yelling at the mule, or whenever I have to kill another snake, I am just going to put my hands on my hips and say, 'Well, fiddle-dee-dee!'"

He barely suppressed a laugh. He liked to see his sister happy and carefree. They hadn't had much to lift their spirits in a long time. "And what am I supposed to say to that?"

"Well, Laurent . . ." Margo said to him, mischief dancing in her honey colored eyes, "Rhett's famous remark to Scarlet was, 'Frankly, I don't give a damn!'"

"That is just wonderful." And it was. "The bank just denied my loan application, and, frankly, I don't give a damn. We don't have enough money to pay the taxes, and, frankly, I don't give a damn. A demented woman from the future just attached herself to me like a burr on a dog's backside, and, frankly, I don't give a damn."

Lettie picked up on his thread and said, "The war is over and the south ain't never gonna rise again, if you ask me, but fiddle-dee-dee! I lost my beau at Shiloh and there's not an able-bodied man under forty with teeth to replace him, but, fiddle-dee-dee! Cleona died and left me to be the cook, and I can't cook worth spit, but, fiddle-dee-dee! Lightning just farted for about the twentieth time, and the smell is putrid, but fiddle-dee-dee!"

He laughed out loud then, and it felt damn good. In fact, they all laughed, and laughed, 'til a companionable silence fell over them, and the only sound was the *clop-clop* of the horse's hooves on the dirt road.

Margo summed up all their thoughts when she murmured, "Tomorrow is indeed another damn day."

*   *   *

God must have a sense of humor . . .

Margo was scared.

From an early age she'd had to be brave. Growing up in a New Orleans slum, there had been no one to help her but herself. Not her absentee father, or her druggie mother. .

She'd been a scrappy little kid, determined to rise above her surroundings, often having to fend off bullies, thieves, and even rapists. She'd been collecting tin cans for pennies when she was nine, a paper girl at age ten, and a babysitter extraordinaire, dish washer, and waitress 'til she earned her way through college.

None of those hurdles or threats had scared her the way this situation did. She could fight the known enemy, but this was totally out of her sphere of understanding. Somehow, some way, she had time traveled to 1870. The longer she talked with these people and viewed the passing scenery, the more she had to accept facts.

But how? Surely time travel didn't exist from a scientific standpoint, did it? The only thing she could offer as an explanation was that it must be some kind of miracle created by God. You could say it was a celestial joke on her.

If that was the case, why? There had to be some reason for this twist of her destiny. Was there something she was supposed to accomplish here? Or was it for her that the change had been deemed necessary?

It was all so confusing.

And it didn't help that the brooding man beside her threw

off erotic heat like a sex furnace. She had to smile inwardly at her corny metaphors. But it was true. He wasn't the best-looking man in the world. And he frowned almost constantly, as if he carried the weight of the world on his shoulders. On more than one occasion, she had barely restrained herself from leaning over to kiss the frown away.

He glanced at her suddenly. "What? Why are you smiling?"

"Oh, Laurent, you really do not want to know."

He tilted his head to the side, then pressed his thigh even closer against hers. He knew. Oh, he knew all right. And she would bet her Victoria's Secret bra he felt the same way.

Best to change the subject before she jumped his bones, with his sister as a witness.

"Do you own slaves, Laurent?" she asked.

Her question surprised him, probably because she had been staring at him like eye candy. "No."

"Did you, before the war?"

"My father did. He died of a heart attack at home a year after the war started. Most of the slaves left on their own."

"Did that bother you? Did you want to go after them?"

He shook his head. "I wasn't a secessionist, but I was never in favor of slavery, either, which was a huge disappointment to my father. In truth, I never wanted to inherit Rosylyn, but as an only son, I had no choice."

"Laurent is being too nice," Lettie interrupted. "He and father had constant fights over release of the slaves. In the prosperous times, he wanted father to pay them as workers."

"Well, no need to worry about that now. Prosperity is gone. Poverty is here to stay."

"Don't be such a pessimist, Laurent," his sister chided.

"A realist, Lettie."

"So, now all the slaves are gone?" Margo persisted.

He nodded. "Oh, there are eight or so blacks still there. They have no other place to go. But they are the old, the very young, or crippled."

And he was taking care of them all, Margo realized. She put a hand on top of Laurent's forearm and squeezed.

He glanced at her, and their eyes held for one brief, sizzling moment.

She laughed and told him, "Here's a great news flash, honey. You've gotta appreciate this. The president of the United States in my time is Barack Obama, and guess what? He is a black."

❁   ❁   ❁

There's more than one way to pique a man's interest . . .

Halfway to Rosylyn, they stopped at a stream a short ways off the road to relieve themselves and the horse.

Margo headed for the stream to get a drink of cold water and splash water on her face and arms, or so she said. Living in Louisiana her entire life, she made too much of the heat, in his opinion.

"Pssst! Come over here," Lettie whispered from the other side of the small clearing.

He walked over, wondering what disaster was about to befall him now. It had been a day above all days so far.

"What do you think of her?"

"Who?"

"Who do you think? Fiddle-dee-dee, sometimes you are an idiot."

He rolled his eyes. "I think she is a bit crazy but harmless. Kinda like Maisie Mae Benoit who used to run naked during Mardi Gras." *Now there is a thought.*

"I didn't mean that. I meant, isn't she wonderful?"

"Wonderful?" *Maybe the craziness is contagious.*

"She has so many stories to tell, and she's going to teach me how to do my hair. She even has some ideas for us to earn extra money."

"Now wait a minute. I don't want her interfering in our business."

Lettie shrugged. "I think she already has . . . just in coming to Rosylyn. One more thing," she giggled, and whispered extra low. "She's wearing a thong. I saw it when she changed her clothes at the market stall."

He blew in and out with frustration. "I can see you're dyin' to tell me. What is a thong?"

"Ladies don't wear drawers in her time . . . uh, place. They wear panties, or a special kind of panties called a thong."

"Good Lord, Lettie! You are wastin' my time, standin' around discussin' ladies' undergarments."

"Dontcha wanna know what a thong is?"

"Hell, no!"

He started to turn away when she said, "It leaves almost all of her buttocks bare."

He stopped and glared at her, but it was obvious she had caught his attention.

"There's this strip of lace that runs up between her . . . uh, crack; so, from the back, it looks like she's wearin' nothin'. And the front is just this little scrap of V-shaped lace coverin' . . ." She pointed to her groin area. "It's scandalous, of course." But then she added, "She's going to help me make one for myself."

Laurent was speechless for a moment, but the image was now planted in his head. "Don't you dare!"

Lettie just laughed.

Of course the first thing he saw when he stomped away was Margo on her knees, leaning over the edge of the stream, her gingham-covered bottom aimed his way. And all he could think was, *How soon can I see the damn thong?*

*   *   *

It was no Tara, but . . .

It was early evening before they arrived.

Margo's first glimpse of the rundown and overgrown Rosylyn was not impressive. But on second glance, she could see how splendid it had once been and could be again.

Rosylyn was not a huge plantation by the standards of the time, but it was large enough. A square French Creole–style house sat on a rise about a football-field length from the river. Its three stories were covered by a broad sweeping-hipped roof with dormer windows on the upper level. Railed galleries

encircled all sides of the second, or main, floor, which were
supported by columns down to the ground level, which was an
open loggia. Clusters of roses, jasmine, and other creepers
grew wildly up the columns. While the upper part of the house
sported peeling, white-painted timber, the bottom was brick
covered with bousillage, a mud and moss mixture, once white-
washed to match the rest of the house.

Farther away from the house could be seen waist-high,
green sugar cane, like a green lake, tassels waving in the
slight breeze, with the sugar house rising above all in the
distance. She guessed that the crop covered several acres, a
small percentage of what might have flourished here before
the war.

The front lawn leading down to the river would once have
been clipped regularly with a scythe but was now mostly an
overgrown jungle of wild semitropical plants and trees, except for about a hundred feet directly surrounding the house.
A necessity, she would think, if they didn't want snakes and
other native wildlife coming indoors.

A horseshoe-shaped drive allowed visitors to ride right up
to the front, but Laurent turned at a lane before that, which
presumably led to the back of the mansion.

Numerous ramshackle outbuildings were scattered throughout the back . . . barn, laundry, blacksmith, carpentry, stable,
smokehouse, pig pen, and chicken coop. Even the old slave
quarters, which appeared mostly unoccupied.

But look. People were emerging from all these structures,
including the back of the house, and lining up to welcome
Laurent and Lettie back. Or more likely, anxiously waiting
for the supplies they carried.

There were about ten people, all ages, and every shade
from almost white to cafe au lait to ebony black. The closer
they got, the more horrified she was, though.

Among the gathering crowd was a man with no legs in a
wheelbarrow-type apparatus, being pushed by a young boy.
Another man was missing one arm. A frail, elderly woman
moved slowly, as if afraid of falling. A young light-skinned
woman, who might once have been beautiful, had a livid scar

puckering one side of her face and a bump on her nose, which must have been broken and healed improperly. A tall, statuesque woman held a newborn baby.

"Laurie! Delilah must have gone into labor as soon as we left this morning."

Laurent appeared less impressed with that fast delivery than he was with two men who were approaching from the sugar fields, carrying hoes. "Looks like Cordell and Ivory have come back." At least these two looked like healthy young men, in their twenties, with no missing body parts.

"They upped and went North expecting to be handed a sack of gold. Ivory left about seven months ago, but Cordell has been gone more than a year," Lettie explained to her in a whisper. "Ivory is the father of Delilah's baby, but I don't think she'll be welcomin' him back to her bed anytime soon. And Cordell left his son Jacob behind."

Margo turned to look at Laurent.

He inhaled deeply, then pasted a thin smile on his face. It was apparent to Margo that he was attempting to put the best face on for all these people who depended on him. Many men would have just walked away from such a huge responsibility. Oh, maybe not from a family member, like Lettie. But all these others? No way!

Her heart constricted with emotion as she continued to gaze at this incredible man, and in that instant, she fell a little bit in love with him.

She squeezed his hand to show her support.

To her amazement, he squeezed back.

This is why I was sent back in time, she realized suddenly. *And I suspect that I am never going back.*

⁎　⁎　⁎

She was always on his mind . . . rather, her thong was . .

Laurent helped unload all the supplies.

And kept watching Margo as she was introduced to the others, taking particular note of her manner in dealing with the almost white Jonas, who had fought for the Yankees and left both legs at Gettysburg. He stood alongside Clarence, who'd been on the Rebel side and lost an arm in the notorious Andersonville prison.

Laurent was especially pleased that Margo listened to them with respect, not pity. She laughed gaily when Jonas, a woodworker, told her he was thinking about carving little naked lady figures to sell in the French Quarter Market since his dogs and cats weren't doing so well. Clarence, who had been an assistant gardener at one time and did the best he could these days with one arm, told her that, if Jonas could do nekkid ladies, he was going to market his juju plants, which increased male virility.

Of course Margo had to go and tell them an outlandish story about some magic blue pill that was popular in her time. The pill could presumably help men who couldn't raise their flagpoles anymore, or help them keep the Grand Ol' Flag waving for an exceedingly long time.

Every male within hearing distance went on alert, ears flapping. He just shook his head. A lady discussing male parts?

Amazing! He should have been repulsed. Instead, he was beguiled, never knowing what she was going to say or do next.

And he was still thinking about that damn thong.

Ivory and Cordell ducked their heads with embarrassment as they walked up to him. He shook both their hands and said, "Welcome back." Their relief was palpable that they weren't to be kicked out on their asses for leaving him in the lurch, Ivory last winter, Cordell, much earlier.

"I'll work real good fer ya, Master Laurent, if ye'll give me a chance ta earn some money," Cordell said.

"Me, too," Ivory chimed in.

"I'm not your master. Never was. Just call me Laurent, or Mister Duvall," he told them, then changed the subject. "Things weren't so golden up north, huh?"

"Pfff! They made us work jist as hard fer less money." Cordell grimaced with disgust. "I ain't got but five dollars in my pocket."

"And they still called us niggers," Ivory added.

"Well, we can certainly use your muscles here. I'm thinking about trying for a late crop of sugar to see if it'll take. I could only get ten acres in with the little help I had."

"Yes, sir," they both agreed, just thankful to be back.

"Congratulations on your new baby, Ivory. Is it a boy or a girl?"

"A girl. Suzette. But Delilah won't talk to me nohow, 'ceptin while she was birthin' the baby. Then she kept cussin' me fer all her pains with names I cain't repeat."

"You didn't expect a brass band from her after leaving her pregnant, did you?"

"Nah, but I expected at least a teeny tiny kiss." Ivory grinned. "And I was here fer the birthin'."

"And, you, Cordell?" Cordell had left his then nine-year-old son Jacob behind, with the best of intentions, hoping to make a better life for the two of them.

"Jacob was happy to see me. I missed him so much. He's off now with the book I bought him in Philadelphia. *David Copperfield.*"

Laurent went into the kitchen to grab a bowl of red beans and rice sitting over a low fire in the hearth.

Granny Belle was in her rocking chair talking to Margo as she chewed on her wad of tobacco, spitting occasionally into the fire. For as long as he remembered, she'd had that cud in her cheek. Next to her was old Cassius, nodding off in his matching rocker. Cassius, who had once been the head gardener, would be going to the promised land soon, according to Granny Belle.

Leaning against the wall, he ate, preparing to be amused as he watched and listened.

"You bake bread *every* day?"

What? You thought we had it delivered?

"Yessirree. Get up at dawn ta mix and knead the dough. Let it rise while ya build a fire . . ."

"Build a fire? From scratch?"

No, from toenails.

"Milk the two cows. Gather the eggs. Feed the chickens. Slop the hogs . . . well, ya kin do that later."

"A cook does all that?"

"You betcha." Granny Belle glanced over at him and winked. "Then ya gotta make breakfast. The mens do like a big breakfast. After that ya gotta decide what ta have fer dinner. Mebbe a chicken. Ya do know how ta kill 'n' pluck a chicken, dontcha?"

He could swear he heard Margo murmur something about what to do with the chicken, and it rhymed.

"The worst part is the guts . . . and the smell of wet feathers."

Margo's face turned a bit green.

"Are ya sure ya handled chickens before?"

"Uh, sure. I just haven't done it lately."

Lady, I would bet my left elbow you don't know one end of a rooster from the other.

"And best ya use the hens. Them roosters is too tough."

"How do you tell the guys from the gals? I mean, do I have to turn them over and check for family jewels?" She laughed at her own humor.

He almost choked on his supper.

Granny Belle just chuckled.

By the sound of things, his crazy lady from the future didn't know spit about cooking, especially over an open fire. Well, he would have to find some other job for her.

And he thought of her thong, again.

Just then, she seemed to notice him for the first time. "Think it's funny, do you?"

"Very funny."

"I can't cook."

"No kidding!"

"Don't be sarcastic."

"I'll be anything I want. You came here under false pretenses."

"Hey, a girl's gotta do what a girl's gotta do." She grinned at him. "Don't worry. I'll make myself useful."

"That sounds promising."

"Are you flirting with me?"

"I don't know. Would it bother you if I was?"

She stared at him, then slowly admitted, "No."

"We'll decide tomorrow where you can best be used, but

there is one thing you could do for me today, darlin'. Well, not now. Later. Tonight."

She eyed him warily, probably thrown by his use of the endearment.

"Show me your thong."

Four

Where was a hot tub when you needed it? . . .

It was only nine o'clock, and Margo was exhausted as she and Lettie trudged up to the third floor, with the maid who led the way frowning at the water she was spilling.

When she'd found out there was a bathtub on the floor where she would be sleeping, Margo had been ecstatic . . . until she learned it had only cold water coming in from an outside cistern. So, she was lugging her own hot water to mix.

"Don't pay any attention to Sophie," Lettie whispered. "She's just a high yaller who was always a house servant, thinks she's better than anyone else. Won't do anythin' but dust and change linens."

Margo wanted to correct Lettie's political incorrectness but decided to pick her battles in this time period.

Sophie was very light skinned and skinny as a rail. Probably more than fifty. And, yes, she was arrogant and almost possessive about the house, remarking on fingerprints and dirty shoes more than once.

"This is the guest room," Sophie said, opening the far door, then pointed to a room across the way, announcing, "the bathing room." She went in to lay down some towels and used a dust cloth in her belt to shine the porcelain sink with its one faucet. As she passed her and Lettie to go back downstairs, she gave them both looks that pretty much said, "Leave the bathing room spic and span or you will answer to me."

Lettie giggled. "She treats me like I'm seven years old when I'm twenty and seven."

"You're the same age as me."

"Really?" Why such a thing was so pleasing to her stumped Margo until Lettie added, "I feel like we're sisters." Tears filled her eyes. "I've been so lonely."

Margo hugged her then. In truth, she'd always wanted a sister, and if she was going to be stuck here, she couldn't have picked a nicer one. Swiping the tears from her eyes, Lettie went into her own bedroom, the first on this floor, and got a nightgown for Margo, one which Margo doubted she would use. It was voluminous, and in this heat, had to be unbearable.

"I'll see you in the morning," Lettie called out and closed her door.

Margo turned the water on in the bathtub, filling it half full before adding her two buckets of hot water. The result was tepid water, but wonderful, she thought, as she took off her clothes and sunk down into the depths. She would have loved a bubble bath, but even she knew that was beyond possible.

She must have dozed. The water was cold and her fingers and toes shriveled by the time she got out and pulled the plug. She dried with the towels Sophie had left for her and arranged the wet cloths neatly over the edge of the tub. She grimaced as she realized she would have to don the same underwear, figuring she would wash them out tomorrow.

Bent over, wearing only her bra and thong, she was about to pick up her dirty clothes and the nightgown when the door opened suddenly.

"Oh, sorry. I didn't know you were in here. I was going to

brush my teeth." There were old-fashioned tooth brushes and tooth powder sitting on the dry sink.

Like a deer caught in the headlights, she just stood and stared at Laurent. He must have washed somewhere else. He was wearing clean clothing, drab as usual, and his wet hair was brushed off his face.

And, hey, he was doing a bit of staring, too. In fact, you could say he was devouring her with his eyes. With dilated pupils, and parted lips, it wasn't hard to figure out what he was thinking.

"So, that is a thong," he finally said in a sex-husky voice.

"It is. How did you . . . oh, Lettie told you."

He nodded. "And I've been picturing it all day."

"Does it live up to your expectations?"

He grinned. "I don't know," he clearly lied. "Maybe you should turn around so I can get the full effect."

It was beyond Margo's understanding why she would even consider such a suggestion, even more confusing was her standing here, practically naked, and not screaming or ordering him out or complaining about him invading her privacy. Truth to tell, his arousal was turning her on. And she didn't need to look down at her breasts to know her nipples were hard and pressing against the white lace of her bra.

Which was exactly where he was looking now. "And that lace torture instrument?" He waved a hand at her chest area.

"A bra. A Victoria's Secret push-up special. A torture instrument, huh? You've gotta be the first man in history to dislike Victoria's Secret lingerie."

"I never said I didn't like it, but surely it is meant to torture a man."

She smiled.

He smiled back and stepped farther into the room, closing the door behind him.

The air practically sizzled with the chemistry they were creating.

"You know, Laurent, I've never kissed a man with a mustache before."

"Is that a fact, darlin'? What a coincidence! I've never kissed a hundred-and-forty-year-old woman."

He made a twirling motion with his hand, indicating he wanted her to turn. Did she have the nerve?

"Okay, here's the deal. We believe in equality between the sexes in my time. I'll turn around if you'll take off your shirt.

The smile he flashed her was pure wickedness. He had the shirt undone and tossed to the floor before she could say Chippendale dancer. And, oh, boy, was he a prime example of southern men . . . Rebel with a real good cause—her. All suntanned muscle and definition. As buff a body as Larry Wilson's, but his physique was the result of just plain hard work.

He folded his arms over his chest and cast her a challenging look.

"If you make a crude mark, or say I have cellulite, I am going to wallop you a good one."

"Do it," he said in a strained voice.

And she did. Slowly. Very slowly. She could swear he moaned and that she could hear his breathing. When she was facing him again, she didn't have to ask if he'd liked it or not.

He told her with one succinct exclamation. "Lord have mercy!"

Without hesitation, she stepped into his open arms. As he began to lower his mouth to hers, his eyes holding her gaze, she murmured, "This is probably a mistake."

"Probably."

"Just one kiss."

"Just one . . . for now."

And then he kissed her. One kiss. One never-ending kiss. It started with his lips learning hers with gentle shaping, but once he got the fit he wanted, he became ravenous, using his lips and tongue and teeth to persuade her to mimic all his actions.

Which she did.

He made a raw sound of satisfaction deep in his throat. His one hand held her in place with fingers cupped on her nape, but when he put the other hand on her bare buttock and drew her closer, she felt her knees give way.

Still not breaking the kiss, he turned and pushed her against the door. His tongue was deep in her mouth, his hands caressing her everywhere. If she was in any doubt about his attraction to her, the erection pressing against her stomach would give her proof . . . hard proof. If he was in any doubt about her attraction to him, the way her hands were exploring his back and shoulders and flat male nipples would give him proof.

How they had gone from zero to raging excitement in minutes was a wonder. It had never happened to her before.

"Margo?"

"Hmmm?" she said against his open mouth.

"Margo? Are you all right?"

She realized then that it was Lettie, and not Laurent, saying her name. Lettie was on the other side of the door, knocking lightly.

Laurent released her lips, reluctantly, and pressed his forehead against her.

In a raspy voice, she said, "I'll be out in a minute, Lettie."

"I was worried. You were in there so long, I was afraid you might be in trouble."

"Oh, I'm in trouble all right," she whispered.

"We both are," he whispered back, nipped her chin, and stepped back.

"You might have fallen asleep in the tub, I reckon," Lettie said.

"I did, but I'm out now." Quickly she donned the huge nightgown.

"She's gone now," he said, opening the door for her.

But she wasn't.

Lettie stood there, mouth gaping at her shirtless brother who strolled past her big as you please and then at Margo's unbuttoned nightgown.

Then she grinned widely. "Fiddle-dee-dee!"

❊   ❊   ❊

Gimme some sugar, baby . . .

Laurent spent the entire morning doing hard labor in the fields.

His father would be horrified. But then, his father had been dependent on the slaves who worked for him. At the height of its prosperity, Rosylyn's thousand acres had supported the Duvall family, the overseer's family, and about two hundred blacks, including a hundred field workers. Now, he had a mere ten acres in healthy cane; maybe he could plant another ten in sugar or some other crop now that Ivory and Cordell had returned to help.

Before the war, there had been more than a thousand sugar plantations in Louisiana. He doubted there were more than two hundred now. Of those, half were owned by northern speculators, either northern by birth or backed by northern money. It was a losing situation without the work force, and the profits weren't sufficient to support paid field hands. Maybe sometime in the future, but not now.

Slavery! He had hated it then. He hated it now. Except he was the slave. Slave to a plantation he never wanted and a gaggle of people, white and black, who looked to him for support.

If that weren't bad enough, sugar growing was dependent on the weather, and God only knew what it would be day to day in Louisiana with its tropical-like climate. Heat and humidity, of course, constant rainstorms known as gully washers, and then the occasional hurricane. He wondered suddenly if there actually would be such a disastrous hurricane to hit the Gulf Coast like the crazy woman had related.

Which of course brought to mind the kiss. The kiss like no other he'd ever experienced. He'd been married to Elizabeth for two years before she died ten years ago. Before the war. Before everything went to hell. Maybe it had been a blessing for her to be taken so early. He'd known Elizabeth from childhood. He'd been fond of her. And, yes, they had engaged in sex on a regular basis, even good sex on occasion, but never had a mere kiss from her turned him raging hot. He needed to control himself or he would be in big trouble. Hell, who was he kidding? He was already in trouble. He would have the woman in his bed shortly, he knew he would, and he could not wait.

"Who ya talkin' to?" asked Cordell when he came up to the water wagon and took a long drink from the ladle sitting in the bucket. By now, the water would be lukewarm, even though seven-year-old Precious refilled the buckets every hour. Precious was a little girl who had wandered down the River Road one day two years ago, with no memory of who she was or where she'd come from, except for her name. No one had ever come to claim her. In between water duties, Precious's job was to pick the caterpillars off the plants wherever she saw them. Another worry.

"No one. Just mumbling." See, now the crazy woman was turning him crazy. "How's it going?"

Swiping a forearm over his forehead, Cordell replied, "We got all the drainage ditches cleared out this morning."

"We've had a dry spell the past two weeks, but I expect it'll rain this afternoon."

"The sugar looks healthy," Cordell remarked.

"God willing," he replied back. The cane was about three feet high now, good for mid-July, and would be ready for harvest in October. Everything about growing and harvesting followed a particular pattern, even the cutting, which always involved only four strokes of the blade, two sweeping vertical swathes to remove the leaves, a horizontal cut to the ground, then a last chop to take off the top. "I've been reconsidering what I told you yesterday. Maybe it's too much of a gamble to try a later sugar crop. Maybe we could try diverting the rain drain off into a rice field instead of just sweeping it off to the swamps."

"Is rice bringing in a good price?"

He shrugged. "Good enough. Better than no crop at all."

Cordell, who had grown up at Rosyln with Laurent, although Laurent was about five years younger than him at thirty-three, scanned the fields with him, then shook his head. He knew what he was seeing. A field crew of himself, Cordell, and Ivory, the only able-bodied adult males, along with Cordell's ten-year-old son Jacob, fifteen-year-old Sulee with her club foot, and twenty-two-year-old Fleur, a once pretty woman with cafe au lait skin, whose mother had thought her daughter's prospects were greater at one of the Creole Quadroon Balls in the city. Unfortunately, her protector, who'd purchased her for a mistress, had a cruel streak, and one of his beatings had gone too far. Delilah would be back helping in the fields once she recovered from childbirth.

A bell could be heard ringing in the distance, and everyone headed toward the house for the noontime meal.

"I'll be there shortly," he told Cordell. "I need a swim to cool off." And wasn't that the truth? Before he could face Margo again, he needed to be cool, calm, and collected.

He could swear he heard laughter in his head.

✿   ✿   ✿

Chillin' out southern style . . .

Margo ran into Laurent, literally, as she rounded a corner of the house, heading toward the dairy shed where milk and cheese were kept cool.

"Ooompfh!"

"Steady," he said, taking her by the upper arms. Which he did not immediately release. "Got your balance?"

Hah! I've been off balance since I first met you. She was staring at his mouth, remembering what that mouth could do. Then she realized that water was dripping from his hair onto his face and neck and that it had seeped into his cotton shirt and pants, showing damp spots here and there. "A bath?" *I wonder if two people could fit in that tub. Hah! I'm not about to lug all those buckets of hot water up two flights of stairs.*

"No, a swim."

"In the river?" *Hmmm. Possibilities there.*

He shook his head and answered distractedly, "A stream runs through the property down to the river. Sometimes, like now, it's deep enough for a cool swim."

"I could use a swim." *And other things.* "Take me with you next time."

"And scandalize everyone from here to Baton Rouge?"

"I think I've already done that."

He chuckled, but the whole time she'd been speaking, his eyes were on her mouth. He was remembering, too.

She licked her lips, just to make sure.

He gasped, softly.

She smiled.

"Temptress!" he said, releasing her forearms.

No one had ever called her a temptress before. She liked it.

"Where are you off to in such a hurry?"

"The dairy shed to get some clabber cheese." The cottage cheese–like mixture was made from the clabber of sour milk.

He arched a brow. "So, you can cook after all?"

"Not really, but I'm learning. If you must know, I'm going to try to make my famous cheesecake, which should be something, baked in a hearth oven without a springform pan . . . wait, what are you doing?" He had linked one of her hands with his and was tugging her forward.

"To the dairy shed," he said with all the innocence of a spider to a fly.

Once inside the small room, which was partially underground and much cooler than the outside, he shut the door and sat down on one of the wide benches. When he pulled her forward it was to sit on his lap, and not across his lap, either, like a little girl, but astraddle, like a big girl, with her dress flipped up, and her almost bare bottom resting on his thighs. *Holy Moly!*

"You're awfully good at that move. Do it a lot?"

"Not nearly as much as I'd like." His palms were running up and down the outside of her arms, from the edge of her cap sleeves, down to the wrist, then back up again, over and over.

"You smell good." He nuzzled her neck.

And caused every hormone in her body to go on red alert. "I had a little sample of perfume in my purse. Jessica McClintock."

"Who?"

"Never mind."

"I had the strangest dream last night," he said.

Oh, my God! Did he just blow in my ear?

"It was me, but not me."

Forget the freakin' dream. Blow in my ear again.

"I had very short hair, almost a shaved head, and I was running and running along a beach."

"That's what Navy SEALs do. It's part of their military training." *Now blow in my damn ear again. Or . . oooooh, yes, lick my neck.*

He laughed. "Fighting men learn to fight better by running?"

She smacked him playfully on the chest. "Jogging develops muscles and stamina."

I can think of a few other things related to stamina, honey.

"Sometimes they go for twenty-mile runs before breakfast."

"You do tell the tallest tales." He put his hands on either side of her waist and pulled her even closer, at the same time spreading his thighs wider.

She saw stars as his erection pressed against the thin silk of her thong. But wait, this was too much too soon. *Slow down, Margo. Slow down.* "What else did you dream?"

He smiled, a wicked I-thought-you'd-never-ask smile. "After that kiss, I could think of nothing else but a repeat performance."

Hallelujah! "I thought about you, too."

She combed her fingers through his wet hair on either side of his head, framing his face. Then she leaned forward and kissed him.

Margo had kissed a lot of men in her twenty-seven years, some of them frogs, some of them really nice guys, like her gay fiancé. But this was different. Just the gentle slide of her open lips against his was an explosion of the senses.

He groaned and kissed her back.

She wrapped her arms around his neck and rubbed her breasts against his chest. With the heat they were creating, his shirt would probably dry. Heck, they would melt the butter, too.

The kiss was alternately soft and seeking, then hard and demanding. It was hard to tell who was kissing whom.

So, it was no wonder that she was so dazed that she had no idea how her dress had been unbuttoned in front, her bra shoved down, and his mouth broke the kiss to come down and suckle at her breasts.

But then, her hands had been at work, too, tugging his shirt out of his pants and exploring his shoulders and back. She even slipped her hands into the back of his pants to caress his buttocks.

They were both out of control, both of them sighing at different touches, moaning to show what pleased, or especially pleased, each other.

Margo was soon undulating her hips toward him, and his tongue in her mouth was imitating her actions below. His hands were on her bare butt, guiding her, as if she needed guidance.

Soon, way too soon, she arched against him in a mind-blowing orgasm, and he clutched her tightly as his erection rode her cleft.

"Oh, my God! Oh, my God!" she cried.

He just groaned, long and sweet.

Then she was slumped against his shoulder, and his hands were soothing her with soft strokes of her back.

"That was incredible," he said, kissing her quickly as he lifted her off his lap.

"Tell me about it!"

With grins, he noted that his trousers had one more damp spot, and she noted that she would have to wash her thong, which prompted him to make a remark about how he would enjoy picturing her walking around bare-assed under her long dress.

Then, just before he opened the door, reminding her to get the clabber cheese, he urged, "Come to me tonight."

Five

Match that! . . .

When Margo walked into the kitchen a short time later, she saw that everyone was seated at the long table eating ham and red-eye gravy, beaten biscuits, leftover gumbo, grits with butter and milk—sometimes called Southern oatmeal— and lemonade. Apparently, there was a lemon tree at Rosylyn. Who knew?

The only ones missing in the kitchen were Laurent and the snooty maid, Sophie. From one of the other rooms could be heard loud voices. Laurent shouting and a female voice whining.

Margo arched an eyebrow at Lettie, who got up from the table and came over. "Laurent came in to find Delilah in the dining room bawling her eyes out, tryin' ta nurse her baby and cut cloth for new clothes at the same time, with no one helpin' her."

"Sophie, I know you've been a house maid at Rosylyn for thirty-some years. We don't need the blasted furniture, that isn't even being used, dusted every day. What we need is for you to sit your skinny ass down and help Delilah with the sewing."

Even though there was silence in the kitchen, except for the clank of silverware on pottery plates, they could not make out Sophie's argument.

"I don't give a good rat's ass, woman! Either help Delilah and start teachin' Fleur, or you can get the hell out of here."

It appeared as if Sophie was weeping now.

Laurent's voice was softer now. "We all have to pull our weight here, Sophie. We all have to adapt."

Lettie and Margo scurried to sit down as they heard footsteps approaching.

"What?" Laurent asked as he entered the kitchen, noting the silence.

They all immediately resumed eating and chatting, and everyone made a special effort not to look at Sophie as she came in and sat by the hearth, next to old Cassius and Granny Belle, who handed her a plate full of food. The three ate from their laps, even though there was room at the table.

Laurent sat down on the bench next to Margo and squeezed her thigh under the table. "Was I too harsh?"

She shook her head. "It needed doing. I had an employee one time, the sweetest girl, but she was always late, and left early, and spent half the day gossiping with my other employees. I had to give her a warning or dismiss her."

"What is it exactly that you do?" Laurent asked as he filled his plate and poured lemonade from the pitcher into a tall glass." Even without ice, it was refreshing.

"I own a dating agency."

"Huh?"

She tried to think of a term he would understand. "Matchmaking. I told you that before, I think."

"You mean that you match men and women together for marriage?" Lettie's eyes were wide with wonder.

"Sort of. Not everyone is looking for marriage."

"What else might they be looking for?" Laurent inquired with a grin, which was soon reflected on the faces of all the other men at the table, even Jacob.

"I could use a little matchmakin'," Ivory remarked, glancing at the far end of the table where Delilah sat, her baby asleep in a cradle next to Granny Belle.

Delilah shot him a glare. "What you could use is a lick of sense."

"Now, Delilah, I said I was sorry."

"Sorry doan count fer nothin'," she remarked back. "How many women did ya poke while ya went gallavantin' off?"

"Delilah!"

Laurent must have thought it was time for a change of subject because he turned to Margo and asked, "Do you make money from matchmaking?"

"Yes, actually quite a bit." She told him how much each person paid to get her services, and there was a gasp around the table.

"I don't have that kind of money, but I sure would like you to match me up with some fella before my hair turns gray," Lettie said.

"Lettie!" her brother reprimanded.

"What? Did you think I was resigned to bein' a spinster the rest of my life?"

"I might be able to help you," Margo offered.

"Don't you dare," Laurent cautioned.

"Or what?" she challenged.

He leaned close to her ear and whispered, "I'll paddle your sweet ass."

"Promises, promises," she shot back, causing him to about choke on the piece of biscuit he'd just put in his mouth. Then, she told him, "It's a natural instinct, Laurent, for men and women to want to meet and mate."

There was communal silence as everyone was all ears.

"I can't believe you said that, out loud."

"Why? Women want to fall in love, marry, and have children. Men want to have sex, marry, have sex, then have children, and more sex."

Laurent burst out laughing and the others followed suit, even Granny Belle, who said, "I declare!"

"What would you like in a man?" Margo asked Lettie.

"That is enough on this subject," Laurent decided.

They ignored him.

"Taller than me and kind. He doesn't have to be good looking, but not repulsive, either. I don't care if he's a Yankee or Rebel. I don't care if he has money, but he has to have enough to take care of me and our children. I'm tired of being poor."

Laurent chuckled and said, "Hey, if you have any rich women available, I'm tired of being poor, too."

"Oh? And what else would you want?"

He just grinned and gave his full attention to the food on his plate. When the others were no longer looking his way, he told her in a voice low enough for only her to hear, "She has to look good in a thong and give kisses that could melt wax."

Granny Belle toddled up to the table with a new tray of biscuits and glanced at her and Laurent, then glanced again. "Lord-a-mercy! What have you two been doin'? Yer lips look bee-stung."

Laurent's face turned red and probably matched hers.

Lettie craned her neck forward so she could see Laurent on Margo's other side. Then she clapped her hands together and exclaimed, "Well, fiddle-dee-dee!"

*   *   *

Wanna play, sugar? . . .

Everyone was asleep, and Laurent was waiting for Margo to come to his room.

He'd bathed in the stream, again, after the evening meal, then shaved off his mustache when he'd gotten back to the house. He wasn't sure exactly why . . . maybe it was a physical manifestation of his unconscious decision to put the past behind him, to move on to something new in his future. Because he for damn sure needed to make a decision about Rosylyn . . . either he did something dramatic to get it back into a profitable position again, or he chucked it all and headed off for new horizons, taking only Lettie with him.

Or maybe it just involved this new, crazy woman who'd entered his life, turning it upside down.

He'd heard Margo splashing in the tub down the hall a long time ago. What was she doing in her bedroom? Why was she waiting so long? If she didn't come soon, he would go for her.

But wait. The soft padding of bare feet in the hall drew his attention, followed by the swish of the door opening. Then it shut with a resounding snap.

He stood before one of the open, floor-to-ceiling windows, one of four in this corner room. It had rained all afternoon, and the air was thankfully cooler than normal.

They would create their own heat.

"You came."

"Did you doubt I would?"

"I would have come for you if you didn't."

"Would you have carried me?" She tilted her head and regarded him saucily. "Rhett picked up Scarlett on more than one occasion."

"Enough with Rhett!" He beckoned her with a forefinger to come closer.

She balked and shook her head.

So, he approached her, slowly.

"Laurent! You shaved your mustache. For me?"

"For me," he said, declining to explain. "Do you prefer the mustache?"

She bit her bottom lip as she studied him. "I like both." She laughed. "There's a very vulgar expression in my time about sex with a mustached man . . ."

He could see by the light from the full moon that she was blushing, a unique occurrence for her, or he would have thought so. "Don't stop now."

"A mustache ride," she blurted out, "and don't ask me to explain."

A grin twitched at his lips. He needed no explanation. "We might be able to accomplish that without the mustache." *Forget might. Definitely.*

She blushed even more when she realized that he'd understood. Shifting from bare foot to bare foot, she tried to find the right words for her next declaration. "I want you to know that I don't do this very often."

"Do what?" Laurent found his brain operating at a sluggish speed, slowed down no doubt by the boiling blood churning through his body, which had been in a state of simmering half-arousal all day since he'd left her in the dairy shed.

"Make love with someone I've just met."

"Do you think I do?" *If you only knew!*

"I don't know."

"The only sex I've had in more than a year has been solitary."

She laughed. "Likewise."

His eyes went wide, and he laughed, too. "You come out with things I've never heard a lady say."

"What? You think women in your time don't masturbate?"

His jaw dropped. He clicked it shut and was about to reply when she continued.

"You want a lady in bed?'

"Hell, no! I am more interested in knowing why you are wearing that shroud."

"It's the only one Lettie gave me."

"Take it off. No, let me." In record time, he had the hem up and over her head. For a moment, it stuck on her arms and around her neck, giving him an up close look at her nude body. No scraps of lace this time. Just all that lovely skin.

She was tall for a woman, though a head shorter than him. Her breasts were large and high. Well, large compared to her slim frame. The areolae and already pearled nipples were a dusty pink. Her nether hair was blonde and curly, a shade darker than her head.

"You are beautiful," he choked out as he tossed the nightgown behind him.

He was barefoot and shirtless, and while he'd been getting his fill of her, visually, she had been a busy bee. Without even being asked, or begged, she was undoing the buttons of his trousers, uncaring or deliberately brushing the backs of her fingers against his erection. Before he knew it, she was releasing his engorged penis while he stepped out of his pants.

He let out a whooshy exhale, attempting to gain some control over his roiling passion.

"Nice," she whispered as she studied him with wanton appreciation.

"Nice?" He laughed and picked her up in his arms just like she'd mentioned. "That is not the way a man likes to have his best parts described." He dropped her on the bed flat on her back, adjusted the mosquito netting, then came down next to her, on his side.

He adjusted her the way he wanted. Arms over her head on the pillow, legs slightly parted. For a second, he just looked, relishing the searing joy of anticipation.

"I think you're amazing," she said.

"That is certainly better than nice." He smiled down at her, trying to decide which pleasure he wanted to enjoy first. Kissing her lips. Sucking her nipples. Wetting his fingers in her woman's dew.

But then she reached over and fondled his "amazingness." His eyes rolled up in his head at the sheer ecstasy. Still, he removed her hand. "We don't want a repeat of what happened this afternoon."

"What did you have in mind?"

"Let's play for a while."

"Sounds good to me. This is a side of you I never suspected."

"Why?

"Because you're so serious all the time. Always scowling."

He made a tsking sound of disgust. "Scary Larry?"

"Oh, yeah!"

He pinched her belly. "Make me smile, darlin'."

"As long as you make me scream."

She did.

And he did.

But he was getting ahead of himself.

He kissed her with a slow seduction while his hands learned all her curves and secrets. The swell and contour of her breasts. The way she inhaled sharply at the mere brush of his fingers over her nipples. The curve of her waist and indentation of her navel. The silken hair below protecting her moistness.

She is wet for me, he exalted. Then, when she attempted to lower her hands to caress him, as well, he murmured against her open mouth, "Not yet. Not yet."

By the time he was ready to enter her, her hands clutched the wood rails of the headboard, and she was moaning and begging him for release. He was in no better condition. The pleasure was almost painful in its intensity.

He knelt between her thighs, lifted her knees, spread them wide, and then . . . and then . . . thank God and all the saints, he pushed himself inside her, filling her. Then he pushed even more as her inner muscles shifted to accommodate him. For a moment, he was still, enjoying just this completeness.

He raised himself on braced arms and stared down at her. He was slick with perspiration from holding back, but beads of sweat were on her forehead and upper lip, as well. Her honey-colored eyes were glazed with arousal, almost wild with want. Her hair was a mass of tousled curls.

"Please."

He was happy to comply.

His long, slow strokes were excruciating and soon cut off. He'd waited too long. When he began to pound in her with short, hard plunges, she was keening and arched her hips off the mattress and up against his belly. Inside, her muscles were convulsing with orgasm, clasping and unclasping, attempting to hold him in.

Throwing his head back, he roared out his own completion, then blacked out for a moment as he slumped onto her body. Her hands were caressing his back when he regained consciousness.

He raised himself to look down at her, astonished at the

sex act that they'd just engaged in, which was not a sex act at all. It was way more than that, more than could withstand examination at this time. He ran the backs of his fingers over her swollen lips and just stared.

"Can I tell you something, Laurent, without you running away in a panic?"

He could not imagine what that might be. "Of course."

"I love you. I don't how or why it happened so quickly, in such odd circumstances. I just know I do. No, don't say anything. I'm not asking for a reciprocal declaration. I just wanted you to know. I love you."

"I'm glad," he said, surprised at himself. He didn't repeat her words. He couldn't. Not yet. Maybe never. But he couldn't deny that her words pleased him and perhaps reflected his feeling that theirs had not been just a sex act.

He grinned then, deciding it was time for more play. "Looks like the South can rise again after all, Scarlett." He rolled over onto his back and pointed downward.

"Well, fiddle-dee-dee!" She grinned and showed him how modern women played, but to his credit, he also showed her, good and true, that the South was not dead yet.

*　*　*

Two could play this game . . .

Margo wanted to make love with Laurent. Of course she did. But more than that, she wanted to lighten his life, to ease some of the pain and responsibility he faced every day, and she didn't mean the physical pain of his leg wound.

"How did this happen?" she asked as she ran her fingertips over the livid scar that ran from his knee to his upper thigh.

"Bentonville. I managed to escape with only minor scrapes through five years of the bloody war, then caught a bullet to my shoulder and a saber cut to my leg at the last real Confederate battle of the war. Talk about bad luck!"

She leaned down and kissed the wound, starting at the knee, then moving slowly upward.

"Whoa, whoa, whoa!" he laughed, grabbing her by the shoulders. "That is too close to heaven."

"I'd like to show you heaven, sweetie."

Mischief and pleasure danced in his blue gray eyes. "Maybe later, *sweetie*."

"Definitely later."

"By the way, there was something else I dreamed last night, aside from the idiots running and running and running. There were explosions. Lots of them. And weapons that must have been guns but unlike any I've seen before. And dead bodies." He shook his head as if to clear it.

"Larry Wilson was a Navy SEAL. The SEALs are among the toughest fighting men in the world in the war against terrorists . . . I'll explain terrorism later. The explosions were probably bombs, and the guns very sophisticated technical weaponry."

"Bad enough I have nightmares about my own war. Now I've taken on another man's war, too."

She smiled. "If you have a bad dream, just call for me. I'll come kiss it better."

He smiled back at her, and, cliché that it was, her heart turned over. "I'll hold you to that promise." But then he grew more serious. "Will you be here then? I mean, will you be staying?"

"I think I'll be here as long as you want me."

He drew her down to him and kissed her, a gentle thank-you kind of kiss. But then it became something different.

In the midst of it, though, he whispered, "And how long will you want me?"

She didn't answer, but she knew immediately. *Forever.*

With his hands holding on to the headboard rails, at her insistence as he'd done with her, she touched and kissed every inch of his delicious body. She loved touching him because he was so sensitive, everywhere. He encouraged her to talk to him, too. To tell him what she liked about what she saw and caressed. To tell him in explicit detail what she planned to do next.

She'd never met a man to be shocked by oral sex, but he was. In truth, she hadn't done it more than a few times before because, frankly, to her it was the most intimate of acts, both to and from a partner, reserved for special people. People you loved. Or thought you might love.

He bucked so violently when she first put her mouth to him that he almost threw her off the bed, but then he threaded his fingers into her hair holding her in place. When he was approaching his climax, she drew back and climbed up to straddle him. Holding his eyes, which had gone from gray to blue with excitement, she took his erection in hand and impaled herself with him. Her body welcomed him with a little miniorgasm, a flexing and tightening of her inner muscles around him. For a moment, the only sound in the room was that of his panting.

"*Sacre bleu!*" he said then, sitting up to take over control of the love play. "Let me," he said huskily and put his hands on her hips, showing her the rhythm he wanted. "Like that, darlin'. No, no, no, slow down." Then, "Harder."

And finally, a long drawn out, "Aaarrgh!"

When they both lay splayed on their backs, fighting to regain their breaths, he turned his head to look at her. "Thank you."

"No, thank *you*," she countered, also turning just her head.

"I hope my sister didn't hear us. You were very loud."

"Hah! You were the one bellowing like an alligator."

They smiled at each other, and he took her hand, lacing her fingers with his.

"At least we don't have to worry about me getting pregnant. Not right away anyway."

He kissed her knuckles. "I didn't think about that. I should have, for God's sake! But you made me mindless."

"I have a monthly packet of birth control pills in my purse. Twenty-five days left."

"I am not even going to ask what you mean. I can only assume it is good news for both of us."

"The best."

"Twenty-five days. Four times a day, maybe five if you are not too weak. I figure we best get to work here, darlin'." He winked at her.

"I'm game," she said.

And much to her surprise . . . his, too, probably . . . they did in fact make love five times that night.

Six

There ain't nothin' a smart woman can't do . . .

For the next two weeks life moved on at Rosylyn following a pattern dictated by the sugar crop.

Hilary Clinton may have coined the phrase, "it takes a village," but, truly, Southern plantations put it to work, even those that no longer had slaves. Everybody had a job, even the little ones. Since it was mid-July and the sugar cane wouldn't be harvested until October, there was a minimal amount of field work required every day, usually only a few hours in the early morning, but the other work went on. Massive amounts of it. Vegetable gardening, which was mostly supervised by Lettie—the flower gardens had been left to go wild long ago, not having the required labor, although Clarence did his best with his one arm to keep it tamed. Clothes made. Fruits and vegetables preserved. Laundry. Planting rice and hay for the horse, mules, and two cows. Even the legless Jonas had jobs to do, like butter churning and sharpening tools.

To her surprise, Margo seemed to fit in, helping wherever

she could, whether with cooking or whatever job she was assigned. Her cheesecake had been a flop as a first try, but it had still been delicious scooped into little dishes like a pudding and topped with fresh whipped cream.

She'd even taught Fleur how to use the tube of makeup she'd found in her purse to cover her scar, and now Clarence was acting very interested in her. Apparently when Fleur had been only seventeen, her mother, a free black, had taken her to one of the Quadroon Balls in New Orleans where wealthy men came to buy mistresses. Fleur's protector had been abusive, almost killing her before she'd escaped. Her mother had refused to take her in.

At night Margo became Laurent's and he became hers, whether it be in his bed, her bed, the storeroom, a stall in the barn, or in the creek one moonlit night. She told him repeatedly that she loved him. Although he didn't return the sentiment, she knew he loved her, too. It was there in his blue gray eyes and in his lovemaking.

She felt as if they were in a holding pattern, waiting for something to happen, which she hated. She'd always been a person who took charge and made things happen, whether it was her escape from the projects or her rise in the business world.

Right now, she was raking rows in the vegetable garden next to Lettie. Delilah, who was still giving Ivory the cold shoulder, had just taken a basket of harvested vegetables up to the kitchen. The poverty at Rosylyn troubled Margo deeply, and she wanted to help, but they had already sold everything of value . . . paintings, silver, even fine clothing. "There sure is a lot of okra here," Margo remarked. "And beets."

"Way more than we can use, even after preserving," Lettie said.

"Can't you sell the excess at the market?"

Lettie shrugged. "You saw how many vegetables there were there. I doubt it would be worth the trouble."

Margo thought about her own business and how she'd taken an existing concept . . . dating agency . . . and turned it on its head. What Rosylyn needed was a new concept. "Why not use what you have and make it into something more marketable? Okra, for example. What else could you do with it? Okra jelly? Okra cake? Okra tea?"

Lettie turned up her nose.

Suddenly Margo got an idea. "How about okra wine? They say you can make wine out of anything. Even dandelion wine. We probably have the ingredients here. Of course we wouldn't have time to age it, but maybe that's okay. Betcha there's no okra wine for sale in New Orleans."

"My grandpa used to make wine. There are lots of bottle and jugs in the storeroom."

"See. It was meant to be."

Lettie just rolled her eyes at that.

"And as for the beets, how about we mix the juice with lard and make a kind of rouge?"

"Laurent would never allow it."

"Laurent doesn't have to know."

Lettie giggled. "How could we hide what we're doing?"

"We'll only work when Laurent is away from the house, and we'll swear everyone to secrecy."

They looked at each other and smiled.

"It's a deal then," Margo said.

Lettie nodded, but still she exclaimed, "Lawd-a-mercy!"

"Another thing . . ."

Lettie groaned.

". . . I've got to find a way of utilizing my matchmaking skills here for profit. I bet there are lots of single men and women who don't know about each other because their homes and plantations are so far from each other. Like you, Lettie. You're too pretty and nice to not find a man to love. Yes, we can go into the matchmaking business, for a fee, of course."

Lettie groaned again, longer this time, but Margo couldn't help but catch the hopeful expression on her face. "How could you . . . *we* manage it? I mean, would you set up an office here in the front parlor or buy a space in the city?"

"No, Laurent would find out. Imagination, that's all we

need here. I know . . . oh, I can't believe I didn't think of it earlier."

Lettie waited expectedly for her big announcement.

"We're going to have a speed-dating party, 1870s Southern style."

"What kind of party?" Laurent asked, coming up behind them from the edge of the sugar fields, where he, Ivory, and Cordell had been clearing more drainage ditches. He was covered with sweat, which dampened his shirt and trousers, and, frankly, he smelled of perspiration, this being predeodorant days, but he looked downright irresistible, and he would bathe later. He was especially attractive when he flashed her a knowing smile, which Lettie saw, and glanced repeatedly between them.

"The party?" Margo said. "Oh, Lettie and I were talking about setting up a garden party here."

"What garden? We don't have a garden. Oh, you mean here in the vegetable patch?" He laughed.

"Don't be silly, Laurent. We'll clear out Mama's flower garden, or else we'll just have it indoors."

"I am not getting involved in a garden party."

"That's the best part, Laurent," Margo said. "We'll do it someday when you have to be away from Rosylyn."

He shook his head at what he perceived to be their foolishness and walked off up to the house.

She and Lettie exchanged glances, then burst out with laughter.

"I am so glad you came here," Lettie said, giving her a hug.

"No more than me," Margo replied, but she was thinking of Laurent and a new idea she'd just had for what they could do tonight. It didn't involve vegetables, but it did involve another crop.

Sugar cane. Specifically, the tassels.

❖   ❖   ❖

Hope floats . . . or something . . .

There was something strange going on.

Laurent wasn't sure what it was, but every time he entered a room, it suddenly went silent. And some of the men were staring at him kind of funny, as if they knew something he didn't.

Plus, the smell. "What is that god awful smell?" he'd bellowed this noontime.

"I was boilin' dirty socks in here this mornin'," Lettie had said, chin held high with belligerence. She'd been lying, clear as daylight.

"Margo?" he'd asked then.

"Sorry. Gotta go. Delilah's waiting for me to help hang laundry."

"What's that you're doin'?" he now asked Jonas, who was strapped to a chair on the back loggia whittling.

"Nothin'," Jonas replied as he jumped as far as he could within his restraints and dropped the object he'd been working on into a burlap bag. Instead, he picked up another piece of wood and showed it to him. It was a deer, complete with antlers. The detail was remarkable. But Jonas was hiding something from him. He couldn't imagine what it might be.

Then there was Clarence who was spending an inordinate amount of time in the flower garden, gathering plants with his one arm but had nothing to show for it in terms of weeding or pruning. "Uh, what are doing, Clarence?"

Clarence, too, about jumped out of his skin. "Lookin' fer herbs?"

"Herbs? Since when did Mama grow herbs in her flower beds?"

"Flower herbs." Clarence raised his chin belligerently, too, daring him to disagree.

Laurent couldn't be too upset over any of this. He had Margo in his bed and in his life these last six weeks. They'd long since run out of her birth control pills, but he could not worry about that, either. If she became pregnant, he knew what he would do. Maybe he would do it anyhow.

He couldn't believe what a difference she made for him . . . for all of them, actually. Suddenly, they had hope. Hell, if a woman could travel through time, anything was possible, even surviving these harsh financial conditions,

which Margo called a "freakin' bump in the road." Some
bump! While Rosylyn was easily self-sufficient in terms of
feeding and housing everyone, it wasn't bringing in any hard
cash. And the tax man did not take sugar or eggs, which
Margo had actually suggested.

He smiled. The woman was a font of suggestions . . . and
information, some of it outlandish, some of it interesting,
and some of it downright fascinating, like multiple orgasms,
G-spots, and oral sex. But he had news for her. He knew a
few things about sex that she didn't.

Tonight he was going to show her the "Rebel's Last
Stand," and he wasn't talking about the military.

*   *   *

You could call them Donald Trumps in crinolines . . .

They were riding in the buckboard, heading toward New
Orleans by dawn a week later. Lettie was driving so that
Margo could make notes on their upcoming Speed Dating
Garden Party.

She was also making signs advertising their wares on the
back of some old letters she'd found in Laurent's office.

Fleur and Sulee, the girl with the club foot, were in the
back of the buckboard making sure the two rosewood tables
with pedestal bases didn't topple over. In an empire style,
possibly even Duncan Phyfe, they were going to be substi-
tutes for yard-sale-type folding tables. Delilah had wanted to
come help, bringing her baby, but they figured her absence,
along with theirs, would be too suspicious.

In addition, there were twenty jugs of wine and twenty-
seven jars of rouge—lard mixed with beet juice—put in
pretty miniature salt dishes and sealed with a thin layer of
wax. Twenty-seven was all they could find. If they'd had
more containers, they could have had two hundred or more.
Oh, well, this would give them an opportunity to study the
market and see what sold, or not.

Jonas had provided them, along with a bunch of intri-
cately carved animals, with fifteen little wooden statues of
naked women, some with really big breasts. She'd teased

him that, if these sold, he might want to offer a few naked men, as well, next time. To which he had laughed and said, "If it sells, I'll make it." The joy of being appreciated and the hope in this legless man's eyes were worth all the trouble they would probably be in.

Fleur and Clarence, who were becoming quite the couple, had worked together on their project. He gathered the juju plants with their alleged Viagra qualities, while she sewed pretty silk sacks with ribbon ties to hold the dried and crushed flowers. At one point, Fleur had whispered to her and Lettie, "It really works."

Margo doubted that. It was probably subliminal suggestion, like the placebo effect, but who was she to argue?

They would have liked to start earlier, but they'd had to wait until Laurent left. They weren't taking any chances. As it was, they'd lied unabashedly, telling him they would need the wagon to visit a neighboring plantation where Lettie had friends.

"Okay," Margo started, "I figure that the most people we should have this first time around is forty . . . twenty men and twenty women."

"First time! Forty!" Lettie shook her head as if it was impossible.

It wasn't. Margo wouldn't let it be.

"And let's see. There's you . . ."

Lettie moaned and her face turned beet red.

"Isn't there some man . . . or men . . . you would like to get to know?"

"Well, the pickin's are slim since the war, but I always liked James Fontenot. He works at the bank in New Orleans. He was a friend of Samuel, my betrothed, who died in the war. James is a widower with two children."

Margo wrote his name down. Not the ideal choice, but a possibility, and, hey, if he didn't work for Lettie, he might for someone else. "And?" she prompted.

"Henri Gaudet is a small sugar planter up the river a ways, handsome as sin, but he is so bitter these days. Like a bear with the miseries. Lost nigh everythin'."

Just like Laurent, except Laurent kept plugging away. They all did. Either that, or lay down and die.

"Come on, give me some more names. Women and men."

So, Lettie went on and on, and the list grew, amidst the four of them alternately giggling, snorting, scoffing, and outright laughing.

"Sue Mae Elliott is a biggety spoiled brat, even with her threadbare clothes. About twenty-five. Probably a mite crazy. Thinks she's still back in 1860, before the war.

"George Saunders, a cotton agent, but, whooee, does he have the beatin'est bad breath!" Lettie fanned her face and the girls in back giggled.

"We'll give him breath mints, or sprigs of mint to chew on."

"Pierre Lawrence hasn't changed his underdrawers since the war started."

"You would know that, how?"

"The smell," Lettie, Sulee, and Fleur said as one.

"That man ain't fittin' ta roll with the pigs," Lettie added.

On and on, they went, eating up the miles, as they came up with their invitation list.

"Does having no teeth bar a candidate?" Lettie asked.

"Hell, no!"

"Margaret Despain is a shrew, very unpleasant. Always was. Almost forty and never married."

"Maybe that's why she's a bitch."

"Harry Torrent has a tic.

"Melanie Sulent has an overbite like a horse.

"Clive Theriot has a wooden leg that creaks.

"Mary Ann Vincent ain't got a lick of sense. She's holdin' out for a rich husband, doan matter if he's old or ugly.

"Devon Hebert is godly good-looking with the whitest teeth I've ever seen, but I swan that man has poked every girl he could since he was twelve."

Fleur made a choking sound.

"What?" Margo asked.

"When I was goin' to the Quadroon Balls, M'sieur Hebert was noted fer his slippery hands and stingy ways."

Margo crossed him off the list.

And Lettie continued: "The Comeaux twins, Jolene and Julia, are sweet, and have had plenty of beaus over the years, but they both want to marry at the same time, neither leaving the other behind.

"Alain Fortier has no arms.

"Jacques Billaud lost an eye and wears an eye patch that keeps slipping.

"Aubrey Cuvier has a glass eye that's kind of . . . well, cock-eyed.

"Charlotte Sullivan hasn't been able to keep her pantaloons up since Oliver Parsons first cornered her in her daddy's sugar shed. Gave her the appetite, if you know what I mean.

"Dawson Sorbet cusses too much.

"George Evers is dog homely and mean as a dog, as well.

"Carter Dulaine is fifty and bald.

"Catherine O'Brien is forty and has a bald spot on top of her head. Hmmm. Maybe she and Carter would make a good pair. Maybe this matchmaking business isn't so hard after all.

"Marilee Fontaine was married to a Yankee and has five children."

"A double handicap."

By the time they were nearing the city, they had their list and a rough draft of the invitations they would be sending out by messenger . . . probably Jacob.

"I think we should charge only one dollar each," Lettie said. "Folks just doan have much money, even for essentials."

"No. If you place a lower value on your service, it will be undervalued. At least five dollars. And I can't believe I'm saying that. I charge five thousand dollars at my agency."

"Per person?" a shocked Lettie asked, even though Margo had told her this before.

"Per person, and they are privileged to be accepted." Still, five dollars times forty people would be two hundred dollars, with little overhead, and that was probably comparable to two thousand dollars in her time. Even though it rankled, she sensed that they needed to start small. Plus, with the money they earned today, she was hoping to exceed five hundred dollars, which was what the delinquent tax bill amounted to, according to Lettie. Laurent balked every time she asked about it.

They arrived at the French Market at noon, which was late for the New Orleans customer who liked to be out of the heat before the afternoon. Still, they were set up quickly and had their products set up nicely on lace-tablecloth-covered tables and damask cloths laid out on the ground.

Business was brisk, and they were sure to be sold out soon. Margo taught Lettie how to give a high five, and they were giving them to each other repeatedly.

Until disaster struck.

Seven

The thing about secrets is they can't be kept...

The first hint Laurent had that something was amiss came when he noticed Fleur and Sulee missing from the noontime meal.

"They went with Lettie and Margo," Granny Belle told him, with a decided cackle. Cassius, who was asleep in his adjacent chair, snorted at the interruption, then went back to sleep.

"Visiting the Comeaux twins? It's only two miles away. Why would Lettie need to take those two with her?"

Granny Belle just shrugged.

Then he went outside and found Clarence and Jonas whispering to each other. When he stepped closer, they stopped, and looked guilty.

The topper came when, as he was walking away, he heard Jacob ask his father, "With all the money they's gonna make fer us t'day, do ya think I could buy me a new straw hat and some of them fancy fishin' hooks?"

Laurent stopped dead in his tracks and turned slowly.

Jacob had a hand clamped over his mouth and tears welling in his eyes for letting slip some secret. Clarence and Jonas appeared guilty as cats with cream mustaches.

He walked back and demanded, "Tell me."

Clarence and Jonas exchanged glances, then nodded with resignation.

Clarence spoke first. "Miss Lettie 'n' Miss Margo went ta market."

Why would they tell me they were going to visit the Comeauxs if . . . ? "What market?"

"The French Market."

Jesus, Mary, and Joseph! "In N'awleans?"

Clarence stiffened with some kind of umbrage inconsistent with Laurent's question. "Is there any other?"

Clarence's insolence rankled. It really did. After all he'd done for him!

"So, Lettie and Margo, and I assume Sulee and Fleur, as well, went all the way to N'awleans . . . for what?"

"Ta sell some things," Jonas spoke up.

"Like your wood carvings?"

Jonas nodded.

That wasn't so bad, he supposed, but why couldn't they have told him that. He probably would have objected—ladies did not set up a stall in a public market—but the motive was certainly kind-hearted. "Do you think your animal carvings will sell for a good price?" *Enough to warrant a long trip and four "venders"?*

"Well, I carved more than deer and horses and dogs this time." Jonas's face heated with a blush.

This was like pulling teeth from a snake. He folded his arms over his chest and scowled. That's what everyone said he did best. "Exactly what did you carve, Jonas?"

"Nekkid women," he blurted out.

"*What?*" Laurent shouted.

"Now doan you be takin' yer ire out on Jonas. We all had a hand in this pot." This from Clarence.

"We?"

"Me and Fleur made juju tea and put it in little silk bags ta sell," Clarence explained. His chin was seeking the sun, too.

"You're selling tea?"

"Not exactly 'tea' tea?"

Laurent crossed his eyes.

"Afro-diss-ak tea."

At first, Laurent didn't understand until he sounded the word out, but then he did. "Oh, my God!" Once he had cursed a blue streak and berated the two of them for keeping secrets, he cooled down. "Is this all? Please. No more secrets."

"Uh . . . did I mention the beet rouge what Miss Lettie and Miss Margo made up? Fer ladies' cheeks. And . . ." Jonas stopped himself from revealing more.

Laurent put his face in his hands, counted to ten, then dared to ask, "And?"

"Jist one little other thing," Jonas said. "The okra wine."

"They made wine? Out of okra?"

"Yep?" Both men said.

"Tastes like horse piss," Jonas said, "but doan tell 'em I said so."

"How? How could they make wine without my knowing?"

"They did it when you were gone in the mornin'," Clarence revealed.

Ah! The odd smells and secretive looks. "What time did they leave?"

"About dawn. Right after you left." Jonas was relaxed now, as if everything was going to be just fine now. It wasn't.

The sly deceiving witches! Lettie and Margo, the witch twins, that's what they are. Lettie never used to be like this. It's all the other witch's fault.

Laurent had soon bathed in the stream, changed clothes, and was down at the wharf catching a flat boat to New Orleans. Steam practically seeped from his ears as his blood roiled with anger. How dare they? How dare she?

Someone was in big, big trouble.

Paddling a female ass never held so much appeal.

*   *   *

It was a good day and a bad day . . .

By three o'clock most of their goods were sold and they were ready to pack up the wagon to return to Rosylyn.

Lettie was almost ecstatic that they had made three hundred dollars so far. Everything was gone, except for one jug of okra wine and three rouges. During one of the lulls, Margo had gone off and bought a half dozen readymade dresses, a bag full of slipper shoes, and four ladies' hats with the money she'd earned earlier from selling her diamond. She planned to share these things with her fellow sales ladies.

Then everything started to fall about.

A woman came up with bright red circles on her cheeks screaming, "I can't get it off, I can't get it off."

Margo had explained to every one of their customers that only a tiny dot would do, but apparently this woman had not been listening.

Then a man stormed up yelling, "Do you know what this wine tastes like? A jug of Mississippi muddy water would be better than this slop."

Everyone who'd indicated an interest in their wine had been offered a thimbleful to taste. Apparently they didn't get the full effect that way.

Next came a heavyset matron dragging her husband by the ear, waving the naked woman carving. "Sinners! Jezebels! That's what you are. Sellin' sinful statues to poor innocent men."

Yeah, right.

But then their biggest trouble arrived in the form of one raging Creole man with blue gray eyes and a limp.

He said something through gritted teeth which they couldn't understand.

"Doan be mad, Laurie," Lettie tried to tell him.

"Get. In. The. Wagon!"

Lettie, Fleur, and Sulee scurried to do his bidding, carrying the last jug of wine, tablecloths, and other items. But Margo stayed.

"Don't test me now, Margo. I might just kill you."

"I have to help you carry the tables," she said.

He didn't speak to her the entire time, even as she returned the money to those three fuming customers. Lettie, the traitor, crawled into the back with Fleur and Sulee.

"I blame you for this," he finally said.

"That's all right. It was my idea, mostly."

"How dare you? Interfering in my family . . . with my workers. You have no right."

Now that hurt. He was treating her as if she were an outsider, not the woman he loved. *If* he loved her, that was.

"I just wanted to help. We all did. Maybe you ought to give that stupid pride of yours a vacation."

"I don't need your help."

"Or your sister's. Or your former slaves. Give me a break. Everyone needs help some time."

"Not by making a scandal of me and Lettie."

"What's the big deal? We became merchants. Where's the sin in that? And we made three hundred freakin' dollars for you, you ungrateful bastard."

"What?" Clearly he was surprised that they'd earned so much. Not proud, like she and Lettie had been, but surprised, nonetheless. "Do you honestly think I would take any more money from you?"

"You have no choice. If you won't take it, I'll give it to Lettie, and she'll pay the taxes."

"Are you crazy?"

"Probably. You've told me I am enough times. Good enough to fuck, but too crazy for anything else."

He made a growling sound of disgust at her language, and the three women in the back gasped. Well, she didn't care at this point. She didn't like crude language, either, but sometimes it was the only thing that would do.

Despite her righteous indignation, she couldn't control the tears that leaked from her eyes.

Laurent glanced her way and said more softly, "Margo."

She put up a halting hand. "No, dammit! You don't want my help, I don't want your pity."

He went still. He hadn't expected her anger in return. Well, good.

So, there was silence the rest of the way, even when Laurent chuckled, then burst out with a laugh at one point, muttering something about naked women, dimwitted women, and okra beer.

When he tried to take her hand in his, she jerked hers away.

No one spoke to her that way and then expected a little kiss and make up. Not even the man she loved.

Maybe this whole time-travel business was a mistake.

Maybe I should try to go back.

But then she sneaked a glance at Laurent, and he glanced back at her.

Maybe not.

❁   ❁   ❁

Stubborn is as stubborn does . . .

Margo would not talk to him for the next two days, let alone make love with him. Hell, no one else would talk to him, either.

He was the one wronged here, and yet everyone blamed him.

With the money Margo had pushed on him when they'd first met, and the money Lettie had forced on him from their crazy market endeavor, he had almost enough to pay the taxes. That should have made him feel good. Instead, he fumed beneath the surface, shamed by his inability to handle the problem himself.

"You're a fool, Laurent," Lettie told him finally, coming up to him by the old slave quarters where he was helping Ivory fix the fence rail around one of the cabins. Delilah was whitewashing the outside. The reunited happy family would be moving in tomorrow.

"What now, Lettie?" He straightened and arched his back to get out the kinks. "What have I done now?"

"It's not what you've done. It's what you've not done."

"Margo," he guessed.

"Yes. She feels helpless here, out of place. Doing business is what she knows, and she tried to help you. We all did. Didn't you ever hear about marriages being a partnership?"

"Marriage! Who said anything about marriage?"

"You better, if she stays here."

On the alert, he asked, "Has she talked about leaving?"

"No, but anyone as bruised as she is won't stick around for more abuse."

"I have never abused any woman, certainly not her."

"Laurent, you and Elizabeth loved each other, I suppose, but almost in a brother-sister kind of way. No, don't interrupt. I might be six years younger than you, but I saw things. Now you're being offered the kind of love you deserve. And passion. Yes, you idiot, I know what passion is. Are you going to throw it away?"

Laurent stared at her departing back, not needing to look behind him to know that Ivory and Delilah had heard it all. But then he really thought about the words Lettie had hurled at him. She was right. Pride didn't warm a man's bed . . . or his life.

Tossing his hammer down, he stomped down to the kitchen, where Margo was making more of that cheesecake slop of hers. She looked up, and looked again.

"Wha-what?" she asked, no doubt noticing the expression on his face, which could be anger, frustration, lust, or . . . love.

"Stand up, Margo."

"Huh?"

Not waiting for her to comply, he picked her up, tossed her over his shoulder, and walked away. He could smell the faint scent of her perfume, a luxury she'd been carrying in her purse when she arrived. He wished he could gift her with more. He would some day, he swore he would.

But, for now, he'd just given every fool at Rosylyn . . . probably up and down the river . . . something to gossip about for the next year.

When he got to the old gazebo, he set her squirming, squealing body down, and said, "We have to talk."

"There's nothing you have to say that I want to hear."

He hoped that wasn't true. He stared at her for a long moment, then opened a vein . . . or was it his heart?

"I love you."

❀ ❀ ❀

I went to a garden party . . .

Margo floated on a cloud of happiness for the next week.

He loves me, was the refrain that rang through her mind throughout the day, no matter what she was doing. And all night long, he told her and showed her.

She couldn't have been happier, except that she hadn't yet told him about today's Speed Dating Garden Party. Oh, he knew they were planning a garden party. "Have a good time, Lettie," he'd said, patting her back. "You deserve a party." He'd even watched as they cleared up the flower garden, exposing pretty flowers and bushes, and about a hundred snakes. "It's a lot of time to waste . . . uh spend, for one day," he'd complained, "but it does look nice."

Every chair in the place had been taken outside. Then, they'd dragged stumps from the woodshed that hadn't yet been cut for firewood. They were being used for small tables, covered by miniature tablecloths, which Sophie, of all people, made for them out of old stained or ripped tablecloths. "Aren't they cute?" he'd said.

Oh, Lord! she'd thought. She'd tried repeatedly to broach the subject, but he kept putting her off, telling her that they needed to put the French Market incident behind them and not bring up any potential problems in the future. So, coward that she was, she'd put it off.

You can always apologize later, the bad side of her brain said.

If he'll let you, the good side countered.

Well, it was too late now. She and Lettie stood in their new dresses, wearing subtle makeup and lipstick, looking over the setting. Granny Belle was making the tea. Sophie had polished an old dented silver service that she'd found, and it was set out on the lower side loggia off the gardens.

Sulee would be collecting money as people arrived, and Fleur would be taking any loose wraps inside. Delilah would be serving. Margo and Lettie would make the introductions and explain the rules.

By three o'clock, the party was almost over, and it was a resounding success. Not one person complained about the fee, some connections were being made, and everyone was having a good time.

"One more round, folks," Margo announced, and forcibly pushed Lettie to sit down at a stump . . . uh, table with James Fontenot, the New Orleans banker with two children. Even Margo had to admit he was hot, knowing he had eyes for only Lettie.

At first, Lettie resisted, but then she smiled and said, "Well, fiddle-dee-dee! All right."

"What did you say, Lettie?" James inquired.

She just batted her eyelashes and smiled in a way Southern Belles must have been doing for ages.

Everything was going to be all right, she told herself, as she gazed at everyone chatting, drinking tea, eating little sugar biscuits, and most of all finding a possible mate.

That was before she got her first look at an incensed Laurent walking over to the flower garden. Someone must have told him.

There wasn't a speck of love in his stormy gray eyes now. Truthfully, it appeared more like hate.

And for the first time Margo realized that this time things were not going to work out, not as planned. Not at all.

❖ ❖ ❖

Fool me once, you're a fool; fool me twice . . .

Laurent had gone by riverboat to Baton Rouge that morning and completed his business with his new sugar agent in record time. Under normal circumstances, he would have liked to stop for a meal with old friends, but today he was anxious to return home.

The boat stopped about ten miles from Rosylyn to pick up a few passengers . . . acquaintances he'd known in the old

days. The sneers they cast his way boded ill for any strength-
ening of those ties.

"Bodine, Steven," he said, nodding.

"Laurent," they both replied.

Then Bodine spoke up, "So how come we didn't get invited to your garden party?"

"Probably because you didn't have the five-dollar entrance fee," Steven told Bodine.

"And you weren't in the market for a wife, seeing as how
you already have one," Bodine countered back with a snicker.

"What the hell are you two talkin' about?"

Bodine pulled a piece of parchment from his jacket and
handed it to him with a smirk. A garden party invitation.

His eyes went wide at what he read. Then he walked
away to lean against a far railing.

Again, they had done it to him again, but this time they
would make him the laughingstock of the entire state. How
could they? How could she?

He felt frozen by the time he got off the boat at his own
wharf and saw that the party was just breaking up. He recognized many of the people who were leaving and waving gaily
at him.

"Too bad you missed a fine party, Laurent."

"It was so good seeing your sister again. You must come
by soon."

"Your new friend is delightful."

"I haven't had so much fun since before the war."

Near the side loggia, he saw Delilah stacking several piles
of coins, then handing them to Lettie who put them into a
small box.

As one, Lettie and Margo realized he was back, and the
guilt on their faces made it clear that they'd known how he
would react, and had done it anyway.

"Leave us," he told Lettie.

"Now, Laurent, be reasonable," Lettie begged.

"Not now, Lettie. Go."

She left reluctantly, leaving him to face Margo alone.

"I won't beg you to understand."

"I don't want any explanations from you," he spat out. "You knew how I felt after your antics at the French Market. I forgave you then, but —"

"You forgave me? You forgave me?" Her voice dripped with disdain. "I did nothing to forgive, except keep you in the dark, and no wonder. You are the most stubborn, ill-tempered brute in the world."

"That makes it easier for me to tell you to leave Rosylyn, first thing in the morning. Keep your money," he waved a hand at the money chest on the table behind her. "You'll need it to get a hotel room in the city, or wherever the hell you want to go. In fact, if you want, I recalled while I was away that there's a sugar planter up Houma way, on Bayou Black, with the name of Etienne Baptiste. Maybe he's one of your relatives. You could go there."

She was no longer looking obstinate. In fact, she appeared wounded. "I love you, Laurent," she said softly.

His heart lurched, and his lungs felt crushed. "Too bad that's not enough." He walked away.

Eight

Had leaving Tara been as hard for Scarlett? . . .

"I'm going with you."

"No, Lettie," Margo said early the next morning as she finished packing up her few possessions into a small canvas carpetbag. "Laurent needs you here."

"He's a fool. Don't go. He'll change his mind, I know he will."

"No. I've pushed him too far this time. Oh, I'm not excusing him, honey. He never gave us a chance to explain. And, darn it, everyone had a good time, didn't they?"

"Yes, and if you go, I'm going to have more of those parties. I am. I don't care if Laurent has a hissy fit."

"Be tolerant of him, Lettie."

"I hate him."

"No, you don't, and I don't, either. He's a good man. He cares about all of you, and he's done it alone for so long that he doesn't know how to give up that control to accept a little help."

"If you feel that way, stay, and convince him to change."

"I can't, Lettie. There is a famous expression in my time."

Lettie swiped at her eyes. "Another famous expression?"

She smiled. "This expression is: if you love someone, you have to set them free."

"I don't know what that means."

"It means that I love Laurent, but my love isn't good for him. He needs to be free of me."

Lettie started to bawl.

A short time later, Margo stood at the end of the wharf waiting for whatever water vessel passed by to hitch a ride to New Orleans, where it had started. She was alone, as she'd insisted to Lettie and all the teary-eyed servants that she wanted to be.

As for Laurent, she hadn't seen him last night after his tirade or this morning. For all she knew he was off somewhere blitzed on okra wine.

She sighed deeply, waved at the approaching flatboat, and told herself, *Tomorrow is another day. Dammit!*

❖   ❖   ❖

Clueless men: the same throughout the ages . . .

Lettie found Laurent in the barn where he was dunking his head in the horse trough. He must have slept here last night.

She shoved him in the chest, almost knocking him over.

"Hey, what was that for?"

"I'll tell you what that was for, you bloomin' idiot. For losin' the best thing you ever had."

"Margo?"

"Yes, Margo. How could you, Laurie? How could you?"

"A man needs—"

"No! I doan wanna hear any blather about men and their pride." Full-out bawling now, her words came between sobs, her nose running. She had a full steam on for all the things she'd stored up to lash at him.

"You don't understand."

"Laurent, let me ask you something? Margo told me one day that if you had your druthers, if you didn't have all of us here, that you would go off to the California gold fields to seek your fortune."

"She had no right to tell you that."

"She had every right. She loves you, and I'm your sister, who also loves you. But don't you see what a burden that puts on all of us, to know we're holding you back? We want to help, for our sakes, as well as yours."

He took her in his arms and held her until her crying died down. "What Margo failed to tell you is that, yes, I did feel that way at one time, but I haven't for a long time. All of you here are my family, and Rosylyn is where I want to be, God-willing."

"And Margo?"

"I'll talk to her."

"That might be difficult."

"Why?"

"She's gone."

Laurent went cold as ice. Yes, he'd told her to leave, but he hadn't really meant it. Had he? Raising his chin, he told his sister, with not just promise, but determination in his voice, "Not for long."

*　*　*

She was dealing for her life . . .

Margo was surprisingly calm.

Between Rosylyn and New Orleans, she'd made some decisions. She was a fighter, not a quitter. But first she needed a plan.

She'd arrived in New Orleans about ten A.M. and registered at the Vieux Carre Hotel. Talk about irony! Then she went to the French Market where she, thankfully, found her jeweler, Mr. Goldstein, and bargained hardy for the sale of her Cartier wristwatch, which was unique in her time, and *really* unique in 1870.

"But I can't afford that kind of money!"

"I can't afford to sell it for less. Keep in mind, there are three carats of diamonds in this thing, in a platinum setting, and the mechanism will probably last for hundreds of years. You'll never find another like this, I guarantee it."

"Six thousand dollars."

She shook her head. "Sorry. Maybe there's another jeweler who can afford it."

"Eight thousand."

"Really, don't feel bad. Maybe I'll travel north to New York City. Bet there are wealthy jewelers there."

He sighed heavily. "Ten thousand then. In paper?" he asked hopefully.

"What do you think?"

So, by two P.M., after a trip to the bank with Mr. Goldstein, she was back at her hotel, waiting for Laurent. Without a watch, she wasn't sure of the time as she waited. But she knew he would come eventually. He had to.

* * *

A hurricane was about to hit New Orleans, and it wasn't Katrina . . .

Laurent knocked on the door of Margo's hotel room.

He felt a bit silly, having donned a suit, the best he had, which wasn't much. Widow-bait clothing, Lettie had teased as she sent him off. But he wanted to do this right.

She opened the door almost immediately, and, damn, she looked as if she'd been expecting him. She was wearing a new dress and that intoxicating perfume.

"You left." *Dumb, dumb, dumb. Where are all the charming words I've been practicing?*

"I did. You told me to."

Since when do you listen to what I tell you? "I didn't mean it."

She raised her eyebrows. "Where were you all night?"

"I tried to get drunk."

"On okra wine?"

"No, I might have gone off half-cocked, but not that far. I tried to drink bourbon, but I couldn't. I tried to sleep and kept having these awful dreams. As if it was me, but not me."

"Like what?"

"I was crying in one of them, staring at a body of water where there was a sinking boat."

She nodded. "That would have been when Larry's wife Bethany drowned. She was pregnant at the time, and he was devastated."

"I felt his devastation. In others, he . . . I mean I . . . was sitting in a tavern with men similarly dressed with almost-shaved heads. They were drinking and laughing, except me, or Larry, or whoever. There was just this overpowering sadness."

"I don't think he ever got over his loss, even after five years."

"But why me?"

"I don't know. Just as I don't know why this time-travel thing happened. I can only believe that it was a miracle, and that God used Larry to get me to you."

"I don't want you to go."

"Why?"

"Because I love you."

There was a flash of emotion in her eyes before she went blank again, hiding her feelings. She was deliberately making this hard for him.

"And?" she prodded.

"Do you still love me?"

"Pfff! Did you think I would change overnight?"

That pleased him, but he didn't dare smile. Yet. "Stay, Margo, and marry me."

She closed her eyes for several seconds and seemed to be praying. In thanks, he hoped. Not for nerve to refuse him.

"Sit down, Laurent. We need to talk." She waved a hand to the small table with two chairs.

He would much rather sit on that big bed over there with her. Or not sit.

Like a good boy, he sat on one chair, and she sat on the other.

She took his hand in hers. "Laurent, what do you really want?"

"To marry you."

She smiled and squeezed his fingers, which he took for a good sign.

"No, I mean about your life. If you had your choice and no financial worries, what would you do? Leave Rosylyn and go to the gold fields? Go abroad? Or stay at Rosylyn and bring it back to life?"

He thought for several minutes, giving it the time it deserved. "I would stay, if I could."

The smile that lit her face then was almost miraculous, but what did it mean?

"Here's the deal, Laurent, and believe you me, I have learned this morning just what a good dealer I am. If I marry you, would you be willing to accept a dowry? Or would you go all postal again?"

"Postal?"

"Would your overinflated male pride accept a dowry?"

He narrowed his eyes at her. This was a trap, he knew it was. "How much?"

"No matter how much money is involved, for me to marry you, it would have to be a partnership, each contributing something. Other than love, you own the physical property, that's your contribution, and my contribution would be , a certain amount of money."

He weighed the two sides of her proposition, but really there was no question. Have her or not? "Yes, I would accept that."

She shocked him then by dropping down on her knees before him and asking, "Will you marry me, Laurent Duvall?" Then she laid her face on his knees and burst out crying.

A short time later, a way too short a time later, they lay naked and sated on the bed, having pledged their betrothal in the age-old way.

"Just how much is this dowry?" he inquired.

"Let's just say we could hire several dozen workers, buy a new horse, or two, perhaps a buggy, and even have a honeymoon in New York City."

"I like that last part best." He kissed her shoulder. "What did you do? Rob a bank?"

"No, just a jeweler. At a bank."

He glanced down at her wrist, recognizing immediately what she had done. "You sold your watch."

"Not to worry, honey, now that I'm here time can stand still."

*   *   *

Meanwhile, back at the ranch . . . uh, base . . .

In the Coronado, California, Navy SEAL special forces office, Commander Ian MacLean bellowed at two of his team members, Justin LeBlanc and Sylvester Simms, "What do you mean, he disappeared?"

LeBlanc shrugged. "He was with us in New Orleans. We had that meeting with the Baptiste babe, and before you know it, he was gone."

"Terrorists?"

"No," Simms said. "We had the police investigate. We searched everywhere ourselves. No luck. Just poof!"

"The odd thing is that Ms. Baptiste has disappeared, too," LeBlanc told him.

"A coincidence?"

They all pondered that question.

"Stranger things have happened," LeBlanc concluded.

The Drowning Sea

Veronica Wolff

With thanks to my dad
and to Patrick, my first mate and big brother,
for explaining how to sail a ship,
and then sink it.

Bheir an cuan a chuid fhèin a-mach.

The sea will claim its own.

One

Iain leaned down and swung his blade. It landed in the thick slab and a familiar jolt shot up his arm. He twisted the handle, pulling the iron through and out. The peat answered with a dull suck.

He stood. Studied his work. He'd been stacking the bricks in low piles. He wiped his hands down the front of his plaid. The muscles in his shoulders and arms hummed. Using his sleeve, he mopped the sweat from his brow and knew a moment of raw pleasure at the kiss of chill air on hot skin rubbed dry. He pulled a deep breath in and savored the scent of dirt and island air in the back of his throat.

There was a scream, and he startled.

The shriek of an animal stuck in the bog?

Another scream, ripping down to where he stood in the belly of the glen. A woman's scream.

He tossed his peat iron atop the bricks, turned, and ran along dry ground. If there was a woman trapped, he had no choice but to run. The bog drowned folk as quick as the sea.

The sound had come from over the hill, where the muck

was thick and wet. Peat looked just like land, until it sucked you in. And then even the bravest of men knew fear. Stuck in the bog, panic seized a man's chest, until the black muck became nothing less than evil itself, oozing from a crack in the earth, pulling all down to greet the devil.

He crested the hill and spotted her. He galloped down, and speed made his strides clumsy. He skidded to a stop.

The prettiest girl in the world stood knee-deep in the muck. He'd only ever seen her from afar, and only a few times at that. She was even more beautiful up close, so lovely and perfect, pale and blonde, like a creature crafted of innocence and fine cream and sunshine.

He knew an eternity as time stalled and stretched in a single pound of his heart. Iain never dreamed he'd ever be within reach of her. He never would've thought it possible, but seeing her now, suddenly everything seemed possible.

She gave a tug to her dark blue frock and frowned.

Fascinated, he watched her bite at her lip, muttering a curse that should grace no high-born lass's mouth.

He felt a smile crook his lips.

She felt his presence and turned.

Her body froze, but her face lit a thousand different ways. Frustration turned like quicksilver into anger. She'd spied his amusement and didn't much like it.

He schooled his features, trying his best to look grave.

The bonny cream of her cheeks flushed pink. How soft that skin would be.

His smile flickered again at the thought, and this time there was no fighting it. He felt the tug of it spread broad across his cheeks.

Her face seemed to narrow in on itself, and she stared, looking as though she'd give him a verbal thrashing if only she knew the right words.

The urge to laugh swelled in his belly. It was a struggle, but he muted it to a low chuckle. "The more you dance about, aye, the more the bog will suck you in."

"I am not dancing." She bit out each word with affronted

dignity, as if she were taking wee nibbles from a triangle of toast instead of speaking in anger.

His smile renewed, and with it her ire.

"If you would be a gentleman, and please—"

Iain Gillespie MacNab was no fool. He wiped his palms once more on his plaid and, in two long steps, was by her side, perched on a sliver of dry earth.

She gave an outraged squeal as he scooped her free of the bog and swung her up in his arms.

"Do you know who I am?" she sputtered.

"I do . . ." He gave her a quick bounce to settle her in his arms and laughed at her indignant squawk. "And I don't."

"What do you mean you do and you—Stop that at once!"

"Stop what?" he asked, giving himself two more seconds before shifting his hand from her rump.

"You know very well what I meant."

"Shall I put you down then?" He made as though to drop her into the muck, taking the opportunity to graze his cheek along her hair. She wore it long and loose, a yellow spill down her back, shining bright in the sunlight.

"Oh. bother."

"Carrying you is no bother," he said grandly, backing away from the bog.

"No, I said 'oh, bother.'" She squirmed, looking down her legs. "That . . . that bog ate my shoes."

He noticed her feet for the first time. Stockings bunched low at her ankles, and the fabric was soaked black, hanging heavy and long from her toes. They were the tiniest feet he'd ever seen on a person full-grown.

"Such wee paws," he exclaimed. "'Tis a wonder you don't blow over in the wind."

She looked quickly away, biting a smile from her lips, and he decided he'd not release her until he teased a full grin from that mouth.

"There's naught for it." He began strolling calmly across the uneven terrain, headed toward the sea. "I'll simply have to carry you home."

She twisted in his arms, shock widening her eyes. "You cannot carry me all the way home."

"Aye, and I can."

"But I'm heavy," she protested, her pale brow furrowing.

"Och, you're no heavier than a bird. And you can't walk with your feet bare."

"You don't even know where I live."

"Aye, I do at that." He purposely, mischievously, avoided her eyes.

"So you do know who I am."

"I said I do and I don't. All know the laird's daughter." He stared at her then, slowly grazing his eyes over her. "Bonnier than the first heather in bloom, hair spilling like honey down the lovely curve of her back."

His smile feigned innocence, but he risked letting some darker thing flash in his gaze. A darker, wanting thing that stiffened his body against the feel of her soft figure held tight in his arms.

"Then why do you say you don't know me?" Her voice warbled and her cheeks reddened, and it gratified him.

"Aye, well, though all ken the fair and treasured daughter of the MacLeod, few are privy to her given name."

"Oh," she said simply.

"Oh. Your name is Oh, is it?"

"No."

"Ah."

He let the silence hang. She'd be unaccustomed to such chatter with a man, and he could tell it flustered her. He liked being the cause of her discomfort. He prolonged it, hoping to see her cheeks flush pink once more.

He imagined she'd flush so if kissed.

For surely the MacLeod's cherished daughter had never been kissed. He smiled at her and winked.

"Cassiopeia," she blurted.

A laugh burst free of his throat. "Cassia-what-a?"

"My name. It's Cassiopeia."

"Now that's not a name to roll easy from the tongue, is it?" He bit his tongue between his teeth and leaned in close to her.

And there it was, the answering pink flush.

His smile faded as lighthearted delight slid into something that put him on his guard. Sweet, bonny Cassiopeia would break a man's heart some day, he predicted.

"No," she allowed, with a small smile. "It's not a common name."

He adjusted his arm under her knees, settling her higher along his chest to make the climb uphill.

Whether it was discomfort from the silence or a polite way to call attention from his momentary exertion, she spoke on. "My father. He is a devotee of astronomy."

"Is that so?"

She caught the wary sarcasm in his tone and her eyes narrowed.

"Och, easy, Cassie, love, I'm a peat farmer and son of a peat farmer. I know not of astronomy."

"Do you sail?"

"Aye, better than I can walk."

"And how do you steer?"

"My boat? By the stars . . . and I see where this is leading."

"Good, then you should know that, if you can steer by the stars, you, too, are a student of astronomy."

"I read the stars better than I read words on paper. I've just never known the Latin for them."

"Greek. Cassiopeia is from the Greek."

"Then good, aye? Your father and I will have much to discuss when I come to ask your hand." He gave her a rakish wink.

Her tone grew instantly wary. "Please don't . . . you'll not . . . please leave my father out of this . . ."

For the first time he wondered what had brought the sequestered MacLeod daughter so far afield. "What brought a bonny lass like yourself to the bog? Dropped from the sky like an angel, is it?"

She seemed to fret over his question, but her darling shrug made him decide to press the issue.

"Truly, lass, it's rare I've seen you outside your family's keep. Trust me," he said, cocking a brow, "I'd remember."

"I don't know . . ." she stammered.

"You don't know." He nodded thoughtfully. "So you *are* an angel."

"No," she replied coyly, fighting a smile. "I just came because . . ."

"Because?"

"I just wanted to see," she said finally.

"Ah," Iain said with mock gravity. "And have you seen?"

"Aye. Look," she said suddenly. She pointed his attention into the distance, but not before he spied the blush warming her cheeks.

Her home was on the horizon, a stern, gray tower rising from a high rock at the edge of the sea. As they neared, he felt her bristle. Glancing down at her pretty face, he saw something pinch at her brow.

"Really," she said, "you cannot carry me the whole way home." Nerves strung her voice tight.

It would be the laird—her father—who'd be the cause. The notion made him defiant, and he pulled her more tightly against him. "You're afraid of your father."

"Aye," she replied, and her plainspoken tone took him aback. "As you should be."

He leaned in close to whisper at her ear, "I fear no man."

He felt her breath catch, or maybe he imagined it, but an urge claimed him all the same. He took the barest nip of that ear, perfect as a wave-swept top shell on the sand.

"Go to the side then," she said weakly. "If you must." She pointed him to an entrance off a small courtyard and what would be the kitchens.

"Oh, I must," he muttered under his breath.

They reached their destination, and reluctantly he let her go. She was shorter than he'd realized, her head coming only to his chest, and he fought the urge to pull her back and tuck her close in his arms. "Your home, fair mistress," he said, sweeping a playful bow.

"You . . ." She froze. Battling a smile from her face, she pointed hesitantly at his cheek. "Oh my."

"Oh your . . . ?" he asked, leaning into her hand. He raised his brows, determined to see that smile in full bloom.

Finally her grin spread. It crinkled the corners of her eyes and set a single, deep dimple on her cheek. Iain thought, until that moment, he'd never truly felt the sun shine upon him.

She rustled in the pocket of her skirts, retrieving a small square handkerchief. Lace trimmed the edges and an elegant blue *C* was embroidered in the corner. "I'm afraid you have a bit of . . . of *bog* on your face."

She gave him an apologetic smile as she began to wipe at his face. Her features were still, her eyes determined, as she concentrated on swabbing the peat from his jaw. He savored the touch of her fingers, gentle and cool.

She was so close to him and, for the moment, unaware. He stared openly. She pursed her lips, and he noticed a faint brown freckle gracing the corner of her mouth.

His chest tightened. He was overwhelmed by the desire to twine his fingers through her hair, to cup her face gently in his hands and pull that fair mouth to his.

"There," she said with a pat to his cheek. Her eyes grew quiet. "How . . . how can I thank you?" She struck him as reluctant as he to part, and it made him brave.

"You can kiss me."

"I cannot!" Though her reply was immediate, awareness flushed from her cheeks down to the top of her deliciously plump bosom.

And he knew then that he *would* kiss her.

He bent to her and whispered, "You're not going to thank me?"

"Of course. I . . . I am very grateful."

"Then just a small kiss." He tapped his finger on his cheek. "Just here."

He leaned close, offering his cheek, and she reflexively pecked a prim little kiss. Whether her response had been involuntary or impulsive, he didn't know. But he felt the breeze tickle her hair against his neck, and a great truth flashed to him in that moment: his life would never be the same.

"Now the other side." His voice seemed to him ragged, uncooperative.

"What?"

"The other side," he told her, turning his face to present his other cheek. "That was only half a thank you after all."

She thought about it this time, and he worried he'd gone too far. But she leaned closer. The fresh, sweet smell of her filled his senses, and his heart swelled.

She leaned to buss his cheek, but he turned his face at the last instant, catching her lips in a quick kiss.

She gasped in surprise. And then, remarkably, she simply swatted his arm, smiling her scold. He felt a bursting in his chest.

"Och, bonny Cassie . . ."

And then it was *his* cheeks he felt grow hot, and she giggled. It was *she*, suddenly, who had the upper hand. She knew it and laughed. It was such a musical, sweet sound. A sound to fill him.

"But I don't even know your name," she murmured, and he decided he'd not rest until he could hear that sweet whispering voice, spoken for only him, every day, for the rest of his days.

"Iain. I am Iain MacNab."

"Iain MacNab," she repeated, her eyes locked with his.

His heart wrenched from his chest at the sound of his name on her lips.

"Say you'll meet me," he whispered. "Say you'll see me again. Tomorrow. And the day after that."

She blushed and looked away.

"At Callanish. Beneath the standing stones." He took her chin gently, tilted her face up to him. The blush still stained her cheeks, but endless possibility danced in her sky blue eyes. "I'll be waiting for you, bonny Cassie. Tomorrow, until forever."

Two

Iain sat down hard at the foot of the tallest stone. Leaning back, he let the cool granite leach the nervous heat from his body. He'd been pacing and sitting and rising and pacing all morning.

Opening his sporran, he peeked once more at the wee treasure he'd brought Cassie. He'd found the shiny, black seed that morning in the surf and had taken it as an omen.

"Naught but a fool's whigmaleerie." He gave a small, wistful laugh. "I'm as silly as a tippling fishwife."

No surprise, that. Cassie's beauty would inspire boyish foolishness in the gravest of men. Iain traced her features in his mind. Could her hair truly have been as shiny as he remembered? Her eyes as bright?

Where was she?

He patted his sporran shut and sighed. "What'd you fancy would happen, lad? Ah, but it would've been nice." The peat boy and the laird's daughter. Very nice indeed.

And very impossible.

"Enough lazing," he grumbled. There wasn't exactly a peat fairy who'd show up to do his work.

He stood and gave a brusque brush to his plaid, and with a last look at the stones, headed back toward the bog.

"Iain!"

The shout rang clear across the field. He stilled. Had thoughts of fairies among the standing stones well and truly addled his mind?

"Iain, wait!"

Had she come? He wanted to believe it but couldn't. Slowly he turned.

But there Cassie was. And God save him, she was running. She'd hiked up her skirts and was running to him as though she were a girl half her age.

He laughed, and she looked abashed, and so he ran to her, too, shouting, "You're the bonniest sight in all Scotland."

They met halfway, and they stood for a moment in silence. She panted from the exertion, her lips trembling with a shy smile. He thought his own smile might split his face in two.

"You came," he said finally. A burst of joy found his hands taking her by the shoulders. He couldn't believe she stood before him. "You truly came, Cassie."

"I . . ." She looked down, and he saw that she kept her skirts gripped tight in her fists.

She was a bashful wisp of a thing. And she'd come, to see *him*, despite it.

"My dress." She frowned and brushed at her clothes, still not meeting his eyes. "It isn't my best, you know. It was hard, yesterday, explaining away the stains on my hem. I needed to wear something more . . . sturdy."

Iain finally registered the practical brown linen she wore. "You fash yourself over your . . . your frock there?" He laughed. "Och, lass, don't you know you're the loveliest creature ever to set foot on this isle?"

The thought reminded him of what he held in his sporran. "Ah, but you must come, Cass. Come bide a wee, beneath the stones." He reached out and gently took her hand.

Her features eased, and her eyes rose to meet his. It knocked the air from his lungs. Cassie's eyes were as blue as he'd remembered. Bluer even. Vivid, like the petals of some otherworldly wildflower.

"Like some lovely fairy you are," he whispered. "Come, Cass. I've a gift for you."

"A gift? For me?" She gave him a look of such guileless surprise, he laughed from the sheer pleasure of it.

"Aye, for you and you alone." He led her to the stones and sat beside her in the heather, pretending to adjust his plaid so as to nestle just a bit closer by her side.

He plucked the seed from his sporran and she gasped.

His eyes leapt back to her face and he studied her, trying to interpret her every aspect, every blink, every breath. "I see you ken what this is."

"*Airne Moire*," she marveled. "A Mary's bean. My father has one. He had it set in silver." Wide eyes met his. "How did you find it?"

"I came upon it just this morning. I walked the shore, thinking of you, of course." He winked. "And there it lay, in the sand."

She looked down quickly, blushing. The sight tugged a low, husky laugh from his throat.

He turned her hand over and placed the seed there. It was black and hard, like a rounded stone, and just the right size to nestle perfectly in her palm.

He couldn't help himself. He brushed her exposed wrist, just for a moment, lightly with his thumb. It felt such an intimate thing, stroking along the fine webbing of veins that lined her delicate skin. They led to her heart, a heart he vowed then and there to make his own.

"Some folk believe they come all the way from Africa," he said, his voice suddenly hoarse. "They say a Mary's bean can float for twenty years."

"Africa?" She scoffed. "My maid says they're fairy eggs. *Uibhean sithean*. You should make a charm from it." She tried to hand the seed back to him. "'Tis very good luck indeed."

"No," he said, wrapping her fingers around the seed. He hesitated, then kept her hand held in his. "'Tis *your* very good luck, Cassie. It's a gift. From me to you."

"But I could never accept such a thing."

"Lass, it's truly but a trifle." He squeezed her hand. It was so small and frail in his. His heart clenched—a heart he feared already belonged to her. "If only you knew. It's the least of what I'd have you take from me."

Three

Iain waited for her in their usual place. They'd been meeting in secret for weeks, always beneath the Callanish stones. He imagined the towering, gray monoliths were their sentinels, guarding them from prying eyes.

Though he knew that none would see them. Lewis folk worked, and hard. They didn't trudge across fields in the middle of the day simply to visit the standing stones. None would stumble upon two sweethearts submerged in the late summer heather.

The wind tossed her hair as she approached. It was long and smooth, and the sun caught it, igniting it into rays of light.

"Cassie, my love," he said, laughing and curling her to him to kiss the top of her head. "Could you not wear a bonnet? You sneak from your father's keep like a wee spy, and yet all of Lewis must see that bonny hair of yours. You're named for a constellation, but I'd swear you shine brighter than any star."

Smiling, she ignored his comment and stood up on tiptoes

for a proper kiss. Her lips were cool from her brisk walk, but they soon warmed at the touch of his skin.

She brought her hand to his chest, idly threading her fingers in the folds of his plaid. "I'm late."

"You're here." He leaned down to steal another kiss. She was sweeter than the ripest fruit, and he could kiss her every day for the rest of his days and never get enough. "'Tis all that matters."

"But your work," she protested. "You need to do your work. I hate the thought that you were here waiting, without me, yet you'll need to leave just as soon. I wish we had more time."

"I went to the fields early. I'll return late," he said dismissively. "It matters not."

He pulled her into the shelter of the stones. They were tall and grave, casting long shadows along the heather that grew thick at their feet.

Iain threaded his fingers with hers and rained hungry kisses at her neck and cheek and mouth as he eased them down. "All that matters is that you're here now."

His knee touched the ground and he froze. There was ever so slight a reserve in the way she kissed him back, and he sensed it at once. "Cassie, love, is there something the matter?"

He pulled away and saw the desolation in her eyes. "Och, I'm a brute," he said, tenderly smoothing the sleeves of her dress. He guided her down to sit side by side in the heather. "I'm like a lad with his first kiss. I'm sorry, it's just I've missed you so—"

"Iain," she sighed with a smile. "I love your kisses. It's not that, 'tis . . ."

"What then?" He traced the hair from her face. "What has your lovely eyes in such a muddle?"

"It's my father."

"Your father," he repeated flatly. He'd known this day would come. Cass had lived a sheltered life. It was only a matter of time before she glimpsed the true heart of the MacLeod.

"My father . . . he's gone too far. I'm afraid, Iain."

Iain had known that the concerns of a daughter anxious of her strict father would someday crystallize into fear. Still, he wasn't prepared for the heartbreak he heard in her sweet voice.

"I know you are," he said gently. "But can you tell me . . . what happened, Cass?"

"I . . . he . . ." She drew a deep breath in, settling herself. "I'd snuck out into the kale garden, to come to you." A smile ghosted across her face and then was gone. "But the cook was out there. And so I hid. She was talking to the other women. I heard them, heard her tell it . . . My father has a . . . a natural child." She'd whispered the last of it. "The mother lives in the village. They said she was . . . unwilling."

His face fell. Such a thing would shock dear Cassie. And pain her. She was so sheltered from the world.

And yet he sensed she longed for more. She yearned for experience, for a life rich with family and friends. He imagined it was what had drawn her so far from home on the day they first met. She sought more freedom, more knowledge. But he wondered if she were ready for what she'd find.

He didn't know why the MacLeod sequestered her from the world. Iain suspected the man wanted to keep her pure in thought and deed, an unsullied treasure whose ultimate value would be measured, not by a father, but by a laird seeking advantage.

Iain shuddered.

"I know," he told her quietly.

He suspected the MacLeod had even more bastard children, though Iain wouldn't share that now. Cassie's mother had died giving birth, and the laird wasn't one to moderate his needs. Iain would spare Cassie this one bit of knowledge, this Pandora's box of secrets that'd been kept from her.

"You know? What do you know? What have you heard?"

"Och, love . . ." He paused. How to say it? He had his suspicions, but there was one child whom he knew without a doubt. "'Tis wee Janet."

"Jan?" Confusion wrinkled her eyes. "Your aunt's child? But your uncle—"

"Died a full year before she was born."

He was silent then, letting the truth sink in. Letting the picture form in her mind. His Aunt Morna's lone blonde girl in a cottage full of black-haired sons.

"Oh," she said simply.

"Ease your mind, love." He stroked her back lightly. "There's naught to fear. But you must never speak of it again. Never speak of it with *him*."

"I already did. 'Tis why I'm late." She worried her skirts in her hands. "I had to know what it means. For me." She shut her eyes then, marveling. "A sister . . ."

Some noxious thing spiked through his veins, his body on instant alert. "You mentioned this to the MacLeod?"

Opening her eyes, she nodded wordlessly, and fear for her gripped his chest. The laird had fathered only one legitimate child, his treasured Cassiopeia, whom he jealously concealed from the world. He wouldn't take her sudden knowledge well.

"You must never speak of it with him again. You mustn't think of her as a sister."

"But he's my father, and—"

"He's the laird before he's your father," Iain said sharply. "He wakes in the morning, and it's the MacLeod who dons his plaid. 'Tis the MacLeod you see at the hearth. Don't be fooled, love. When he makes a decision for you, it's the MacLeod deciding. Not a father."

Iain grew cold, remembering her original words. "What did he do to make you afraid?"

"He raged," she whispered. "'Twas as though I'd never truly seen him. He grabbed me. Shut me in my room."

Iain's fists flexed. No man would touch her in anger. Not the MacLeod, not any man, if he could help it.

He registered what must've happened next, and his eyes grew wide with disbelief. "And you snuck out?"

"I did. But I'm afraid of what will happen when I return."

"We must go back at once." His mind raced. Mindlessly, he stroked her hair, thinking of a plan. "We'll fetch a cloak to cover this bright, bonny hair. We send you in as you went out, through the kitchen gardens, and pray folk will think they've seen a scullion."

"Not yet," she said quickly, and the plea in her voice took him aback. "My father's gone to see some lord about his cattle. He won't be home 'til nightfall. Please, Iain."

It was the sound of his name on her lips that swayed him. "As you wish it, love."

They sat in silence for a while. Cassie lay in the heather, resting her head in his lap. Iain stroked her hair, stroked down her back, willing her nervous heart to calm.

He loved her so. He'd never known such contentment. He didn't want it ever to end. He would make himself worthy of the beautiful girl lying near him in the heather. And then he'd take her away, far away from this man whom she feared.

He'd always dreamt of having more, of being more. And now that he'd met Cassie, he'd been working day and night. She said she loved him as he was, but he'd not make a formal proposal of marriage until he could stand before the MacLeod and ask for her hand like a proper gentleman.

"There's a parcel of land," he began tentatively, "near Stornoway. The earl there fought with my father, for Charles, in the wars. The king rewarded him with lands. I've been in contact, and he tells me he'd let me buy a parcel. I'd be more than merely his tenant. He tells me I could act as his factor, like."

He paused, hesitant. Her breath had stilled. Would she want this life that he imagined for them? Cassie was accustomed to a castle. She was queen of his heart, but in choosing him, her kingdom would be a mere cottage. "I'd build a fine home. 'Twould be small, but it would do for two. Or more," he added with a wistful smile, "if they were small."

She was silent for a time, and he didn't press her. He simply continued to stroke her hair, memorizing her every curve and shadow as she lay in the heather. What did she think of his plan? Would she see herself in it?

"My father . . ." She hesitated, worry knitting her brow.

"Your father is *my* concern now, lass. If it kills me, I'll not abide you living in fear of any man." His hand stilled on her back. "I'll work night and day. I'll do whatever it takes to deserve you, to have you. Even if it means I must steal you away in the night."

Slowly she turned. Her head still resting in his lap, she looked up at him, and the adoration in her eyes made his heart soar.

"You ease my soul, Iain Gillespie MacNab."

He leaned to kiss her, and she stopped him with a gentle finger to his lips. Gravely, she said, "But you must make me a promise. Here, by the standing stones. Promise me. Whatever happens, promise always to meet me, just here. As long as you live, promise to come to me, just here, come what may."

"I promise you," he said quickly, earnestly. He took her hand tightly in his. The air around them felt charged, fraught with the intensity, the solemnity of the moment. Even the stones themselves seemed larger, colder, more ominous. "I promise you, Cassie, my only love. As long as I live, I will be here for you. Come what may, you *shall* call me husband. I swear it."

He looked up at the slabs of granite, hovering like silent monks tall above them. "And may the stones themselves seal my vow."

Four

"You're a wee Diana."

"Diana?" Cassie turned her face up to him. Bright and bonny, she was a slip of sunlight nestled on his arm.

Confusion flickered in her eyes, as did something else. Some feminine thing. The quick jealousy that takes a woman at the mention of another.

"Aye." Iain bent, kissed her yellow hair. "You're not the only one versed in myth, my wee Cassiopeia. Diana, the huntress."

She betrayed a flash of relief, then pure pleasure at the comparison.

He slung the brace of rabbit over his shoulder. Rabbit she'd trapped herself. He made as if to bend beneath its weight, and Cassie giggled.

Iain had not a care by her side. Cut peat, cruel lairds, fathers and their bastards. It all slipped away when sweet Cass was near.

The feel of her at his side was irresistible. He pulled her close. Smoothed his free hand along the swell of her hip.

Their secret meetings had continued for months now. He'd memorized her every curve, and yet he couldn't get enough. Would never get enough.

He kissed her forehead, cool in the late-morning breeze. "When will you make me an honest man, dear Cass?" he whispered into her hair. "I'm close, love. By the end of the season, I'll have enough to get our land. 'Twill be modest. And we won't have help. Just you and me. But it'll be ours, Cass."

He was a patient man. He'd save his money, bide his time. He'd buy their land and build their cottage. And then he'd propose properly, on bended knee, as good as any gentleman farmer.

She'd say yes, how could she not? Cassie was his, just as he belonged to her. It was a thing he knew, indelible and forever, like the tides or the rising sun.

His hand ran over something thick and hard in the pocket of her skirts. "What's this, then?"

"Bread." She tilted her chin in ready defiance, as if he'd have a problem with a mere heel of bread.

"Bread? Are you mounting a wee feast?"

"No. Yes." She looked away. "Well, if my father isn't going to do right by my sister—"

"Your *half* sister," he reminded her. "Your father's by-blow."

Cassie flinched at the term.

A familiar nagging fear eclipsed the light in his heart. She'd heard the talk and had sought out his Aunt Morna to see for herself. She'd found a cottage full of hungry souls, and it'd lit a fire beneath her, transformed her. His Cass, the bonny crusader. It was only a matter of time before she mustered courage enough to press her father directly. "'Tis a dangerous topic to be caviling on about," he warned.

She feared the MacLeod. As she should. But hers was a daughter's fear. She'd known only the firm hand and quick temper of a father. Cassie didn't truly understand what it was to fear her father the laird, the man. A chief who'd not appreciate being held to task for a child born on the wrong side of the sheets.

"Fine. Half sister," she amended in the saucy way he recognized and, Lord save him, loved so well.

She'd passed her girlhood under lock and key. And yet, in her isolation, she'd bloomed like some hothouse flower. Flourishing in unexpected ways. The laird's sheltered daughter had developed all the piss and vinegar of a village scamp.

"Is this what the rabbit is about?"

"I must bring all I can," she insisted. "There's never enough food on Morna's table, and wee Jan is growing like a weed now. She walks!"

"Aye, they've a habit of that," he said darkly.

"Well, I've not known many children."

Her voice was dispirited, but he had to press his point. He knew his words would sting, but he needed to make her understand. "You're still so young yourself, in your way. I beg you to have a care. Stealing rabbit from your father's land—"

"It's not stolen. I'm the daughter of the MacLeod. Everything on the land is mine, or might as well be."

"Aye, that's as it may be, but pilfer enough from your father's territory and someone somewhere will take note. It's a hanging offense, Cassie."

"Don't be ridiculous! My father would never hang me."

"Of course he'd not." He sighed. How to make it clear to her? "But they'll be wanting to blame someone."

She ignored his words, and he shook his head in defeat.

Like a cloud blown clear of the sky, she quickly brightened, and he knew there'd be no more talk of such things that day.

And curse him, but already he felt his attention pulled back to the curve of her hip and the swell of her bosom pressed firm at his side.

"Don't you want to know how I did it?"

"Aye," he conceded, eyeing the rabbits. "I have wondered."

"I found the den and set a wee trap."

"A wee trap, eh?" He gave her rump a squeeze. "Just as I set for you in the bog?"

"Iain MacNab, you be serious!" She gave a swat to his arm.

"Oh, I'm nothing if not serious." He pulled her closer,

leaning down to speak low in her ear. "My trap was years in the making. Set by the fates themselves, generations ago."

He pulled from her, cupped her chin. His tone grew somber as he gazed intently in her eyes. "You see, 'twas the fates themselves who sprinkled heather all along the isle. And the heather turned to dirt, and the dirt to peat. And the peat and I, we both waited. Waiting and watching for the day when the most beautiful, the truest and the sweetest of all women crossed our path. 'Twas the most mysterious, the most potent of traps, set to snare my one true love."

"And did it?" she asked weakly. "Snare your one true love?"

"Did it? Oh aye, Cassie." He took her shoulders gently in his hands. "Did it indeed."

He studied her, studied this most miraculous of gifts before him. Cassie, so lovely and kind. She was an open book and a riddle both. She who broke and mended his heart every day, a thousand times a day.

"Do you not know it, Cass? How very much I love you?" He kissed her tenderly on her brow. Kissed her hair, her cheeks, her eyes. "For I do love you. More than my life, more than this earth, more than heaven above, you are the beating of my heart and the breath in my lungs."

"As I love you, Iain MacNab." Her voice was a sigh on the wind, strained tight, as if speaking freely might loose the very soul from her body.

And, in it, he heard eternity.

He didn't know how to contain himself. How to contain this feeling. This love for her. This want. He kissed her then, but tenderly, his lips merely a whisper over hers.

Iain pulled away. Her eyes were still shut, her lips slightly parted. He memorized her face, and he knew the image would be imprinted upon him forever.

Her eyes opened, and meeting his scrutiny, she smiled at once. Cassie gave her head a tilt. "But do you still want to know about the rabbits?"

His laugh was loud and joyful. "Och, Cassie, my love,"

he boomed, hugging her close. "Your wee hunting victory is the *only* thing I want to hear about."

"Well," she began, lowering her voice as though about to spin the tallest of tales. "I found a den. Not far from the keep. It's off the kale garden, and so I can sneak out, none the wiser. I've been watching it for weeks. Until finally. Finally I made a wee trap. I wove it out of reeds," she said proudly. "And this morning, sure as eggs, two rabbits scampered out and—"

She was too much. Too sweet, too innocent, too fine.

He dropped the pair of rabbits tied at his shoulder. "And . . ." he said huskily, scooping her up and carrying her from the drove path.

She squealed her surprise and pleasure as he rolled them into a nest of deep bracken. The ferns were damp and cool, webbing over their heads like curtains of green lace.

"'Twas it a trap like this one? Or was it more like a wee basket you made with your reeds?"

"Aye." Her voice wavered. She licked her lips.

"Aye like a trap, or aye, a basket?" He traced errant wisps of hair from the delicate arch of her brow, stroked them from her forehead. "And I must wonder, perhaps they didn't ken they'd been trapped. Mayhap they thought themselves still in their den."

Her hair spread like a halo around her, exposing her throat, her neck. He leaned down, tasted her, nuzzled her. He whispered in her ear, "And do you ken what wee bunnies like to do in their dens?"

"Eat wee turnips?" Her voice shook, and their laughter was a momentary respite from the tension between them.

"Aye, but what is it that makes them hungry?" He tenderly nipped at her, and their desire raged anew. Her heart pounded against him, and he pressed closer to feel it. That was *his* heart beating in her chest. "What it is that whets their appetites?"

He felt her legs grow loose, opening to him. She sighed his name, and he had to grip her hips, needing desperately to hold on to something that would anchor him to this earth.

She was unschooled in the ways of the flesh and yet . . .
Instinctively, she spread her legs. Instinctively arched her
back, offering him her breasts. And he knew. Cassie was like
tinder ready to spark, and God help him, the wildfire would
consume them both.

His body grew tight. He was a patient man. But, he realized, not *that* patient. She was the bride of his heart. He had
to have her as his wife in truth, and soon.

He nibbled at her pale throat. Dipped his head lower.
Lower than he'd ever allowed himself to go. He traced kisses
along the neckline of her bodice. Her skin was soft and full
at his lips. Her moan nearly unmanned him.

He needed to stop but couldn't. He wanted so desperately
to pull her gown from her, to take those breasts in his mouth.
He'd waited so long to taste her softness. Every renegade
brush of bosom along his side or against his arm, had him
fantasizing what it would be to palm her bare flesh. Feel her
silken skin under his fingertips.

He slowly kissed her until he reached the center of her
bodice. The neckline dipped down, exposing the merest hint
of a crease between her breasts.

He could fight it no longer. He traced it with his tongue,
echoing the V of her gown. He dipped in and down, between
her breasts. The soft give of flesh in his mouth drove him
over the edge.

His body raged, hard for her. He knew he should stop. He
needed to stop. Before he was no longer able.

And yet, he couldn't bear to. Not yet.

Slowly, he drew his hand from her hip, brought it to her
waist. An image flashed to him, a fantasy, the vision of his
hand just there, guiding her on a dance floor.

Someday they'd be wed. Someday he'd guide her in their
first dance. Someday that would come to pass.

The thought brought him back to himself. He'd not take her
in the dirt like an animal. When their time came, he'd see her
atop fine linens with a down-soft mattress beneath her.

He inhaled sharply. Pulled his head up to meet her gaze.
Her eyes were half lidded from pleasure, and he almost let

madness take him then. To see her lust echoing his? It was sheer gritted will that kept him in check.

He gave her what he hoped was a light smile, yet he knew the shadow of his wanting was still in his eyes.

He needed to stop, but he had to take just one bit more. Just one kiss, before they rose from the bracken.

He'd ferry her wee trophies to his aunt's table. He'd be carefree and easy, working his fields and saving his coin, patiently waiting until the last anxieties about her father were wiped from her brow.

He'd pretend he didn't long for her day and night, pretend he was more than half a man without her. He'd let one more day pass without pressing his suit. Too hard.

But first he'd kiss her, just once more.

He leaned close, pressed his lips to hers. His heart galloped in his chest, but still, he kept the kiss sweet. Tasted her but lightly.

Cassie twined tender fingers in his hair, and the gesture pricked some sharp emotion. It ached in his throat, filled his heart.

And he marveled how always with Cassie, each time, every time, each kiss was always better than the last.

Five

"And you're certain your lass survived the day without you?" Gordie's tone was somber, but his eyes glowed with amusement as he rowed their small fishing boat to shore.

"Aye," Niall agreed with his brother. "I didn't know they could even be apart."

"Enough, lads, enough." Iain beamed. He loved his friends' ribbing. He'd have more of it. He'd have the whole world poke fun at him. He was a fool in love, and love wasn't proud. "Though I will grant you, a day in your company is a pale substitution for my lovely—"

"Uugh." Niall pretended to be ill over the side of the boat.

"Och, more of *this*?" Gordie said. "Best haul her in, Niall, before the sot gets started again."

The young man was stringing up their huge haul of fish. A large haddock slipped from his fingers, dropping into the bucket with a splash. "Why do *I* always have to haul her in?"

"I'll take her this time, lad," Iain said. He slid into the water, rope in hand, to tug the boat onto the sand. His plaid floated around him, the wool heavy with seawater. "Age before beauty, aye?"

"He *is* crazy with love," Gordie marveled, and the brothers rolled their eyes.

The chest-high waves bobbed the boat in erratic, staccato movements as Iain pulled her through the surf. When they reached the shallows, his mates leapt out to join him, helping to tug her in the rest of the way.

"A good day, aye?" Niall said, admiring the garlands of haddock and cod.

"What say you, Iain?" Gordie tossed the last of their haul on the shore and sidled up to his friend to help capsize their boat on the sand. "Do you think a creel of herring will dispose the laird to you?"

"I still don't believe the lass is truly willing to marry him," Niall muttered.

"The lass has a name. And, aye," Iain said proudly, "Cass will have me indeed. She gave me a scare, though." He was silent for a moment, remembering. "Said she told her father she loved me."

Gordie and his brother gasped, standing still where they stood in the sand.

"Aye," Iain said, "'Tis true. I thought my heart would fail me when I heard. But damned if the old cad didn't warm to the idea."

"The MacLeod?" Niall asked, astounded.

"We are talking about the laird, correct?" Gordie shook his head in astonishment. "Your lass *is* a determined one."

"That or crazy." Iain shrugged. "Either way, it seems the MacLeod isn't entirely opposed."

"Or he's not yet tried to kill you outright," Niall muttered.

"She told him your plan, is it?" Gordie dusted the sand from his hands. "About the lands you're eyeing in Stornoway?"

"Aye, I think that must've been the trick." Iain bent to

rake his fingers through the sand. He'd spied a shiny black ridge, and dug it free. A mermaid's purse, Cassie's favorite.

I'll take you away, across the sea. You can be my mermaid, he'd told her once. He couldn't get over the fact that his dream was so close to hand.

A distant shriek ripped down to where they stood. They stilled, rigid, looking up the beach to the grassy hills above. A woman ran to them, shouting and gesturing wildly.

"Morna?" Iain muttered. His aunt?

As she grew closer, her screams became clear. "Run!" she cried.

"What—?" Iain was frozen in place.

She was on the sand now, racing to them, her skirts hiked high at her knees. "You must go! Run! They say you've stolen."

Gordie stiffened, stepping forward to speak for his friend. "What's the meaning of this?"

"They say he's stolen," she panted, reaching them by the shore. "From the laird."

"Stolen?" Gordie and Niall asked in unison.

"The rabbits," Iain said dully. Though he knew it wasn't rabbit the MacLeod was worried about. "They'll accuse me of stealing the rabbits."

Morna's face fell. That meat had graced *her* table.

"Don't fret," Iain told her quickly. "Surely Cass will speak up for me. Clear my name." He gave a firm nod, certain she'd clear it up.

"Cass . . ." Morna faltered. "Cassie can't, Iain."

He stared. The words didn't make sense. "What?"

"She's to be married. To the Lord Morrison. They've taken her already."

His heart stopped. Surely he'd heard wrong.

"That's not true," he said. "She's marrying *me*. Cassie is promised to *me*. There's been a mistake."

His aunt's wordless and pitying look told him there'd been no mistake.

And then Iain did run. He raced up the beach.

He'd stop her. Save her.

"You can't!" Morna screeched at his back. "She's gone. Protect yourself, boy! The laird wants your neck!"

But he charged up the beach to face what he would. The mermaid's purse left crushed behind him in the sand.

Six

"Are there any who would speak for the peat boy?"

Iain struggled, and the rope cut into his wrists. He was trussed like a beast. A knot of men held him, facing off a crowd of villagers who'd not meet their eyes.

Iain watched his townsfolk. Saw their fear and their pity. All kept silent.

Cassie kept silent.

"Iain Gillespie MacNab has been accused of stealing," the Laird MacLeod announced.

Iain scowled. This wasn't about any rabbits. If aught had been taken from the MacLeod, it was his daughter.

"The peat boy has stolen from me. 'Tis a hanging offense. Though, man that I am, I might extend some measure of mercy." The laird's voice was a baritone snarl from the side, and Iain twisted his body to see him. The MacLeod was big and burly, with a chest like a barrel, and the yellow of Cassie's hair twined with the white of his years. *Measure of mercy.* The man disgusted him.

Iain's eyes flashed to Lord Morrison standing by the

MacLeod's side. Morrison was older. A man smelling of snuff and foul breath. He was the man who was to wed his Cassie.

Fury swelled in Iain's chest until he thought he'd burst from it. "Take me," he shouted suddenly. He'd go to his death willingly, if it would save sweet Cass from this vile arrangement.

Iain looked at her. So terrified and alone. Would she not speak? He could bear the worst of all tortures, if he could only hear her voice once more.

"I beg you," he implored the laird. "Spare your daughter. Take *me*. Hang me. Do what you will."

Cassie stared at him, her eyes wide with horror. She gave small shakes to her head as though trying to communicate something. Why would she not just speak? What had they done to her?

Morrison stepped closer to her, wrapped a possessive arm around her.

Rage, frustration, heartbreak . . . a tumult of emotions boiled in his veins, hissing from his throat, sounding a single word. "Cassie," he cried, then louder, "Cassie!"

And still she only stared, fear and that mysterious intensity in her eyes. His heart gripped.

"Cassie?" He cursed the crack in his voice, sounding a plea now. "Please, Cass, love. You don't have to do this. He can't make you do this."

"Shut it, boy," the MacLeod snarled. "Will none speak for him?"

Iain knew the others wouldn't speak out. None would raise a voice against the laird. Even if they knew he was in the wrong.

"The peat boy has broken the law, and he will suffer the consequences."

A rustle whispered across the crowd. Iain saw his aunt's face. She alone opened her mouth to speak. Iain gave a frantic shake of his head to silence her. His aunt had enough troubles.

Two from her houseful of boys clung at her skirts. She

held the youngest, her only girl, in her arms. Yellow hair shone like spun silk on the child's head.

It was the laird's child Morna held, the laird's child laid on her by force. Did the man destroy *all* he touched? Iain wrenched his head to spew the curses that raged in his chest. "Damn you!" he growled to the MacLeod.

Cassie's father came up behind him. A pair of hot, beefy hands gripped his arms where they were tied at his back. He leaned close, whispering in Iain's ear, "I'll mind your Auntie Morna after you're gone, peat boy. She's a willful bird, but if I take her in firm hand, I find she always obeys."

Iain's eyes flicked along the crowd, finding his aunt once more. Terror contorted her features.

His gaze went back to Cassie. His Cassie, still unbearably lovely, even in her grief, weeping in silence like some mourning angel.

The laird spoke again in his ear. "Aye, I'll see Morna submit. Just as Morrison has made my wayward daughter come to heel."

Some final part of him shattered, cracked like a glass vial, dumping acid into his veins. Iain gave a tug to his bonds. If it weren't for the rope tying his wrists, the laird's neck would already be snapped.

The MacLeod took Iain's hands, wrenched them. There was a popping and pain exploded white like a burst of sparks. But Iain ignored the pain, struggling wildly now. He felt the bones of his arms strain at their sockets.

He was being torn from his Cassie. His eyes were for only her now. He shouted for her, and again. But still she only stared in silent agony. He saw fear in her gaze, and dread.

She gave another small shake of her head. Was she telling him to move on? That she'd moved on? What of their promises, whispered beneath the standing stones? He fought to breathe.

Iain watched in horror as she tucked down, curling herself into Lord Morrison's side. Did she turn away from Iain, from their love? Was she turning instead to this old swine for comfort? Did Cassie forsake Iain already?

Ice lodged in his belly, already roiling with bile, and he felt violently nauseous. Was she choosing riches over *peat boy*? Or did she simply prefer the weight of an old man's body?

"Cassie, my love." His voice was small then, anguished. A mere sigh on the breeze.

"Did you truly think I'd let my only daughter wed a peat boy?" Laird MacLeod gave him a shove. Toward a cart.

Where a cage awaited him. The cage where he'd live, until they stretched his neck at the end of a hangman's rope.

"No!" Cassie screamed, finally. The anguish in her voice hit him all the more savagely for her silence in the moments before. "You promised!"

"Hush, girl," her father spat. "I said I'd keep him alive. I never promised to keep him free."

A cawing sounded over their heads. The invisible net of tension that'd held the crowd spellbound snapped. All looked up, whispered among themselves. The voices grew louder and braver.

"Three gulls," a woman cried. "Three gulls means death."

His aunt shrieked. She'd think it portended *his* death. She didn't know Iain wished for precisely that. If he died there, then, he'd not have to bear the image of Cassie turning to the old lord. Not have to bear her betrayal.

"Iain!" The shock of hearing his name snapped him from his thoughts. It was Gordon's voice. Gordie, his lifelong friend. And though it didn't fill the void in his chest, Iain felt his heart beat once more. "Look sharp!"

Three gulls were an omen, and Gordie took advantage of the distraction. He burst through the line of villagers, a dirk in his hand, his brother Niall close behind. Guns swung from their sides. Iain recognized the old matchlock muskets. They'd belonged to the boys' father.

Their matches were lit. Iain could smell the burning cord. Niall's was tied around his wrist and it swung as he ran. The rope singed a woman as he passed, and she screamed, startled.

The humming of the crowd boiled into loud, confused

chatter. People pushed in different directions, beginning to panic.

Iain's eyes went to Cassie. Lord Morrison took her shoulders in hand. Her body canted at an unnatural angle, tucking closer to his chest.

Was she, even now, pulling closer to the old man?

And then Morrison turned her, wrenching her away sharply. There was a flash of silver between them.

Cassie's hands clutched at her chest. Vivid scarlet bloomed along the ice blue of her dress.

"Cassie!" Iain choked on his scream.

Her eyes met his. A thousand things flashed there. Love, sorrow, desperation, terror, apology—all conveyed to him in her single glance. And then, like a snuffed candle, those vivid eyes went blank.

Iain felt her go. Her soul, which had been tied tight round his heart, snapped from him. Cassie, inexplicably, was simply gone.

He couldn't make sense of it. He stood, frozen for what felt an unbearable lifetime in the stretch of a lone heartbeat.

And then he saw the blade jutting from her perfect breast. "No!" he howled, watching helpless as she crumpled to the ground.

Grief seized his body and he cried out, arching back hard, like a baying wolf. He knocked back into the laird, and the man stumbled and tripped.

Gordie rushed in, taking the MacLeod's place at Iain's back. Iain felt the cold kiss of a dirk slicing him free of his bonds. Felt a musket shoved into his hands. The wood was cool, and he realized his palms had been sweating and hot.

Two of MacLeod's men sprang toward them, slamming into Gordie from the side. His friend caught himself before he fell, spinning into a crouch, his dirk in hand. Gordie was quickly backed up by a knot of villagers.

It seemed not *all* had stood with the laird.

The sound of hissing steel drew his eyes. Iain whirled in time to duck the wide swing of the MacLeod's broadsword.

The musket was warm now, in his hands. He guessed

Gordie would have it loaded, the match already set for firing. Iain raised it, pointed it at the laird.

The man grew still, his sword poised in the air. "If you think I'll let you live, peat boy, you think wrongly. You stole from me. Cassiopeia was mine to give to Morrison. But she's dead, and so you've stolen from him, too."

Iain's response was quick, and his voice had the calm certainty of a man already dead. "Cassie belonged to no one."

He fired.

The crack sent the already nervous crowd exploding hysterically in all directions. Yet the scene before him remained slow, a sluggish, surreal unfolding of events. The laird's body reverberated from the gunshot. The lead ball to his chest splayed him open, propelling his shoulders back, spinning MacLeod to the dirt. And to hell below.

There was one other man whom he'd see dead that day. Iain scanned the crowd; it was pandemonium. But Lord Morrison was nowhere in sight. He'd surely run, like the coward he was.

There was a cry, and Iain recognized Gordie's brother. The boy's voice had not yet changed and its frantic pitch rose above the din. Niall was in trouble.

Iain tossed the musket down. He'd gotten a shot off, and the weapon was no good to him unloaded.

Niall was cornered against the cart. An unarmed man stalked him, circling like a cat ready to pounce. The boy was terrified. He still held his father's musket, and it was near as tall as he. His hands shook as he tried desperately to slide the match into the thin clamp of the gun, but the cord trembled in his useless fingers.

Ramming the man aside, Iain leapt to Niall's aid. He grabbed the musket and pulled the match from where it was tied about the boy's wrist.

Iain shoved the match into the serpentine clamp. But he saw too late that Niall's trembling hands had spilled black powder over the pan, along the top of the weapon. Too late he saw the shadow of it, smudged black along his hand.

The match caught the powder. There was a strange eternity

between the feel of his body catching fire and the thunderous clap of the explosion. He'd covered his eyes, he guessed, for he smelled the acrid smoke before he saw it, a thick gray cloud that enveloped him.

And it burned. White-hot pain. *He* burned. It seemed his brow melted with it, his hand was paralyzed from it.

"Christ, Niall, what have you done, lad?" Gordie was suddenly by Iain's side, shouting.

Iain felt his friend's hand on his good arm. Felt him pull. The three of them broke free of the mayhem, and they ran.

And they ran to the water, where a small sloop awaited them. Awaited *Iain*.

A privateer in search of a cabin boy, paid in potatoes and whisky to wait for Iain's escape.

But there *was* no escape, Iain thought, as the boat pushed into the Atlantic. He studied the burnt claw of his right hand, held clenched in a bucket of seawater as if it were a foreign thing, separate from his body. No, there would be no escaping who he'd become.

MacLeod had been wrong. Iain MacNab wasn't a thief.

But now he was a killer.

Seven

He leaned down.

Would she stop him? Would she let him kiss her?

It would be their first. He would be her first, if she let him.

His heart pounded in his chest. Cassie was so lovely, poised before him. Her eyes clung to him, her lips gently parted.

Might she? Would she?

He eased closer. She was soft and warm in his arms. The breeze drifted across the wide, treeless field, chasing to the Callanish stones, swirling her scent to him, something like sunshine and sugar and fine things. The experience of her bore into him.

"May I kiss you?" he whispered, and wondered if that truly could've been his voice. It sounded ragged, unused.

"A simple kiss? Is that what this is about?" She leaned into him, her eyes lit with mischief. She reached around his neck, twining her fingers in his hair.

His skin shivered at the sensation. His body went rigid, frozen with disbelief, with joy.

"Why, Iain MacNab, I think I will—"

* * *

"MacNab!"

There was a pounding.

"MacNab! Sir!"

He woke with a start. *Where?*

The ship. It bobbed and pitched gently. Timber planks creaked overhead.

He was somewhere in the North Sea.

Twenty years gone by. Cassie dead these twenty long, hopeless years.

There had been pounding, he realized, and scrubbed his hand over his face.

"Aye, I'm coming," he shouted. His voice was hoarse from sleep, and he put enough snarl in it to send whoever the man was away. "Bang once more and it'll be your stones I nail on my door as a knocker."

"Aye, John . . . MacNab . . . *Sir.*"

John. He scowled and rolled from his bunk. He took a slug of ale from a pewter tankard. It was sour and flat, but it washed the sleep from his throat.

He was John now. Not Iain. He was a man without a country. And so bore the Englishman's version of his name.

Never again would he be Iain. Iain, the name he'd heard so often on his mother's tongue. A proud name. A Highland name.

If Cassie would never again speak it, then never again would he hear it.

He tipped the empty tankard up. Light from the porthole glimmered across the pewter. He tilted the mug until he saw his reflection waver dully on its surface.

His eyes flicked from the reflected shadow along his cheek to the matching scar on his right hand. Both burnt forever black from that powder charge exploded in his face, so many years past.

He would only ever be John now.

Black John MacNab.

Eight

There was a thump on the timber overhead. The sound of a man dropping from a height. Then another thump, followed by the heavy patter of running.

MacNab pulled himself from his thoughts and heard the shouts he knew would follow.

The schooner. His men would've spotted the schooner again. The one they'd been chasing. But it kept eluding them. Two masts, full-sail to the wind, disappearing like a wraith in the fog.

Her hold was full of goods. A cynical smile curled the corner of his mouth. "Goods" were precisely what he was after.

He quickly rolled into his plaid, knotting it at his shoulder with a leather thong. He refused to wear the traditional sailors slops. Though their billowy leg and cuffed knees enabled a man to climb the rigging with ease, MacNab much preferred navigating the deck in his *breacan feile*.

And though his clothes were of the Highlands, his colors were not. His was a custom tartan, black and gray, unique to him alone. Colors to match the coal black sheen of his scars and the shadow of a storm-roiled sea.

The shouts intensified, and he flew from his cabin up onto deck. He was greeted by a glorious sight. They'd found that big beauty of a schooner. With a crisply elegant topsail and a greedy belly that'd be full for the taking.

The schooner tacked hard to port in an effort to escape. MacNab saw her name up close, painted red on the stern. *Morrison's Pride*. A chill beaded his skin.

A memory flashed to him. His Cassie, tucked into the arms of Lord Morrison. He remembered the way she burrowed into him.

Surely the name was mere coincidence . . .

The bigger ship caught the wind and pressed full speed, but their efforts would be hopeless. Though just a one-mast cutter, MacNab's *Charon* was sleek and fast, bearing twelve guns and forty souls, and she sliced through the water like a shark.

"Ready about!" MacNab shouted. He bound across the deck to the wheel. The timber planks were polished to a honeyed sheen, smooth like glass beneath his bare feet.

His first mate stepped aside quickly to let him take over steering. The wind whipped, and seawater pricked sharp and cold on his face. MacNab tasted brine and found he'd a smile on his face.

"Hard a-lee!" he shouted again. He spun the wheel, and the canvas grew slack. Sails flapped madly and the rigging clanged, making a sound like a storm-whipped flag.

The boom swung about, and his crew instinctively ducked. There was a sharp snap, and then a single heartbeat of perfect silence as the wind caught the sails once more.

"Man the guns!" he cried, and men scattered to their stations. He'd get a broadside off, aimed straight for the *Morrison's* rigging. The trick was to disable the schooner enough to board her, but not so much that she'd fetch a lesser purse. "Fire as she bears!"

Soon the rhythmic thumping of the starboard guns shook the deck, six claps of thunder cascading fore to aft, *boom,*

boom, boom. Plumes of gray smoke cleared, revealing the *Morrison's* foremast splintered but not sheared through.

"Flank! Flank!" MacNab ordered, and his *Charon* came about hard, slamming into the side of the larger ship. The impact resonated up the wheel to his shoulder. He let a grin flash.

The cries of *Morrison's* crew rose over the din like screeching gulls. They ran about in a mad attempt to rally. He'd take advantage of their disorder and strike fast. End it fast.

"Hoist the grapnels!" he called, and lines flew up and over, their hooks snagging in rigging, in sails, on timber. Men swung and leapt onto the schooner's deck, their violence graceful, their faces ecstatic. MacNab gestured to his first mate to take back the wheel, and he followed quick on their heels.

He grabbed a rope and leapt, unsheathing his blade as he flew, a slow-motion ballet over a sliver of open sea, roiling gray and white beneath him. He landed on the deck, looking for a fight.

A few of his sailors were climbing the rigging, skittering across the ratlines like monkeys, slicing as they went. Thick hanks of rope whistled, plummeting to the ground, and canvas fell at their feet in a thunderous ripple.

The schooner was his for the taking.

"Mercy," he ordered. "We give quarter!"

A pirate maybe, but he was no barbarian.

He bounced on the balls of his feet, ready to dive into the melee. A loud bark of a laugh called his attention aft. One of his sailors had just run a man through. He waved his broadsword triumphantly in the air.

But that's not what held MacNab's attention. The man who'd been stabbed was staggering along the deck. Blood seeped through the blue of his thigh-length fitted jacket, and the grisly pattern of it burst and spread like a blooming flower.

Another image flashed to him, the same rich scarlet on blue. In his mind's eye, he saw Cassie's hands gripping at her chest. He remembered the terror in her eyes, and then worse, the emptiness.

Pain skewered him, and MacNab wished it were a sword that'd impaled him, rather than these unbearable memories.

He bared his teeth. He needed to focus on the task at hand. "If there's a devious dog among them," he snarled to his men, "send him by the boards."

His crew clamored a blood lust that MacNab pretended not to hear.

He sliced through the waning chaos, eager to blood his sword. But already only a handful of fights remained. Across the deck, knots of men knelt, yielding, accepting MacNab's mercy.

A man stood across the deck, gesturing wildly. He seemed the only one yet to realize the battle was nearing a close. His basket-hilted sword gleamed white in the sun. A full-skirted coat and tricorn hat announced him as the captain.

MacNab glided to him like a magnet.

His body cast the other man in shadow. The schooner captain turned, and his puffy, red face blanched gray.

Every muscle in MacNab's body seized. His breath stalled in his lungs, and his eyes froze, cold and flat.

"You," MacNab hissed. He gave a violent shake to his head. The moment he'd dreamt of for so long was strangely, finally here. For once, some odd trick of fate had smiled upon him. He would avenge his Cassie.

He swung his blade down hard, and it was sheer luck that Morrison managed a block in time.

"Peat boy." Lord Morrison's eyes widened. The man was old now, and full at the waist. His white hair had loosed from its knot and it haloed cheeks that were pink with effort. "You're a pirate."

Peat boy. MacNab scowled. That part of himself was gone. Long dead. A tidal wave of memories buffeted him. He held his breath. Withstood them. Willed them to wash over and past.

He was Iain the peat boy no more.

"I prefer the term privateer." MacNab spoke with forced nonchalance, delivering a hard, diagonal slash. He decided to toy with the man, enjoying watching his lips pale and cheeks redden from exertion. "So much more"—he swung his sword, aiming for the torso—"dashing, aye?"

Commotion at the foredeck splintered their attention. A mass of young men and boys stumbled from the hold, blinking away the shock of sunlight.

The haul of *Morrison's Pride* was set free.

It was what MacNab had been after. A load of boys and young men, stolen from Scotland, headed for indentured servitude somewhere in the Caribbean.

It sickened him. He snarled, slamming his sword down in a vicious crosscut.

Morrison parried, and with a shrug, admitted, "I've become a . . . gentleman of fortune."

MacNab unleashed with renewed hatred, his strikes growing less playful and more intent. He struggled between the urge to murder and the desire to see justice done.

"These boys . . ." Morrison stopped speaking for a minute, weathering a fresh torrent from MacNab's sword. "Mere Glasgow urchins. It's better this way. For them. In the Indies." Each phrase was accompanied by the clang of steel.

"You traffic in slaves." Iain fought the urge to end the man's life with a single, simple sword thrust. But he wanted Morrison afraid, humiliated, demoralized.

"Is this about Cassiopeia?"

Grief sucked the air from MacNab's lungs. It was always about Cassie. Everything was about Cassie. His heart felt like smoldering coal.

MacNab reeled, and Morrison took advantage, stepping forward on a thrust. "She proved useless in the end," the older man taunted.

And so the Lord Morrison sealed his fate. His death would be a different sort of justice. He'd stolen Cassie's youth, her joy. Stolen *her*. *Cassie*. Dear Cass, gone twenty years, dead by this man's hand.

MacNab was done toying with him.

Morrison must have seen the shift, sensed it, because fear seized the man's face, opening his mouth and pinching his eyes. "Oh . . ." he gasped, shuffling a desperate sidestep.

MacNab shadowed him, assailing him, thrashing him, his sword relentless. His fury was a palpable thing. It wavered black at the edges of his vision. Their conversation was over.

"I am done." MacNab's blade whined as it whipped through the air. It caught the thick flesh of Morrison's shoulder. "This is done."

The lord winced. His eyes flared, like that of a desperate animal. He spoke, frantic words, more cutting than any sword. "She was worthless. I gave her a test ride. She lay like a dead thing beneath me. A cold fish. 'Twas like tupping a haddo—"

MacNab's blade stole the words from his enemy's throat.

Nine

"I love you," he told her, gazing down on her, her head in his lap. Iain combed his fingers through her smooth, yellow hair, spread it along the heather like rays of sunlight. He'd never tire of the soft silk of it in his fingers. "Aw, Cass, love, I could stare at you forever."

She curled into him. Her delicate hand reached up and wrapped around his thigh. She gave it a squeeze. "I imagine you'd eventually get hungry, aye?"

His laugh was sharp, pleased. Iain let the wanting steal over him. It was a powerful thing, his desire for her, and he kept it at bay, hidden close, like the blood that pumped just beneath his skin. He let that darker thing sound now in his voice. "There are other ways a man can sate his hunger."

He shifted, adjusting the slightest bit. He'd stiffened like a beast in heat, and he'd not startle her with his relentless, insistent body. That was his secret to keep.

Until they wed.

He traced her face, fighting the urge to meld his hand lower along her body.

"Oh, indeed?" Her voice trembled and her cheeks flushed hot pink.

Such a lovely innocent, his Cassie was. He treasured her. He'd take it slowly, savoring every moment . . .

❦ ❦ ❦

He opened his eyes. His head was buried in his hand. His other hand lay clenched in his lap.

"But which?" The words came to him through a tunnel, reverberating like the clang of a bell. "Sir?"

"Which did he say?" Another man had spoken.

"Orkney. Sure as eggs is eggs, 'twill be Stromness Harbor."

The voices came from a distance. His mind fought them. They'd been discussing their course. He'd put head in hand to think.

It was ships and harbors.

Not courtship, nor heather, nor the sweet, silken feel of Cassie in his arms.

He felt the thin wisp of fabric wadded in his fist. A delicate handkerchief bearing the letter *C*.

Though it rose from the depths of his soul, the sound he made was slight, like the creak of ship's timber. It was anguish.

"Captain had too much whisky last night," a man ventured. The others laughed merrily.

"Sir?"

"What?" His voice was a jagged snarl.

He raised his head. There was the ship's mate, two sailors, the cabin boy. All stared, confident in him and waiting for orders.

How long had he been lost in thought? A heartbeat? Two? It had felt like a lifetime.

"Will we be docking off Orkney?" a sailor asked.

MacNab could only muster a blank stare.

"The boys, sir. We need to drop the boys," the first mate said. The other sailors called the man Patch, though MacNab had never understood why. His mate was neat as a pin, in

possession of both eyes, and with nary a stitch out of place.
"But Morrison's men, they're blackguards one and all.
They'll fetch a tidy bounty. As for the schooner—"

"Aye," MacNab said, remembering. They'd captured the
schooner. That prize alone would fetch a lavish sum. He'd
installed a skeleton crew, and the two ships were sailing in
tandem. His men would be paid well when they pulled into
port. "Aye, to the Orkney Islands. To Stromness. As for the
boys, we'll use a portion of my purse to get them back home
to Glasgow."

MacNab jammed the handkerchief back where he kept it
forever in his sporran. He held his hand before him. Studied
it, fisting and opening his fingers. He eyed the patch of tight,
grizzled skin, black like charcoal.

He stood and caught his reflection wavering in the glass
of the porthole. A matching scar darkened his brow and temple, like the shadow of his memories.

Abruptly, he grabbed a bottle of whisky. The sea rolled
and the *Charon* pitched, and the amber liquid hit the side of
his tankard as he poured. It spilled into a small puddle on the
table.

He'd avenged Cassie. His life was no longer of use to him.

But he had men who depended on him. His eyes went to
his first mate. MacNab had failed Cassie. But he could make
it so that another could build the life that'd been denied him.

"Go above deck," he ordered Patch. "Set a course for Orkney."

Ten

"I said, will you have the purse in gold or men?"

The first mate was staring at him, and MacNab realized he'd been asked a question. He pushed away from the rail, studied the leaden sky and scowled. "Gold," he answered, distracted.

"Good on you," Patch said quickly, nodding. He waited for some response from his captain, then clarified, "For getting these slavers, Black John. Good on you. Morrison was a bad man."

"We're all bad men," MacNab muttered darkly.

He spun on his heel. A group of sailors were congregated on the foc'sle. He called to them.

"Aye, sir," they answered in unison, springing to their feet. A silver flask was quickly pocketed. It didn't escape MacNab's notice.

"Lazy dogs," he growled. "Drink on your own time. Snap to. The wind's down. Hoist the yard. Let out the sails." His eyes flicked from the uniform gray of the sky to the limp sheets of canvas overhead. "Unfurl the bloody lot of them.

We need to catch the wind or we'll be dead men pulling into Stromness Harbor."

"Speak not of dead men," a voice grumbled from behind.

MacNab turned. Sailors were a superstitious lot, and Haddie, the cook, was the worst of them. He was a benign old sort, so named for what felt like the only food he ever prepared. Haddock chowder, haddie pie, smoked haddock . . .

"You'll call the reaper himself to the ship," the old man warned again.

MacNab registered his words, but he couldn't muster a care. *The reaper himself?* His muscles clenched. 'Twould just bring relief. "Shut it, Haddie. Save your tripe for the mess table."

"I hear you can buy wind on Orkney," the ship's boy said.

"Aye, 'tis true," a sailor chimed in. "I've seen it myself. The wind seller. She sells it, tied in knots upon a thread."

"Och, lads," Haddie grumbled. "'Tis the Lewis witches who are the most powerful of their kind."

"Shut it," MacNab ordered. The only thing that tried his patience more than foolish superstitions was the mention of his home isle. "Shut the devil up, the lot of you."

"Black John," Haddie hissed, frantically shaking his head. He made a warding sign with his fingers. "Speak not of . . . *him*. You can't call on him, that way."

"What the dev —"

Haddie hissed again. "You say his name, you call him to us. You say his name and seal our fate."

"Superstitions," he grumbled, then was distracted by a ruckus above. A man was tangled in the rigging, his leg stuck through the webbed net of the ratlines. "Bloody hell. 'Tis the bloody drunken sailor who seals the fate of any ship

"You"—MacNab pointed at a gaping seaman—"up, now. Man the sails. We're losing wind."

The sound of birds cawing carried to them on the still air. All eyes looked up to see three gulls reeling overhead.

"Three gulls." Haddie made the sign of the cross. "'Tis death herself. A sign. Someone will die. I warned you, Black John. You called her to us."

MacNab's body stiffened. *Three gulls.* The memory cut him. He thought back to another day. Another death. "What did you say?" he asked the cook in a dangerously quiet voice.

Haddie stared, terrified. MacNab didn't know whether it was the gulls or his own ire that scared the old cook more.

"Damn you and your gulls," MacNab told him. "Damn it all to hell."

Haddie flinched.

"I'll not have the fears of fishwives spread on my boat."

"You've sealed our fate," Haddie whispered again.

"What did you say?" MacNab grabbed him by the collar. "Answer me."

"Black John," the first mate pleaded. "He's just an old man, aye?"

"Do you all believe such foolishness?" MacNab pushed the cook away. He eyed his crew, all silent, frozen in place. "The lot of you. Are you *all* fools?"

MacNab stared, his blood running cold. He flexed his hand and then rubbed it over his sporran.

"You have the deck," he snarled to Patch, then turned and stalked below to his cabin.

Eleven

She dug her delicate fingers into the neckline of her bodice.

Iain's eyes widened. "Och, lass, whatever are you—"

She plucked her handkerchief from her corset and began to wipe at some bit of dirt on her hands.

"Ah" Inhaling deeply, he gave a quick clearing shake to his head. "You'll be the death of me, Cassiopeia MacLeod."

Iain studied the bit of linen she held. "Ohh," he said, "I remember this." He took it gently from her fingers. Gave her a broad smile. "You wiped my face with it. On the first day we met."

"Aye, and I had a time of it getting the stain out," she snapped saucily. "Had I known you'd come to me every day smudged with some bit of bog on you, I'd have spared myself the trouble."

"You sassy girl." He grabbed her, growling and nuzzling at her neck.

She laughed, a lighthearted trill that thrilled him.

Cassie held the handkerchief out. "Well, would you like it?"

"Oh, I'd like it." He cocked a brow, giving a more wicked meaning to his words than what she'd intended.

"Iain!" she gasped with mock outrage. *"I meant my handkerchief. I'd like you to have it."*

"You would?"

She gave him a pert little nod. The look in her eyes was that of a cat who'd eaten all the cream.

"Why ever is that?"

She gave a quiet shrug. *"I hate . . . I hate when we part. I'd like to think you had some reminder of me."*

"Cassie, love." He grew serious. *"How could you ever think I'd need any reminder? Don't you know I think of you every moment? The sun reminds me of you. The moon in the sky, the wind off the sea. I could roam far, far from here, 'til the ends of the earth, and still I'd need no reminder of you."*

* * *

He groaned. There'd been knocking.

"Sir?" The first mate sounded tentative, calling into the cool dim of Black John's small cabin.

MacNab smoothed the delicate square of linen along his thigh, tracing his finger gingerly along the faded *C*. He folded it, and folded it again, returning it to his sporran.

"Aye, come." His voice was tired. *He* was tired.

"We can't find the wind, sir." Patch stood stiffly before him, respectful, waiting.

His mate wasn't a bad man. An Irishman, MacNab believed. He wondered what unlucky whims of fate had brought him just there. To be the first mate on such a ship, working for such a man. Patch was neat and upright, with a head of smoothly combed black hair and sailors slops that were, though not crisp, kept remarkably clean. His shoulders were pulled back, hands clasped behind, and MacNab noted the bearing of youth—tensile, robust—still writ on the man's bones.

MacNab wished for once to have the walls of formality down. He'd ask the mate what strange chain of events brought him to choose such a hard life. He'd advise him to leave, to take his portion of the *Morrison's* bounty and build a cottage on a square of land somewhere. Find a wife to fill it with bairns.

His mind went to his own bairns, robbed from him on the day he lost Cassie, wee blond babes who'd never be.

"We can't tack, sir," Patch continued.

MacNab snapped back into the moment. He flexed his hand and scrubbed it over his brow and eyes. He could ill afford these daydreams. These musings and memories that plagued him.

He rose from his bench. "How far are we from the coast?"

"Close now, and drifting closer," Patch said. "A current pulls strong, into the firth. The helmsman worries we'll run aground on the shoals."

The air on deck was utterly still, and with it came an eerie quiet. There was no slapping of water, nor cawing of birds. The sails hung slack in their rigging. He looked to starboard. The sea was a smooth sheet of mercury, like a vast looking glass stretching clear to the horizon, where it seemed simply to curve and fade into a haze of white.

He turned a slow circle, sweeping his eyes across the distance. The schooner that'd been known as *Morrison's Pride* sailed ahead of them, manned by what crew he could spare. And just beyond her, a ghostly mass wavered above the water. The Isles of Orkney. Their intention was to sail up along the eastern shores, circling around and back down to Stromness.

MacNab's eyes narrowed. "What the devil?"

Leaning against the rail, he extended his spyglass. He couldn't believe what he was seeing. *Morrison's* stern had just jutted to the right, so sharp and so sudden it was as though the helmsman had spun the wheel, aiming them straight for the rocks.

"Why do they not tack starboard?" Patch asked, aghast.

"They can't," MacNab said simply. "There's no wind to carry them."

"But she'll run aground."

"Aye." MacNab's voice was grim. "She'll run aground."

Morrison's Pride began a slow spin, moving lazily in the water, her bow pointing now to larboard, now to starboard, and back again, in a ghastly and languorous dance.

All hands stilled, watching in horror. They knew it was the *Charon*'s own fate they witnessed.

A great collective breath sucked in, so loud it was as though the wind had picked up once more. But it was simply his men bearing the sight of their prize schooner as she slammed into the rocky coast.

A terrible sound like felled trees carried to them across the still air. Rocks chewed into the *Morrison's* hull, a great screeching and groaning, followed by the screams of her men. She'd pitched hard but hadn't sank, and MacNab was grateful to see the crew scrabbling across the deck like crabs, clambering onto shore.

"We'll never make it," Patch muttered.

MacNab turned his back on his prize. The crew he'd installed on the schooner would live to see another day. He had his own crew to save now.

As though suddenly gripped by a giant hand from the deep, the *Charon* herself stuttered, tossing men stumbling on their feet. A horrible shuddering scrape thundered in the lifeless air. They'd drifted into one of the shoals.

"We'll never make it," Patch said, louder now.

"Aye. We'll head through."

"Sir?"

"Through," MacNab said, turning to face his crew. Some strange charge stirred his blood. He felt alive for the first time in so long. Awakened by the prospect of facing his death. Eager for it? He shoved the thought quickly from his mind.

He needed to save his crew. They'd lost their prize, but he could save his men. "We sail through the Pentland Firth," he told them. "Set a course for Stromness *through* the firth."

Blank and frightened eyes met his.

"But, sir," Patch murmured for MacNab's ears alone. He'd not dissent before the other crewmen. "The firth—"

"I ken the stories." The Pentland Firth was a narrow and

treacherous channel. Unpredictable tidal swells spun whirl-pools and wrenched towering waves from water that moments before might have appeared as smooth and still as polished stone. It was some of the most perilous sailing in the world, and none but a few sailors were mad enough to brave it.

"Step lively now," he shouted. "All hands to the larboard rail. Patch, fetch the topsail."

His mate stared for a moment, bewildered.

"We rig a sea anchor," MacNab said. "Toss it over the larboard side."

The first mate's eyes grew wide. A buzz rose instantly, the still air humming to life. All sailors knew about sea anchors, but few had ever attempted one.

"A . . . a sea anchor?"

"Aye. The wind may be dead, but the current pulling into the firth is strong. We submerge the topsail. The current catches it . . ."

"And," Patch finished, his understanding dawning, "you believe it'll pull us from the rocks and shoals. Like a great underwater sail."

"Aye, exactly that."

Patch's brow furrowed. "But even if we can hitch the current, it'll drag straight into the firth."

MacNab flexed his hand. He'd deal with *that* when it came. "One concern at a time."

He turned to stare over the rail, eyeing the deceptively glassy water. There was stillness at his back where there should've been an explosion of activity.

He spun his head, shooting a black gaze at his first mate. "You heard my order. Topsail. Now."

Men scrambled to action, skittering up the rigging like spiders. Patch alone faltered. "We can't do this," the mate said quietly, emboldened by his fear. "I beg you. The Pent-land Firth . . . it will mean our deaths."

"You'd have us dash up along the rocks instead?" MacNab challenged. "'Tis a cowardly course. If we wait, and drift, praying like a bunch of pious widows for a breath of air, we are only allowing the fates to decide."

He shaded his eyes, looking toward the narrow channel
between the Orkney Islands and the Scottish mainland. "Sailing through the firth is a gamble, but the prize is our lives.
I'll not just bob and float like a lame mallard to be pitched
onto the shoals."

His gaze went to the sailors clambering back down the
rigging, topsail in hand. "And if a course of action means our
death, then so be it."

Patch gave him a single, stark nod. MacNab had known
he would. Just as he hoped he was making the right decision
and not sending this good man, this veritable stranger, this
shipload of strangers, to a watery grave.

The *Charon* skidded again, and this time the groaning of
timber was otherworldly. The boat pitched and heaved, and that
great underwater hand was a fist now, punching at the hull,
sending her in a sluggish spin, stern first, toward the rocks.

Sailors scrambled to him at the larboard rail, and MacNab
led them, tying off ropes, making a great kite of the topsail.

"Now!" MacNab shouted, and they cast the sea anchor.
"Pay her out slowly, now."

The canvas dropped to the water like a dead weight, but
its descent below the surface was maddeningly slow. It fluttered like a ghostly swath of kelp, drifting and sinking.

There was a sudden tug, a snapping of ropes, and the sail
faded into black. His men shouted their excitement, their feet
shuffling across the deck, holding desperately to the ropes as
though to the leash of Cerberus himself, as the sea anchor
dragged them to the railing.

She caught the current and righted herself, propelled into
the Pentland Firth. MacNab caught movement out of the
corner of his eye. A few of the Irish sailors crossed themselves. He saw Patch's hands were clenched fists at his sides.

The real challenge had just begun.

They whipped fast into the channel, and the air, the sky,
everything, simply felt . . . different. Charged somehow, and
ethereal. Like they'd crossed an invisible threshold, leaving
the world they'd known, traversing into some other, stranger
place. One of forfeits and penance.

MacNab shook his head hard. *Stay sharp.* There was no time for these relentless reveries.

He smelled the wind before he felt it. A prick of fresh air in his nostrils. And he gazed into the far distance to where the water seemed to boil, churning the surface, cutting across the firth like a great ruff of lace.

"'Tis the *muir bhàite*," a voice said from behind him. Haddie had come above deck, and the old man was oddly still at MacNab's side. His superstitious panic had quieted. He sensed it, too, MacNab saw. This eerie passage taking them to someplace *other*.

"The *muir bhàite*," Haddie muttered again. "The drowning sea."

•

Twelve

"Belay the main," MacNab ordered. The firth tossed waves like a petulant girl her hair, and he'd batten the *Charon* down. Something was coming, something greater than any storm. "Lash it to the mast."

He didn't like the strange swath of turbulent sea that cut directly across their path. They had too much momentum; they were cruising straight for it. They had to quit the current.

"Cut the sea anchor," he called, and he saw panic flicker in his men's eyes. The situation was grave indeed if they were to sacrifice such a valuable swath of canvas. "Cut the lines!"

His men sliced the *Charon* free of her underwater sail, but it wouldn't be enough. More than simply heading into a channel, it was as though they'd entered a tunnel, one that was subject to different wind, waves, and weather.

A renegade wind smacked them. It keened through the rigging, a sharp blast, come and gone like the shriek of a woman. An eerie silence reigned once more.

"'Tis a demon sea," someone shouted.

"Focus like the men you are," MacNab growled. "Furl the sails." They needed to draw in all the sheets. The wind they'd been lusting for was beginning to nip. If it grew as big as he feared while the sheets were unfurled, it'd snap the mast in two. "I'll not risk the mast."

MacNab edged forward and clung to the bow. The vein of water continued to roil in the distance, and it mesmerized him. They were closing fast.

"'Tis the sea witch," Haddie said. The old man's tone was calm and steady, as if he'd glimpsed the future and knew there was no turning back. "She lies yonder, in the depths below, grinding salt for the sea."

As if summoned, the first wave seemed to rise straight up from still water, coming at them from the side. The ship simply bobbed low at the stern, pitched, and then a great white claw curled up and over, grasping at the rails, pulling the *Charon* down hard. She hung sideways for one heart-stopping moment, then bobbed sharply back to starboard, sending the men skittering over the deck and snatching desperately at the lines to keep themselves aboard.

"Grab the lifelines," he shouted, doing a quick headcount. MacNab was relieved the watch had changed over an hour past. There were only nine hands on deck, plus his mate and Haddie. "The lines," he yelled again, and his men scrambled for the rails, holding tight to the weather lines.

And then, inexplicably, they were struck from the opposite side. It was violent, like the sudden slap of a raging mistress, vengeful and giddy with her anger.

And then the water began to boil. The waves dwarfed them and the *Charon* became merely a child's plaything tossed about. Another wave struck them, and another.

Water swelled up to gorge on *Charon*'s timber, flooding her. Froth swirled along the deck, and for a strange, still moment all was serene and white, as though there'd been a light dusting of snow. And then the froth whirled, receding quickly like a recoiling snake, trying to suck the sailors back into the depths.

"Tie off the mainsail!" MacNab shouted to those few men clinging to the yards above. "Belay the sails."

His eyes scanned the mast. It struck him as a pitiful, reedy thing, ready to snap like a piece of rotted wood.

An enormous swell rolled beneath them, and the ship heaved, pointing upward. The horizon spun away, until all they saw was the leaden sky through a haze of mist. She slammed back down.

How long would the *Charon* last? How long until they crossed this unending swath of turbulence? His eyes scanned the deck. MacNab was tired, his own heart grown cold, but he'd not suffer his men. "Man the lookout!" he ordered. "Where does this end? Tell me where this godforsaken churn ends!"

The ship's boy hurtled up the lines to the crow's nest. The men's chaos stilled for a moment, as all stopped to watch him lean forward, squinting and concentrating on the horizon.

"Gurge!" the boy screamed suddenly, pointing frantically in the distance. "A gurge!"

Whirlpool.

"Swilkie, she's called," Haddie said ominously. The old cook wove the lifeline around his fist, bracing for the worst. "The swallower."

MacNab had no time to contemplate this. He heard gasps and spun, already feeling the growing shadow at his back.

A mountain of water came for them, an enormous wave barreling across the firth, so magnificent it seemed a living thing, a monster risen from the deep. Black, marbled with white, and impermeable as stone. The wave was death incarnate, and it was a thing of beauty.

She brought with her a rumble of sound, like an angered god, and a fierce blast of wind struck them. It was a wind straight from hell, but cold, so cold.

"Hang on," he bellowed uselessly. Noise filled his head— the cries of his men, the groaning of timber, the wailing of the wind in the rig.

And then the wall pummeled them.

They knew an eternity of silence. For a moment they

were merely helpless bits of flotsam, weightless and mean-
ingless, and all wondered if this would be their grave. But
the wave pulled back with a hiss, leaving them human again,
with their human sounds. Sounds of men scurrying, of torn
sails flapping—mundanity so utterly out of place from the
unearthly majesty of moments before.

MacNab surveyed the damage. Miraculously, the mast
still stood. But the jib had torn free from the rigging. It'd
been the foremost sail, a triangular sweep reaching from the
top of the mast to the very tip of the bowsprit. It hung now,
in front of the *Charon*, dangling dangerously close to the
waves. If it went under, caught water, the ship would capsize
in an instant.

"Cut the jib!" MacNab shouted, but Patch was already at
the bow, edging his way out along the sharp point of the
bowsprit.

And just beyond, the vortex churned, drawing them ever
closer. It swirled madly, an eddy crafted of pure darkness,
with an angry mouth of white froth waiting to swallow them.
It thundered, ravenous.

Patch eased along the knife-edge of the bowsprit. Another
wave struck them, and all held their breath as the first mate
was submerged in a wall of white.

It receded, and all sighed relief to see him clinging there
still. He had a wild-eyed look, hanging desperately from the
point of the bow, shrouded in sea spray. Patch's hand patted at
his waist, but his dagger was gone, ripped free of its sheath.

The lines were a hideous snarl. Patch shook the curtain of
hair from his face and was trying to make sense of them
when the next wave struck. It came at them from leeward,
and the nose of the *Charon* dipped dangerously low. The first
mate slid. His hands slipped free of the slick wood and the
men gasped as he plummeted down to the seething water.

But just before his head hit the waves, the line snapped
taut. He swung like a pendulum, swooping over the open sea
then back again, perilously close to the hull. Patch hung,
upside down, his leg tangled in the rigging.

One of MacNab's crewmen was at the rail in an instant,

kicking off his boots, getting ready to inch out onto the bow-sprit.

"No," MacNab told him. His eyes went to his first mate. Patch was a good man, deserving of that cottage and wife. MacNab trusted only himself to save him. "I'll do it," he told the sailor. He pulled his knife free. He curled his toes, feeling the solid connection between the *Charon*'s timber and his always-bare feet. "This is for me to do," he repeated.

Biting his dagger between his teeth, he climbed out. The bowsprit was slick, but MacNab clung to it with hands and feet and knees, edging closer to where Patch dangled. He'd have only seconds to save him before they were hit by an-other wave.

He kept his dagger clamped hard between his teeth. It would be the thing that'd save his ship; he couldn't lose it. The blade dug into the corners of his mouth. The feel of sharp steel on his skin gave him focus.

They'd lost their prize money when they'd lost the schoo-ner. But he could save the men their lives.

MacNab wrapped his legs tightly around the bowsprit, as though clinging to a tree trunk. He snatched the line from its pendulum swing and wrapped it about his arm and fist. It bore Patch's weight, and it cut into the muscle of MacNab's forearm.

He heaved the line in, and his first mate jostled up, closer to the bowsprit. He heaved again, straining with the weight. Each yard of rope MacNab gained, he wound around his arm, until finally Patch was close enough to curl up and grab hold of the bowsprit.

Patch met his eyes, and MacNab nodded to the ship, ges-turing for him to get back on board. If anything happened to MacNab, he knew his first mate would be the *Charon*'s only chance at survival.

He looked away the moment his first mate reached the rail. Angry welts crisscrossed his arm and fist, rope burns, rope slashes. But MacNab didn't feel them.

He knew only the dagger in his teeth and the sail dangling

dangerously below. He set to work, clinging with legs and feet, slicing the lines free.

There was a sharp crack, and for a moment, MacNab thought a thunderstorm was to be their next trial. But then he felt the next crack in his hands. He felt the slow creaking of wood as the bowsprit began to fracture beneath him.

"MacNab!" Patch shouted.

He looked up. The men gestured madly to him, waving him back on board.

"We'll cut the lines from the deck," another shouted.

Sailors were already frantically cutting away at the lines, from the deck, from the mast, trying to free the jib.

But MacNab knew it wouldn't be enough, the lines were too snarled beneath him.

In his gut, he felt the slow surging of the water, as though the sea herself were drawing in a great breath. Another wave was coming. It would catch the jib, drown them all. His men would never get the lines cut in time. He needed to lean down, severing *below* the tangled mass.

The bowsprit creaked again, and he saw the fissure crackling up the thin stretch of it. Still, he clung with his legs, hugging the wood. His plaid flapped in the wind, the wet wool slapping hard against his thighs.

He reached below the snarl and sliced line after line, until only one was left. He sensed the wave surging. Felt the pull of the water on the jib. He cut the final line free. There was one last deafening crack.

The *Charon* heaved back, freed of her weight. The bowsprit snapped. The wave swallowed the jib, the bowsprit, and MacNab.

Thirteen

MacNab's body spun, and he felt it as a slow flight through space.

I am lost. The thought crept to him, quiet, unassuming.

He closed his eyes, and the whole of his life came to him, clear, bright, and heartrending.

Gordie, dear Gordie. Where was his friend now? His aunt, Morna. Did she still live?

And Cassie. At the end, there was only Cassie.

The others were mere flickers, stars in the night sky. But Cassie was his sun. Brightness and warmth. He hadn't been alive, not truly, since she'd died.

Snippets flashed to him. Her shining, yellow hair. Their first kiss. Her saucy smiles. A promise made beneath the stones.

He spun, and it was as though the sea swirled up to meet him. But it was aggravatingly slow, this death. Still he spun, and still the memories came.

Finally, blessedly, he struck with a hard smack. The waves swallowed him. Water forced its way into his sinuses, down his throat. It was sharp like glass, invading his body.

But the pain was nothing to these final memories that impaled him. He saw her, over and over, and her sweet voice filled his head. His only, his lovely Cassie.

His body spun in the water. He felt a tug at his core. The vortex seized him. Swilkie, the swallower. He spun faster.

Finally.

Rest.

And then he spun down into blackness.

❖ ❖ ❖

"Iain," someone shouted. "Iain!" It was Gordie's voice.

Pain swept him. Would he never be free of the memories? Did they follow him here, down to hell?

"Shake him," a voice like his aunt's said.

Something yanked at his hair. Iain opened his eyes. His aunt's daughter, the little blonde baby Jan, pulling on his hair with chubby, sandy fingers.

He blinked, looked around, dazed. What of the *Charon*? Had he shipwrecked, landed back on Lewis somehow?

His eyes went back to Jan. "But you . . ." he stammered. Jan should be over twenty and a woman grown by now, yet here she sat, tugging his hair, a smear of sand clinging to her drooly chin.

Iain dropped his head onto the beach. *Hell.* He'd landed himself in hell, where he'd be forced to live and relive his painful memories throughout eternity.

"He opened his eyes," Morna said. "Iain, lad, are you alright?"

He lifted his head again. Looked down to his hands in the surf. They were the hands of a young man.

There was mumbling at his back, but he ignored it. He pushed himself up to sitting and flexed his hands before him, marveling. His black scars, gone. His fingers traced his face. It was smooth.

Was it a dream? Was he in hell? He surely hadn't earned heaven.

"He's not in his right mind," Niall said.

"Ach, our Iain is harder to kill than that, aye?" Gordie laughed, and Iain's eyes went to him.

Gordie was cuffing his brother on the shoulder. Neither of them was a day older than when Iain had fled, so long ago.

"Where am I?" he asked, bewildered.

"The boat, lad. We've sunk."

"Are you certain he's alright?" Morna leaned down, plucking Jan from the sand.

"We were on our fishing day, remember?" Niall said.

"Thank God he's alright," his aunt muttered. "And thank the heavens I saw the wave as you lads went out. I've never seen the like. 'Twas like the sea witch herself come to sweep you away."

Their fishing day. His eyes scanned Gordie and Niall, studied their clothing, desperate to remember. Was this *that* day? The day he'd returned to find Cassie promised to another?

How could it be? Was he dead? Was this real?

A thousand thoughts skittered through his mind. Of churning seas, whirlpools, and sea witches, of the laird he'd killed. The image of Cassie's dress stained scarlet with her blood. And clear like the sun through parting clouds came the memory of a promise made beneath the Callanish Stones.

"We didn't go fishing?" Iain asked, wonderment in his voice.

"No, lad." Gordie and his brother exchanged worried looks. "We left not an hour past."

This *was* that day. The day they'd fished. The day he'd returned to find Cassie promised to Lord Morrison.

Hope blazed to life in his chest. Perhaps it was a dream, perhaps not. All he knew was that, if less than an hour had passed since they'd left on their fishing boat, there was a chance he could find Cassie, get her. Take her before Morrison had a chance to.

Iain jumped to his feet and ran.

Fourteen

Rocks bit at his feet, the cold air scored his throat, and his plaid was heavy and wet, slapping against his pumping legs.

Iain ignored it all, even ignored the feel of his body, suddenly young and taut and fast.

His only focus was Cassie.

He didn't know what was happening to him. He wondered if his soul weren't wandering in some netherworld, while his body lay drowned on the bottom of the sea.

But he pushed that thought away. He was here now, in his young man's body. And he would do what he should've done when he was young in truth.

He ran along the coastline, cresting hills, jumping rocks, to get to MacLeod's tower. It emerged on the horizon, sitting high on its cliff-top perch, a rocky outcropping jutting into the sea.

The castle loomed grim and gray, but what had once evoked fear now simply spurred him on. He should've faced the laird in his own domain long ago.

He loped around the back to the kale garden. His heart

clenched, anguished at the memories. Cassie'd had a whole world apart from him, one in which she'd sneak through this very garden, doing things like listening in on maids and trapping rabbits. Sneaking out, coming to *him*.

One of the cooks gave him a startled look, and Iain hushed her. But it reminded him of where he was. He might be in a dream, he might be in heaven or hell. Either way, he imagined stealth would serve him best, until he could puzzle it out.

He ducked into the kitchen and gave his eyes a moment to adjust to the dim light. His heart pounded in his chest as he caught his breath. He'd run hard. He looked down in amazement at his body. *Young again.* Dream or no, it felt good to be young again.

He heard a shout. A man's voice loud in argument. Iain crept onto the stairs.

Muted voices came from above. The dining hall? He tiptoed up, running his hand along the cold, dank stone of the spiral staircase as he went.

"He stole." It was the laird's voice, speaking with disdain.

"No, father," a woman entreated. Iain's heart flipped in his chest. *Cassie?* Could it truly be her? It took all his will not to run up the stairs to her. "Iain didn't steal. It was I—"

"Do not contradict me, girl. If I say the peat boy stole from me, then the peat boy stole from me."

"Will you hang him?" a second man asked.

Iain scowled. *Lord Morrison.* He knew an instant of vertigo, so strange it was hearing the voice of the man he'd recently killed.

"I'll hang the peat boy—"

"Father!" Cassie screamed. "It's my fault. You can't hang him. We wish to marry. He is my one love, my true love."

Iain's heart soared to hear the words. He had to see her, had to see with his own eyes his Cassie, young again. He snuck higher up the stairs. He couldn't believe she lived. If this indeed was hell, he embraced it. He'd endure the wrath of Lucifer himself for one more moment in her presence.

"What do you know of love, chit? You know naught. Wait"—the laird's voice grew steely—"has he soiled you?"

The room stayed silent.

"Bedded you," he snapped. "Has the boy bedded you?"

"Of course not!"

"Good," Morrison chimed in. "Because our bargain is off if your girl is no longer a virgin."

"What *bargain*?" Cassie asked hesitantly.

"You marry Lord Morrison, and I'll not hang your peat boy. That's the only bargain you need concern yourself with."

"So?" Morrison demanded.

There was a shuffling, then Cassie spoke, her voice barely a whisper. "I will."

"Louder, girl."

"I'll do your bidding, but you must swear to keep Iain alive. Swear you won't hurt him."

There was a grumbling, and MacLeod snapped, "Calm yourself, Morrison. I've a dungeon with the boy's name on it. Nobody will stand in your way."

"I don't trust you, MacLeod. Our agreement isn't final until I've had a chance to confirm she's a maiden still. I'd not buy a horse before putting it through its paces, and I'll not wed your daught—"

Iain didn't give Lord Morrison a chance to finish. He flew up the rest of the stairs, angling for a fight.

His eyes went straight to her. It *was* Cassie. The same Cassie of his youth, sweet and lovely, but with a look of fear pinching her brow. He swayed on his feet.

"How can it be?" he whispered. "Is it truly you, lass?"

"What's the meaning of this?" MacLeod unsheathed the dagger at his waist and stalked to Iain.

"No father!" Cassie shrieked.

He tore his gaze from her. They might all be ghosts, or flesh and blood brought back to life, he didn't know. But he did know he needed to act. He'd once chosen a path, and it'd been the wrong one. Was this his chance to change his destiny?

He'd save Cassie. Cassie *would* be his bride. He'd sworn a vow beneath the Callanish Stones.

A light flickered in his mind. Was it the standing stones

that had brought him back? Was his promise more sacred even than magic?

The laird stopped, waiting and staring, a look of bemusement on his face. "What do you propose to do now, peat boy?"

Revulsion curdled his belly. And not because the laird spoke words of disdain for *him*. To Iain, the man had been dead for decades. But to see him treat his daughter so? Like chattel, or livestock, the MacLeod traded Cassie to another man.

Iain had killed the laird once, was it his destiny to kill him over and over for all eternity? He faced the MacLeod head-on, realizing with dismay that he was armed with naught but his wet plaid and bare feet. Still, Iain snarled. He flicked his eyes from the laird to Morrison and back again. "I suppose you'll not talk this through like men."

Iain rubbed his hands together and flexed his fists. Cassie gasped. He wondered distantly if it was the conspicuous absence of a weapon that had startled her.

He snuck another look at her. He couldn't keep his eyes from her.

Morrison stepped to her side and placed his hands hard on her shoulders. Cassie turned from Iain. She canted her body, tucking herself into the old lord.

Iain's vision wavered. It couldn't be. The image was so like that moment, before, by the cage, when Cassie had turned her body from him. Iain had been trussed, helpless. And helpless he'd watched her die.

And now, here, again she'd turned from him.

He'd been helpless then, but he was a helpless boy no more. Was she seeking comfort from the old man? Iain stepped toward her. She might not want saving, but damn the girl, he'd save her anyway.

But Cassie shocked him then. She pulled away from the lord, his dagger gripped in her small hand.

Iain reeled. She *hadn't* betrayed him, that day. She'd been trying to *save* him. His sweet, maddening Cassie had thought to slay the lord with his own blade.

He laughed. It was a manic laugh, relief and joy and disbelief. And sadness, too, for having ever doubted his Cassie's love.

He'd never make that mistake again.

Iain had the body of his youth, but he'd the experience of an old salt. He felt the laird rush at his back. He smiled. *Fool.*

Iain let the man attack. He was eager for it. He braced, feeling the MacLeod charge from behind.

Another time flashed to him, the MacLeod at his back with Iain trussed like an animal. It had happened so long ago, and yet, somehow, it appeared that it had never happened. He gave a shake to his head. He'd not contemplate the ways of time and the universe. He had a man to fight.

He felt a rush of air, saw the shadow of the laird's upswept dagger arm. But Iain simply stepped back, into the attack. In a single motion, he pivoted, grabbing the MacLeod's out-stretched arm, twisting it down, and wrenching it back up again.

A look of shock seized the MacLeod's features. It'd been MacLeod's own force that thrust the knife. He toppled, stabbed in the heart by his own blade.

Cassie yelped, struggling. Lord Morrison was peeling her fingers from the hilt of his dagger.

Iain rushed to her. She'd died for him once. Vivid in his mind was a sky blue dress, stained scarlet with her blood. She'd not spill a drop more, so long as he lived.

He pushed between them, and Cassie fell away. Iain grabbed Morrison's throat with one hand, and stilled his blade arm with the other. He'd crush this vermin with his own two hands.

Fury blinded him to all but the man before him. Iain tight-ened his grip. The small bones of Morrison's wrist crunched, and his dagger dropped to the ground.

The lord clawed at him, gasping for air, his mouth work-ing wordlessly as Iain squeezed his throat, crushing the air from his body.

Words echoed in his head. *Worthless. Test ride. She lay*

like a dead thing. "I killed you once, Morrison. I'll kill you again. And again in hell, if need be."

Cassie was suddenly there, by his side. Iain knew a moment of panic. Then he saw that she'd snatched Morrison's dagger from the floor.

She stood, driving it into his belly, splitting the lord open like a gut fish. "Rot," she snapped. "You'll not ride me, you . . . you . . ."

She stared at Morrison with unseeing eyes as he fell to the ground. Finally Cassie broke.

She wept and shivered, and Iain pulled her close. "Hush, sweet Cass."

He shuddered. To hold her once more was a relief so profound, he thought he'd expire from it. A part of him waited, to wake up or to disappear from this moment like a puff of smoke.

But he didn't. And Cassie remained solid and warm in his arms. He hugged her closer still, kissing her hair, her brow. "Och, Cassie, love. Are you alright?"

She wrapped her arms more tightly around him and wept, and he let her. "Hush, now. You're safe now. You're safe with me."

"But!" she gasped suddenly, raising wild, panicked eyes to his. "How will we explain? Morrison, my father . . . You'll be blamed—"

"Hush, lass." He stroked her hair, pulling her back into him. "Nobody will come for me. We'll tell folk they killed each other. That it was a fight over . . . *property*." He shook his head, disgusted.

Cassie nodded gravely, turning her head to look at her father's lifeless body. Her face crumpled, but the tears had stopped.

"I'm sorry," he told her quietly. "I tried . . . He came for me, I tried not to kill him, but . . ."

"I know," she said simply. She scrubbed the damp from her face and repeated more loudly, "I know, and it's alright."

"But he was your father."

"Aye. And I imagine he'd have traded me for a cask of

good claret and twenty head of cattle." She looked up at him, raw sincerity in her eyes. "No, Iain. You are the only man I belong to."

"Och, love, you belong to none but yourself." He gave her a broad smile. "I'm not that great a fool to think I could ever own such as *you*, Cassiopeia. But I will ask you the honor of being my bride." He grasped her hand in his. "Will you, Cass? Will you finally, finally be my wife?"

"Aye," she whispered. "I've merely been waiting for you to ask it."

"As I have been waiting. Waiting quite some time indeed . . ."

She smiled back at him then. Tilting her head, she asked, "You do ken, I'm a very wealthy bride?"

Iain laughed, long-buried joy erupting from deep in his soul. "You are all the riches I need, Cassie."

Epilogue

Cassie watched her husband sleep. It was one of her favorite things. She'd always been a restless soul, her mind needing but the barest nudge to set it spinning from dusk till dawn. But not her Iain.

He had only to shut his eyes and think of sleep for it to come. She fully believed it was his hours in the fields that brought sleep with such ease. That and his pure soul.

She rested her head dreamily on the crook of her elbow. Nobody was luckier than she. Her Iain had an honest and joyful heart. And he also happened to be the handsomest man Cassie had ever laid eyes on.

She sensed he had secrets, but those would come, in time. Cassie had kept a couple secrets herself.

She fought the urge to touch him. To trace those muscles so hard-won. In marrying her, he'd inherited quite the bounty, but still he insisted on applying himself physically. He loved walking the hills, surveying their lands.

Not that she paid *that* any mind. She was the one who benefited, Cassie thought with a smile. Often, she'd rub his shoulders and arms at the end of the day, working those thick knots of muscle, impermeable as granite under her fingertips.

She stifled a giggle, remembering the first time she'd done it. The feel of his bare skin in her hands—how she'd swooned! She should've been ashamed at her reaction to him, mounting her husband as she had, like she were a mare and he some prized stallion. But the feel of him, his broad and healthy strength . . . She purred a little sound of contentment, remembering.

No longer able to resist, she tentatively reached out to trace the hard silhouette of his upper arm. He may have a gentleman's title now, but he had the body and the sun-kissed skin of a man. He could go back to peat farming for all she cared. She'd not complain.

It was his looks, after all, that had first attracted her to him, so many years past. Someday she'd confess her secret to him. Someday admit how she'd eyed him from afar.

She'd first spotted him when she was but a young girl. Even then, he'd stood out from the others. He'd been young still himself, and yet he'd already had much of his height. Standing tall over the other boys, with a body made of straight limbs and strong edges, Iain was like a prince from a fairy tale.

And his hair. She sighed, relishing the fluttering in her belly. That thick, gorgeous hair, the color of burnished copper. There was a day she'd seen him at market, and the sun had caught that hair and set it afire. She'd been desperate to know if his eyes would match. For years, she'd wondered if those eyes would be as blue as the sky or brown like the fields. Or even darker still, mysterious like the sea at night.

She'd been such a foolish, lovesick girl. The memory tickled her, contented her. There were so many memories of him, etched in her heart. Playing them in her mind, in these wee hours, it was as though she could relive a story whose happy ending she was assured.

She'd spied him again, a couple years later, and he'd grown even taller, and broader, and the sight of those long, straight limbs and that auburn hair had her body thrumming in shocking and unexpected ways.

For so long, in secret, she'd wondered who he was. It had become too much, though. How she'd begged her lady's maid to find out his name! Iain MacNab, she'd told her, and Cassie had swooned from the very sound of it. She'd imagined it matched the man: strong, upright, steadfast.

She had seen him again and was desperate for just one glimpse more. It was what had brought her so far afield on that day, the day they first met. She'd snuck out, braved the bogs, and spied on him hard at work. And what a glorious sight he'd been.

His broad shoulders flexing with each strike of his peat iron. His plaid, so proud, fluttering in the breeze. His strong and steady legs. She blushed at the memory.

And then she accidentally sank into the bog. She'd been mortified!

But then *he* appeared, cresting the hill, a smile on his face . . . she'd thought her heart would stop.

He'd swept her out, easy as you please, and that thrumming she'd felt before was nothing to the melted butter she became in his arms. And finally—finally!—she learned the color of those eyes. Wondrously, amazingly, they matched his hair. His hair and his eyes, the same striking rich auburn. Like gingerbread. They'd warmed for her, their edges crinkling.

She'd been lost then. She was his from that very moment.

Cassie had never met anyone like him. Everyone else seemed so . . . ordinary. But Iain was nobler, somehow. She'd known it from the start. All eyes went to him when he entered a room, as though folk naturally looked to him for guidance. He was special, so good, so courageous.

So very handsome.

And he was hers. She smiled.

His eyes fluttered open, and she stole her hand back fast to her side. Too late, though. He'd spied just what—and who—had woken him.

He smiled his crinkle-eyed smile and Cassie's heart kicked. Would she ever get over this feeling?

"You're up with the birds this morning." He tugged her possessively to him for a kiss that stole her breath. Iain pulled away and chuckled, sensing her reaction to him.

"What has you roused, wife?" he asked, his voice mischievous and hoarse from sleep. He stretched and looked to the window. The sky had lightened to dark gray, but full dawn was still a half hour away. "'Tis too early to get to work." He pulled her on top of him, kissing her shoulders, her neck. "Whatever should we do?"

It became immediately apparent to her that Iain knew exactly what it was he thought they should be doing.

She nestled her body down, just right, over him. He moaned, closing his eyes, jarred by a surge of lust.

She wriggled her hips for good measure, settling her weight fully upon him, loving the sudden control she'd won. She gave him a little feline smile of satisfaction, and he gave her a dark and hungry look in return. He'd know exactly what she was doing, and he'd not stop her by any means.

"But your mates had said they were off to fish today," she said innocently. "Are you certain you don't have a mind to catch them and go for a sail instead?"

"Och, no, bonny Cassie," he answered quickly, adamantly, laughter in his voice. "Trust me, lass, I've lost my taste for the sea."

He kissed her hard, growing serious, and rolled her beneath him. Now it was Iain's turn to nestle his body just so. He smiled wickedly at Cassie's gasp.

"No, my bonny, bonny bride. On land, in sky, in the sea, the only creature I have a mind to catch I hold already in my arms."

Sixteen Decades

Trish Jensen

To Chris White,
for making me laugh even during thunderstorms,
and for helping me brainstorm the funny.

One

"Okay, who's missing?" Sheriff Ty Coltraine asked.

Fannie Mae, the madam of Little Fork's claim to fame, The Rooster Ranch, scowled up at him, her smudged lipstick and caked-on makeup not doing her scrawny little eighty-year-old butt any favors. Tonight she was wearing a hot pink chiffon number that clashed a little with her flaming red Farrah wig hair. "Like I'm going to name names."

"How am I supposed to find this person if I don't know who I'm looking for?"

Fannie laughed. "I'm guessing you'll figure it out right quick."

Ty sighed. "One of your girls, a client, your dog, what?"

"Let's just say it was a friend who dropped by to say howdy."

"Was this friend male or female?"

"Don't get many female callers. Oh, a few now and then but—"

"When's the last time you saw him?" Ty interrupted, before she could elaborate.

"Around eight." She pointed at the chalkboard that held the evening's menu. Each of the ten bedrooms were numbered and named; names like Little Bo Peep, The Dungeon, Room Service, and—

"Ten Little Indians? Good Lord, Fannie."

She shrugged. "Different strokes. Anyways, he was heading to six, The Court Room, but he never showed. None of the girls have seen him, so he didn't take any detours."

"How do you know he didn't just change his mind and go home?"

"Beemer's still in the lot. And his clothes are still in the dressing room."

"I know I'm going to regret asking this," Ty said. "But what was he wearing the last time you saw him?"

"Judge's robe."

"Excuse me?"

"The Court Room? Duh, Ty. If you'd come around once in a while, blow off some steam, you'd be a much happier sheriff. And a handsome man such as yourself? Stunningly handsome, if my old eyes do say for theirselves." When he just raised an eyebrow, she added, "He was wearing a judge's robe. Nothing else."

Ty glanced up the *Gone with the Wind*–type staircase just in time to see Little Fork's mayor, Tony Fitch, starting down the steps. At the sight of Ty the mayor made a U-turn and hauled his hefty ass back up, as fast as his black stilettos could carry him.

Good Lord! Well, if nothing else, Ty's hometown certainly wasn't boring.

He shook his head, knowing for a fact that the next town council meeting would be interesting. "Okay, you and the staff scour the house top to bottom. I'll have a look outside."

"You really need to take a good look inside, Sheriff. Yer Pap sure did."

Ty chucked her on the chin. "Which is why, Fannie darlin', I'm avoiding it at all costs."

* * *

Ty was about to open the Dumpster when he heard it.

"Help!"

His head jerked around at the sound of the weak female voice. He glanced around the dusty, sandy backyard of the Rooster, but no weak female in need of help jumped out at him. He shook his head, figuring it might have been a fake cry coming from one of the windows above. From what he'd heard, many a customer of the Ranch enjoyed the helpless female fantasy. He was pretty sure that was what the Little Miss Muffet room was all about.

He went back to using his Maglite, searching the grounds around the Dumpster, hoping to find any clue to help him discover what had happened to the male "friend" who'd disappeared earlier.

"Please, sakes almighty, might anyone be of some assistance?"

Same voice. And he could have sworn it dropped to almost a whisper and ended with, "You filthy cretins."

Definitely didn't sound like a man.

He swept the yard with his light, landing on the shed at the far left corner of the Rooster's property. Moving slowly, trying to keep his boots from crunching up too much noise, he approached the shed.

From prior experience dealing with the Rooster, he knew the shed was where they kept many, many different outfits for the ladies. It certainly didn't hold gardening equipment. Neither the front nor the back of the mansion had a speck of greenery, save for the huge Don't Come Again cactus in the front yard. He was sure that wasn't the real name of that monstrosity, but it certainly fit its job description.

Little Fork Medical Center could attest to that.

Ty swept the area one last time as he neared the old wooden shed that truly looked like it had been here since the beginning of time. Nothing moved. The evening was amazingly windless, cloudless, and cool for early May, although the moon was a tiny sliver, offering no help whatsoever.

He reached the shed and noticed the padlock on the door. It was rusted beyond rusty, as if it had been there forever. And yet, the last time he'd been here it had looked brand spanking new. Nevada weather was harsh, but that harsh?

He knocked on the door. "Hello?"

He heard scrambling and rustling and finally a woman saying, "Oh, praise be! Please, help me."

"Who are you?" he asked, as he tried the lock. It didn't budge. "What's your name?"

"I . . . I . . ." the woman said, voice growing weaker. ". . . am so hungry."

Hungry for what was the question. "Are you one of Fannie's girls?" he asked. "Is this like a rescue game? 'Cause I'm not a client. And I'm not playin'."

He popped a couple of Skittles in his mouth.

"Fannie? No, no my mother's name is Elizabeth. Please, get me out of here."

Ty pulled out his cell and punched in the number to the Rooster. He, unfortunately, knew the number by heart.

When one of her male bouncers answered, he said, "This is Ty. Who's this?"

"Hi, Sheriff. It's Boner."

Of course. "Well, Boner, I'm in your backyard. I mean, the Rooster's backyard. And I need the key to the lock on this shed back here."

"The shed ain't locked."

"I'm standing in front of it. I know a padlock when I see it. Get me the key."

"I swear, Sheriff, the shed ain't been locked for weeks. Fannie got tired of always having to open it for people, so she took it off and threw it away."

"Well, someone put it back on. And they stuck a girl in there before they locked it. Any of your girls missing?"

"None that was scheduled to work tonight. Can't rightly say about those who have the night off."

"Okay, well, thanks, Bo . . . thanks."

"Any day now would be wonderful," he heard from the other side of the door.

"Okay," he said. "Hold on, darlin'. We'll get you out of there. Other than hungry, are you hurt?"

"My head seems to be pounding a bit."

Ty got on his phone again and called his deputy. "Jinx, I need EMT at the Rooster. Backyard shed. And I need a bolt cutter. 911-like. For both."

*　*　*

After surveying the entire perimeter of the shed, hoping to find another way in, Ty returned to the door. "Darlin', you still hanging in?"

"Darlin'? I'm not your darlin'."

"Okay, what should I call you instead?"

There was a long hesitation. "Who are you?" the woman asked.

"Your white knight, come to rescue you. What's your name?"

"M. . . . Magg . . . uhmm. Margaret. Margaret Prescott."

"Are you in there alone? M . . . mmm . . . Margaret?"

"I have no idea, Sir Lancelot. And I'd prefer not to know."

Ty squinted his eyes. The woman had an accent, but he couldn't place it for anything. It was stilted and just plain weird. Sort of British, but not.

"Do you know how you got in there, Margaret?"

"Indeed."

Her voice was growing fainter, and he called again to find out the status of the bus and the cutters. Five minutes out, both ways.

"How would that be?" he asked.

"What?" she whispered.

"Hang with me here, dar . . . Margaret. Who locked you in here?"

"The sheriff."

"Excuse me?"

"The sheriff. At least, that's what he claimed to be."

"What did this sheriff look like? Do you remember?"

"How could I forget? Well, he was wearing all black. Which, if you ask me, was not a good look on him."

So someone was dressed up as a sheriff. He'd have to discuss that little fantasy with Fannie. That definitely wouldn't do.

"Okay, Ms. Fashionista. What else?" he asked.

"He . . . was quite tall. Well over six feet."

"Fat? Thin?"

"He was . . . well muscled but most assuredly not stocky."

"Okay, a tall dude. How about his features?"

"His features. On first inspection, he was spectacularly handsome. Stunning, actually."

Ty groaned. Fannie's words almost exactly. "This is a joke, right? Fannie put you up to this? Trying to lure me in?"

"Do I sound like I'm joking, White Knight? I think I'm bleeding. My head feels sticky. This bad man was not joking, either. I'm scared. And c-c-cold."

And she sounded like she meant it. Her teeth had started chattering.

"Tell me more about him so I can find him."

"He . . . had dark hair."

Ty held a hand up to his head. "Long or short?"

"Short, compared to the others. Cut behind his ears. Oh, and he had a freckle on his left earlobe."

Ty's fingers immediately went to his left ear. The one with the freckle on it.

"Eyes?" he asked.

"The most striking feature. A very deep green."

Check. This *had* to be a practical joke. Although the woman didn't sound like she was joking.

"A-a-a-and he had a dimple in his chin. Unmistakable. Does this sound like your sheriff, sir?"

It sure as hell did. It sounded like him. But he knew for a fact he hadn't put this woman in this shed. "Not really," he said, because he was afraid to scare her even more. "But we'll find the SOB. I promise." *Because I want to find out who's impersonating me, too.* "You're sure he said he was the Little Fork sheriff?"

"He said he was the law around these parts. And he was very arrogant about it, I might add."

Shit. Ty had used those words before when he'd had to.

And he'd been called arrogant more times than he could remember. Except for the people who knew him well, many others misconstrued his shyness as arrogance. Which he'd allowed to happen, because no one in Nevada wanted a shy sheriff.

"And he smelled like a spittoon. That man jawed on tobacco until the smell was coming out of his skin."

Ty almost yelled "Hallelujah." He'd smoked exactly one cigarette in his life, when his father forced it on him. He felt sick for two days running. Chewing on it? Even his father hadn't been that bad.

"Margaret, you are a dang good witness," he said, wishing he could hug her right now, whether she was a prostitute or not. Strange thing was, he hadn't seen a spittoon anywhere except in those houses that re-created the old west. Even Fannie had a huge sign on her front door warning customers they weren't allowed to bring tobacco of any kind into her establishment, or they'd get the cactus.

"I . . . I'm hungry."

Considering the circumstances he was impressed she had an appetite at all. "Sorry, all I have on me are Skittles. But we'll get you out and be stuffing Big Macs down you in no time, Margaret."

"Big who's? Macs? The rumors were true then? I didn't believe it, but . . . oh, my Loosie! You're . . . you're cannibals?"

Oh, my Loosie? Ty would have laughed if he hadn't heard a distinctive thump behind the scarred wooden door. "Margaret?"

No answer. He knelt down. "No cannibals in this town, Margaret," he said. "I mean, we aren't going to make you eat a Mac! How about a Whopper?"

"Oh, my Loo . . ." he heard. And then there was nothing.

Apparently not a fast-food fan. Depending on her condition, he could bring her to Fanny at the Rooster to fill her up, except it seemed that it was a good bet someone from the Rooster had dumped and locked her in this shed. But why?

This was no game. He heard the fear and desperation in her

voice. But someone—who looked uncannily like Ty—was running around impersonating him. And assaulting women. That someone was in for a very big comeuppance when Ty got hold of him.

Ty knew Little Fork was fairly loose. He should. He'd lived here his entire life, except for the three-year break to jam in that degree at Oregon State in public safety and law enforcement. And then back to his hometown to do what his forefathers had been doing since Little Fork was part of the Utah Territory: enforce the law in what had mostly been a lawless town.

His father, his grandfather, and all the fathers before *that* had sucked at law enforcement, in his opinion. Brutal, crooked, and too full of themselves. It would break their hearts to know that their progeny was actually trying to bring real law and justice to their honky town.

Good. The bastards.

"Pizza?" he asked, just to try to get her talking again.

Nothing.

"Margaret, my name is Ty. Tell me where you're from."

"Philadelphia," she whispered.

"Hey, Philly! How about those Eagles?"

"Eagles? What eagles? I've not seen any eagles in Philadelphia. Except in paintings, of course."

"Not big on football, eh? How about the Phillies?"

"Phillies?"

"Not a sports fan, are you Maggie?"

"I'm . . . a teacher."

"Oh, well, that's great. What subject?"

"Subject? I teach them all of the subjects."

"Oh. What year?"

"Year?" she said, so softly he almost missed it.

"What year do you teach? Kindergarten? First grade?" He figured if she was teaching all subjects, she must be teaching the little crumbcrunchers. Which for some dumb reason he found endearing. He'd always admired anyone who could stand to put up with thirty or so restless kids for an entire day. Even though he coached Little League softball, and truly enjoyed it, he was darn ready for the parents to take the kids home after practice or games.

Now that he thought of it, his very first crush was on his kindergarten teacher, Ms. Taylor. Man, she'd been so pretty and she'd smelled like heaven.

Ty shook his head. Now wasn't exactly the time to wax nostalgic. "Look, help is coming, I promise. Just stick with me here. Tell me something about yourself. Talk about anything."

Silence.

"Tell me about your students. Tell me a joke. Something."

There was a pause, and then he heard her take in a deep painful-sounding breath. "Um, well, okay. Ben Franklin walks into a pub . . ."

Ty lifted his head. "You went with the joke?" he asked, chuckling.

"Ah, you've heard it then. I thought perhaps that one hadn't made it out to the territories yet."

The territories?

"But I suppose jokes travel as fast as the Express."

The Express? As in Federal?

"Nope," he said, "haven't heard that one. So old Ben walks into a pub. Strange, seems to me I learned in history that he pretty much lived in pubs."

She laughed softly, but it got cut short by a low moan. "My . . . head."

"Posse's on its way, Ms. Prescott."

"Posse? But . . . but, I'm not a criminal, sir! I know the sheriff said so, but it's not true. I just came to take possession of property that is rightfully mine."

Ty sat back on his haunches. "Property?"

She either didn't hear him or was on a tear and decided to ignore him. "I thought I was inheriting a ranch. I mean a real ranch. Cows and chickens and land. Imagine my horror. A bawdy house! Of course, knowing my father, I suppose I shouldn't be surprised. Still, I was looking forward to that ranch . . ." she trailed off. Ty's head was spinning. This woman was either batty as hell or had sustained one helluva whack to the noggin.

Senior Deputy Jinx Davis, Ty's best friend since they shared space in the Med Center's nursery thirty-two years ago, came racing from around the mansion, bolt-cutter cradled in his arm like a long football. Which of course made sense. Jinx should have been a pro football player. He was even drafted in the first round out of college. Only a body dropped from a hotel room seven floors above and landing right on top of him changed his plans drastically.

"What the hell?" Jinx asked, as he stopped short in front of Ty. "And get that damn light out of my face."

"Someone locked a lady up," Ty said, nabbing the cutters from Jinx. He knocked on the door again. "You still with me, Mags?"

"If you're speaking to me," a scarily weak voice answered, "I'm not you're darling and I'm not Mags. Well, Maggie, if you must. Miss Prescott would be preferable."

Jinx turned to Ty and raised his eyebrows. "Well, la-freaking-da!"

"Definitely a little uptight," Ty said in a loud voice as he worked the lock. "Aren't you, *Miss Prescott*?"

The only sound greeting him was a ladylike sniff.

It took longer than he liked, and she'd gone totally silent by the time the lock snapped. He shucked it and pulled open the door, shining his light on the lump on the gritty ground.

They both stared at the woman passed out dead and then back at each other.

"She's wearing petticoats," Jinx said.

"I see that. And how the hell would you know what a petticoat is?"

"I pride myself in knowing all about female fashion."

"Since when did petticoats come back into fashion?"

"They didn't," Jinx said as they both stared down at the unconscious woman.

"Holy shit," they whispered in perfect unison.

❈   ❈   ❈

"Okay, Fannie, tell me right now what's going on around here."

"You tell me, cowboy," Fannie Mae said. "You just cost me a night's worth of business. What with all those sirens blaring up to my place. You'd think the Rooster was on fire or something."

"Who beat the hell out of your new girl and then locked her in the shed out back?"

"New girl? What new girl?"

"Little school marm? Calls herself Margaret Prescott? Pretty? Blonde? Except for the red covering her head from all the blood."

Fannie stared up at Ty in shock, which was a brand-new look for Fannie. He'd never seen *anything* faze her. She was four feet nothing and skinny as a stick, but he'd lay odds on her anytime against anyone. Including himself.

Her real name was Stella Pruce, but she'd recently taken on the moniker of Fannie Mae because she figured she took clients' money, made sure they were screwed, then kicked them out.

"Ty, I'm sure I don't know what the hell you're talking about. I haven't taken on a new girl in months. And the school marm thing just doesn't attract that many of . . . my friends."

"She looks like she walked straight out of *Little House on the Prairie*."

Fannie shrugged. "I'm sure I don't know who she is, and I'm sure I don't know who locked her in my shed. I take it there were no signs of Lester?"

"Lester? Lester Pipps? *That's* who your missing 'friend' is?"

"That's privileged information, sonny, so keep your trap shut."

Oh, he'd keep his trap shut all right. Especially for Lester, who up until right now had been his dentist. "No sign of Lester. Maybe he got lost in one of your secret passageways."

"You know, that's a possibil—hold it, how did you know about the secret passageways? You haven't come farther into this house than the foyer in your entire life."

"Rumors," he said, not wanting to tell her the truth. That his father had told him all about the place when he tried to bring Ty here for his sixteenth birthday.

She looked him up and down. "You're looking a little disheveled, sweetmeat."

He knew that. Once over the shock of the sight of the woman all dressed up in old west attire, he'd fallen to his knees, making sure Margaret still had a pulse. And then checked her for injuries. Other than dust smudges all over her forehead and cheeks, he'd only found one problem. A bad and bleeding abrasion to the back of her head. Someone had whacked Miss Margaret but good.

"Fannie, *someone* assaulted a woman and locked her in your shed out back."

"I swear I know nothin' about it, Ty. And I know *everything* that goes on around here."

"Anything unusual happen tonight? Other than Lester going missing?"

"Every night is unusual. It's why I love this joint. But this kind of thing," she said, putting a fist to her temple, "does not happen at my establishment. You *know* I'm clean and a straight shooter."

"That I do, Fannie. But something bad happened here. I'm going to need to talk to all of your people working tonight."

"Fine."

"And a list of all the clients—"

"Not a chance in Hades, Sheriff," she said, straightening to almost four-one.

"I can get a warrant before you can say 'French maid or baby doll?'"

"And I can lose my accounting files before you can say 'Please Fannie, let me keep at least one testicle.'"

If Ty wasn't so upset for that pretty blonde, he'd probably chuckle. He was not in a chuckling mood.

"She claims that 'the sheriff' was the one who locked her in the shed. I don't take kindly to anyone imitating a law enforcement officer, Fannie. Especially a woman beater. Have any friends with a cops and robbers fetish?"

"A couple of inquiries. I always send them over to Lacie in Reno. There's just not enough interest to devote a room to that one."

"Do you keep an old-time sheriff uniform around? An all-black one?"

"Yes," she said slowly. "But it's not for customer use. It's hung behind the bar in the Founders room. Framed and under glass. But I was just in there having my nightly constitution. And it was there, untouched." Suddenly she laughed. "Matter of fact, Ty, it belonged to one of your great-grandpappies. Jesse Coltraine. He was the one who took over possession of the Rooster in the early days. Then sold it off to a private concern."

Great. Another stellar point in his family's history.

"I don't see much funny here, Fannie. Don't you care that someone assaulted a woman on your premises?" he asked softly. He knew he was playing the ace card, because one thing Fannie would never abide was physical harm to anyone in her domain.

She wilted back down to four feet nothing. "Is she going to be all right?"

"Seems like a fighter to me. I think Miss Prescott will be okay. Jinx says Doc Sanchez came right away."

Fannie gave him a weird look. "Prescott? Her name is Prescott?"

"So she said before she passed out. Why?"

"The Rooster was opened by a Prescott. James Prescott. When he passed in 1850, he left the place to his daughter. But she disappeared within hours of arriving to stake her claim. At least that's the legend. And that's when Jesse Coltraine took over the property."

Ty got a very strange, hot sensation in his stomach. "Do you know the daughter's name?"

Fannie stared up at him. "Yep. It was Margaret. Margaret Prescott."

Ty swallowed. "Fannie, as strange as it sounds, looks like Miss Margaret just returned to Little Fork."

Two

Maggie knew she was in a very strange dream. But something of a wonderful one at that. She'd never seen all the doodads this dream had before, a bunch of whirring things and tube things and needle things. But for some reason she didn't care so much. After so many months of crossing the continent in that horrendous coach, and then minutes or even hours of being locked up in that awful shed, she was finally warm and comfortable. Even though she'd been poked and prodded in this dream like some kind of pin cushion.

Everything in her dream looked clean as her mama's linens. And very, very strange. In a most fascinating way.

This needle in her arm for instance. It was attached to a long tube that led up to a big bag of something liquid that the nurse had said the doctor ordered.

"Miss Prescott?" a man's voice said.

"Hmmm?" she said, knowing the very last thing she should be dreaming about was a man in her room. *So what?* It was her dream and she was sticking to it.

After all, everything else was so odd. Her doctor was a

woman! Imagine that. And a Mexican to boot. Her mother would be so proud.

"Ms. Prescott?"

Okay, that voice was real. Unfortunately, her dream seemed to be over.

She squinched one eye open, then the other. Standing beside her bed was about the best-looking Negro man she'd ever laid eyes on. Okay, not only a man in her room, but a black man at that. What a scandal this would cause back home. Apparently not so much here, seeing that Dr. Sanchez was standing beside him, smiling. "Am I still dreaming?" she asked.

The exotic, pretty woman laughed softly. "No, I think you're quite awake. Ms. Prescott," the dream doctor said. "This is Deputy Jinx Davis."

Maggie's gaze slid back to the man. "Deputy?"

"You can call me Jinx," he said, flashing a smile that could melt Philadelphia snow. He had a badge on his shirt, which made her shudder. But he was nothing like the brute of her nightmare. He wore beige-colored, neatly pressed pants with a matching beige shirt that, the sleeves of which he had folded up to right below his elbows. And his face was kind. And somewhat dizzying.

"Deputy Davis?"

"Jinx," he said.

"You're a free man then, Jinx?" she asked, feeling suddenly shy.

He winked at her. He actually winked! "No woman's been able to shackle me yet. Why? You want to try?"

"Certainly not!" she said. "I don't believe in that barbaric practice."

The doctor and the deputy glanced at each other. Maggie wondered what she'd just said that warranted such a reaction.

The deputy pulled up a chair and sat down. "If you don't mind, I need to ask you some questions, Miss . . . oh, hell, may I just call you Margaret? Formality's not my thing."

"Nor mine, Deputy. I mean Jinx. I'm Margaret." She pulled

the covers up closer to her chin, because it was obvious she was in some kind of strange sleeping garment and not her traveling clothes. "Maggie, actually."

"That's good," he said, smiling again. "Because Ms. Prescott is a mouthful."

That was about the third time she'd been called a Mizz. Probably a regionalism. "What questions do you have for me, Jinx?"

The doctor put up a hand. "I have some other patients to be looking in on. I'll be back to check on you later, Maggie. Is that all right with you?"

"Yes ma'am."

The doctor laughed. "It's Sonia."

And with that, the doctor left her alone in her bedroom with a man. Forward thinking, indeed. She didn't think even her mother would approve of this. But she felt strangely comfortable. The deputy had warm eyes. Unlike that green-eyed monster who'd dragged her from her rightful home and into a shed. "I don't know what more I can tell you, Jinx. I . . . already told that other man everything I knew."

He pulled out a strange little notebook and a writing utensil unlike any she'd seen. "First, how's your head feelin'?"

Her hand went to her head, and she felt the scratchy cloth wrapped around it. "It doesn't seem to hurt at all. As a matter of fact, nothing seems to hurt. I feel kind of . . . like I'm in a very strange dream." She eyed him. "You aren't a dream, are you?"

"I've been called a dream once or twice," he answered, grinning again. "But not tonight. Tonight I'm on business. And I'll try not to keep you too long, okay?"

"Yes, certainly. I have so many questions of my own. But too confused at the moment to make sense of any answers you might provide."

"Plenty of time for that." He pulled the chair even closer to her strange bedside. It had metal bars on it. And buttons with strange symbols on the sides. "Ty tells me you said a sheriff was the one to toss you in that shed. And was probably the one who whacked you, too. Is that what you're say-ing?"

"That's right."

"Did he identify himself as the sheriff of Little Fork?"

"He did indeed."

"Is it possible that he was just playing one of Fannie's games at the Rooster?"

"That's the second time someone has mentioned a Fannie. I've never met a Fannie here. And I'm sorry, but I don't know what you mean by games. He wasn't playing a game when he dragged me from the house. Or if he was, it was a horrible one."

"Did he assault you?"

Maggie laughed, even if this was no laughing matter, and laughing hurt like the devil. "Deputy, is this bandage wrapped around my head not proof enough? Do you think I did this to myself?"

"I mean sexual assault, Maggie."

Her mouth dropped open. "Sexual assault? You mean, did he force unwanted attentions on me?"

"Yes, that's what I mean."

She laughed again. "Oh, Jinx, that's so silly. I mean, look at me. Who would want to do that to me?"

He sat back in his chair. "Just about any sick bastard around, that's who. Other than that god-awful outfit you were wearing—"

"It was my traveling gown! And I'd come a very long way, sir. And I'll have you know I sewed it myself."

His lips quirked. "Sorry, no insult intended. Are you with a historical wild west traveling troupe or something?"

Correction, her head was beginning to pound. It was like they were talking two different languages. "I was traveling alone. I came to claim my inheritance."

"Which is what?"

"The Rooster Ranch, just as I told the other man."

"The Rooster Ranch is owned by Fannie Mae Tipwell, Maggie. As it has been for as long as I've been alive, and then some."

She shook her head, then immediately regretted it. "No. My father left it to me. I have the papers right here." She looked around for her clothes. And then it hit her. She sure as Hades hadn't undressed herself. And the papers had been tucked in her garter. "Where are my belongings? There are papers. I swear. Legal papers."

Jinx's brown eyes probed hers. "Okay, we'll deal with that later. Right now I'm more interested in catching the person who did this to you. This is real important, Maggie. What did this man look like?"

"Hi, folks, how's our patient?"

They both turned to the doorway of the room and Maggie's head swam. She pressed one hand to her temple and pointed a shaking finger with the other. "There's your man, Deputy. It's him. Shoot him."

* * *

Jinx had to physically force Ty into the hallway outside of Maggie's room. Which wasn't easy. Ty had two inches and probably ten pounds on him. And Ty had something else. Outrage.

"Hold on, hold on, hold on, buddy! Chill. Let's talk."

"I never hurt that girl, Jinx! I *found* her, for chrissakes!"

"'Course not, Ty*ler,*" Jinx said, dragging his bud down the hallway. "There's things you need to know. But not right by her door, okay? Settle your fucking ass down."

Ty stopped fighting him. "Someone is playing a colossal joke on me, J. And I'm pissed off."

"My thinkin' exactly. But let's talk this out. How about some of the dee-lightful coffee they have in those vending machines?"

"It just gets better and better," Ty muttered.

* * *

Ty sat down on one of those plastic chairs in the vending area, holding the disposable coffee cup in his hands. "What the hell is going on, J.?" he asked. "She looked at me like I was the devil."

It bothered him more than he could say. Even with the gauze wrapped around her head, Margaret Prescott was beautiful. And touched him in a way he couldn't explain. Unconscious, she'd been so helpless and needing her Sir Lancelot. In the hospital bed he'd watched her for a few seconds, and she seemed confused and yet enjoying herself. And then she'd taken one look at him and nothing but terror had filled her big brown eyes.

"Ty, she's a very strange duck," Jinx said.

"How so?"

"I'll let Doc fill you in," Jinx said. "I'm not sure you'd believe me if I told you."

"Oh, goody," Ty said. "Where is she?"

"Right here, Ty," Doc Sanchez said. He hadn't even heard or noticed her walking down the hallway, which just went to prove he was off his game. She was a beautiful woman, with hair as dark as his, but long. As usual, she had it up in a bun as she always did in the hospital. When she'd come to town a few years back, they'd dated for almost three months. But by mutual and happy consent, they'd decided they made better friends than lovers. And as far as he was concerned, she was the best doctor LF Med had. Which is why he'd been very happy when he'd learned she was on call tonight.

"So what's the news, doc?" he asked, standing.

"Sit down, Ty. I don't want you falling over like a big old oak."

"She's not dying, is she?" he asked, dropping back into his chair. The thought of that poor girl expiring made his stomach do somersaults. Especially while she still believed he was the one who'd assaulted her.

Sonia laughed. "No, although why not is something of a mystery."

"The wound was that bad? She lost too much blood? What?"

"Nope, other than needing a transfusion and fluids, she's completely healthy. All of the tests—CAT scan, MRI, X-rays—show her brain is perfectly normal. Sort of."

"Sort of?"

"Either she's confused from the head injury, or we've just entered *The Twilight Zone*."

Ty was getting frustrated. "Spit it out, Sonia!"

"I asked her the usual questions. Her answers were a little strange."

"Such as?"

"Such as I asked her what year it was. She told me it was 1850."

"Okay, she was in costume. Maybe she was still playing a role."

"I don't think so. I asked her who the president was, and she told me it was, of course, Zachary Taylor."

"Oh boy. Was Zachary Taylor the president in 1850?"

"Did you flunk history, or what? Yes, he was the president. Until he died in July of that year. So in her mind she's living during Taylor's presidency."

"That whack on the head did a real number on her," Ty said. "Right? She's an actress and is still working her role?"

Sonia shook her head.

"There's more," Jinx said.

"I asked her what her birthday was, and she told me it was May seventh. A week from now. So she has her days right."

"But . . . ?" Ty asked, dreading the *but*.

"She says she was born in 1828."

Ty swallowed. "Well, she's aged well."

"She has indeed. Every single part of her confirms that she's what she thinks she is. Twenty-two years old."

"She has to be faking something."

"If you say so," Sonia said. "But when Danie and I undressed her, I found these on her garter belt. A garter belt, Ty! No woman in her right mind would be wearing one unless they were working for Fannie. Look!"

Ty stared at the papers Sonia handed him. A copy of a will of a James Prescott, and the deed to Prescott's ranch. The Rooster Ranch.

"Holy shit, right?" Sonia said.

Ty and Jinx looked at each other. "Holy shit," they said in unison.

* * *

Ty wasn't allowed to see Margaret the rest of the night. So he spent it looking for Lester, which was a waste of time. Lester had come face-to-face with his wife having a good old time with someone in the Bo Peep room, and had been so upset, he'd fainted in the back elevator. Since Lester's wife was Ty's accountant, Ty was figuring he now needed two new professionals, one for his teeth and one for his taxes. Make that three, since he also apparently needed a lawyer.

Finally the doc gave him the go-ahead to visit Miss Margaret at noon the next day. As Sonia said, her brain was just peachy.

Except she kept insisting that Ty was her attacker.

And she thought she was born in the nineteenth century.

And he was beginning to believe it. Which pretty much meant that he was probably the one who needed that CAT scan.

He felt a little strange as he approached the room. He was damn sure he was mad at her for fingering him for something he was obviously innocent of doing, but he was also sure she'd been attacked by someone who she thought looked like him. He hated the thought of upsetting her.

So he brought a nurse, Louise Ledbetter, along with him.

Louise went in and fussed over her, then said, "I have someone who needs to talk to you, Margaret. I'll stay here a few seconds, okay? But I do need to make med rounds shortly."

"It appears the entire continent has been in to see me. What's one more?"

"How about me?" Ty said.

"You!" she breathed, sitting up straighter in her bed. "I thought Deputy Jinx shot you!"

"You *hoped* he shot me. Unfortunately for you, he works for me. Wouldn't have looked good on his resume."

"His . . . what?"

Damn, she was so pretty. And damn, so scared of him.

He looked back at the nurse. "Louise, would you ever allow me to harm your patient in any way, shape, or form?"

"I'd shoot you first, Sheriff."

Ty looked back at Maggie. "See? You're safe."

"I'd feel safer if she'd just go ahead and shoot you."

"You're a bloodthirsty little thing, aren't you?"

"And you are an awful brute."

"Of course I am. I only saved your life. For which you have yet to thank me."

"Thank you! I'll be my mother's uncle before you get a—"

"Margaret, I need to make my rounds with other patients," Louise said. "Do you want me to make him leave?"

"I want you to shoot him."

"Since I can't do that, would you like him to leave?"

Margaret glared at him for several seconds, then said, "No. I'll kill him myself."

Louise backed out slowly, looking back and forth between them like they were aliens. Which one of them just might be.

"How comforting to know," Ty said. "And I'm shaking in my Nikes, you tiny little wimp."

She apparently took offense. Her face went beet red and she made fists. "I will see you in jail before I leave here."

"Possibly, but you'll be the one behind bars for fraud."

Her anger died. "Fraud? What are you saying?"

Ty felt like a total shit. So he switched gears. "By the way, you never finished your joke. Ben Franklin walks into a bar . . ."

She stared at him. "That was you? At the shed? Why did you hit me and then help me? It makes no sense. Just like none of this makes sense. Everything here makes no sense. Sir, what is going on? Fraud? What kind of fraud?"

"Maggie, darlin', you tell me."

She opened her mouth, but he stopped her with a hand. "I know, I know, don't call you darlin'. I'm still calling you Maggie, though, so get used to it. So tell me, pretty Maggie, why have you come to my town? And why are you accusing me of something I absolutely didn't, and could not have done? I was at Barby's Blue Moon watching the Rockets game right about the time you were assaulted. I have at least twenty witnesses."

Shaking her head, she said, "Once again, I don't understand most of what you're saying. But I understand accusation and I understand alibi, but I saw what I saw."

"It wasn't me, Maggie. You have to believe that. I've never hurt a woman in my life. And I sure as hell wouldn't hurt someone as pretty as you are."

She gave a short snort. "Do not even try to appease me with false flattery, *Sheriff*."

"It's Tyler. People call me Ty, though."

"Among other things, I imagine."

The quirk in her lips was heartening, even if she was trying to insult him. It meant progress. "Ty Coltraine. Sheriff of Little Fork. And I don't fake anything."

She cocked her head a little. "That's not what you said your name was when you met me at the Rooster."

"What did this imposter say his name was?"

"Imposter, maybe, but you are the spittin' image."

"Another conundrum."

"When *you* met me inside you said your name was Jesse."

Ty tried to keep the shock from showing on his face. But his heart was thumping something fierce. "Since my name isn't Jesse, and I don't have a twin named Jesse, then it wasn't me. But Jesus . . ."

"Jesse, not Jesus. And don't try to call on Him now. Your goose is cooked, Jesse."

"Ty. My name is Ty."

She held her arms around her shaking body. "I might be in a very strange dream that I can't seem to get out of. I mean, a TV? With moving pictures? What in Hades is that all about?" She seemed to shore up a bit and get her courage back up and running. "But when I get out of this dream, you are going to be burnt bread, mister lovely looking Sheriff." She started punching the call button.

Louise came running into the room, puffing. "What's wrong?"

"Arrest this man!"

Ty sighed. "Louise, what's my name?"

Louise glanced worriedly back and forth between law enforcement and out-of-her-mind patient. "Sheriff Coltraine."

"Hah!" Maggie said, then held a hand to her head.

"What's my first name, Louise?" Ty said, just about seeing why his imposter bonked Miss Prissy Prescott.

"Ty," Louise said.

"Not Jesse, right?" Ty barked.

"No . . . although I don't know your middle name."

"And no one ever will," he said, completely irritated now, no matter how pretty the patient who *he'd saved* was. "But it sure as hell isn't Jesse."

"Do you need anything?" Louise asked glancing back and forth between the two of them.

"A bottle of whiskey," Ty said.

"Make that two," Maggie said.

"I'll look into it," Louise said. And then ran from the room.

*   *   *

"Maggie, look at me closely," Ty said. "Do I really look *exactly* like your attacker?"

Maggie took her time, because looking him over was no hardship. As it hadn't been the first time she'd laid eyes on him back at her father's ranch. Well, brothel.

He had the most amazing green eyes. They were hard to forget. His hair was the same gleaming black, but cut much shorter than before. The strong cheekbones were the same, the lips just as hard, and of course there was that dimple in his chin.

"You're sure you don't have a twin?" she asked, for some stupid reason wanting to believe that he was, indeed, innocent.

"No twin."

"An older brother, perhaps?"

"A younger sister in California. No brothers."

"Well, then this imposter did a mighty fine job, Sheriff."

"My name's Ty. Now look closer."

With pleasure. She didn't know why she believed him, but she did. Or she wanted to. Or she was out of her mind.

"Well, your hair is much shorter. When was the last time you've been to a barber?"

"Two weeks ago. And my 'barber' is my mother. She can verify this. What else?"

"You . . . look a little younger than you did yesterday. I would have guessed your age at late thirties if someone had asked. Now you appear to be more like thirty."

"Thirty-two. What else?"

Maggie opened her mouth, then shut it again and looked away.

"What else, Miss Prescott?"

"My students call me Miss Prescott. You're welcome to call me Maggie, seeing as you already took that liberty."

She snuck a peek at him, and the smile on his face was fairly breathtaking. Her heart started drumming even more than her aching head.

"I appreciate that, Maggie. I'm honored. Please help me some more. I want to find the man that did this to you."

"Well, your teeth are much whiter. And . . . and your smile is different. It's nice. You don't smell like a spittoon. And, really, your eyes are kind. His weren't."

"Beginning to believe I'm not the bad guy, Maggie?"

"Grudgingly."

He chuckled, and that pretty much changed Maggie's mind. His chuckle was nothing like the mean man's chuckle. It was warm and rich. The mean man's laugh was . . . evil. She shuddered at the memory.

"Maggie?"

He cupped her chin and gently turned her face toward his. Their eyes met, and just seeing the concern in his was her undoing. "I'm so confused," she whispered. "Everything, *everything* is so different here."

"Different how?"

She took a deep breath. "When I arrived, all was as I'd

expected. Rugged. Wild. But I look around now and things are so strange in here. Your medical facilities are so much more advanced than even Philadelphia. And we have always prided ourselves on being ahead of other cities. How does no one know what is happening in the territories?"

He pulled up a chair. "What's different here?"

"Look around! That TV thing! What is that all about? Who are all of those people and how do you get them in that little box? By the way, I'm especially taken with those people on something called *Days of Our Lives*. But, oh, my Loosie, the clothes those women wear! And what are those little metal things they use to talk to people who aren't even there?"

He pulled out his little metal thing. "Like this?"

"Yes, what are those?"

"Cell phones."

"See? I have no idea what those are." She gestured around her. "All of these new-fangled boxes that beep at you. You seem to be so far ahead of us Easterners."

"You have no idea."

"Excuse me?"

He took her hand. "Maggie, something very weird is going on here. If my theory's correct, prepare for a little shock."

Maggie put her free hand to her heart. "How much of a shock?"

He hesitated. "About sixteen decades worth."

"Excuse me?" she said again.

"What year do you think this is?"

She frowned. "What year do *you* think it is? Why is everyone asking me about years and presidents and birthdays?"

"How old are you, Maggie?"

"Where I come from, that's an insulting question, Sheriff. A gentleman *never* asks a lady her age."

"You're really cute when you frown, Maggie. Glaring, not so much. I apologize. But thank you for even calling me a gentleman. Never been called one before."

"My shock at *that* news is overwhelming."

* * *

Okay, he was falling for her. There wasn't a good reason on God's green earth, but there you had it. He was falling for a smartass nutcase.

Ty loved women. But he'd never loved *a* woman. Other than his crush on his teacher when he was a kid, there'd never been a single girl who made his heart go bang. Lower parts went bang a lot, but never in his heart or his head.

Suddenly, his heart was pounding in a way he'd never felt before. It was sort of uncomfortable, and wildly exciting.

And it was the most stupid thing he could possibly imagine. Why her? Why now? Why so hard? It made absolutely no sense. None of this made sense.

Ty shook his head. "I'm guessing you're about twenty-two," he said.

"So why are you asking me? You've obviously been speaking to the doctor."

"I have. I just wanted to hear it from you."

"Yes, I'm twenty-two," she said, looking exasperated. "I'm unmarried because I'm not marriageable. I haven't been happy, as much as I love to teach children. I wanted to find a new life, a new dream. So when I learned the news that my father had left me a ranch out west, I thought my hopes and dreams had come true. Instead I've landed into a nightmare. Happy now?"

Ty's pounding heart dropped straight to his toes. "No, Maggie, that doesn't make me happy. Who the hell told you that you're unmarriageable?"

She looked away, out the window. "No one needed to tell me. A spinster knows these things."

"A *spinster?* At twenty-two? Around these parts that seems almost too young for marriage."

She glanced back at him, her whiskey-colored eyes wide. "Is that true? Or are you humoring me . . . Ty?"

"Cross my heart," he said, making the gesture.

She watched him for a second. "What was that?"

"You've never heard the phrase, 'cross my heart and hope to die, stick a needle in my eye'?"

She pursed her lips for a moment, then obviously couldn't help it and burst out laughing. Her laughter was light, sweet, and genuine. "That's silly. Why would you hope to die? Or stick a needle in your eye?"

Ty couldn't help it; he grinned, too. "I think it's a children's saying. It just means that someone is very sincere about what they're saying."

"Oh, I see," she said, her lips still twitching. "So are you married, Ty? Seeing as we've become familiar enough at this point to be rude and nosy."

She was taking to this nosy notion rather quickly. "Nope."

"Do you have a sweetheart?"

"Yep, her name is Josie."

"Oh."

She glanced out the window and he realized her profile was just as pretty as her face straight on. And with her head bandaged, her long lashes, cheeks, nose, and stubborn-looking chin were all the more pronounced. And her lips were a man's dream. He didn't know if it was wishful thinking, but she looked disappointed.

"Josie and I have been together for four years," he continued. "Ever since I rescued her as a puppy."

She turned back to look at him and once again wishful thinking had him seeing happiness where it probably didn't exist. "Your sweetheart is a puppy?"

"Well, she's four, so technically not, but she hasn't seemed to have read the memo yet."

She smiled. "What kind of dog?"

"Heinz 57."

"What?"

"She's a mutt. I have no idea. But she's big and shaggy and her favorite food in the world is hot dogs."

"Hot dogs? You mean she—"

"No," he said quickly, wanting to kick himself for forgetting she was still in this 1850 amnesia fog. "Hot dogs are a kind of sausage. Not one real dog is harmed in the making of this product."

"Oh! Do people eat them, too?"

"Are you kidding, they are the staple of foot—err, sporting events."

"I would like to try one sometime."

"I'll make dang sure that you do." He took her hand again. "You know, maybe you can still find that dream you came out here looking for."

"How would that be, Sheriff?"

"Ty."

"How would that be, Ty?"

He took a breath. A deep, deep breath. "By recognizing you're not just in a different place, but also in a different time."

"Excuse me?"

"Maggie, do you honestly believe it's 1850?"

"Of course. What do you believe?"

"Take a deep breath, sweetheart."

She began to protest but then just huffed and sucked in a deep breath. She blew it out slowly and then said, "Okay, I'm ready. What should I believe?"

"That it's the year 2010."

Three

Maggie's laughter was adorable. Or possibly hysterical. Ty wasn't sure which.

"Two thousand and ten what?" she asked. "Bottles of beer on the wall?"

"I don't know how, I don't know why, Maggie, but this is definitely not 1850. This is the year 2010."

"You . . . you people are playing with my mind."

"Or you're playing with ours."

"You're a twit."

"And you're batty. Do you think we made up all of these gadgets to make a fool of you?"

She looked around. "I don't feel so well."

"I don't blame you. You're like a zillion years old if you really believe what you're saying. None of us know what to think."

Her eyes filled with tears. "You don't believe me?"

Ty stood over her and grabbed her shoulders. "We believe you. I want to believe you. But nothing you're telling us makes any sense, either."

She stared into his eyes. "Which one of us is right, Sheriff?"

He shook his head. "The strange thing is, Maggie, I think we both are."

"How is that possible?"

He let go of her, because she felt too good under his fingers. Sitting down, he kneaded his forehead. "You know how you said your attacker was named Jesse?"

She shuddered. "Yes."

"My great-great-great-grandfather's name was Jesse. Jesse Coltraine. And he was the Sheriff of Little Fork—"

"—in 1850," she finished for him.

"Yes. The man who attacked you died about one hundred and thirty-five years ago."

"So I've been locked in that shed for sixteen decades?"

"So it would seem."

"I've aged fairly well, then."

"So we've all noticed."

She swallowed and was silent for several long seconds. Finally she looked up at him. "Do you know the last thing my mother said to me, before she disappeared?"

"What, Maggie?"

"She said, 'Maggie you're going to go far.'"

"She sure was right about that one."

Her laughter was shaky. "I don't think this is what she meant. She was hoping I'd live to see the day when a woman had the right to vote. Do women have the right to vote now?"

"Not only allowed, last election," he said, showing less than an inch between his thumb and forefinger, "we came this close to electing a woman president."

Her mouth dropped open, and then she did something he totally did not expect. She started laughing, and then looked up at the ceiling. "Wish you were here, Mama."

* * *

"Dr. Sanchez says I'm free to go," Maggie told Ty the next morning.

"That's terrific!"

"Yes, terrific," she said, looking like someone had just kicked her puppy.

Ty pulled up a chair and sat down. "What's wrong?"

"You're kidding, right?"

"Umm . . . no. Most people are thrilled to get out of the hospital."

"Well, most people don't wake up in a strange world with no place to go and no money to buy clothes that closely resemble the ones people on the TV wear," she said, waving vaguely toward the set that appeared to be tuned in to *Dr. Phil*.

"Oh . . . of course. I hadn't thought of that."

"Are you positive my money's worthless?"

"Well, you might be able to get a good price for it on eBay," he said. And before she could say, "What in Hades is eBay?" he held up a hand. "I'll teach you that later."

Her eyes filled with tears. "I'm frightened."

He felt gut-punched and moved to her, sitting down on the edge of her bed and taking her shoulders. "Who wouldn't be? If I were in your situation, I'd be terrified. But honey, we'll figure it out."

"Where am I going to go?"

He grabbed a tissue from the bed stand and wiped her tears as gently as he could. "Well, let's see. I'm pretty sure you wouldn't agree to bunk down at my place."

She smiled briefly. "You'd be correct, cowboy."

"Josie will be there to chaperone."

"Josie's a puppy.

"Adult dog. Very responsible."

"Who didn't get the memo about growing up."

"Do you remember *everything* people tell you?"

"Of course. If it's interesting enough to pay attention."

"Josie will love you."

"Probably, because I love animals. But I'm certain that Josie is very much loyal to her daddy. She'll either eat me or turn me over to you on a platter."

He couldn't help but grin, even if disappointment was stabbing at him. He'd really hoped she'd take his offer to stay with him. "You're an amazingly resilient woman, Mags. And you're going to find a way to get through this. But whether you like it or not, for right now, you need to accept help."

In the couple of days she'd been here, he'd witnessed her soaking up everything around her, including some of the lingo. She was a little sponge and it was quite a sight, not to mention tiring, to be around her as she questioned everything and tried to reconcile it with all she'd known.

Dr. Pendergrass, their local shrink, had come to see her the night before and had left, shaking his head. His analysis was that she truly believed everything she was saying, that she gave details of her life in Philly that even the most astute historian wouldn't know. The doc was as mystified as everyone else who'd come in contact with her. And just as taken with her. Which was sort of irritating.

He'd been thinking a lot the last couple of nights about just what he was feeling for her. And why. It wasn't just her beauty, although he'd be lying to himself if he didn't consider that a huge plus. It was more like she was a puzzle. And every piece of her attracted him. Her unquenchable thirst for knowledge. Her brutal honesty. And if what she was telling him was the truth, her courage in traveling to the "territories" to forge a new life for herself. That had to be one bold move for a woman in the mid-nineteenth century.

And now her vulnerability. She was alone, penniless, in a strange new world. She needed him, whether she liked it or not. And he needed her. Whether he liked it or not. Or understood it.

"I'm guessing that bedding down at the Rooster wouldn't be acceptable, either," Ty said.

"Yes. Very kind of her to offer," Maggie said, "But I think not."

"Fannie's been here to see you?"

"Oh, yes. She's . . . quite unique. But very nice. And she was so concerned that someone had hurt me on her property."

"Which might still be your property, too. We'll talk to Neil Douglas. He's the property lawyer in town."

"There's no way I'm taking the Rooster from her, Ty. What happened was not her fault. And obviously happened a year or two before she was born." She smiled behind her sniffles. "Sorry, that wasn't kind. She's adorable."

Ty felt himself falling even more. "True, but I still think we need to straighten matters out about that."

"Want to hear something funny?" she asked, but didn't wait for an answer. "Except for the blonde hair, she looked almost exactly like Misty."

"Who's Misty?"

"The woman who was . . . managing the Rooster when I first arrived. She was also tiny, up in her years, and wore lots of that easy, breezy beautiful makeup stuff."

"Too much TV, Maggie."

"I don't think so. It's all so fascinating. Do you know there's this tiny little green lizard animal who talks and sells insurance?"

"Maggie . . ."

"And I discovered a news channel. And you're right, it's the year of our Lord, 2010."

"You mean you didn't believe me?"

"Let's just say I like independent verification."

Ty was a little insulted but shrugged it off. After all, if he'd been knocked in the head and then told that it was the year 1850, he'd want more than one person saying so.

He also knew she was stalling, scared to death, probably. But they needed to decide on her next move. "If you refuse to stay with me," he said, "you're refusing, right?"

"With some regret, because I love dogs, yes."

"Fine," he said, and sounded disappointed even to himself. "Then we have a couple of nice hotels in town, but they're all casinos, and I'm not sure you're ready for that yet."

"I've seen betting houses before."

"Not like these, you haven't, darlin'. Trust me, you're not ready."

She took the tissue from his hand and wrung it, staring down at her hands. "I do."

"You do what? Feel you're ready?"

"No, not that. I'm probably barmy, but I do. Trust you."

Ty cleared his throat to get the choky feeling out of it. "I'm glad."

"Don't go thinking it's because of your charm or anything," she added.

"Oh, I'd never presume such a thing, ma'am."

"And don't call me ma'am," she snapped. "I'm not *that* old."

"Well, if we did the math—"

"No math!"

"Then if I can't call you ma'am, I'm heading right back to darlin'."

"Seems I couldn't stop you if I tried."

"You have tried. Darlin' is a term of endearment."

She huffed. "I said I trust you, not that I find you endearing."

He sure preferred the spark of annoyance in those big brown eyes over fear. "I'm pretty sure most women find me endearing."

"As *if*."

He stared at her for a couple of seconds before bursting out laughing. "Where'd you learn that one?"

"Last night. A moovee channel. It was actually quite funny."

"You are amazing, Ms. Prescott."

She pointed at him. "I now know what Mizz means, too! It denotes a woman who might or might not be married and doesn't consider her marital status anyone's business. Correct?"

"Correct. I still prefer darlin'."

"I'm sort of getting used to it."

And he was getting used to her. Quirky, weird, whatever. She was so cute and wacky and beautiful. "Anyway, back to the trust thing. You're sure? You realize I'm not the bad guy?" He *so* did not want to be the bad guy in her mind.

She waved her hands in the air. "It's just that everyone I've met here seems to think you're trustworthy, so I'm taking *their* word for it."

"But not mine?"

"You . . . look too much like the bad guy. But I'm going to be down with that. He wasn't you."

She apparently had been watching MTV, too. "I'm so glad you're *down with that*. Because it sure as hell wasn't me." He stood up trying to think. "And I'm taking care of you, sweetheart."

"Why can't you just call me Maggie? Do you hate my name? Or are you just trying to insult me?"

Ty plopped his hands on his hips. "I don't know. Maybe because Maggie's so personal. It's your name."

"More personal than darlin' or sweetheart?"

"Those are the overall kind. Those are the 'I think you're really pretty' kind."

"Oh, really? Ya think?"

Ty reached over and grabbed the remote control, clicking the power button. "You are watching *way* too much TV, Maggie."

"There you go. You managed to call me by my name. Was that so hard? Oprah says—"

"Maggie . . ." he growled.

"I don't want to go, Ty," she said softly. "Where am I going to go?"

Ty didn't know. He had a couple of ex-girlfriends who might take her in, but he was a little afraid of what they'd tell her. Not that he'd been a *bad* boyfriend, just not real attentive. He had a tendency to forget about them for days or weeks at a time as other things occupied his mind. No, he didn't think he'd want to let her get an earful from any of them.

And then it struck him. He snapped his fingers. "Of course, I have just the place."

"Which is?"

"My mother's house."

"Your mother lives here? In Little Fork? Of course. She cuts your hair."

Man, this woman had amazing recall. "Sure does. Well, she lives right outside of town."

Maggie shook her head. "I couldn't impose."

"Impose? Believe me, she'd be thrilled. She loves having company."

"But . . . I need to repay her somehow. I can't just let her care for me without some recompense."

"Believe me, she'll find a way for you to pay for your keep. How would you like to learn how to use a computer?"

"Computers I already know," she said, with a blasé wave of her hand. "They use them all over here. But the Inter . . . net? I hear that all the time, but don't know what it means exactly."

"Live with my mom, you'll learn it for sure. That's how she's shoring up her income."

Maggie's eyes lit up like she'd just been handed a million-dollar winning lottery ticket. "I believe I'll enjoy your mother very much. Does she have a TV?"

Four

"I can't do this!" Maggie yelled.

"You can," she heard Ty bark back at her. "Maggie, it was the best I could do on the spur of the moment. Jackie was the only gi . . . friend who seemed about your size."

Maggie took a deep breath. She *could* do this. After all, the women she'd seen on that TV wore much less than this. But these jeans things? This top wasn't so bad. It was a sweater-type thing, and more comfortable than any she'd ever known, but it had a neckline that allowed much of her chest to be exposed. "My grandmother would have a cow!" she yelled.

"I'm betting your grandmother *did* have cows. And chickens. And sheep."

"And goats. Like that commercial where the guy marries one. You people are weird. My mam had goats but never presided over a wedding with one. Oh, wait, there was that time—"

"Too much information!" Ty yelled. Then, "Maggie, we need you to come out already. Unless you want to wear what you came in with."

"As *if*!"

"I'm suing the producers of *Clueless*," she heard Ty say. "Get out here!"

Maggie took a deep breath and then threw aside the curtain. "The first person to make a comment gets your ass blued."

No one made a comment. Not one single person. Standing outside her hospital room were Ty, Jinx, and Doctor Sanchez. They all stared at her like she was a ghost or something.

"Well, happy now?" she asked.

"Holy shit," all three said in unison.

❖   ❖   ❖

Yes indeed, Ty was happy. Miss Margaret Prescott was one beautiful one-hundred-and-eighty-two-year-old woman. And she wore a pair of jeans as if she were modeling for them. Her legs were longer than he'd have guessed, her hips slim, waist even slimmer. Ty didn't dare stare at her chest, but he got a good enough eyeful as his gaze moved quickly up to her flushed face to know she should be right proud of her breasts, too.

"Well?" she said.

"You look"—Jinx hesitated—"very nice, Maggie."

Ty cleared his throat. "Yes . . . nice."

Sonia backhanded both of them in the stomach, then stepped forward. "What the Neanderthals are trying to say is you look fabulous. How do you feel?"

"Very strange. In my day women didn't wear breeches."

"Are you uncomfortable?"

"No. But why are they staring at me?"

"Because they're *men*. And because the last time they saw you dressed, you were looking a little Laura Ingalls-ish."

Maggie made a mental note to write down Laura Ingalls and research what that meant. "Is everyone going to stare at me like this . . . outside?"

Sonia winked. "Well, I'm pretty certain you'll have people staring at you, Maggie, but not because you're out of place."

"Then . . . why? My head is no longer bandaged."

"Because," Sonia said, handing Maggie over to Ty, "this is a small town. And you're a new face in town. So people are going to wonder who you are."

"Oh, no!" Maggie looked up at Ty imploringly. "We mustn't tell them. They'll think I'm straight out of the lunar bin."

"Loony bin," Ty said, who appeared to have finally regained his vocal faculties. "And no they won't. You're Maggie Prescott, formerly from Philadelphia, and you've come to visit an old friend of your mother. Having taken to the place, you've decided to stay. Well, stay until you decide you want to move on, at any rate. I'm assuming you'll want to . . . return home?"

She laughed. "Return to what?"

"Philadelphia?"

"Do I want to return to Philadelphia? I'm sure it isn't anything like I've known."

"Ben Franklin still hangs out around just about every corner in Center City," Jinx said.

"He's an imposter."

"Of course he is, darlin'. But he's the most popular man in town. Except, maybe, the next coach who brings home the Lombardi Trophy," Jinx said.

"The . . . what?"

"Look it up on Wikipedia," Ty said.

He put an arm around her shoulders, and even though she should have, she didn't shrug him off. It felt too safe, secure.

He pulled her closer to his warm, wonderful-smelling body. "We'll figure out what you want to do in time, sweet. Right now, let's get you home."

*   *   *

"I've never felt so . . . so . . . exhilarated!" Maggie told Ty, as they whipped down Main Street in his automobile. "There's just . . . so much to see! I mean, I've seen places like this on the TV, but in person they're just . . . amazing."

"Want me to slow down?" he asked, glancing over at her with one of his half grins.

Maggie stared at him for a second, everything else around her not nearly so interesting. How could she ever have mistaken him for the filthy brute who'd dragged her from the main hall of the Rooster? Even his hands on the round steering thing seemed gentle.

"No," she said, wrenching her gaze from him back to the vibrancy of this new world. "We'll return later and walk the streets, like those people are doing."

"We will, will we?" he asked.

"Unless you don't want to. I could ask Jinx to escort me."

"I don't think so."

"Why not? It's apparent that there's no crime in coloreds and whites spending time together any longer."

"The color of his skin has nothing to do with it," Ty said, stopping when one of those hanging lights turned red. "And coloreds is not a politically correct term any longer, Mags. You need to figure that one out."

"Yes, you're right. I must learn how to describe people differently."

"Actually, describing people by their race or color just doesn't do anything good, Maggie. People are people."

"Oh, my mother would have loved you, Sheriff Coltraine."

The light turned and he shifted into gear. "I wish I'd met your mother, too," he said, glancing into the mirror stuck to the glass window in front of them. "I'm sure I'd have loved her."

"Not many people loved her. She drove most crazy."

"Ah, so you take after her."

She scowled at him, even though he was looking everywhere but at her, so missed her displeasure. "And do you take after your great-great-great-grandfather?"

Instead of sticking it to him, she seemed to have amused him instead. Which was irritating, because she was definitely going for the punch in the stomach.

"Sure as hell hope not, Mags. I admire your mother. Don't have a speck of admiration for my male ancestors."

"How do you know you'd like my mother?"

"She created you, didn't she? Sounds to me like she was working for a better future for women and the world in general. My male ancestors would have hated her, because they wanted to keep everyone but themselves and their friends down."

Maggie felt that wonderful warm, melting sensation flow down her body. "So then, why should I not invite Jinx to stroll down the streets of Little Fork? Maybe have lunch in Tina's Diner back there?"

A muscle jumped in his jaw. "Because he's my best friend, and I would really hate to have to whoop him to a pulp."

Maggie smiled, swinging her head the other way so he wouldn't see it. She wasn't exactly clear on the ways of men, but she was fairly certain that statement meant that he felt possessive of her. Which made her feel a little giddy. As they'd made their way out of the hospital, she'd seen many of the female nurses look at him as if they'd like to eat Ty up. A jealous streak unlike anything she'd ever known had welled up in her. But it was overcome by her happiness that he'd been holding on to her possessively. So many emotions. So many new and exciting sights. So many adventures yet to come. Or so she wished. Wished profusely.

They turned onto a road called This Way and within minutes had left the town behind and were heading into the beauty of the country. There were mountains all around them, some still snowcapped. And the plant life all around them was so exotically sparse compared to the lush greenery of Philadelphia. Which made it so different and lovely.

"This is beautiful country."

"It is," Ty agreed. "So is Pennsylvania. Just in a different way. We're mostly considered desert here."

"How do you know what Pennsylvania looks like?"

"I've been there before," he said, then pulled up a hidey hole in between their seats and plucked out a pair of dark glasses, shoving them over his eyes. "I took several training seminars on CSI at Penn State."

Maggie took out one of those little pads Jinx gave her and added CSI and Penn State to her growing list of things to check out on the Internet. Louise had told her all about how to find out any information you wanted on the superhighway. She wasn't certain what all of those things were, but she'd be damned if she didn't learn them. "Did you fly to Pennsylvania on one of those airplane things?" she asked.

"I did."

"Like a bird in the sky."

"No, like a big machine in the sky. But it has wings. They just don't flap like a bird's wings do." He glanced over at her, the small smile still in place, but his eyes were completely covered by the glasses. "The Wright brothers. Kitty Hawk. Write those down."

She did. "Would it be okay if I go strolling or taking lunch with Sonia?" she blurted out.

He chuckled. "Sure."

"But not Jinx."

"Right."

"The difference being?"

"The difference being he's my deputy. And he could get called to work at a moment's notice and leave you stranded."

"And Sonia, the doctor, wouldn't have that same problem?"

Ty hit the stop pedal on his car pretty hard, and for once Maggie understood the necessity of having this strap over her body. He turned to her and pulled off his glasses. "I don't want you going out with another man, okay? If you're going strolling with anyone, it's going to be me."

"But you said you didn't want to."

"I changed my mind."

"Why?"

His green eyes bored into hers. "Just because."

"Well, now, that's understandable."

"Maggie, you're starting to piss me off."

"Tell me the truth, Ty."

He hesitated. "You've been abused by men in the past. I don't want any man to hurt you again."

"And Jinx would? I have a hard time believing that, seeing as he's been nicer to me than—"

Ty took her face in his hands and kissed her. She didn't know all that much about kissing and kept her lips tightly closed. But, oh, it felt good anyway.

He pulled back for a second, looking at her with smoke in his eyes she'd never seen before. "Relax, Maggie. Relax your mouth."

She did, and before she knew it her insides were exploding. His mouth moved over hers, their lips connecting in a way she'd never known. His lips were alternately hard and soft. He pushed them against her, and then he stepped back some and just kissed parts of her. Not just her lips, but her face, too. She was in heaven.

Before she wanted him to, he ran his thumbs over her face and then let her go. "*That* is why I don't want any other man strolling you around town."

Dizzy didn't even begin to explain her feelings. While he seemed so normal, putting those glasses on his face again, and moving that stick to put the automobile into motion, she was holding on to anything she could grab to keep her steady. "Oh, my Loosie," she whispered.

❋   ❋   ❋

Ty felt like a total shit. He'd never lost control like that before. He just hated her egging him on about spending time with Jinx. Or anyone, besides him.

He'd love to believe that it was purely protection for a person who'd been battered in his town, but that would be stupid. A jealous monster had risen up through him, and he wanted to imprint himself on her. He wanted her. Exclusively, totally, he wanted a woman who by all he knew shouldn't even be here.

It wasn't even how pretty she was. He'd had pretty. It wasn't that she was smart and curious. He'd had smart and curious. It wasn't even that she was vulnerable. Or maybe it was. He'd felt something of the same protectiveness with Josie, his dog. But he sure as hell had never wanted to make love to his dog. Right now he'd give anything to make love to Miss Margaret Prescott.

Make love. Another strange thing. He should be thinking "have sex." He wanted to have sex with her. Except that didn't seem right, either. He wanted to make love.

"I'm really sorry about that, Maggie. I don't know what I was thinking."

"I'll take a wild guess," she said. "You wanted to kiss me."

Leave it to Miss Margaret to cut to the chase. "Yes, I wanted to kiss you."

"Good, because I wanted to kiss you, too. But I think I need better practice."

Ty almost lost control of the car. "You do? I thought it was pretty damn good once you chilled."

"Once *you* chilled, cowboy. I didn't know how to kiss. You had to *chill* to teach me."

He let his blood stop boiling before he said, "There's much more to kissing than what we did. That was just step one."

He shoved the left turn signal on.

"How many steps are there?"

He looked to her. "At least six."

"Before we arrive at your mother's, might I learn at least step two?"

Ty had never shifted his car from four to neutral before, but he did it now.

❊ ❊ ❊

Tyler's mother's home was stunning in its simplicity. It was a sweeping, white, one story with large, black shutters, but the roof was unlike any she'd ever seen. It had windows in it. And the shingles weren't shingles, really. At least, not like any shingles Maggie had seen before.

Ty apparently had noticed her interest because he said, "Solar power."

"I'm sorry?"

"My mom's house runs on solar power."

Maggie got out her little notebook and wrote the term

down. She'd noticed that sometimes her constant questions got on people's nerves, including Ty's, so she'd made it her mission to start learning all of these things by herself.

She pointed to what looked like a long glass house to the left and rear of the house. "Hot house?"

"Or greenhouse. Yes. My mom also grows all of her own vegetables and flowers. She's big on gardening."

"And it shows," Maggie said. "The landscaping around the home is scrumptious."

"Scrumptious, huh? Louise teach you that one?"

"Yes. That's what she called you. I liked the sound of it."

"You realize scrumptious implies loving the taste of something? Wanting to just eat it up?"

"What's your point?"

Ty chuckled as he took her elbow and guided her down a clay-colored walkway. As they got closer to the door, Maggie started getting nervous. The house seemed so elegant, and she was dressed in these jeans things with her hair pulled back in a ponytail. She felt like the house itself, and its owner, deserved the respect of her guests wearing something much more formal.

Ty reached for the knob, but the large black door swung open before he could touch it.

"About time!" said a woman, who must be Ty's mother. And she couldn't have been further from what Maggie had expected if she'd been a goat. About the only thing she and Ty had in common was that twinkle in the eyes that threatened mischief at any moment. But her eyes were a stunning blue. Her hair was light brown and cut around her face in that wispy style Maggie had seen on TV. It suited her. And she was at least three inches shorter than Maggie's five-seven, and about a foot shorter than her son.

But what really stunned Maggie was what Mrs. Coltraine was wearing. She had on what Maggie could only describe as very tight black britches, tucked into very tight, shiny black boots that came right up to her knees. Her white shirt looked like a man's, with buttons holding it together top to waist where it was tucked into the pants. The scary part was, in one hand she was holding a hard, black hat and in the other she was tapping a short whip against her thigh.

Mrs. Coltraine eyed her from the sandals on her feet right all the way up, but stopped abruptly at Maggie's mouth. "Tyler Isaiah Coltraine! You've been kissing the poor girl! And from the looks of her lips and cheeks, it was no step-one kiss. It was at least a step-two, maybe even a three, yes?"

Maggie felt more mortified than she'd ever been in her life. "I'm sorry, ma'am, I asked him to. It's not his fault, Mrs. Coltraine."

"Thanks for the great welcome, Mom," Ty said. "And you might want to lose the riding crop. I'm betting Maggie's scared to death that you'll be using it on her."

Ty would win that bet.

"Oh, please, honey," his mom said, dropping the whip and the hat onto a table beside the door and dragging Maggie into the house. "I sure as hell didn't mean to embarrass you. And forgive me. I was out working the horses."

"You have horses?" Maggie asked.

"Eight of them. Do you ride?"

"Oh, yes!" And then she looked at the woman's outfit again and said, "But only sidesaddle."

"Oh, honey, if you can ride sidesaddle, you can ride dressage. If you ask me, I don't know how women ever managed to stay on a horse sidesaddle."

"I'll teach you if you teach me," Maggie said.

Mrs. Coltraine's face lit up, and Maggie almost gasped. How she hadn't realized before that Ty's mother was utterly lovely she couldn't imagine.

The woman took her arm and started dragging her farther inside. "You're forgiven for kissing this girl, Tyler," she threw over her shoulder, and Maggie giggled.

She turned back to Maggie and said, "Come on in. We'll fix up that scratched face right quick. Tyler, go away."

"I'm not going anywhere until she's comfortable."

"Are you comfortable, Maggie?"

"Do you have a TV, Mrs. Coltraine?"

"My name's Bree. And yes, TVs in almost every room in

the house, including the bathroom. Don't want to miss *NCIS* during my bubble baths."

"Oh, I think I've seen that one. The very good-looking but grumpy secret agent?"

"Special agent, but yes, that's it. I'm totally hooked."

"Do you have a computer?" Maggie asked.

"One desktop, three laptops."

"Do you know about the Internet?"

"Who doesn't these days?" Mrs. Coltraine stopped. "Well, except for a few people, I suppose. But if you're interested, I'll teach you all about it."

This was just getting better and better. "Do you like to go shopping, Mrs. Coltraine?"

"What woman in her right mind doesn't?"

"Do you know how to sell things on a place called eBay?"

"Do I ever!"

"May I please work for my room and board while here?"

"You don't need to do that."

"I can't stay unless I pay you back somehow. I can clean. I can cook. I can bathe the horses. I can help in the hot house. Please?"

"Well, if it's that important to you, you have a deal, Maggie."

Maggie looked back at Tyler, who had the dazed look of someone who'd just been knocked upside the head. "I'm comfortable."

"But—"

"But nothing, son of mine," Ty's mom said. "You don't get her back until you actually deserve step four."

"Do I get supper?"

"Only if you plan to take her out. I've got a date."

"With who this time?"

"Is it any of your business?"

"Yes."

"Fine. I'm going out with Trevor Witherspoon."

"This is your third date with him. I don't like it."

"Tough noogies. Now are you taking this poor girl out?"

"I'll take her out."

"You're taking her to Le Duex, so dress appropriately."

"No!" Maggie said. "I have nothing to wear."

Mrs. Coltraine—Bree—gave her about a five-time over. "Think I've got just the thing. Ty, go home and dress up."

"Oh, but what if it doesn't fit me?" Maggie said.

"What size is she Ty? Four? Six?"

"The clothes were Jackie's," Ty said. "I eyeballed it. I don't know sizes."

"By the time he gets back here," Bree said, "it'll fit you. Ty, skit."

"Right," Ty said, still looking a little out of it to Maggie.

"Ty, you don't have to do this," she said.

"Of course he doesn't," Ty's mom said. "I can set you up with—"

"I'll be back in three hours," Ty said, giving his mother a look that Maggie couldn't even name. It wasn't anger exactly. Maybe more like exasperation? But when his mother winked at her, she stopped worrying and felt excited about it all. She was going on an unescorted date! With a man Louise called a dreamboat!

Five

When Maggie opened the door that evening she totally forgot about how self-conscious she'd been while Bree had made it her mission to turn Maggie into a "sex kitten." Another term she'd scribbled in her notebook to look up at the first opportunity.

He was dressed in what apparently was a modern-day man's gray suit. Underneath it was a white shirt she now knew was called Oxford style that brought out the swarthiness of his skin. And a gray, navy, and black striped necktie. The word scrumptious didn't even begin to cover it. She could, quite simply, gobble him up.

Unlike this morning, he appeared to be freshly shaven, and emanating from him was a fresh, masculine scent.

And then she realized that while she'd been staring at him, he'd been staring at her right back. And it suddenly occurred to her that he'd fixated on her legs, which, for the first time in her life were bare from just above the knee to her toes. She had an immediate desire to cover them. A man had never seen her legs before.

As Bree had been hemming the dress—which she referred to as the perfect little black number that was a must for every woman's wardrobe—Maggie had protested that she couldn't possibly wear something so, so revealing, but Bree had kept assuring her that this dress was more demure than she'd see on any of the other women in the restaurant tonight.

Maggie had stared at herself in a full-length mirror. Bree had been right that it was quite demure up top. At least from the front. The neckline actually came up to her neck, and the sleeves were long. That was the good news. The bad news was that the back was made up only of crisscrossed strips right down to the waistline. And then, of course, there was the issue of her legs.

She'd seen, of course, as they'd driven through town earlier that day, that many, many women were wearing shorts and exposing much more of their legs than she was now. The problem was, these were *her* legs, and she had no idea if they were good legs or bad legs.

She'd also wanted to put her hair up in a bun, as she was so used to wearing it back home. Bree had insisted she wear it down.

Back home. So much had happened, she hadn't really thought of Philly as home the last few days. And she didn't have time to think of it now, because a scrumptious man was standing in front of her, staring at her legs.

"You look . . . very nice," she said, giggling inside at the understatement.

It looked like it took him effort to drag his gaze from her legs to her eyes. "You look beautiful," he said, his voice sounding a little grainy.

"I feel a little self-conscious."

"Please don't, Maggie. I'm going to be the envy of every man in that restaurant."

She smiled, feeling a little better. "You exaggerate, sir."

"No exaggeration, Mags. You ready?"

"No."

"You hungry?"

"Starving."

"Well, we're not going to put anything in your tummy standing here."

"Will there be those hot dogs things at this restaurant?"

He laughed. "I sincerely doubt it." The disappointment must have shown on her face because he added, "But I promise, I will get you those hot dogs real soon. Okay?"

He stepped aside and waved his hand. "After you."

Maggie took a deep breath. "Here we go," she said, and walked over the threshold. Hearing his swift intake of breath, she turned back. "What?"

"Oh, Maggie, trust me, I will be fighting off every man in Little Fork."

Fortified, she smiled up at him. "Aren't women of the twenty-first century supposed to do their own fighting?"

"I'm making an exception for you," he said, putting his hand on the small of her back as they walked to the car. "Because you haven't had enough practice."

"You're full of it," Maggie said.

"Louise again?"

"Sonia."

He held open the door and she felt awkward a moment while slipping into the seat, because the dress slid up her thigh a little as she settled in. But as he pushed closed the door, she distinctly heard him say, "Thank you, Mom."

＊   ＊   ＊

"Oh, that was simply wonderful!" Maggie said, slipping a little more gracefully into the car this time. Which Ty thought was a shame, because her thigh stayed hidden from view.

He tipped the attendant, then jogged around to his side of his Miata and into the driver's seat before some other guy tried to jump in first and kidnap her. He'd been right on the money. She'd charmed every single man in the restaurant, from the maitre d' to their waiter to the ten or so acquaintances who'd stopped by to say hello. Normally on a date he didn't mind disruptions from people who wanted to say hello. Tonight he'd wanted to tell them all to eat dust.

Very unusual for Ty. His male ego, of course, usually enjoyed the idea that he was the envy of other men. Not tonight, no, sir. He'd simmered with jealousy every time Maggie had turned her thousand-watt smile on another guy.

"Glad you liked it," he said, trying to keep the annoyance out of his voice. Of course he was happy she'd had such a good time and was willing to try foods so new to her. The problem was, her delighted laughter had enchanted every man in the place. And if she hadn't noticed a few of the glares from women at other tables, he certainly had.

"I want to thank you," she said, laying her small hand on his arm.

"You already have. About fifty times, but who's counting?"

"No, I don't mean for the meal, although that was wonderful. I mean for the way you smoothly answered the questions about who I was and where I'd come from."

It had been more like, "Where'd you find this little beauty?" accompanied by the occasional leering wink. He'd wanted to punch every single one of them.

"So what was your favorite part?" he asked.

She laughed. "The truth?"

"Of course," he said, praying she wasn't going to say it was all the men trying to flirt with her right in front of him.

"All of the jealous looks I was getting from all the women," she said. "I've never been envied before."

That surprised and flattered the hell out of him at one and the same time. And it was really cute. "Well, honesty deserves honesty, Mags, so I have to tell you they weren't jealous of you being with me; they were jealous of their dates being more interested in you than them."

"Men are so dumb," Maggie said on a sigh.

"We are *not* dumb. You're just a little . . . naïve."

"I might not have a lot of practice, cowboy, but I know when a woman is wishing that she was sitting in my seat. That blonde with . . . Digger, I think his name was . . . looked like she wanted to eat you. And wanted to poison my meal."

"That would be Shelley. She owns the flower shop in town."

"Well, Shelley has the—what did Louise call it?—the *hots* for you."

Ty groaned. "Remind me to kill Louise."

"Are you denying it?"

"Shelley's been dating Digger for months," he said.

"Wow, that was the worst way of not answering a question."

"Let's go on to your second-favorite part?"

"My second favorite is that I'm in this car, with you, and Shelley's not."

Ty took his hand from the gear shift and threaded his fingers through hers. "That makes two of us."

Her soft, soft hand squeezed his. "So where are we going now?"

Ty glanced over at her, and by the light of the street lamp saw the wide-eyed excitement in her brown eyes. "I figured you'd want to go home to my mom's."

"Oh. Okay."

"But if you don't," he added quickly, "we can do something else."

"I would love to! That is, unless you're too tired. I mean, I realize you've had some trying days."

"I'm not tired at all," he said, happier than he could say that she didn't want the night to end. "Want to catch a movie?"

"You mean, in a real theater?"

"Sure. Miller's has late showings."

"But that would involve just watching a movie, right? We wouldn't be able to . . . talk . . . or anything?"

"The other people in the theater might take offense at us talking . . . or anything"

"Then, no, I don't think I'm in the mood for the theater."

"Want to get some ice cream?"

"After that flambé thing? I couldn't eat another bite."

"Okay, what sounds like fun to you?"

"Maybe someplace where you could show me step three?"

Ty nearly ran a red light, staring at her instead of the road. He screeched to a halt and reluctantly disengaged their hands to shift. "Really?"

"I know it's so very forward," she said, "but I really don't care."

"You hussy!" Ty said, grinning to make sure she didn't take offense.

"Maybe so," she said, lifting her chin and meeting him eye to eye. "Seems to me there's only one way to find out."

"Well in that case," he said, "how'd you like to meet my dog, Josie?"

Her smile was breath-stealing. "I'd love to."

* * *

Ty flipped the switch that turned on the gas fireplace and then returned to the couch. He poured them both a glass of cabernet then sat back and watched what the light from the fire did to Maggie's hair. There were about fifty shades of blonde in it, and if he didn't know better, he'd think that someone had just done the most perfect color job on her.

She'd kicked off the heels she'd been wearing, tucked her legs under her and rubbed her feet.

"Those shoes . . . take some getting used to," she said, then took a sip of wine.

"I was actually surprised at how well you took to them," he said. *And them to you.* What those heels had done to her legs should be illegal.

"Expecting me to fall flat on my face?" she asked.

"Let's just put it this way," he said, "I wasn't just holding on to you because I love the feel of you under my fingers. But it was kind of nice to have an excuse."

She laughed softly, then sipped again. "Mmmm, this is delicious."

Oh, how he wanted to taste that wine on her lips. But something was bothering him, and before he or they did anything she'd regret, he wanted to clear the air. "Can I ask you something?"

"Certainly."

"What do you see for your future?"

"What do you mean?"

"I mean . . . have you given any thought to trying to go home?"

"To Philadelphia? I'm fairly certain I no longer have a home in Philadelphia."

"I meant home to 1850."

Her mouth dropped open. "Is that even possible?"

"I don't know. Hypothetically, let's say that it is. Would you want to?"

"I . . . I don't know. I'm here for a reason, Ty. I don't know what it is, but I know that I'm here. I'm supposed to be here."

You're here for me, is what he wanted to say. *You're here because I need you. You're everything I didn't know I was looking for.* Instead he asked, "Do you miss it? Any of it?"

"I suppose I miss the familiarity. I knew who I was then. I knew my place. But . . . I burned bridges in Philadelphia when I quit my job and sold my family home. But Little Fork in 1850 was not so kind."

"I hope you're finding us a much friendlier bunch now."

"Oh, most definitely. But do I belong here? Or should I try to return to Philadelphia? See what the city is like now."

"It's filthy."

She eyed him. "Is that so?"

"Well, not *all* of Philly. But parts are."

"Which parts?" she asked, sounding more suspicious by the second.

He waved. "I don't know *exactly*. But the point is, neither do you."

"I could find out on the Internet."

He was beginning to hate computers. "I suppose. But you'll need money to get back there and find a place to live,"

"Didn't I tell you?" she asked, sitting up straighter. "Your mother took photo-paintings of my money and clothes and then put them up for action—"

"Auction," Ty corrected, now not feeling so grateful to his mother, suddenly.

"Yes, auction. And before she left she checked and told me that people had already placed bids. She said even she was shocked at how quickly the bidding had started. She said there must be a huge demand for pre–Civil War mementos."

She cocked her head and looked at him a little sadly. "Imagine that. I missed an entire war."

"You've missed several of them, darlin'."

"So I've heard. But one that abolished slavery? I so wish my mother had lived to see that. She so hated slavery, Ty."

"It's gone, Maggie."

"But she never got to see that," she said, and Ty hated the sadness in her eyes.

"You told me she disappeared. Do you know what happened?"

"My mother made a lot of people angry. I can think of any number of people who would want to quiet her. But she was never found, and no one was ever brought to justice for her disappearance."

He could tell she was becoming melancholy, and he didn't want to go there. "I'm so sorry." He searched for some seamless way to change the subject but was stymied. He knew what it was like to lose a parent, but he hadn't exactly liked, much less loved his father, so he definitely couldn't claim that he could relate.

"But you know what?" she added, after another sip of wine. "Even going back in time, if it's possible, my mother would still be gone. I'd be going back to a time when I was trying to change my life, to find something new and exciting."

Excellent segue. "Well, you've certainly found that here."

"To say the least! Then again, it's an entire new world everywhere."

Uh-oh. "Well, I know Little Fork might not be as exciting as other places, but it *does* have its moments."

"It certainly does," Maggie said and set down her wine.

"Like right now," she said, crawling over to him and coming nearly nose to nose. "What is this thing that I feel whenever I'm around you?"

"I don't know," he said. "Describe it."

"You make me feel all tingly. Do you feel tingly, too?"

"I feel like my insides are going to explode," he said, because he didn't think telling her that she made him horny as hell whenever she was near him was a great idea.

"Is that a good thing?"

"It can be. Or it can get damn uncomfortable."

She sat back on her ankles. "Uncomfortable? That doesn't sound good."

He threaded his hands through her silky hair, cradling her face. "It's only not good if you don't want me to touch you. Because I really, really want to touch you."

"You're touching me now," she said, in a bare whisper.

"I want to touch you all over, Maggie. Every inch of you."

She sucked in a small breath. "I think . . . no, I know I want you to. But is it okay if we start with you teaching me step three?"

"My pleasure," Ty said, and kissed her.

After several incredible moments of tasting her, smelling her, feeling her, he sat back. "Maggie," he said, his voice an almost croak, "I don't understand any of this. All I know is that I want you. But I can't do this."

Her eyes looked kind of foggy. Her lips looked deliciously swollen. "Why?"

"You're a . . . you're . . . innocent. It scares me."

"I don't feel innocent, Sheriff. I feel . . . I don't know how to describe it. Louise would know."

"We're not consulting Louise on this matter."

"Maybe I could look it up on Google?"

He officially hated computers. "Mags, this is just you and me. You are not going to learn about making love on the Internet."

"Actually, your mother showed me this page that had—"

"Nothing you needed to see. And nothing to do with this

moment." He was going to confiscate his mother's computers. "What do you feel about me?"

Maggie looked directly into his eyes. "You saved my life. You gave me this new life."

"So you're grateful?"

"Of course."

He sat back and away from her, his heart killing him. "Then this can't happen, Maggie. Gratitude is a bad reason to have sex."

"What if the reason is I want it to be you?"

He looked at her, sitting there with her eyes pleading, her lips half open, and her body almost quivering. "You're sure?"

"I'm not certain about anything right now, Sheriff, except that I would very much like to see you without clothing. I just don't know if I want you to see me without mine."

Ty started slowly, pulling off his shirt first. She stared at his chest for a long time, and Ty had to keep himself from fidgeting.

"I have figured out what scrumptious means. You are scrumptious, Ty," Maggie said, still staring at him.

"Maggie, I don't know about this. I don't want to hurt you."

"Do you want to make love with me?"

"Oh, God, Maggie, yes."

"I'm a little scared, Ty."

"So am I Mags. I think I love you. But I don't want to hurt you."

"You won't hurt me. Will you, Ty? Make me learn how to love."

Ty stared at her for a moment, then pulled her to her feet. "My bedroom and bed are this way, Mags. You can let me take you there, or you can stop right here. I could also make love to you right here, but I want your first time to be in my bed. It's your choice."

Maggie looked around. "I think I'd like the first time to be in your bed. The next time I could have rug buns."

He opened his mouth to correct her but decided her description might just be more accurate than she knew. "Come with me, Mags," he said, meaning that in more ways than one.

He led her into his bedroom. She looked around and said, "This is so like you. So . . . just made for a man."

Not in the mood for a description of what exactly that meant, Ty sat her on his bed.

"Are you afraid to let me see you?" Ty asked.

"Are you afraid to see me?"

"Hell, no. I'd give anything, Maggie."

"Then see me. But I'm not all that good to see."

"Says who?" he asked, dying to see her.

"Ummm, says me?"

"May I be the judge of that?"

"You may."

"Then take off that dress, Maggie. Please."

She hesitated, but then shimmied out of the dress like an honest-to-god stripper. And what he saw left him breathless.

"The rest," he whispered.

She was hesitant, but then pulled off her bra over her head, instead of unclipping it

"You are so beautiful. The panties please."

She hesitated for a second, and then pushed down the black matching panties and stood before him, naked and stunning, and not able to look at him.

"Your turn," she said, eyes still studying the floor. "I want to look at you, too."

He was very certain that his cock was going to scare her. "Let's lie down and just let me touch you for a while."

"No, not fair. I'm standing here completely unclothed. You have to be the same."

"Maggie, I want you so much. I'm afraid of worrying you."

"I'm not worried, Ty," she said softly. "I'm very certain of what I want. I would not be standing here like this if I didn't know."

He started unzipping his slacks. "I don't want to hurt you."

"You won't."

"How do you know?" he asked, as he kicked the slacks aside and moved to her.

She finally peeked downward and whispered, "Oh, my."

"Say no now, and we're done."

"How's that going to . . . fit inside me?"

"Because I'll make sure your body wants it to."

He saw the fear in her eyes and reached for his pants. "Okay, not tonight, Mags. No way am I going to scare you."

She reached for his arm. "But . . . you didn't say anything about hurting me."

"I can't guarantee not hurting you. I can guarantee trying not to. But scaring you is different. I'm already doing that, and can't live with it."

She grabbed his arm. "It has to be you, Sheriff Coltraine."

His insides dumped all over themselves. "Why?"

"Because for whatever reason, you love me, Ty. I want to be with the man who loves me, not the one who leers at me."

And he did. He loved every inch of her. She was so soft and smelled so good and had a body that was every man's fantasy.

He pulled her to him, and every part of him was touching every part of her.

Not only that, but she apparently loved being touched. As he kissed her skin and touched her, she made soft noises. Gasps. Lovemaking sounds.

He picked her up and laid her on the bed. Then fell down beside her and began worshipping every inch of her.

"I love this," she whispered. "I never want you to stop."

"Maggie, I need to be inside you. But I want you to need me inside you, too."

"I want it. I know what this is. I want it."

"Let me help you get used to it, okay?"

"Please. But hurry up, okay?"

He buried a finger inside her, then two, while stroking her with his thumb. She looked at him with such pleading eyes, and then cried out when he ran his tongue across her.

"Are you sure, baby?"

"Oh, my, *yes*."

He moved up and spread her legs even farther. He felt her and knew her body was ready. So he did what he'd wanted to do for a long few days. He made love to her. She came first, with an orgasm that was obviously new to her. He had an orgasm just watching her. The rest of the night was so much the same, and so much different. And Maggie loved every difference. Ty was too dazed to know anything but he never wanted this to end.

Six

Two days later Ty left his office to pick Maggie up at his mother's house. After forty-eight hours of not seeing her, he'd been miserable. He'd checked in on her plenty, but he'd been so busy, he hadn't been able to be with her. And he desperately wanted to be with her.

But she'd never given any indication in any of those conversations that she was missing him. In fact, she'd always been impatient to get back to her new next adventure.

And then this morning after his shower he'd emerged to find a text message on his cell.

I have just discovered what a one-night stand is, cowboy. If you don't want me to believe that's what happened, you better find a way to get your ass over here.

Even as he dialed the phone in a panic, he was definitely kicking himself for thinking ensconcing Maggie at his mother's house had been a good idea.

This morning he'd announced to his deputies at their

weekly meeting that he was going to take a few days of vacation. They'd all looked at him like he'd gone over the edge. In the eleven years he'd worked for the Little Fork PD, he'd never once taken a day of vacation.

But Helen, one of his two female deputies, had piped up while the others just stared at him, speechless. "I think that's an excellent idea, Ty. You might not have noticed, but you've been awfully grumpy the last few days."

"I have not," he'd barked. Then took a deep breath. "Well, maybe. Which is why I think a couple of days of vacation is in order."

"He's in loooooove," Jinx had chimed in.

"You're fired," Ty responded.

Jinx just grinned.

"In love, huh?" Marlie his deputy, second in seniority only to Jinx, said. "Could it be that pretty girl he rescued from the Rooster?"

"Meeting over. Jinx, you're in charge of the roster."

"I no longer have a job, I believe."

"You're re-hired until after I get back."

And with that Ty had stalked out of the room, and thank the Lord and pass the butter, no one said another word.

So now Ty had at least a couple of days to convince Miss Margaret Prescott that she belonged in Little Fork. Little Fork 2010, not Little Fork 1850.

And she belonged to him.

After the other night, one of the best of his life, he'd had to do some true soul-searching. He had to realize that as impossible as it seemed, he'd fallen hard for a woman who'd dropped into his life from two centuries ago.

The woman who he'd instantly pegged as a prissy, smart-ass pain-in-the-ass was anything but. Well, the smartass part still held true. But he liked that about her.

Actually, he *loved* that about her.

He also loved her mouth. The woman was one fast learner.

And her body. And her scent and her greedy need to explore new territory. Including making love. He was almost certain she'd loved making love.

Ty shook his head and jumped out of the car, jogging to the front door.

Normally he walked right into the house, but for some reason he felt the need to ring the bell instead.

She answered with a wide smile on her face, her hair up in a high ponytail and . . . "Wow," he said.

She had on a pair of pale pink shorts and a white tank top. She was barefoot and her toenails were painted pink. She looked flushed and extremely proud of herself.

"Hi," she said. "You're not in your cop duds."

"And you're in my mother's shorts."

"Nope, these are mine! Come in!"

"Where's my mom?" he asked.

"She and Trevor went to Reno for the day."

His eyes were glued to the back of her legs and her amazing butt. "Umm, well, that's nice."

"It really is. I don't know why you disapprove of him, Ty. He's a very nice man."

She turned suddenly and, not paying attention to anything but that swinging backside of hers, he ran right into her. She almost fell back, but he grabbed her arms just in time.

They stared at each other for a moment, and then he pulled her to him and kissed her before she could protest. His mind and body both exploded, responding to her obvious welcoming kiss.

She nipped his lips, demanding entrance, and then sucked softly on first his upper, then lower lip. Ty held her closer and engaged her tongue in mouth foreplay. Her arms wrapped around his neck and she broke the kiss, then began nibbling on his ear. Her breasts pressed against his chest, and it was all he could do not to pick her up and carry her over his shoulder to her bedroom.

"God, Maggie," he rasped in her ear. "What you do to me."

"I feel what I'm doing to you," she said, laughing softly against his neck. But then she stepped back and looked him over. "You look very, very good. I've decided I love you in jeans."

"Good," he said and tried to pull her back to him.

But she stopped him with a finger to his sternum. "You seduced me. And then you never called me. Your mother and I agree that you're a brat."

The fact that she'd told his mother about their night was kind of scary. "I was going to. I was on duty the last two nights. I told you that."

"But you didn't *ask me out again*."

"I'm asking you out right now," he said desperately.

"Oh, sure," she said, turning her back and walking up the three steps from the foyer into the living room. "After I had to threaten you."

"I'm on vacation now, Maggie. I took a few days off so I could be with you," he said, following her.

She flopped onto the couch. "Your mother says you never take a vacation."

His mother talked way too much. "Exactly!" he said, holding his hands out wide. "See? That's how much I wanted to spend more time with you."

Her frown turned into a smile. "Is this true?"

"Have I lied to you yet?"

"Yes."

"When?"

"When you promised you'd feed me a hot dog."

"Want to go have a hot dog with me, Maggie?"

She jumped up. "Yes!"

Ty checked his watch. "You know, if we leave now, we can catch a baseball game. The Nevada Forkers are playing the Spikes in about twenty minutes."

"Do they have hot dogs at these games?"

"Only the best in Nevada."

"Well then, let's go!"

Ty eyed her. "Do you want to get dressed?"

She laughed. "I *am* dressed, silly man."

"In shorts."

"Yes. As just about every other woman in this town wears at this time of year."

"But your legs."

She looked down at herself. "What's wrong with my legs? I thought, after the other night, that you liked them."

"And so did every other man who saw them. And that tank top."

"The problem with the top is what? I'm wearing a braw-zeer."

"But . . . aren't you uncomfortable with . . . you know . . . your arms and shoulders exposed?"

"As your mom says, 'when in Rome.' "

"I might have to kill my mother."

Maggie laughed. "Suck it up, cowboy."

He didn't want to suck it up. He preferred when she was too shy to allow an ounce of skin showing. Unless it was for him. But if he was going to talk her into staying in this year, in his town, he was going to have to get used to her catching up with the twenty-first century. He just sort of wished she wasn't catching up so damn fast. "At least put on some shoes. You won't be allowed into the stadium barefoot."

"Stadium? Do I need to write this one down?"

"Put on shoes and learn for yourself."

❄   ❄   ❄

"So those clothes are yours?" Ty asked, as they headed down toward the Forker's stadium.

"Yes!" she said, smiling. "At least they will be officially mine when the bidding on eBay ends. Bree was sweet enough to lend me some money, which I'll be able to pay back when PayPal pays up."

"So the bidding's going well?"

"Oh, Ty, as it stands now, I'll have more money than I ever dreamed possible."

"Well, good," he said, not meaning it for a moment. With money, she could go anywhere, do anything. It was a totally selfish feeling, wanting her to be tied to Little Fork. And yet he couldn't help it. "And what are you going to do with your new-found fortune?"

She was quiet for a few too long seconds. "I . . . haven't decided."

"Buy a house?" he asked. "I have a friend who's a real estate agent. I'm sure she could find you the perfect place."

"Or . . . I could travel."

"Or you could travel," he said. *Not without me you won't*, he didn't say. He had no right to try and tie her here. Not when she was discovering an entire new world. But as long as she was here, he could damn well try to show her the benefits of making Little Fork her hometown.

*   *   *

"This is amazing!" Maggie said, licking mustard from her fingers, then wiping her hands with a paper napkin.

"I take it you like the hot dogs," Ty said dryly. "Want a fourth?"

"Oh, I couldn't possibly. Not for at least another inning."

"The way this game is going, that means about another ten minutes."

"Sounds about right," she said, lifting her new sunglasses and smiling at him. "I'm having so much fun."

She took another sip of soda, then grabbed his hand as the sound of the bat cracking a ball filled the air, and she followed the ball soaring over the stadium. It hit the stand at the far end of the field. "Home run! But why isn't that man running around the bases?"

"Foul ball," Ty said. "They have to get them in between the posts for it to count as a home run."

"And you say you teach this sport?" she asked, trying to draw him out. He'd been unusually quiet the last couple of innings, and she wasn't quite sure why. When they'd first arrived, he'd been answering her questions and seemed to be enjoying himself. But in the last minutes, he'd gone almost mute.

Did he hate wasting his vacation time on her? Did he wish he was somewhere else?

"I *coach* Little League softball to kids. This is semi-pro ball."

"Do you enjoy coaching them?"

He smiled for the first time in innings, and all she wanted to do was touch the dimple in his chin. "I enjoy it a lot. I love watching them learn and work hard to improve. I love being there the first time one of my kids makes a base hit. Or an out."

"I bet watching the first home run is pretty freakin' cool, too," she said.

He finally laughed. "Yep, it's pretty freakin' cool."

"That's how I felt about teaching."

He turned his head to face her. She regretted the glasses that hid his amazing eyes. "Do you miss teaching?"

"I do."

"You could teach again."

"Oh, Ty! Teach what? It will take me years to catch up with modern schooling, with the world."

"I bet you could teach pre–Civil War history just about better than anyone could."

"Yes, I suppose so. But I researched, and teachers now have to have college degrees and certificates to be hired."

"True. I don't suppose your resume would qualify," he said, and then went silent again.

"Ty," she asked, laying a hand on his muscular thigh. "What's wrong with you? Do you . . . want to be somewhere else? Because if so, just tell me."

"Jesus, Maggie," he said, his head dropping.

"You do. That's all right," she said, cursing herself for the catch in her voice. "Then go. Please. I'll find a way back home. I'll hire one of those car taxis."

She pulled her sunglasses down over her eyes, so he wouldn't see the moisture she felt gathering there.

He grabbed her hand. "No, I don't want to be anywhere else, Maggie."

"Then what's wrong? Tell me, please. Am I embarrassing you? I mean, I know people have been looking at us a little strangely. I'll try not to ask so many questions. Or I won't ask any at all."

"Dummy," he said, putting his arm around her and pulling her against him, making her almost spill her drink. "The problem is, I *don't* want to be anywhere else."

"But you'd rather be here without me."

He lifted his sunglasses and then hers, so they were looking straight into each other's eyes. "I'd rather be anywhere as long as it's *with* you."

She blinked. "And this is a problem how?"

An organ started playing, and there was no way he'd be able to say something without shouting. So she watched him glare up toward the loudspeakers, then back at her, swallowing hard several times. Everyone around them stood up for some reason she couldn't fathom. So they seemed alone down on the bench, cocooned in the bodies surrounding them. Finally he leaned over and whispered, "Because I don't know what I'm going to do when you leave me."

Seven

"Where *are* you taking me?" Maggie asked, laughing. "Are you kidnapping me, Ty?"

"Sort of."

It was the day after the baseball game, and Ty had shown up at eleven o'clock in the morning at Bree's house. Before Maggie could say "Boo!" Ty had swung her around and tied a silk scarf of some sort over her eyes.

She'd panicked and tried to fight him at first, but he'd said, "Shhh, sweetheart. This is a fun surprise."

"But why must you blindfold me?"

"Trust him, Maggie," Ty's mom had said. "You'll like this surprise."

"Are you sure?"

"Have I steered you wrong yet?"

"Well, Ty wasn't as happy with the shorts I bought as you said he'd be," Maggie replied.

"Oh, he was happy," Bree said. "He just didn't want to share how booty-licious you looked in them with other eyes."

"Booty—"

"That's a good thing, Maggie," Ty said. "Come on, you adventurous little soul, just go with the flow."

And she had. Because after what Ty had said to her at the baseball game yesterday, after an evening of sharing Chinese food and lovemaking in front of his fireplace, how could she not?

The man was amazing. Admittedly, as gentle as he'd tried to be their first night together, the making love part had been painful. But also wonderful. She had not had any idea how special it could be to have a man be part of her, inside her. And the way he'd touched her and tasted her had been magnificent. Last night had been even better. It amazed her that she felt so free with this man.

In her time, making love before marriage made a woman a very, very bad person. But she didn't feel bad at all. It was so . . . freeing. So . . . right. Her mother had always told her that she'd know when the time was right. She'd known even then that what her mother was saying was a scandalous opinion. One not shared by very many people. But if her mother was here right now, Maggie knew she'd approve. Just as Ty's mother had approved when she'd confided in her.

Oh, how she wished her mother had come on this journey with her. Then again, she was certain her mother knew about this. Maybe even orchestrated it somehow. She'd wanted so desperately for Maggie to have freedom. Joy. Choices. And Maggie felt like she had all of these things right now. Not to mention a very handsome man who seemed to like being with her. As much as she loved being with him. Imagine that? *Mom, you'd like him.*

"I have to tell you," she said, as the wind whipped through her hair, "being blindsided—"

"Blindfolded."

"Fine, being *blindfolded* is not my idea of a good time."

"Oh, you'd be surprised. Ever made love with a blindfold on?"

She snorted. "As *if*."

"I hate to tell you Mags, but that little saying is *so* twentieth century."

"Meaning what?"

"Meaning it's outdated. Nobody says that anymore."

"Oh. Well, the point being, you know darn well we've never made love blindfolded."

"We might have to try it sometime."

"I don't think so. I like looking at your body."

"And how glad I am of that."

"Ty?"

"Hmm?"

"Why didn't you let me answer you yesterday? After the sweet thing you said?"

"Because I wasn't ready to hear your answer. And I'm pretty darn certain you weren't ready to give me one."

"But—"

"No buts, okay? Let's just enjoy today."

"How can I enjoy it, when I can't see it?"

"You'll see it soon enough," he said, bringing his car to a halt and yanking on the brakes.

The air was suddenly still and quiet, except for the sound of birdsong. "Are we here?"

"We're here."

"Where's here?"

"You, Miss Prescott, are about to find out."

She heard him come around the car, his shoes crunching against some kind of gravel.

He opened her door and helped her out. She punched him lightly in the gut. "Ow! What was that for?"

"It's Ms. Prescott to you."

He laughed and started guiding her to their destination. "Step up."

She did, and they were now on concrete or something solid. He guided her, his one hand on her waist and the other on her shoulder, and Maggie reveled in his fingers on her body. In just a few short days she'd grown to love his hands on her. All over her.

Finally he stopped her and said, "Ready?"

"I'm not sure."

He chuckled, and then whipped the silk from her eyes.

"Surprise!" a bunch of people yelled, and Maggie boggled at the sight before her. About thirty people were standing around the pool on the back patio of Bree's house. There were colored balloons everywhere and a big sign that read, Happy Birthday, Maggie!

"Oh, my!" she said, her hand going to her heart.

Ty grinned at her and kissed her cheek. "Happy birthday, sweetheart."

"I . . . I'd forgotten."

She didn't know whether to laugh or cry. Among the people smiling at her were Jinx and Sonia and Louise, several other nurses from the hospital, Bree and her boyfriend Trevor, Fannie Mae from the Rooster, and a dozen or so others she didn't recognize.

Jinx approached, a lovely Asian-looking woman on his arm. He handed her a glass of what looked like champagne. "Happy birthday, Maggie," he said and kissed her on the cheek, also.

"I don't know what to say," she said.

"How about, 'let the party begin'?"

"Well first, thank you. Thank you all," she said.

"And?" Ty nudged.

"And . . . let the party begin!"

✳   ✳   ✳

Ty sat in one of his mom's pool lounge chairs, watching Maggie. She looked so damn pretty in a flowery sundress and sandals, an outfit, he was certain, his mother had coerced her to wear for the day.

After her initial shock, Maggie had embraced the celebration in a way he hadn't expected. She'd switched roles from invited guest to party hostess in a flash and was walking around thanking everyone and chatting with them.

People migrated to her like lemmings to a cliff. Just as he had. Only he was afraid he'd be the one to jump off.

Yet every so often she'd look around until she spotted him, then she'd toss him a heart-melting smile before returning to the guest who was trying to soak in her aura.

Jeez, he was out of his mind. *Her aura?* Man, he'd listened one too many times to his mother's view of the world.

The afternoon slowly melted into evening, and yet only a few had left Maggie's party. It seemed they couldn't get enough of her. He had that in common with them.

"Earth to Ty," he heard.

He blinked and dragged his gaze from Maggie to Jinx, who pulled up a chair beside him. "Hey," Ty said. "Thanks again for helping my mom pull this together so fast."

"Not a problem. The problem's you."

"What? How so?"

"You've been grilling for most of the afternoon, and then you just plunk yourself down. You've been sitting here staring at her for the last half hour straight. Shouldn't you be mingling? Maybe by her side?"

"I want her to have fun."

"Well, I see your point, because you sure as heck aren't a barrel of laughs these days. What's up with that?"

"I'm PMSing," Ty said.

"Very funny, pretty boy."

Ty took a swig of beer, then made a face. It had grown warm since his last sip, which was probably at least thirty minutes ago. "I want her to be happy."

Jinx glanced over at the crowd surrounding Maggie. "She looks pretty happy to me. *Glowing* in fact."

Ty suppressed a snarl. "What the hell is that supposed to mean?"

"Not a thing. Just that she's having fun. So why aren't you?"

Ty looked at the man who'd been his best friend since they'd been in diapers. "Because it's not fair to ask her to stay here."

"Why not?"

"Are you serious?" he asked, dropping the beer bottle on the table beside him. "Look at her. This is a whole new world. She deserves to see it. She's insatiable about learning it all. I have no right to try to keep her here."

"Have you asked her to?"

"' Course not."

"Maybe you should."

"Do you have fuzz in your ears? I told you, she wants to explore the world."

"So go explore it with her."

"My job is here. My life is here. I can't just pick up and go galivantin', J."

"I'm thinking you've built up enough vacation time to take a trip around the world and have enough left over to see it again."

"What if she doesn't want me with her while she explores?"

"Again, dipshit, *ask* her."

"I'm afraid of her answer."

*   *   *

Maggie glanced over at Ty again, wondering what was wrong with him. As far as she was concerned, this had been *such* a perfect day. Nobody had ever had a birthday party for her. Her mom always did something special, of course, but never an actual party.

Her heart panged. Her mother would have loved this. She would have been initially shocked at the scandalous attire, maybe, but she'd have adjusted quickly, Maggie was sure.

She would have especially loved that a man had cared enough to do something so wonderful for her daughter. Maggie glanced over at Ty again. Their eyes met, and he smiled at her. But the smile didn't quite make it up any further than his lips. What could possibly be bothering that man?

Determined to find out, Maggie excused herself from the crowd and began marching over to him.

"Margaret?"

Maggie stopped in her tracks and looked over her shoulder. Fannie was standing there, holding a brightly colored gift that almost matched the sundress-type thing she was wearing. Today her hair was blonder than Maggie's, in what she'd told Maggie was her Marilyn Monroe 'do. Maggie had made a mental note to search the Internet for Marilyn Monroe later to see what that meant.

"Oh, Fannie, that's not for me, is it?"

Fannie grinned up at her. "It is, although I need to give a little background, so you understand it."

Although Maggie had loved all of the gifts she'd been given today, a gift that needed background sounded intriguing. "Cool!" she said.

"I've been doing a little research, Margaret, because I wanted to figure out how much I owe you."

"Owe me?"

"It might be a little late, but I'm thinkin' your claim to the Rooster is legit."

"Oh, Fannie, I have no desire to stake—"

"Well, missy, I'm stakin' it for ya, then."

"But—"

"No buts about it. Although I'm not a dummy. I'm not just handin' it over to ya. But I most surely am going to pay you a sum. Just haven't figured that sum out yet."

"Honestly, Fannie—"

"No arguin'. The Rooster's a right profitable little business, and I'm an old lady who doesn't believe in taking so much money with me. I can afford it, and you deserve it."

Maggie stared down at her. "I . . . don't know what to say."

"Say I can buy out your share. And we'll all be happy." Fannie tapped the gift. "But this is something different. While I was researching the history of all this I came across something interesting. You say your mama's name was Elizabeth, yes?"

"Yes, it was."

"Did she have any kin? Besides you?"

"No. None. It was just the two of us. Oh, and my father. But he . . . died."

"Oh. Then maybe this isn't quite the gift I thought it would be. In my researchin' I came across an Elizabeth Prescott who lived during the twenties. I thought maybe she'd be a relative. When did your mama pass on?"

"I . . . I don't know. She disappeared. I always thought that maybe she'd made some folks really mad and they kidnapped her. She was . . . a bit of a hell-raiser," Maggie admitted, smiling at the memories. "I've been meaning to try to look for an obituary somewhere, but there just hasn't been time."

"I found one. For Elizabeth Prescott."

Maggie's heart flip-flopped. "Is it in there?" she asked, looking at the present.

"Yes. But this one died in 1945, Maggie."

Any hope Maggie had that it was her mother's vanished. "That wouldn't have been possible. She couldn't possibly have lived that long."

"I'm sorry. Mebbe this was a terrible idea."

"May I see it anyway?"

Fannie seemed reluctant to hand it over, but she finally did. "I was hopin' this might be a relative, but it doesn't sound like there's much chance of that."

Maggie carefully undid the wrapping. It was so pretty she didn't want to destroy it. She opened the box and, sure enough, it was an obituary from the Philadelphia Enquirer, dated July 21, 1945. Maggie started to read it, but then was caught by the picture. This woman had been the spitting image of her mother. Only . . .

"What is this outfit she's wearing," Maggie asked in a whisper, lowering the box so Fannie could see.

"Why, that's a flapper outfit. That picture must have been taken during the twenties. She look familiar?"

"Yes, she does. This is my mother, Fannie. But how is that possible?"

"How is it possible you're standin' here, missy?"

*   *   *

Ty watched Maggie hug Fannie tightly, jump around with what looked like utter elation, then almost run around the pool toward him. Hell, she seemed so high as a kite that he guessed she could have walked right over that water.

She skidded to a halt in front of him and Jinx, her eyes dancing and a little watery all at the same time.

"That must have been one helluva present, Mags," Ty said.

"Oh, it is. Unbelievable even. But I . . . don't want to talk about it until I research a few things." She put the box behind her back with a nervous, excited laugh. "Your girlfriend's very nice, Jinx. I approve."

"In which case, I might marry her, Maggie."

She laughed again. "I'm never wrong about these things, you know."

Jinx stood up. "I'm betting that's the God's honest truth. So I best get back to her before some bozo tries to horn in. See what you can do about this lump."

"I'll do my best." She took the seat Jinx had just vacated. "Thank you for the party, Ty."

"I was just responsible for driving you around while everyone arrived. My mom and Jinx did the rest."

"It was your idea."

He looked at her. "Who told you that?"

"Your mom."

"Blabbermouth."

"She just wanted to give credit where credit's due."

He couldn't help it. He reached out and took her hand. "You've got me real curious about what's in that box. But I'll respect your privacy until you're ready to show me."

"That's just one of the reasons I lo . . . like you so much, Ty."

His heart swelled a little. "Having fun, sweet?"

"I'd have more fun if you'd join me."

"I wanted to give you space."

She tilted her head. "Why?"

"So you could enjoy yourself without me suffocating you."

"Suffocating me? How would you being by my side suffocate me? It would have helped. I'm not all that great with names."

"Bull. That brain of yours soaks up everything you see and hear."

"It doesn't when all I'm thinking about is where you are."

Ty swung his legs over the side of the lounger. "I'm a jerk."

"No comment."

"I'm so sorry, darlin'. Let's go circulate."

Her smile beamed. "Excellent. Would you like a hot dog?"

"You mean there are some left?"

She slugged him in the arm. "I've only had three."

"How your tiny body manages to handle all the food you—"

About six pagers went off at once, and Ty looked around to see all of his deputies checking their messages. Then Jinx came trotting over to him. "Trouble at the Rooster. We've got it covered."

"What is it?"

Jinx glanced at Maggie, then back at him. "We'll take care of it."

"What is it?" Maggie asked.

Jinx sighed. "Seems someone's been locked in the shed."

Maggie gasped.

Ty grabbed her and hugged her. "I'm so sorry, Maggie, but I'm going to have to go check this out."

"I'm coming with you."

"No way," Ty and Jinx said at the same time.

"Way," Maggie said.

❖   ❖   ❖

"You aren't getting out of this car," Ty told Maggie for about the tenth time since she'd strapped herself in.

"I know, I know," she said, sounding exasperated.

"Why would you want to come, Maggie? You were having fun at your party."

"I don't know. I just . . . had to."

"That shed holds nothing but bad memories for you."

"I know, but . . ."

When she didn't finish, he said, "But what?"

"I was thinking. If I want to go back to where I came from, maybe that shed would hold the key to getting there."

Ty's heart dropped out of his chest. "So you've decided? You want to go back?"

"It's not a matter of want. It's a matter of whether I'm meant to."

"How do you figure?"

"Do I belong here? Or back there? Or maybe some other time altogether."

"I figure since you landed here, then here's where you're supposed to be."

"Or maybe, just maybe, I was meant to glimpse the future so that I could go back and maybe . . . I don't know, work to make it happen. Maybe even sooner. Maybe without so much bloodshed."

"Maggie, much as I respect you, I don't think you alone will be able to change the world."

"I know, sounds presumptuous, doesn't it? But who's to say? My mother worked all of her life to change things. And she *did* make a difference. Small perhaps, in the scheme of things, but she did. And she'd wanted me to carry on with her work. I didn't see it that way then. But maybe that's what this whole thing is all about."

"Would you be happy back then now? Now that you know what you know?"

"Not happy, perhaps. Not as happy as I have been here. Especially if I go back after my mother disappeared."

"So . . what? You want me to conk you in the head and lock you in the shed and see if that sends you back? I couldn't do it, Maggie. Not just because there's no way I could hurt you. But I can't stand the thought of living in this world without you."

"Why, Ty?"

"You came here for a reason. I honestly believe that. And I'm selfish enough to believe part of that reason is that you and I were meant to be together. Part of it is that I believe you're meant to teach children the history of the woman's movement. Your mother was a pioneer. What better way to honor her than to teach kids about her struggles? About women's struggles?"

"Or maybe go back and teach children about the possibilities for the future."

He felt shattered. "Would you miss me?"

"Incredibly."

They pulled up in front of the Rooster, amazingly the first to arrive. Ty turned to her. "I won't stop you if you want to try. But I can't help you do it, Maggie. Please don't ask me to."

"I won't."

He took her head in his hands and kissed her hard. "Stay here. Think about it some. Don't make any rash decisions. That's all I'm asking. Okay?"

"Yes, I'll think about it."

"Thank you."

He got out of the car and strode to the front steps of the Rooster, not looking back. He couldn't stand to look back.

❀   ❀   ❀

Maggie waited until Ty had headed inside this mansion that at one point in time was supposed to belong to her. And then, her heart breaking, she got out of the car and started making her way to the backyard.

She didn't know if she was plumb nuts or what, but she had to see that shed. She had a very big decision to make. And she couldn't do it without seeing where this strange, wonderful adventure had begun.

❀   ❀   ❀

Once again, Fannie had no idea who'd locked someone in her shed, or where the lock had come from. All she knew is that one of her girls had come to work, claiming she could swear Lester was locked up back there.

So Ty waited for Jinx and the bolt cutters and called for a bus. He realized he'd forgotten to grab his flashlight from his trunk, so ran back to the car to get it. The car was empty.

"Shit."

❀   ❀   ❀

Maggie stood in the shadows, only the light of the moon illuminating the shed that had been her hell . . . or her salvation.

She could hear a man yelling for help, banging on the door. At least he didn't sound like he'd been smacked senseless as she had been.

Maggie's mind was in a jumble. She wished, so much, that her mother were here to tell her what she should do. Lord knew she didn't want to leave this place, this time. And the thought of leaving Ty was almost unbearable.

And if she *did* go back, at what point in time would she land? She was almost positive that with a little more research she'd find that somehow, remarkably, her mother had also gone forward in time. If this was what she thought it was, her mother had lived to see women get the right to vote. She'd seen women begin entering the work force into jobs that had always exclusively been for men only. "Oh, Mama, tell me what to do," she whispered.

She walked slowly toward the shed, thinking maybe if she'd just touch it, she would get answers. But she was so dang afraid of what the answer would be.

She reached the shed and heard the man's angry demand for help. "Shh," she said. "Help is coming. Sheriff Coltraine is on his way."

"Oh, thank the Lord. When I get my hands on Bertha—"

She lifted her hand to touch this magical shed.

"Maggie, no!" Ty yelled, running to her, his light shining ahead of him. "Maggie, please wait!"

Her hand dropped away from the shed. And she stepped back.

He skidded to a halt in front of her. "You promised you'd wait."

He looked so scared, so upset, that she put a hand to his face. "I . . . thought maybe if I touched it, and I go, then I'm meant to go."

"Sheriff?" the man yelled. "Get me the hell out of here!"

"Help's on its way, Lester. Just hang in there." He placed himself between Maggie and the shed. "You hurt, Lester?"

"Just my pride, Sheriff. But can't rightly say how healthy Bertha's gonna be when I get hold of her."

"Don't do anything I'd have to arrest you for, Lester."

Ty took Maggie's arms and pulled her farther from the shed. "If you're going to experiment, I'm coming with you," he said in a low growl.

Her mouth dropped open. "You'd do that? You'd come back with me?"

"My life is wherever you are, Maggie."

"Oh, Ty!"

"Who'd have thought it. A couple of weeks ago I was thinking I'd probably die a bachelor, because I couldn't seem to fall in love. And then you . . . dropped by. Now I can't imagine my life without you in it. I know I'm not much, but—"

"Not much? Oh, Ty, you so underestimate yourself. You're an honest, upstanding man. With your paternal history, you could have turned into your father, but you didn't. You saw him for what he was and you went the other way. I admire that so much about you."

"Excuse me," Lester yelled. "Prisoner here!"

"Hold your pants on, Lester," Ty yelled back. "If you had in the first place you probably wouldn't be in there!"

Maggie giggled. "You're funny, as well. I love that about you, too."

He looked into her eyes. "Do I . . . make you happy, Maggie?"

"More than I ever expected in my life, Sheriff."

"Then please don't touch that shed unless I'm holding your hand. Whatever the future or the past holds, Maggie, I want to spend it with you."

She stared at him. "Are you saying . . ."

"I bought the ring two days ago. I just wanted to wait until I knew for sure you felt the same way. If I asked you to marry me, what would your answer be?"

"Oh, Ty!" She threw herself at him. "Yes, most definitely yes!"

"Then we need to go back to my place to get it before we . . . touch the shed."

Maggie looked over her shoulder at the place where this strange, exhilarating journey began. "I see no need to tempt fate, Ty. I belong here. With you. I believe my mother would have loved you. Not as much as I do, but she'd be happy."

"What makes you think so?" he asked, his heart near to busting out of his chest.

"As soon as you get Lester out of there, I have something very interesting to show you, Ty."

Ty glanced at the shed. "Jinx'll be here soon enough for Lester. It's time to start our life together. I'm taking the rest of your birthday off."

"Why, Sheriff," she said, fanning her face. "I'm flattered."

"Yeah, well I've heard tell men in love tend to get goofy. Is that true?"

"I wouldn't know. But I can't wait to find out."

They started walking toward his car. "So what's this big surprise?"

"Tell me everything you know about flappers," Maggie said, threading her fingers through his. "Right after you tell me you love me."

"I love you."

"And I you, Ty. Now, about flappers . . .

Keep reading for a preview of
Sandra Hill's next romance

Even Vikings Get the Blues

Coming Fall 2010 from Berkley Sensation!

Double or nothing . . .

Rita Sawyer prepared to set her body aflame and catapult through the fifteenth floor window of the burning skyscraper. A master of double tasking, she also pondered whether she'd have time, or the inclination, to shave her legs before her date this evening with her ex-husband's brother.

Well, it wasn't a date exactly. Darron wanted her to meet the latest love of his life, Dirk Severino. *Darron and Dirk. Doesn't that say it all?* In addition, he was bringing along the "perfect man" for her. His words. Presumably heterosexual, and with a job. Absolute essentials for her as a twenty-eight-year-old veteran of the dating wars.

Darron was suffering major post-divorce guilt—on his brother Scott's behalf, of all things—and had made it his mission in life to find her a mate to make up for his hound dog brother's betrayal during Scott and Rita's short-lived marriage. To her embarrassment, after plying her with Fuzzy Navels last week, Darron had discovered that she hadn't been with a man in more than two years, not since the divorce. It was none of his business, of course, but Darron was a busybody from way back.

To be honest, she was still raw and angry over Scott's infidelity, whether it was one time, as he'd laughably claimed, or dozens, as she rightly suspected. Adultery was adultery in her book. She'd seen what it had done to her mother. Rita had suffered the pain herself.

She'd known Scott since kindergarten. Darron, too, who had been younger. She'd seen Scott at his worst, and it wasn't even when she'd caught him in bed with a fellow architect. Think seven years old and green snot. Therefore, she shouldn't have been surprised when he'd turned out to be an adulterous snot when he grew up. Females had been drawn to his blond good looks from a young age. As if that was any excuse!

Actually, she had her own ulterior motive for meeting with Darron tonight. He was a top notch financial advisor, and Rita was facing monumental money problems since her mother had died and left her with medical bills out the wazoo. It wasn't the long bout with cancer that caused all the problems, but the experimental treatments not covered by insurance—for which Rita had gladly taken out loans—and the year she'd spent as a caretaker when she'd had no income. Unfortunately, it was all in vain. Collection agencies now had her on speed dial. And, no, she still wouldn't accept alimony from Scott the Snot.

"Scene three, take two. Lights! Camera! Action!" Larry Winters, the director of this latest spy thriller starring Jennifer Garner and Hugh Jackman, shouted through his bullhorn.

Whoosh! Bursting into a ball of flame, Jennifer went sailing through the glass and the air with expertise, landing on a trampoline that looked like the roof of another building, from which she then front-flipped onto yet another rooftop, aka a padded platform. Of course, it wasn't really the fifteenth floor, but rather the third, and it wasn't really a skyscraper, but a set prop, and it wasn't really Jennifer Garner, but Rita Sawyer, her stunt double.

"Cut!" the director yelled. "That's a wrap! Great job, Rita!"

Immediately, a technician began hosing down her flames while others were peeling back her flameproof wig along with the tight cap which protected her short, spiky blonde hair ala the singer Pink, two nomex jumpsuits, and gloves. Still others wiped the flame-retardant gel off her face.

"Hey, Rita. Got a minute?" Dean Witherow, the producer, called out to her. "I have a couple gentlemen who'd like to meet you."

Noticing the two military types in the visitors' area, probably consultants on the film, she sighed with resignation. Folks were fascinated with her after witnessing some of her stunts, especially men who fantasized about what she could do in bed. Being a proud lady of the SWAMP, as in Stunt Women's Association of Motion Pictures, she'd heard it all. One lawyer from Denver once asked, before they'd even got to the entree in a fancy L.A. restaurant, if she could do any kinky stunts during sex. Jeesh! And, yes, she could, actually. Not that she'd told him that.

After a quick shower in the doubles' trailer and a change of clothes to jeans and an Aerosmith T-shirt, she walked up and let Dean introduce them. "This is Commander Ian Mac-Lean and Lieutenant Jacob Mendozo. They're Navy SEALs stationed at Coronado."

Seals, huh? I've heard they can be kinky on occasion. They're certainly buff enough.

But then she chastised herself. *Unbelievable! I am flippin' unbelievable. If I don't go ga-ga over Hugh Jackman, why would I be ogling these two grunts?*

Her eyes widened with interest, nevertheless. Like many others in this country, she had a proud appreciation for the good job SEALs did in fighting terrorism.

The one guy, the commander, was in his early forties with a receding hairline that didn't detract at all from his overall attractiveness. He was too somber for her tastes, though.

Lieutenant Mendozo, on the other hand, was *whoo-ee* sex personified. From his Hispanic good looks to his mischievous eyes, he was eye candy of the best sort. And she'd bet her skydiving helmet that he knew his way around a bed, too.

Rita Sawyer, get your mind out of the gutter.

Maybe I am suffering from sex deprivation, like Darron thinks.

"Were either of you among those SEALs who got in trouble for riding horseback into Afghanistan a few years back? I saw it on CNN."

Both men's faces reddened.

"We don't talk about that," the commander said.

Which means yes. "Why so shy? It was really impressive."

"The Pentagon didn't think so," Lieutenant Mendozo explained with a wink—a wink his superior did not appreciate if his glare was any indication.

"Heads rolled," the commander agreed with a grimace. "With good reason. Necessity might be the mother of invention, but in the case of SEALs, they better be private ones."

"What he's trying to say is that a SEAL scalp is a coup for many tangos . . . uh, terrorists. It's important that we stay covert. That episode in Afghanistan was a monumental brain fart."

"Well, it's been nice meeting you. Maybe you can—" she started to say.

"We have a proposition for you," Commander MacLean interrupted.

Gutter, here I come. She laughed. She couldn't help herself.

"Not that kind of proposition."

"Oh, heck!" she joked.

"I'm a happily married man. In fact, my wife would whack me with the flat side of her broadsword if I even looked at another female."

The lieutenant smiled in a way that indicated *he* wouldn't mind that kind of proposition.

But wait a minute. *Did he say broadsword?*

"Can we go somewhere for a cup of coffee?" the commander suggested.

Or a cool drink to lower my temperature.

Soon they were seated at a table in the commissary.

"So, what's this all about?" she asked, impatient to get

home if she was going to make her "date." Now that her initial testosterone buzz had tamed down to a hum, she accepted that these two were here on business of some sort, not to put the make on her.

"How would you like to become a female SEAL?"

She choked on her iced tea and had to dab at her mouth and shirt with the paper napkins the lieutenant handed her with a chuckle. "You mean, like GI Jane?" she finally sputtered out.

"Exactly," Commander MacLean said. "It's a grueling training program. Not many women—or men for that matter—can handle the regimen."

What a load of hooey! "Why me?"

"The WEALS program, Women on Earth, Air, Land and Sea, needs more good women who are physically fit to the extreme. With terrorism running rampant today, Uncle Sam needs more elite forces, and our current supply of seasoned SEALs is deploying on eight to ten combat tours. Way too many! So, we're recruiting special people under a mentoring program. Bottom line, we need a thousand more SEALs over the next few years, and a few hundred more WEALS."

"I repeat, why me?"

The commander shrugged. "We want the best of the best. Men and women who are patriotic . . ."

I do get teary when the National Anthem plays.

". . . adventuresome,"

Did they hear about my wrestling an alligator? Jeesh! Can't anyone keep a secret? It was an accident, for heaven's sake! I fell on the damn beast.

". . . extreme athletes,"

You got me on that one.

". . . controlled risk takers,"

That one, too. Stunt doubles take risks, but well-planned, safe-as-possible risks. But, boy, is he pouring it on!

". . . intelligent,"

I barely passed calculus, and how intelligent had it been to marry a serial adulterer?

". . . skilled competitors who enjoy challenges and games,"

Does he see "Sucker" tattooed on my forehead?

". . . people who love to travel,"

Yeah, like downtown Kabul is my idea of a Club Med vacation.

". . . men and women with a fire in the gut."

The fire in my gut comes from the enchiladas I ate for lunch. And worry over paying my bills.

"Only one in a hundred applicants make it through Hell Week, you know."

And you think I want to put myself through that? "You've gotta be kidding."

Both men shook their heads.

"Each WEALS trainee has a mentor to get them through the process," Commander MacLean added, as if that made everything more palatable.

"And my mentor would be?"

The sexy lieutenant gave her a little wave.

Okay, I'm officially tempted.

But not enough. She'd read about Hell Week. She'd watched Demi Moore get creamed in *G.I. Jane. Who needs that? No. Way.* She started to rise from her seat. "I'm flattered that you would consider me, but—"

"Plus there's a sizeable signing bonus," Lieutenant Mendozo added.

Rita plopped back down into her chair. "Tell me more."

And she could swear she heard the cute lieutenant murmur "Hoo-yah!"

Keep reading for a preview of
Veronica Wolff's next romance

Devil's Highlander

Coming Summer 2010 from Berkley Sensation!

Marjorie skittered down the steep path, purposely descending too quickly to think. The specter of Dunnottar Castle felt heavy over her shoulder, looming in near-ruin high atop Dunnottar Rock, a massive stone plinth that punched free of Scotland's northeastern coast like a gargantuan fist. Waves roiled and licked at its base far below. Chilled, she clambered even faster, skidding and galloping downhill, unsure whether she was fleeing closer to or farther from that grim mountain of rubble the MacAlpins called home.

She shook her head. She'd sworn not to think on it.

She'd done entirely too much thinking already. Much to her uncle's consternation, she'd chosen her gray mare, not his carriage, for her ride from Aberdeen. She'd realized too late that the daylong ride offered her altogether too much time to brood over what felt like a lifetime of missteps. And she hoped she wasn't about to make the grandest, most humiliating one of all.

She was going to see Cormac.

Whenever she'd thought of it—and she'd thought of little

else on her interminable ride—she'd turn her horse around and head straight back to home. But then those same thoughts of him would have her spinning that mare right around again, until her horse tossed its head, surly from the constant tugging and turning.

She reached the bottom of the hill, where the knotted grass turned rocky, its greens and browns giving way to the reds and grays of the pebbled shore. The beach curved like a thin scimitar around the bay, its far side concealed from view by the ragged hillocks and blades of rock that limned the shore as though the land only reluctantly surrendered to the sea.

Marjorie slid the leather slippers from her feet and set them carefully down. She wriggled her toes, leaning against the swell of land by her side. The pebbles blanketing the shore were large and rounded, and looked warmed by the late afternoon sun. She stepped forward, moving slowly now. The water between the stones was cold, but their smooth tops were not, and they sounded a soothing clack with each step.

She was close. She could feel it.

Cormac. *He* was close. Amidst the gentle slapping of the waves and the sultry brine in the air, she sensed him.

She'd not needed to stop in at Dunnottar to ask his siblings where to find him. She and Cormac had known each other since birth, and Marjorie had spent every one of her twenty-three years feeling as though she were tied to him in some mysterious and inextricable way. Though they hadn't spoken in what felt like a lifetime, she'd spared not a penny nor her pride to glean word of him, writing to his sisters for news, aching for rare glimpses of him through the years.

She'd offered up the prayers of a wretched soul when he'd gone off to war, and then prayers of thanks when he returned home whole. And God help her the relief she felt knowing he'd never married. She couldn't have borne the thought of another woman in Cormac's arms.

No, Marjorie knew. Alone by the sea was exactly where she'd find him.

She screwed her face, shutting her eyes tight. There were many things she knew.

She knew that Cormac blamed her. To this day, he blamed her, just as she blamed herself for the foolish, girlish dare that had ripped Aidan from their lives. Because of her silliness, the MacAlpin family had lost a son and brother that day. And Marjorie had lost more still than that: She'd also lost Cormac.

She froze again. What was she thinking? She couldn't do this. She couldn't bear to see him.

But she couldn't bear not to.

The draw was too powerful to resist. Her feet stepped inexorably forward before her mind had a chance to stop them. She told herself she had no other choice. Events in her life had led her just there. She needed help, and Cormac was the only man with skills enough to come to her aid.

The hillock at her side dropped away, revealing the far edge of the beach. Revealing Cormac.

His shirtless back was to her, his *breacan feile* slapping at his legs in the wind. He was hauling in his nets. A fisherman now, as his sister had said. Hand over hand, the flex of muscle in his arms and back was visible even from a distance.

Gasping, Marjorie stumbled back a step, leaning into the rocks for support. She'd told herself she came because he could help her. But she knew in that instant the real reason she'd come: The only place for her in this treacherous world stood just there, down the beach. *Cormac.*

She'd willingly suffer his blame, suffer his indifference; yet still, like the embers from a long-banked fire, she knew Cormac would give her solace, despite himself.

She hadn't moved, hadn't spoken, but he turned, as though he'd felt her there. Her hand went to her chest, reminding her heart to beat, her lungs to draw breath.

He turned away, abruptly, and tears stung her eyes. Would he spurn her?

But she saw he merely bent to gather his nets, dragging them farther up the shore where he carefully spread them out.

Relief flooded her. She scrubbed at her face, gathering herself, and tucked errant wisps of hair behind her ears. She knew it was purely a nervous gesture; the strong sea wind would only whip her curls free again.

She tempered herself. This meeting would not go well if she were this vulnerable from the start. But of course she was this vulnerable, she thought with a heavy heart, considering all that had recently come to pass.

She took a deep breath. He'd seen her. She couldn't go back now. She *wouldn't* go back—Cormac was the only one who could help her.

Marjorie picked her way toward him. He stood still as granite, waiting for her, watching her. His dark hair blew in the wind, and his brow was furrowed. Was he upset to see her? Simply thoughtful?

Suddenly, she regretted the absence of her slippers. She loved the sensation of the smooth rocks beneath her feet, but now felt somehow naked without every stitch of her clothing. She fisted her hands in her skirts. She imagined she'd always been sort of naked before Cormac, and there was nothing that could truly ever conceal her. He was the only one who'd ever been able to read her soul, laid bare in her eyes.

He was silent and still. What would he see in her eyes now?

She felt as though she'd forgotten how to walk. She made herself stand tall, focused on placing one foot in front of the other, but she felt awkward and ungainly, unbearably self-aware as she made her way to him. *Lift the foot, place it down, lift and down.*

He was not ten paces away. He was tall, but with a man's body now, broad with muscles carved from hauling nets, from firing guns. That last gave her pause. She spotted the fine sheen of scars on his forearm, a sliver of a scar on his brow. He'd been long at war. What kind of a man had he become?

Inhaling deeply, she let her eyes linger over his face. She was close enough to see the color of his eyes. Blue-gray, like the sea. Her heart sped. She forced herself to step closer.

She'd been unable to summon an exact picture of him in her thoughts, but now that he stood before her, his face was as familiar to her as her own. There was Cormac's strong, square jaw. The long fringe of dark lashes. But he was somehow foreign, too. The boy had become a man. A vague crook had appeared in his nose, and she wondered what long-ago break had put it there. Where had *she* been the moment it happened, what had *she* been doing while he'd been living his life?

She stopped an arm's length from him. Intensity radiated from him like the sun's glare off the sea.

Her throat clenched. She couldn't do it. What had she been thinking?

He blamed her still. He didn't want to speak to her. He didn't welcome the sight of her.

The silence was shrill between them. She swallowed hard, wondering how best to get herself out of there. How to gracefully back out, to never, *ever* see him again.

For Davie. She had to do this for Davie. That thought alone kept her anchored in place.

Cormac opened his mouth to speak, and she held her breath.

"Ree," he whispered, in the voice of a man. "Aw, Ree, lass."

Her every muscle slackened. Her fear, her disquiet, stripped away, leaving Marjorie raw before him. Hot tears came quick, blurring her vision.

"Cormac," she gasped. "It's happened again."

Also from *USA Today* bestselling author

Sandra Hill

VIKING UNCHAINED

"Sandra Hill has truly outdone herself."
—*Night Owl Romance*

"Ms. Hill had me rolling with laughter with
every turn of the page. She breathes life into her
characters and makes the reader wish they were real.
I dare say anyone who reads this story will come
away with a smile." —*Coffee Time Romance*

"Hill goes a-Viking again! It's a blast!"
—*Romantic Times*

M448T0409